"MY GOVERNMENT CALLED ME—
AND I ANSWERED!"
CAPTAIN LOU ALBANO SAID

Rick Harrison couldn't believe his eyes. The dude was big, wide as a table at the shoulders, and wore a garish Hawaiian shirt. Not exactly your standard CIA garb. "I take it you're going to show me a few moves," he said hesitatingly.

"Baby, I'm going to show you, throw you, flip you, trip you, suplex you, and duplex you. I'm going to teach you wrestling from the inside out, from the medulla to the oblongata, from the spinal to the sternum and back again!"

With that, Captain Lou stripped off his Hawaiian shirt and jumped into the ring. "Let me tell you like it is, Harrison!" he bellowed. "You're in Uncle Sam's Super Concentrated Wrestling Training Program starting *now!*"

And before Rick could open his mouth to answer, Captain Lou lowered his head and came at him from across the ring like a charging rhino.

BODY SMASHER

BY JAN STACY

ZEBRA BOOKS
KENSINGTON PUBLISHING CORP.

ZEBRA BOOKS

are published by

Kensington Publishing Corp.
475 Park Avenue South
New York, NY 10016

First printing: March, 1989

Printed in the United States of America

Chapter One

The truck shot through the night like a spear flung into the moon-splattered German countryside. An immense chromium cylinder attached to a gargantuan diesel cabin unit, the U.S. Army Hazardous Materials Transport was far larger than even the largest commercial Mack truck. Had any German farmers in this sparsely populated region been out tending their livestock at three in the morning, even though they were used to the NATO transports and convoys that had been coming through for nearly half a century, they might have done a double—or even a triple—take at the monster truck, with its huge red crosses and skull-shaped symbols painted on each side as it tore by, stirring up leaves into the air.

But not a farmer was yet up at this ungodly hour of the morning—the very time that trucks such as these made their nocturnal migrations. For the transports were *not* to be seen, lest they remind a sleeping world of the poison that they carried in their midst, the burning death that crawled through their dreams, slithered within their deepest nightmares.

"Lieutenant Hawkins, I swear I can feel that fucking stuff back there burning my ass," the driver of the truck, Corporal Lang, exclaimed. He was just nineteen, and sat ramrod straight in front of the high-tech display panel dashboard. "I mean, can't you? Can't you just feel it burning like a campfire toasting marshmallows? Only we're the marshmallows. 'Cause I can. I sure as hell can. They didn't tell me this was going to be no suicide mission."

"Shut up," the lieutenant replied, not sitting nearly so straight, his body in fact sprawled halfway down in the raised leather seat with its chrome armrests. Buttons and dials were along the sides, like some kind of astronaut's chair. But then the lieutenant had made this trip dozens of times. This was the corporal's first. The regular driver had taken sick. Said it was the flu. But Hawkins knew it was the clap. The fool had caught it from some fraulein up on the Ubenstrasse. And now the lieutenant had to put up with this—

"Lieutenant, Lieutenant—can't you feel it? I mean can't—"

"Listen, pal, for the fifth time tonight—and this is the last time, Corporal Asshole or whatever your name is. We're totally protected from that—that stuff back there. Why the hell do you think this truck is as big as Moby Dick's dick? It's so we don't roast ourselves—or screw up the whole countryside. Tell you the truth, I don't even think the brass gives a shit about us. After all, soldiers are expendable by their very definition, right? But they can't be frying Germans all over the stinking place. So that's why they made this son-of-a-bitchin' *ve-hi-cle* so thick. There's a foot of lead, a foot of concrete, then a few more feet of something else, then there's chain blankets made of . . .

"Oh hell," the lieutenant suddenly said in disgust, mostly at himself. Who cared what the asshole thought. He turned in the seat, and rested his head against the edge of the huge window that curved around the whole front of the truck like a jet cockpit, trying to find a comfortable position—which he couldn't. The driver's cabin of the Hazardous Materials Truck had been designed *not* to be comfortable, to make sure that whatever fools were driving it didn't fall asleep, crash the damned thing, and poison half the country.

"Why the hell am I even talking to you?" the lieutenant mumbled as he squashed his face into his arm, which was pressed against the window. "Even if you *do* get fried—you're in the U.S. Army Tactical Weapons Force now, sonny boy. You ain't got no choice in the matter. Unless you want to jump out that there door and try to make a run for it. Then, of course, I'd have to shoot you right in the back with this here .357 magnum pistol under Regulation 1072AA— which states that any asshole dumb enough to try to flee this truck for *any reason whatsoever shall be terminated immediately. Terminated,* Corporal! Do you know what that means?" The lieutenant didn't hear anything for a few seconds. Then there was a loud gulp followed by a second one, both of which were audible even above the loud purr of the eighty-five-foot-long,twelve-foot-thick moving cylinder of manganese-chrome which hurtled along the Autobahn at nearly seventy miles an hour.

"Shiiit," the corporal snarled under his breath, his face lit up by numerous green and red and amber dials which constantly read out information on the truck's status—everything from speed to outside temperature to tire pressure. A yard to his right were another set of panels, all computerized, with constantly moving readouts monitoring the material—the plutonium— that was sitting in the back, riding along like caged starfire, imprisoned fragments of the very burning coals of hell.

"I don't even know what all these mean," the gawky-faced corporal grumbled softly, not really daring to address the lieutenant directly. He looked as skinny as a rail in his tight uniform, with his collar pressed tight as a piece of folded paper. His narrow shoulders, thin neck, and even longer straight face gave him a slightly cadaverous look even though he wasn't out of his teens. The pallor of his face, brought on by his increasing anxiety over the cargo, didn't add to his good looks any.

"No one told me I was signing up for any glow-in-the-dark parties. I mean when I joined up they promised me that I could—"

"Listen, Corporal," Lieutenant Hawkins shouted, suddenly sitting up and turning toward the driver, whose eyes were focused like a madman's on the road ahead pierced by the triple-beam headlights of the transport's multiple-lighting system. "I've had it—you hear me? I got a fucking headache, my guts are doing the Olympics in my pants, and I gotta play around with a bozo like you. Now you drive—that's what you're here for, okay? They said you were the best fucking driver they had over in munitions transport. That you knew the X-7 display panel and multi-gear system like you studied it at Harvard. So this here vehicle just happens to have that system, all right? Let me worry about all the rad readouts on the board here. I'm keeping an eye on everything—don't worry. But no more talk—or I might just *say* you was trying to flee—and plug you right here in the truck."

With that, his face slowly started fading from red to pink, then back to the pasty white it usually was. Hawkins then slid back down in his seat, and misjudging his speed, slammed his head against the amber-tinted window with a wicked thud. But he didn't make a sound—just gritted his teeth and stared out at the thick waves of stars that rolled across the purple-black German sky like a million spilled jewels on a velvet rug. Maybe he'd shoot this moron after all. Although he knew of course he wouldn't, the lieutenant allowed himself to imagine it—taking out the huge .357, aiming it at the twerp's head, pulling the trigger. It would be most satisfying. In fact the thought gave him such a good feeling that he felt his eyes close a little, his brain start to slip into soft painless darkness.

Corporal Lang gnashed his teeth violently as if trying to grind them down before he reached twenty. This was a bum deal. Being the top driver of the most recent group of transport drivers who had just been sent to Europe from the States had seemed like a blessing, with all the perks and everything. But now? Shit! He knew what radiation could do. He hadn't seen every Godzilla movie for nothing. How the hell did the lieutenant think monsters were born anyway? Every time it was out of radiation. The giant ants in *Them*—radiation. *Gorgo*—radiation.

He tried to relax. The Dexedrine pills he had taken to keep him up through the forty-hour drive had also made him quite jittery and half-crazed. His heart felt like it was beating nearly out of control, and his eyes were unmoving beads glued to the line in the road ahead. He tried to relax. But couldn't. He swore he could feel the stuff—whatever the man said—burning into his back, like he was lying on his stomach at the beach under crystal-clear skies soaking up the sun. He kept glancing nervously over at Hawkins and the display panel on his side of the cabin. The bastard sure as hell wasn't keeping an eye on anything. What if the whole load back there *did* go up? What if his testicles *were* burned down to the size of overdehydrated raisins? What if . . . The corporal madly went through an endless stream of possibilities, not one of them pleasant.

An hour later, at exactly 4:02, the lieutenant's multi-function wristwatch, as big as a rich woman's bracelet, went off with a low beep. He snorted, rattled around in his sleep against the window making sputtering noises, and then opened his eyes.

"Shit, what a moment to wake up." He grinned over at Lang. "I was with Marilyn Monroe—and we were playing this game of strip poker—and I'd gotten her down to her undies—and—I was reaching for her and she was all smiling and coming toward me as naked as you can get and . . . And I had to wake up."

"Who's Marilyn Monroe?" the corporal asked, glancing over nervously at the lieutenant.

"Damn!" Hawkins exclaimed, slapping his hand against his head like he was swatting a fly. "Fucking guy hasn't even heard of Marilyn Monroe. Man, I don't know if this world is worth saving." He snorted again, rubbed his bloodshot eyes, and tried to focus on the dark road ahead lit by the multiple beams of the truck's headlights. "Anyway—I woke up for a reason. Up there—see that light by the edge of the road about two miles up? Just about a hundred yards past it is a pull-off from the road—we're stopping there. Gonna get some food, coffee."

"But, Lieutenant Hawkins," Corporal Lang said nervously, not wanting to incur the man's wrath again. He knew the guy might actually haul off and slug him. And judging from the thick arms and broad shoulders of the career Army man, the kid would be turned to silly putty that would slide down the high-tech cabin walls. "I was specifically told by Colonel Jaspers not to stop for anything. Not even slow down until we reached Marseilles—and the transport ship."

"Listen, kid," the lieutenant said, letting out a long exhale of air. He didn't want to get angry right now and ruin his appetite. All he wanted was a double platter of some sauerbrauten, some dumplings, some blood sausage. "There are rules—and then there are rules. *All* the guys stop here. How the hell we going to go fifty-plus hours without food, no coffee, no—nothing. You know what I'm saying? The brass knows about it. It's okay. I swear. Colonel Jaspers may have said not to slow down—but he meant if other cars or trucks come nearby. Not for this."

"Well, I guess—if you—say—" the corporal stuttered. He slowly started applying the brakes as he shifted out of twelfth gear. A computer-guided grid on a screen just in front of the stick showed him the exact angle at which he was shifting—making sure he did it correctly.

"Sure, sure, kid, don't worry about it," the lieutenant said, rubbing happily at his ample stomach as he licked his chops thinking about just what the hell he was going to get. The thought of food put him in a much better mood. "In fact, we'll just let bygones be bygones. I'll treat you to chow. Whaddya want? This place has got dumplings that'll kick your ass, schnitzengrubbel that kings would die for. Pastries, got every damn thing. It's the only twenty-four-hour diner this side of West Berlin. Damn lucky it's here."

The corporal's eyes lit up. The food sounded horrible—benzedrine made him not want to eat. But coffee, sweets—*that* he could go for. They came up to the diner, which was well lit with a number of fluorescent lights flashing on and off in German, announcing this and that particularly rich and sinful delight on the menu tonight.

"Past it—past it," Lieutenant Hawkins exclaimed, waving his hand. Lang had almost started turning into the big parking lot in front of the place. It was fairly empty now, only about a half-dozen cars, though it could hold over a hundred. "Down the road more— about a hundred yards. We can't actually park right with the other cars—give somebody a heart attack to see a truck this big and mean-looking after all the dumplings he just quaffed down." The lieutenant laughed, anticipating the thick rich foods that clogged the arteries so efficiently.

"There, see, over there!" Hawkins pointed out the branching road ahead used for emergency repairs, picnicking, urinating, whatever, that led off the highway and curved around about fifty yards before coming back on it again. There were no lights here as in the parking lot, and the lieutenant reached over and dimmed the truck's lights, turning them down via a computerized keyboard as he tapped in some numbers. The beams fell from white to a dim amber, just bright enough so that Corporal Lang could see to steer the huge rig.

"This is good," Hawkins said after a few seconds. They had completely disappeared from sight of the highway. "Now stop, and keep the lights down like this." As the corporal pressed the brakes with his foot to bring the rig to a complete stop, he misjudged it a little, and the whole truck lifted up on its tires for a second and squealed hard.

"What the hell, what the hell's going on?" Voices rang out from behind the steel-gridded gate behind the driver's seat. The alternate crew slept in the back of the large cabin, with two bunks, a small refrigerator, even a TV and mini-toilet. A whole little motel built right into the transport system, enabling the vehicle to go days without stopping if need be.

"Just a food stop," Lieutenant Hawkins yelled out as he turned halfway around in his seat and spoke through the grid addressing the groggy inhabitants behind him. "The usual?" he asked.

"Yeah," both men snorted back. "And make mine triple coffee, black as tar. I'm going to need it," one voice groaned.

"Damn right." The lieutenant laughed as he turned forward again. He reached down and pressed in the eight-digit number into the keyboard on its side—the passcode that would open the titanium armored doors capable of stopping a bazooka shell. "At least you will

14

by the time we all finish eating. Lock me out, pal," the lieutenant said to Lang as the door hissed open with a whoosh of air, and slid back on pneumatic ball-bearing tracks. "And don't open it for no one less they give the password."

"And what the hell is the password?" the corporal asked with a smirk.

"Food, asshole, food," the lieutenant cracked back with a laugh as he jumped down and headed off down the road in darkness toward the restaurant. It was a route he knew well, having walked its gravel surface a hundred times before. The early morning service staff was there and the head waiter, all 350 pounds of roly-poly, red-faced German bourgeoisie, smiled and pumped his hand, eagerly awaiting the cash which would be left behind in a few minutes. Lieutenant Hawkins squeezed the asses of a few of the flush-cheeked, basketball-bosomed frauleins who were rushing around getting ready for the day's explosion of activity. He did it in a perfunctory way, not really in the mood. But he knew they got hurt if he didn't squeeze or try to squeeze something. They smacked their lips lewdly, balancing trays of water glasses with both hands. He had actually cornered one of them once a couple of years earlier behind a china closet, and she had let him do a few things before she ran off squealing. But it was all tease and run. Probably made a man even hungrier. Sold more sausage.

The restaurant was one of the most popular of the entire region. But because it was early, his orders were filled fast, the smell of the heavily seasoned dishes filling the air. And within twenty minutes he had two huge shopping bags full of the stuff, the steaming odor so powerful that it made his stomach growl like a caged beast and his brain go dizzy. As he headed back away from the restaurant and drew past the outer storage warehouse, where the light grew thin and the shadows thicker, a voice suddenly hissed from the darkness.

"Psst, buddy, give me a hand, will you?" The shape was in darkness, but he could see that it was wearing a U.S. Army uniform.

"What the hell?" the lieutenant said, looking over, startled. He had been peering down into the bag as he walked, thinking about its contents. He stopped and turned toward the voice, stepping around the edge of the warehouse to get a better view. Suddenly a fist was hurtling toward him. He had enough time to see it coming from about a foot away—but not enough time to move even one inch out of the way. The thick knuckles of the fist slammed into the base of his nose and instantly collapsed his cartilage structure into silly putty. The force of the blow cracked the whole front of his face into fractures that spread out beneath the skin, creating bloody spiderwebs of red as the capillaries burst apart like overloaded balloons.

But the lieutenant didn't have time to contemplate the terrible searing pain of the blow. For as he stumbled backward, a second pair of hands flew out of the darkness. And these hands held a length of piano wire which was slipped around his throat, wrapping tightly around it in a second. The hands pulled back hard in each direction and the wire dug deep into the lieutenant's thick neck, seeming to disappear into it. Hawkins's face grew red as an apple, as his eyes bulged nearly out of his skull like eggs about to pop. The hands suddenly pulled extra hard and twisted the wire over itself. Hawkins's eyes stayed open and took on a vacant look.

In the transport, Corporal Lang sat staring at the dashboard in a daze when there was a knock at the door. He looked over, reaching across for the release button.

"What's the password?" he suddenly yelled out, chuckling, letting his hand hover over the button. Now

16

he'd get the bastard.

"Open the fucking door, man. I got the food." The corporal let his hand descend and the door whooshed open with a low throaty hiss. Corporal Lang sat up again, and the figure entered holding the large food-filled bags in front of him as he placed them on the black leather seat. When Lang turned back a second later to see just what kind of culinary treasures had been brought back, his eyes met dead cold eyes. And they weren't the lieutenant's.

"Die, Army pig," the voice whispered with an ice coldness. Suddenly the corporal felt a terrible wrenching pain in his gut. He looked down and saw the man's hand poking right through the bottom of the bag with a long razor-sharp scalpel in his hand. As the corporal sent the message from his brain to his lips that it was time to scream, the attacker's other hand slammed over his mouth so that Lang's teeth bit right into each side of the palm, sinking in a good half inch, crunching bone. But even as he stared wide-eyed the knife hand ripped up, across his midsection, and then down again. Suddenly the corporal's whole stomach was just a waterfall of red stuff that bubbled out from the center of the dead thing that had been a man.

The assassin ripped the knife out as he saw that the GI was dead. He pushed the bag of food forward out of his way on the seat and it tumbled into the bloody pool of Lang's guts, wieners, dumplings all mixing into the red broth of death.

"Food's here," he yelled out putting his hand over his mouth to muffle his voice. Then again, louder, as the still half-dozing men behind the grid slowly got up again. One of them leaned forward, sliding it back.

"Son-of-a-bi—" he began to scream, but didn't have a chance as a whole wall of silenced 9mm slugs tore into his head, driving him backwards like a mule had kicked him in the face. As the second man rose from his cot, he

17

too was cut down in mid-motion, scissored across the chest and neck with bloody holes. The killer didn't even wait to see the death quivers of the corpses that danced around their beds. They weren't a threat to him any longer. He jumped back out of the truck cabin and down onto the road. He whistled twice, loud, and within seconds a smaller truck pulled out of the shadows of some woods. It came up to the back of the long cylinder of chrome.

The moment it stopped, several men covered from head to toe in thick white radiation gear leaped out and began working fast, synchronized as if they had trained for this night a hundred times. Two of them took up gun positions behind the truck, setting up a 7.2mm machine gun, while another ran ahead, so that the bend in the road was protected from both ends. Even as they set up their guard positions, another man rushed forward and jumped up into the driver's seat. He looked around for a few seconds getting his bearings, and then saw the input keyboard that commanded the truck's many functions. With the skilled, quick fingers of someone who had performed the task countless times before, he slammed in the proper code, then stopped and jumped back down out as he heard a whirring sound coming from the back. The truck began vibrating quickly.

It took about a minute for the big cylinder to open back like an egg hatching, both sides falling away, sliding beneath the truck, pulling back to reveal three glistening cannisters, each about four feet high and two feet wide, that stood on the flat steel surface that formed the inside of the truck. The remaining rad-suited figures came forward and stood for a few seconds as if hypnotized by the sight. They knew what was contained within those steel eggs. What starfire burned just inches away from them capable of turning them back into the powder from which all things had sprung.

"Come on, you bastards, move it," a voice screamed out as a man moved out of the shadows. "We haven't got all night. There are constant late night Army shipments along this road—and they all stop at this diner. There could be another at any moment."

The white-suited figures, with visors like deep-sea helmets covering their faces, broke into units, two of them heading toward their own smaller truck while the other two jumped up aboard the now-opened transport and over to the nearest of the cannisters. The larger truck whirred and the pulley system in back pulled around so it was over the cannister. One of the suited figures took a huge clamp hanging down on a steel cable and placed it in the eyelet on top of the cannister. The steel egg was slowly raised up as the two suited figures pushed it out and away. The load was swung around and then inside the second truck, this one a Ryder Rental truck, fifteen feet long and beat-up as a ghetto wall, covered with graffiti, slashed in some places as if a metal-eating animal had been teething on its cheap aluminum walls.

The block and tackle system worked well enough, and within a minute the cannister was detached inside the truck and set along one wall. Then the next one was moved with equal ease. It was on the final load that disaster struck. For as the two men aboard the Army truck pushed out so the cannister swung free—the hook somehow dislodged from the end of the object. The load dropped down eight feet to the road and slammed hard into some rocks half buried in the dirt. The shock ripped the top from the cannister, popping it free with a sudden outward rush of superheated air.

The two suited men at the edge of the truck stood frozen in place as a blinding white light bathed them from below. It was the light of the gods, the burning eye of the Deathgiver himself. The pure eye of a hell that

19

mortal man was not meant to stare directly into, never directly. And as they were bathed in the rays of the deadliest substance known to man, the very fuel of H-bombs, their flesh began turning red beneath their rad suits. From red to purple, then on to brown. Then the flesh began bubbling up, and the bubbles popped with sickening sounds as both figures just stood there as if they were glued to the flat back of the chrome Army transport.

The men in the rental truck looked on in abject horror, protected from the direct force of the rays, which were directed up and toward the burning victims. Their white suits were never meant to survive the burning heat of such close proximity to the concentrated element. Suddenly both burst into flame and they moved, waving their hands around like burning scarecrows. Their screams could be heard in the restaurant a hundred yards off.

"Let's move. Get the hell out of here," the leader of the group screamed from the front of the rental truck, which had the two cannisters already loaded aboard.

"But those two, they—" one of the men protested.

"They're as dead as you can get, you fool—" the man screamed from within his own suit, his breath fogging up the inside of the mask. "Now move!" He waited a few seconds and then ordered the driver forward as the others just made it into the back.

They were already moving by the time the guards posted at each end came tearing back and leaped through the doors, which they pulled shut even as the truck wheeled past the big chromium flatbed and the bodies burning at the side. They moved out onto the main road as the purple light of dawn began trickling down from above, and were quickly gone. Only the drone of the rebuilt engine could be heard in the distance as the rental truck slowly hit cruising speed down the nearly empty Autobahn.

20

Chapter Two

Colonel Wendell Parker stared down at the dozen or so eight-by-ten glossies strewn around the high-tech steel and black marble desk that curved in nearly a full circle around him. His color was a few shades paler than it had been before he had looked at the photos. Parker had seen a lot of death in this world, more than most men even dream of, and he had seen many ways to die. But this—this was of a new order.

"How'd they even scrape them off the top of the truck?" he asked the man who stood at a sort of half attention on the far side of the desk, his hands folded behind his back though he wasn't a soldier. None of them were, down here a thousand feet below the ground—the headquarters of D2—the most secret of the CIA's counterespionage units. Though many of those rushing around the huge information-gathering room that Parker sat in the center of had been in the service before they came here, now they were engaged in the mental aspect of war—leaving the physical for younger men.

Colonel Parker, head of the entire 200,000-square-foot operation that took up twenty levels below a normal-appearing hillside in southern Virginia, looked again, this time lifting a large magnifying glass that made his face suddenly appear huge and distorted to the younger man standing across the shining marble desk, a blue-suited agent who looked more like an accountant with his straight-cut hair, his gold watch worn just beneath the edge of the tailored double-breasted suit, than the second-in-command of D2. Parker looked closely at the photographs of the radiation victims, the etched lines that ran from the sides of his eyes tightening up, lines engraved by the countless battles he'd fought—and lived through. He ran his fingers through the graying hairline, receding but still hanging on, his fingers moving like nervous spiders threatening to pull out the hair.

"Damn," he muttered as he stared at the high-resolution pictures of the plutonium-melted corpses. That was one of the perks of working for the CIA—you got to see all the best photos of every bloody assassination, car bombing, and execution that took place around the world. And with the plentitude of information-gathering equipment at his disposal, Parker sure as hell didn't find himself wanting for bad and ugly news. He glanced up for a moment as he saw a red light blinking frantically on and off on one of the rows of computer banks that filled the curved walls of the circular War Room, 150 feet in diameter, a good 30 feet high.

The War Room, where Parker was supposed to lead the fight against domestic terrorism both of the home-grown variety and imported. For with the Iranian troubles, the East Europen riots, the you-name-it, there were plenty of angry people out there, and they were starting to come over to America. The U.S. had somehow, almost miraculously, escaped much of the more violent terrorist activities that had been rocking the rest of the world for the last twenty years. But that

22

was all changing. The times, they are a-changing. And getting worse. The floodgates were breaking down. And Wendell Parker was supposed to be the one to stop it all. Little Boy Red, White, and Blue with his finger stuck in the fucking dike.

"Check out that dispatch, would you, Saunders?" Colonel Parker said, as he nervously glanced around at the rest of the beeping, blinking, scrolling, buzzing network of computers, telephone lines, FAX machines, and video receivers tuned in to dishes far above and miles away. Perhaps the most sophisticated collection of such fully interfaced—and functioning—intel apparatus in the world. Yeah, a lot of toys, Parker couldn't help but think to himself as he let his eyes sweep around the room. Every light, every beep meant something going wrong somewhere on the planet. And everywhere around the floor men and women took down notes, culled through the flood of data, trying to pick out the necessary, the revealing, the hidden clue to some bloody plot being hatched.

Parker again ran his fingers back and forth through his gray James-Dean-style hair. He was still wearing the front with a half bop the way he had since he was a just a teen ready to kick anyone's ass. He put down the magnifying glass but continued to stare at the pictures of the melted men. They must been exposed for a while before the radiation source was removed, for the whole front of both had just melted. From their foreheads, down their faces, chests, and legs. Their features had slid down as if they'd been made of mud. Their faces were something from a nightmare, teeth hanging at all crazy angles, one eye fallen down to about nose level—if the black coagulated holes that were in the center of the faces were noses. It was hard to tell just what the hell was going on. He wished he hadn't seen them now that he had. He would remember it always.

23

Saunders came back to the desk. "How did the techs who showed up get the damned cannister closed if it was spitting out so much rad juice?" Parker asked, at last throwing the picture down hard on the table and vowing not to look at the damned hypnotic master-piece of death again.

"It was really only the opened top of the container—which those two had the interesting experience of getting suntanned by—that was lethal. The techs, when they showed up about two hours later, were able to close the thing using a remote-control robot they've been working with—adapted from police bomb-removal systems. And by the way, Colonel," Saunders went on, "two more people got roasted. A couple of restaurant employees who came out to check the noise thought there was a fire, and tried to squirt the cannister out with fire extinguishers. You ever see foam hit pure plutonium? They both got steamed to death, scalded red as Cape Cod lobsters. Fell back screaming before they could get melted like the hijackers. But it didn't take 'em too long to croak."

"How many more were taken?" Parker asked tiredly, not really wanting to know. "Cannisters, I mean."

"Two, sir," his subordinate replied calmly, handing him a printout from one of the Telecom computer pickups from NATO. "And this is the information I was waiting for from U.S. Army Intel in West Germany. Although two of the hijackers were melted, we know from witnesses and evidence found at the scene that there were at least five, maybe six more. And they knew what the hell they were doing. Had rad suits on and everything. These two just got a little unlucky."

"A little unlucky," Parker echoed, shuddering and leaning forward to get a cigarette from his right-hand drawer, though he had sworn that he was giving up the disgusting habit. But if there were shipments of plutonium on the loose, it seemed as good a time as any

24

to backslide a little. He lit up and glared at Saunders hard, daring him to say a fucking word about the Parliament 100, full-strength—no light, low-tar, or any of that shit.

"Believe it or not," Saunders went on, moving his lips in the odd, almost motionless, way that some of the American upper classes affected, perhaps in imitation of their British "ancestry," "they were able to get chemical analyses done on some of the residue that was left. And found—in the boots of one of them—a rosin that's used in weight lifting. Stuff has an extremely high burn temperature—so some of it survived the irradiation intact."

"So what the hell does that mean?" Parker asked, looking annoyed as he took a deep drag and tried not to listen to the clicking, typing, and shouting coming from every part of the room. It was getting too noisy in this place already and they'd only been in operation down here two months now. Heaven help him when the joint really got rolling.

"Well, sir, the World Weight Lifting and Wrestling Games are being held soon in New York. There'll be thousands of contestants from around the earth. If someone had the idea of pulling something there—it would be catastrophic. Unlike any terrorist act we've seen before. A new level. A Hiroshima of terrorism. Something I don't think any of us even want to think about."

"You can say that again," Parker mumbled softly. He hadn't thought somehow that he was going to be in the thick of it so quickly. Not even time to get his damned books completely unpacked and set out. No time to quite know where the hell everything was, or just how it functioned. For this was new to all of them. There had never been a system quite like it before. How would he assemble all the data being spewed out at him into some sort of coherent picture? How would he turn a jigsaw puzzle of blood into a road map of counter-insurgency in five easy lessons. That was all that Parker had to do.

"All right," Parker said, making a sudden decision that he knew would make him or break him as head of D2. "This is Priority One—this whole hijacking thing here. Anything to do with these two, or with the plutonium, I want to know. Everything else you handle, or give to Richfield—he knows what the hell to do. I want a meeting in twenty minutes in Conference Room A. Get me some physics boys, transport people, security, and training personnel. All, you hear me? The department head of every unit in this place. And I mean now! You got me? They don't show—they're out. We're in combat mode now."

"I got you," Saunders replied with a sudden respect in his voice for the colonel. He had only been with the man a few months, and it was the first time he had seen him really exert his authority. And Saunders knew from experience—it was the only way. Someone had to be the fucking chief.

Exactly twenty minutes later, Colonel Parker was pacing around a soundproofed, bug-proofed, wall-to-wall-carpeted meeting room off to one side of the War Room. He kept running his fingers along his scalp, knowing as he did that he shouldn't, for every few strokes a hair or two came out—and he wasn't sure they'd return.

"Now let me get this straight," he addressed one of a dozen men seated around the long cherry-topped table. All their collars were open as the air-conditioning wasn't quite working right. "You're telling me that the plutonium these guys took could in fact be the fuel core of an atomic bomb?" Parker sounded incredulous.

"That's about the size of it," a roly-poly, flush-cheeked fellow said, looking up from the calculations he had been madly computing in the minutes before the

26

meeting. "There is definitely enough material in those two cannisters to do the job."

"But I thought it was extremely hard to build an A-bomb," Parker said, angrily slamming his right hand onto the desk so that it actually hurt. He reached in his jacket for another cigarette, lighting it wildly so it caught halfway down the cylinder of tobacco, wasting nearly half the butt. "I mean, that's why hardly anyone has them."

"Sure it's hard," the physics man said, looking straight up at the colonel as he closed his black notepad. "Damned hard. But it's *possible*. You just asked me if that stuff *could* be the core of an A-bomb. And the answer to that is—yes, it could. *If* they could get some U-238 that was pretty clean. *If* they could mold the right charges of atomic material and explosive in the right patterns so as to cause detonation when imploded. *If* they could figure out how to arm the damned thing and set it off without blowing themselves to kingdom come. *If* a hell of a lot of different factors were present and they were incredibly lucky—*yes*—they could pull a Hiroshima in New York. Or anywhere, for that matter. Atomic bombs, as I remember, aren't too prejudiced about where they go off."

Parker ran halfway around the table, startling some of the seated experts. He rushed up to a mustached fellow in his late fifties wearing a feathered hat such as are traditionally worn by Mafiosi and rich men playing golf. Doctor Claiborne was a legend around the Agency. As brilliant as some kind of Sherlock Holmes when it came to filtering out meaningful intelligence information. And as mean as a junkyard dog when he was in a bad mood, which was nearly always. Today he seemed almost cheerful, perhaps because there was a real emergency—instead of the administrative bull that he'd been involved in lately.

"Tell me, Doctor Claiborne," Parker nearly exploded, "have there been hijackings of other materials that could be used in the construction of such a bomb?"

"Oh, horseballs, man," Claiborne barked out with a harsh laugh as he adjusted his bow tie to make room for the rise and fall of his bulging Adam's apple. "Do you know how much stuff is stolen, unaccounted for, missing from munitions and nuclear weapons stockpiles? Let's put it this way, Parker. Since we've started keeping records—and that was only really only in the late sixties—it's estimated that over a hundred pounds of bomb-quality fueling materials have been lost one way or another. Enough for about fifty low-yield nukes."

"A hundred pounds," Parker echoed back in disbelief. "I had no idea—"

"No one does," Claiborne barked out again with his sharp sarcastic laugh, as if all the world was a joke to him, a big sick joke. As if he just stuck around so he could expose it even more, show the worms and the vermin that ate beneath its surface. "All the intelligence agencies have pretty much agreed not to make it public knowledge. With the amount of free-floating high-rad materials out there, can you imagine the panic worldwide?"

"So you're saying—" Parker began as he stood back, trying to digest the last piece of information.

"I'm saying that, hell, yes, there's plenty of stuff floating around. We've even heard rumors that there's a small but growing black market in the fuel cores and detonation systems for these weapons. You'd be surprised what's up for sale—or barter—these days. But to be even more specific—*yes*—I have a feeling about this one. I don't think that they're planning to use the plutonium on its own—as a poison that might be introduced into a reservoir or a subway system, for example. The high-tech operation that they pulled

28

off—and carried out, by the way, from start to finish in twelve minutes—all indicates highly trained and pretty fucking ice-veined individuals. I mean, their two pals got roasted into inedible Sloppy Joes—and they still continued the operation. I'd say—you better start looking for an A-bomb being assembled somewhere on the European Continent, final destination unknown."

Colonel Parker stood almost frozen for about thirty seconds as if he were contemplating the universe. Then he turned and spoke in a soft voice but with a tone of absolute and crystal-clear authority. A tone that made every man in the room suddenly sit a little straighter in his chair, made his ears rise up to hear each word.

"All right. Everyone in this conference room is now on this project. Project Pluto we'll call it, for lack of a better name." A few men groaned and made protestations that they had their own projects already in full gear.

"Now—some of you don't know me. So I'll explain the situation right here and now so there won't be any confusion in the future." Parker stood at the head of the table now so every eye could see him, his full six-foot-two, 195-pound frame standing tall. He looked commanding. But then he had led men through the hells of the swamps of Asia, had been hunted down like a dog by the Khmer Rouge, had . . . Colonel Wendell Parker had been around. And that experience, those dark blue eyes like the tips of waves in an approaching winter storm, made them all listen closely, if only out of a fear of the man.

"Now we can all stay relaxed—but you gotta do what I want—when I want. This is a war. We're in combat, men, you understand? And what we do as a team, instantaneously and without question, could affect the lives of millions of innocent people. This is primo, AAA, ultra, whatever the fuck you want to designate it. I don't care *what* you're working on. Let

29

your subordinates handle it. If there are actual lives involved, see me privately. Otherwise don't even mention it. I'll oversee the entire operation. We'll meet three times a day, morning, afternoon, evening. On call twenty-four hours. Any questions?" He looked around to make sure they were getting the message. They were.

"Now first things first. We've got to formulate the right questions before we can even begin to get any answers. Write down what I'm saying, and then divide the questions up among yourselves by area of expertise. One: Why have these materials been stolen, and where and when are they going to be used? Two: Where are these materials at present? Three: What does it take to build a bomb—men, supplies, et cetera? Four: What does it take to detect such radioactive elements—geiger counters, equipment from planes, dogs, whatever the hell it is?"

"Are you saying, sir," one of the high-explosive experts asked with a half-twisted smile, "that we should have packs of dogs sniffing their way across Europe searching for these cannisters?"

"If that's what it takes, pal," Parker said, forcing himself to laugh to show he was a regular Joe and they should stay loose, when he felt like slamming the guy for the remark. "Just think of the consequences, okay? Just review your old archival films of the effects of Hiroshima and Nagasaki. Take a look at the burned bodies, the twisted skeletons etched into the sides of walls. It can't happen here. You understand me? It can't!" Colonel Parker's eyes seemed to grow even stormier, glowing with an angry luminescence. "Because *we* may be the only bastards who can stop it. And I'm not going to go down in history as the man who allowed an American city to go up in a fucking mushroom cloud."

Chapter Three

The pre-dawn East Harlem street was dark and cold, frigid with the kind of chill that can slice right into a man's backbone, make him shiver to the hidden depths of his soul. Sheets of steam rose in swirling patterns from the manholes here and there along the potholed streets with their mounds of garbage lining the curbs like insidious monuments to poverty. The sky overhead was black, impenetrable, like pounded metal all twisted and angry as if it might unleash a hail of ice or rain or snow at any moment, depending on the belligerency of its dark mood.

But the wide-shouldered figure that walked forward, clad only in black turtleneck sweater, jeans, and motorcycle boots, didn't tremble or even notice the cold. He was too busy making sure he didn't step on rats, puddles of slime, or any other of the flotsam and jetsam that lay everywhere in one of the most rundown parts of the city. The human garbage too—drunks lying on their pieces of cardboard, junkies crouched Buddha-like in nodding meditations in doorways trying to savor the last opium dreams of the night before the harsh morning winds slammed into their flesh and brought them back to the dark realities

31

of another dismal day. All in all, it was just about the most wretched morning that Rick Harrison had ever seen.

His whole body suddenly tensed as a large black rat rushed out of a pile of garbage and ran right across his path like a black cat. Only this was a rat. That somehow seemed a lot worse. And suddenly Harrison was shivering and the world felt very cold, the battered steel skies pressing down like dirt onto a corpse. The rat stopped about ten feet ahead, stood up on its hind legs, opening its small but tooth-packed jaws, and hissed at him.

"Rat—get the fuck out of here, rat, before I take off your damned head," Harrison yelled, reaching down into a mound of debris and grabbing a bottle, which he quickly broke at the wider end and then held back as if preparing to throw it. But the flash of jagged glass took the macho out of the foot-and-a-half specimen of filthy vermin which looked like it had fought in Nam, so beat up was its face—one eye gone—so mottled its hide, with chunks of fur missing all over the place. But tough as the old boy was, he scurried off, disappearing beneath a car-sized pile of garbage on the other side of the cracked street.

Harrison kept the bottle gripped in his fingers, letting it dangle at his side as he walked forward cautiously one step at a time. Talk about a bad night, he thought darkly to himself as his brown eyes surveyed the street ahead and the alleys between the broken-down, boarded buildings that stood all around him like an audience of brick corpses. A night perhaps to die. A night maybe to win a thousand bucks, another voice said inside his brain, this one a lot more aggressive—and hungry. The figure loomed in his mind. A thousand bucks—how big a pile of tens was that? Why, he could hardly hold it in one hand, he lied to himself, making his legs push on through the windy street as spires of newspapers and dust rose all around him in violent flurries.

It was only the thought of the mini-fortune that lured him on, even through the dust and the stink. Setting his hard chin even harder, he pushed on with a stamping gait searching for the basement door that "the event" was taking place in. That slimy little bookie Karver had said his opponent was just a big fat slob, a janitor who'd gotten a few muscles carrying garbage cans. Shouldn't be any trouble. Right, no trouble. So why was the action all on the fat Puerto Rican? Something was wrong. Something stank. But money has lured men down into mineshafts, into crocodile-infested rivers, to the moon and back—and so it had little trouble luring Rick Harrison down a puke-coated set of dank stone stairs that looked like they descended into the subterranean storage tanks of hell itself.

A pockmarked face appeared suddenly out of the shadows at the base of the steps behind an iron door half hanging off its heavily rusted hinges.

"Who sent you?" the tight little lips squeaked out, as behind him the sounds of a number of other men were faintly audible.

"I'm one of the damn contestants," Harrison said with a scowl, still not feeling too good about the whole thing. He stepped through the door before the guy could say yes or no. And standing six feet four and weighing a good 260 pounds, Harrison had the sheer size that made the skinny, weasel-faced lackey step quickly out of the way.

"Hey, the broken bottle—can't carry that fucking thing inside in your hand." The thug started to reach inside his coat jacket, but Harrison looked down and laughed.

"Sorry, sorry," he said. "I didn't even know it was

33

there." He heaved it back up the stairs behind him, and it shattered into pieces on the sidewalk above. Then he held out both hands in front of him as if for inspection by the junior Al Capone guarding the door.

"See, Ma, clean nails." He smirked and walked past the guy as the guard grunted and let the rod fall back into his shoulder holster.

"Big bastard's lucky I don't plug him," the guard blustered to himself as he turned back toward the basement door and stared out waiting for more ghostly figures to appear out of the sour fog.

Harrison moved carefully along the basement walkways as there were cracks in the concrete flooring. Plaster was threatening to explode down from gaping tears in the low ceilings above. He followed the sound of the voices ahead. The ceiling was lit with just a couple of low-watt light bulbs every sixty feet or so, so it was hard to see. The steam leaking from numerous pipes that crisscrossed overhead didn't help matters any. At last, after going down two long corridors and then through a small room, he entered into a long square chamber with a wire cage in the middle of it. Inside the cage two men were slugging it out like there was no tomorrow. One of them was winning and the other one was losing. And losing bad. His face looked like it was auditioning for a ketchup commercial—as the ketchup. But still the sucker fought on, throwing his fists out uselessly in front of him, like a drunk trying to clean a windshield.

His opponent was big. Fat, but big as a mountain. And he didn't seem too concerned about whether or not his smaller adversary lived or died. For the huge ham-hock fists just kept flying forward like jack-hammers pummeling the man, driving him back, back, until the body slammed up against the steel cage and the crowd of men—nearly a hundred of them all

34

cursing and holding wads of bills in their hands, teeth chewing on cigars, cigarettes, and joints—let out a collective scream. For the end was near.

As Harrison made his way to the edge of the crowd and stopped, he saw the last few seconds of the bout close up—and wished he hadn't. For the fists flew in like missiles over and over. The man's nose, teeth, everything seemed to just crack and disappear into an ocean of red. At last the huge attacker seemed to tire of the proceedings and stepped backward. With the cessation of the barrage of blows that had actually been holding him up, the other man sank down like a sack of sand, his eyes rolling up and back in his head like fruits in a slot machine. His face, neck, and shoulders were coated in blood, and when he hit the concrete floor face first, there wasn't a hell of a lot more to damage. The door of the cage was opened and the unconscious man's handlers—or brothers or whatever they were— dragged the red rubbish out along the floor and into another part of the large underground fight room, where they would try feverishly to administer whatever minuscule first aid they could.

The victor walked around the inside of the cage banging hard on the walls with his huge fists.

"Alll riiight! Alll riiight!" he bellowed as those who had bet on him cheered, and those who had not booed— although they did so from the safety and anonymity of shadows further back in the crowd. "Who's next? Anyone else? That's only two tonight. Come on!" the big man screamed, his face getting red, his eyes blazing like little neon-lit jewels. He was huge. Harrison could see that even more now that the fellow had stood up. A good seven feet tall and wide as a brick shithouse. He was fat too, big dripping folds of the stuff hanging from his chest, giving him the appearance of immense breasts. His stomach resembled some huge growth, a

35

cancer cell gone mad and grown to 400 pounds rather than just normal human flesh. Harrison could see that the guy was completely out of shape, not even muscles detectable beneath the thick fat. But at that size, you didn't have to be strong. King Kong didn't need Nautilus training.

"Ahh, there you are, Harrison," a voice suddenly spat out at his side. Harrison looked over with distaste. It was his "manager," if the lying, thieving, pimping son-of-a-bitch who stood in front of him holding a whole sandwich of money in his right hand could be given such a title. He trusted the man about as much as he did the rat that had crossed his path. But the guy had helped him make money at a few of these "fights" before. Not that the slime gave a damn about his well-being. Where there was money to be made even wolves sat down beside each other. This was Harrison's fourth fight. He wasn't exactly looking for the title. But a few bucks on the side never hurt matters any. And this was more than a few.

"A thousand, right?" the "arranger" said, waving the bills near Harrison's nose. He could see the fat pig looking at him with an amused expression as if he knew Harrison had to take the dough.

"It's fifteen hundred now, pal," Harrison said with ice in his voice. "You said the guy was just a fat old super who got strong lifting garbage cans. This guy's been eatin' his Wheaties, man. A fellow could get hurt playing around in there."

Fat Lip Louis looked around and saw the crowd going wild screaming for someone to go in there with the sucker. Yeah, he could still get some action. "Sure, Harrison," the fixer said with the grim smile of the executioner. "No sense being greedy. After all you're the one in there—not me. I'll spring for fifteen hundred."

36

"And that's win—or lose."

"Of course, of course—like always," Lip said with a big drooling smile, reaching over to pat Harrison's arm. Harrison moved quickly away, not wanting to get the slime's oil on his own flesh.

"And I want you to take five hundred of those winnings and bet them on me. What are the odds?"

"What—what do you mm—mm—" the fixer stuttered, not wanting to tell him the truth, that the odds were huge, that he probably wasn't even coming out of the cage the way he went in.

"The odds, asshole," Harrison said, starting to rip off his turtleneck sweater from over his head. "What the hell are they?"

"Ten to one, man."

"Cover me," Harrison said with a smirk. He knew the bastard didn't want to take the bet. But he also knew he had no choice. Without waiting for an answer, Harrison thrust his sweater into the man's chicken chest. "Make sure no one steals it." He started through the crowd, walking slowly. He wasn't in any great haste to climb inside the cage.

"Well, look what we got here," the huge fellow inside boomed out with a laugh, banging his fist hard against the gate so that the whole contraption wiggled around with loud clanking sounds which echoed around the basement walls. "A mouse is coming up to challenge the Super." So the guy really was called the "Super," Harrison thought with a laugh. At least the fixer hadn't lied about that, probably the first time in his life. The whole place seemed to erupt first in chuckles and then loud laughter as the crowd saw Harrison's physique. As he walked through them, they parted like a Red Sea of greedy gamblers. He was big himself, very big for an average man—but nothing compared to the tub of lard that stood awaiting him with a huge smile on its

37

tooth-busted mouth.

"Shit," Harrison mumbled under his breath as he opened the steel-mesh gate and stepped in. This was like a Christian feeding himself to the fucking lions. He'd have to take at least a tenth of his winnings and invest in some intensive psychiatric care—if he didn't lose all his brains in there. Harrison turned to close the cage, and sensed the sudden charge of the porkpie of death from across the twenty-foot cage. Somehow he was able to twist his body out of the way and to the side, though he still took much of the blow that was aimed at him by the Super's elbow. The force of the strike, which had been aimed for the back of his neck—and had it hit it probably would have killed him—instead struck his shoulder. It felt like a bone or two had been cracked, and Harrison spun around like a top for about three steps until he slammed hard into the cage wall.

But fortunately for him it was on the side away from the charging giant, giving him a chance to clear his senses. The Super flew past his would-be pancake and right into the door, which was just clanging shut and closing into place. He hit it so hard that the whole cage shook for a few seconds and seemed to almost lift up a fraction of an inch. Then the Super flew backward again and fell down onto his back in the center of the square concrete floor. Harrison was just coming out of his fog when he saw the big lug slam down just feet away from him. It was his chance. He rushed forward, leaping straight up into the air and coming down with the heel of his boot onto the man's throat.

The right hand shot up out of nowhere, the long thick arm quivering like jello as the cellulite-rippled flesh jiggled wildly. But though it took a shot from the boot, the hand was able to deflect Harrison's attack, and he found himself flying onto the cement floor, barely avoiding getting his face smashed in as he shifted enough to take the landing with his shoulder, rolling over quickly a few times. The training he'd gone through in the service—though it had been years now—was paying off. Harrison was a little surprised how easily he had taken the roll.

And he came up out of it just as fluidly, suddenly feeling a second wind sweep through his body, a feeling like he'd had in the old days. He also felt a streak of meanness, of wanting to hurt the bastard who had sucker-punched him. Wanting to make him feel a little of the same. As he turned, Harrison saw that the Super was again coming in, screaming and slamming his branch-sized arms in the air. The guy had no attack plan at all. He was just a bear, an amoeba-brained fighting machine. Harrison waited until the last second and then shot fast to the right, unleashing a mother of a left hook into the attacker's midsection. But the fist merely sank into what felt like jello. And the huge ugly Super merely grunted as Harrison ripped his hand back and danced away quickly. He was a few yards behind the man when he turned, confused for a second and not seeing where his victim was.

Then he caught sight of Harrison again and his face lit up like a kid finding a Christmas tree in his living room.

"Ahhh, there you are, mouse," he said with a smile. "See? Already you play better than the others. How long will this last? Maybe even a minute." He laughed again, in a way that Harrison didn't appreciate, to say the least, and then started forward again. This time Harrison rushed in—but just as the Super closed his hands around his neck, Harrison ducked low and unleashed a quick flurry of punches, stiff jabs and strikes, moving out again and past the attacker. But when he stepped back, the obese fighter just laughed. Not one of the shots, which had taken his other opponents to the floor in writhing pain, had done any real damage. It was no use. He couldn't even reach any vital points through all the damned fat. What a joke. Harrison could see that he was just getting the guy angry.

And sure enough, the Super stopped and turned with a decidedly non-amused look. His smile vanished and he grimaced. He wasn't used to being hurt. Not at all.

"Now you die," the mouth spat out, and he charged forward like a rhino on speed, screaming at the top of his lungs. Harrison knew this was it. One way or another they'd get it over with. He waited until the last possible second, leaving his body exposed as the man reached for it with death darkness in his eyes. At the very last instant, just as he felt the fists touching his skull, Harrison turned and twisted, grabbing one of the outstretched arms. It was one of the most basic combat judo techniques in boot camp. But like most basic things—it worked. He took almost all the motion and kinetic energy of the Super and was able to get it airborne with a twist of his whole body. The great load of lard sailed clear across the caged square and rocketed into the steel-mesh fence on the far side. This time it actually bent the whole fence in as if it had been hit by a cannon shell. The Super stood there, his face and chest pressed against the gate as if he was trying to squeeze himself through. His knees wobbled crazily but he just wouldn't go down. The guy was tough. He began to turn, his face bleeding in numerous places where it had hit the steel mesh, and started pulling out a long blade from inside his belt.

But Harrison wasn't about to give the bastard a chance to get it together. He raced forward, jumping up from his crouch and pulling his arm all the way back, unleashed an uppercut with every ounce of strength in his body. The hard fist made contact in the dead center of the throat. There was a whole curtain of fat there too, like the jowls of a diseased rooster—but not enough. Harrison's punch seemed to push the pasty throat straight in about six inches, and the doughy face was suddenly turning a ghastly red, then purple, while the man stopped in mid-stride and threw his hands around his neck as if they somehow might help get the plumbing back in order. He crumbled to the ground as blood and muck flowed out of the foaming mouth, and made ghastly sounds like a dog being stuck with pins. The Super wasn't getting up again—not today anyway.

Harrison slapped his hands together in disgust. He didn't know if he was going to keep doing this, he thought with a sudden deep repugnance for the whole damned scene. He wiped his mouth as he felt a little trickle of blood sweep down one side, a present he'd picked up along the way. He walked over to the cage and flipped up the lever on the door, pulling it back with a bang. Where the hell was Lip? Harrison scanned the crowd, which was stunned, most of the faces drained white as they looked angrily at him. Tough shit. He was supposed to lose his face so they could make a few bucks? He just wanted his own blood money.

There—he saw the little worm trying to slither out of a doorway at the far end of the basement. In a flash Harrison was through the crowd and caught up with the fixer, grabbing him hard with his right hand around the neck.

"Going somewhere, Lip?" he asked angrily. And the look in his eyes made the hustler grow even a little paler.

"Just going to my back room—for cash to pay for the bets I covered. You're first."

"Damned right I am—because I'm coming with you. Let's go. You pay *me* first—then worry about the

41

others. I don't care about them." He accompanied the squirming bookie/manager/pimp down the darkened hall to a small room where a drunken fellow was standing guard in front of the door. Inside, Harrison stood over him as the fixer opened a safe behind a concrete cinderblock wall. He took out the money—$6,000—looked at it longingly—and handed it over to Harrison, whose own eyes took on a gleam. That was $6,000 more than he'd had when he woke up this morning. It almost made it all worth it. Almost.

"Wait a minute—that should be sixty-five hundred, as I figure it," Harrison said. He counted the money a second time and enjoyed the feel of the fresh bills in his hands. There was nothing like the scent of a freshly minted bill. Nothing. It was the very perfume of life.

"Five hundred dollars for manager's fee. I'm your manager. I gotta make a living too, right?" The man looked desperate, the ratlike eyes retreating even further into the man's skull as he frantically tried to think of how he was going to cover the bets he'd taken at ten to one. There weren't a lot of them—but those there were were more than he could handle.

"And if you got any more 'Supers' in the future," Harrison said as he turned and headed out the door, stuffing the money down into the front of his pants and pulling the turtleneck back on over his sweat-coated and bloodied chest, "don't call me, I'll call you."

Chapter Four

Harrison's brain clicked like a calculator on overdrive as he thought about what he would do with the six grand. It had seemed like a fortune when Lip had handed it to him. But already, as he walked back toward his pad along the mist-shrouded, freezing streets, the money seemed to shrink in his mind like clouds that break up even as you look at them. There was fifteen hundred bucks back rent. He owed the corner grocery about five hundred in credit. There was the six hundred he'd borrowed from Garth, the two hundred . . . Well, at least he was less poor than he'd been.

Harrison wondered if the dawn would ever break, or if the night would just get darker and colder. He could feel it now, through the turtleneck, the air biting at his sweat-covered face. It was only October, but damn, it felt below freezing. He hailed a cab heading down the avenue, and lo and behold—maybe because his clothes didn't have holes in them like most of the neighborhood's curb-sleeping residents—the cabby stopped.

"All right, pal, that's an extra twenty just for stopping," Harrison said in a good mood. See that? Already he was riding in taxi cabs. It felt good.

"Downtown, pal—down to the East Village, B and 7th Street." He leaned back, savoring the relative warmth of the seat, of the engine's motor, which sent out gas-created heat right up through the steel frame. The cab hit the East River Drive and shot like a rocket down the east side of Manhattan as Harrison looked out the window at the sliver of moon still hanging onto the lip of the horizon, refusing to fall and make room for morning. The salty air from the river felt like expensive perfume on his nostrils, the call of the seagulls arguing in the gray mists above the river sounding like angelic choirs singing "money, money." Yeah, everything felt better with a few bucks in your pocket. Why, the world almost seemed—at least for the moment—nice.

He fell into a trance, spacing out on the reflecting patterns of water and light, and suddenly the cabby was leaning around and talking to him.

"I said that'll be ten-forty, pal, plus that there twenty you mentioned." He chomped on some kind of dark cigar and Harrison could see the black swamp within the mouth—not the pleasantest sight at five in the morning.

"Sure, pal, sure." Harrison yawned sleepily, reaching into his pants and ripping out two twenties. "Keep it all, keep it all, my good man," he said magnanimously, liking the feeling of wealth it gave him to so easily dispose of bills that only a short while before he would have fought tooth and nail to keep. But things changed.

"Yo, thanks, mister," the cabby said, actually awakening slightly from his permanent half stupor— the only way he could survive the horns, the red and greens, the dizzying effect of the lead and monoxide. But the bills made his eyes widen about double their usual size. He liked to measure his life by the job. And he'd just done damned well. The cab sped off with a

44

little squeal of tires as the cabby suddenly decided to push it. If the day was starting off so good—maybe he could make a fucking bundle today. Omens—you had to feel the omens.

Harrison took out his keys and scratched his stubbly chin a few times, realizing he felt beat as shit, ready to sleep for about a year. He headed down 7th Street, not a soul in sight except for an old man sprawled at one side of Harrison's front stoop beneath a baby carriage which he apparently pushed around during the daytime. It was filled to overflowing with the junk the sleeper had collected. Harrison didn't disturb him. The poor bastard needed his beauty rest. He walked into the hallway, the single light bulb dangling from the ceiling above like it was about to pop with an explosion of little shards onto the uneven tile floor below. Someday, he knew, the damned thing would explode right as *he* passed beneath it. Life was like that.

He headed up the creaking stairs of the six-story tenement. He was on the sixth floor, which felt like it was about a mile off as he climbed up past the graffiti-emblazoned walls on the floors below. Dogs barked in an apartment on the third floor. They always did, damned mutts never slept. Harrison stumbled up to his door and fitted the key in. He opened it and stepped inside. And knew something was wrong.

From out of the shadows just the other side of the door, where he kept his coats hung, a shape launched itself as if from a catapult and came flying right at him. The face was masked, the eyes burning like twin death stars, and even as the figure flew, a stick held in the attacker's hands came hurtling down out of the darkness like a baseball bat looking for a home run. Harrison somehow found the speed to get the hell out of the way. He ducked—dropped like a stone would be more accurate—falling almost flat on his face as the descending stick came shooting past him, missing his

45

head by inches. But the attacker was well balanced and recovered from the miss, pulling the weapon back and holding it up at an odd angle across his chest Samurai-sword style.

"Come on, you bastard—what the hell are you doing in my pad?" Harrison asked angrily, tightening his right hand up into a fist and starting forward. He was in no mood for bullshit.

"Just wanted to see if you were still the same tough son-of-a-bitch that I once knew," the voice behind the mask said with a throaty and satisfied laugh. "And you are." He threw down the pole and pulled off the black cotton gauze mask over his face. He looked hard at Harrison, letting just a trace of a smile flicker back and forth across his lips as if an electric current were running through thcm.

"Parker! Colonel Wendell Parker. What the hell . . . What's going . . ." For one of the few times in his fast-talking life, Harrison was totally tongue-tied as the other man came quickly forward, both arms outstretched. The two men grabbed each other's shoulders, hugged hard, looked at one another again, then took a few more hugs. There was something about sharing death with another human being that forges a bond with him. Changes something forever more. And Harrison had not only come right up to the jaws of the Grim Reaper with Parker—the bastard had saved his life more than once. He stood back and surveyed the man.

"Damn, it's good to see you," Harrison said, slapping Colonel Parker once more on the shoulder. "But what the hell was all that insanity with the stick and all? You nearly gave me a heart attack."

"Had to see if you still had it," Parker said, with a laugh, reaching for a cigarette and lighting it fast with a guilty little twitch. "Didn't make sense to send you out there if you couldn't handle the action."

"Send me out? Couldn't handle the action? What the hell are you talking about, you maniac?" Harrison laughed, stepping back and switching on the overhead light so the contents of his disorderly, clothes-littered fourteen-by-twenty room were lit with a soft golden glow.

"It's a mess in here," Parker said with a mock grimace as he looked around at the archetypal bachelor pad, with old food rotting away in bowls on a table and socks unwashed for months.

"Last time I remember, Parker"—Harrison laughed, going to the refrigerator, which chugged away like a thing alive at the far end of the room in a little cubicle kitchen—"your face was in the mud and your clothes were covered with mold and swamp slime." He chuckled as he tossed a can across the room. "But like they say, those who live in dirt houses shouldn't throw mudballs—or something like that."

Parker laughed too, at the memory of the two of them slithering along like lizards for days and nights at a time through the infernal Asian swamps. Now it seemed interesting in a detached way, amusing in retrospect. Then it had been pure hell.

"Well, things change." The CIA chief laughed, coughing out a little geyser of blue smoke. He glanced at his wristwatch, which shimmered gold under the beating light of the bulb. "These days, believe it or not, I'm as orderly as they come. Got to be. I'm responsible for the lives of hundreds of men, agents around the world. I'm a big cheese now, my friend. How it happened I couldn't even really tell you. But it has and . . . Oh, shit, let's not talk about me. I had to come out myself to even track you down. My 'operatives' couldn't quite make the connection. Not that it was that easy for me to find you either. You leave a trail like a snake through the woods. It's *damned* good to see you, Harrison," he said softly, holding

47

his can of beer, his eyes a little misty for just a fraction of a second, a rare and unusual occurrence.

"Come on, pal," Parker said after drinking down half the can, "let's go have some fun. What's it been—ten, eleven years? Got to be some after-hours clubs around here, right?" He punched at Harrison's arm again, in good humor. As the two stood there together, they both realized that they each might care more about the son-of-a-bitch standing in front of them than anyone else in the world. Their years of combat together had left a deeper imprint than either had quite realized.

"Sure," Harrison said, feeling so much adrenaline flowing into his veins from the mock attack that his heart was still beating at about double its usual speed. He wasn't going to fall asleep for hours anyway. "But it's on me," Harrison said, pulling out his wad of bills and hiding them beneath a floorboard in the corner. Such was his trust for the man in his room who he hadn't seen for over a decade that he didn't think once of checking to see if Parker was looking.

"No, no, on me, I insist," Parker protested. "This is all on Federal Government money—you kidding me? You want to spend your own bucks when you can be spending your tax money?"

"Yeah, right," Harrison replied, realizing that he had to be sensible too. He wanted to hold on to that money for as long as he could. A nest egg, as it were. "You're on, man." He chuckled, taking off the sweated-up turtleneck and putting on another clean one, then a thick leather jacket over it all. "And I know just the place. You'll love it. Avant garde up the ol' kazoo. Jazz, chicks with only half their clothes on spouting poetry, nude tapdancing . . ."

And true to Harrison's words, Colonel Parker wasn't disappointed. He was led through the dark innards of an old loft in Soho that was decked out so it

48

appeared to be one of the old coffeehouses of the past, complete with black cats and bearded beatniks playing bongos. The club was packed too, which was amazing considering the hour. Parker swore he saw familiar faces—people from movies, TV. He couldn't even place them, but fame was written all over them. The two men found an empty old wooden booth in the back of the place, with hearts and "I Luv Susi" carved all over it—coffeehouse circa 1960—the real thing.

"Just bring us two bottles of the absolute best of whatever you have," Harrison said to the waitress as she bent down low so her full breasts pressed out against her black leotard top. She chewed gum with fervent energy as she wrote down the order.

"Two of the best of whatever," she repeated in a bored nasal tone. "I'll see what they got," she said, blowing a half-bubble and walked off, wriggling her hips to the backbeat that was coming out of two huge throbbing jukeboxes set up toward the front of the loft, each playing different songs.

The two men turned their heads around, both noticing that there sure as hell were a lot of young, attractive women floating around the place wearing everything from gowns to jeans to—nothing, Harrison saw as a swab of light from one of the turning disco diamonds in the ceiling lit up a portion of the dance floor to reveal an entirely naked couple, man and woman, dancing away like they were in another world.

"All right, man—my kind of place." Parker laughed as he hit his hand on the table. In a minute the waitress returned with a bottle of private-label Kentucky bourbon and plunked it down on the table along with two glasses and a bottle of olives.

"That'll be one hundred ninety-seven dollars," she said without blinking to the CIA man, who handed her a plastic foldout of countless credit cards from inside his jacket. "Take fifty percent of the bill for a tip,"

Parker said with a smile to the shapely bargirl.

"Yes, sir," the waitress replied, her mouth still chewing as it took her a second to realize that that meant a C-note just for her. "Hey, thanks a lot, mister." She looked at him hard, her demeanor suddenly growing a lot slinkier, catlike, like a female in heat when she smells cash. "Maybe I'll come back and uh— help you do in that bottle." She spoke in what was supposed to be a sexy Mae West accent, but which came out sounding more like a Queens secretary whose adenoids had been removed. Still, both men looked hard as she strutted off moving her hips in exaggerated circles around behind her.

"Damn." Parker laughed, pouring himself a glass of the bourbon and raising it high in the air.

"Damn." Harrison laughed, pouring a full portion of the dark golden liquid.

"To war," the CIA chief said with a harsh laugh.

"Nah, I can't drink to war," Harrison answered. "But I'll drink to the memories of war. The memories of how in the midst of all that blood and horror, the friendship between two men was as strong as forged iron. To the memories of war."

"Yeah, the memories," Parker echoed softly, his eyes again growing a little damp. What the hell was wrong with him? The Hawk could never turn soft. He clanked his glass hard against Harrison's and then pulled back, drinking the whole load down fast, wincing his eyes together to squeeze the moisture away. There was no room in his life for such luxuries as tears. Not when he had to send men to their deaths every day. Not when he might be sending Harrison to his.

The two men drank and talked and drank and talked some more. The club didn't even get going until the sun rose. And it just seemed to grow more and more crowded. The night-life denizens in their myriad of

50

colorful and outrageous costumes, most of indeterminate sex, just kept rolling in like Disneyland had been evacuated. But the two men didn't even notice the parade, so wrapped up were they in their war stories. It was after they had been going at it for about two hours when Harrison's voice rose for a moment above the din of the dancing, screaming crowd.

"You want me to what?" Harrison suddenly laughed incredulously. He took another half glass of the bourbon down in a single gulp.

"You heard me right, Harrison. I want you to work as one of my field operatives—as part of a wrestling team—and do deep penetration work for me. The pay will be worth it, man. I promise you." Harrison didn't, couldn't say a word. The world was crazy. Too crazy. He just stared down at the flaming wax candle in a bottle in the center of the red and white checkered plastic tablecloth and got a weird smile on his face.

"What the hell are you doing these days anyway, man? I mean let's be honest here," Parker said slurring his words a little as his eyes searched around for their hip-swaggling waitress. The bottle was heading on empty.

"Well, I'm doin' lots of things," Harrison slurred back, the whole world a blurred rainbow of dark warm color. "I'm in a band—play synthesizer. Didn't know I cud play—did you? Damned good I am. Maybe even have record soon." He hiccupped up some bourbon and took another quick slug, seeing that his glass was getting low. "Teach some self-defense courses at the YMCA in midtown—and occasionally"—he looked down a little sheepishly—"I take on tough-man fights—you know, for a few bucks. Jus' had one tonight as madder of fact—and won me a bunch of money."

"How much money, Rick?" Parker asked as he

51

caught the waitress's attention and ordered another bottle. "How much you made tonight? Come on, I'm your pal." He leaned forward on the table, his elbow sliding across the greasy surface. "You kin tell me."

"Six," Harrison said, holding up seven fingers. "Six fuckin' thousand bucks. That ain't hay." He waved his finger in front of Parker's nose and laughed again.

"I'll give you ten times that amount, pal." Parker grinned darkly, leaning even closer so his head was nearly touching Harrison's. "Sixty grand per annum— half of it payable up front. Whadda ya say, whadda ya say? It'll be fun—like ol' times?"

"What the hell you want me so bad for?" Harrison asked suspiciously, coming out of his drunken stupor for a moment.

"Can't tell you right now jes what it's for," Parker said apologetically, waving his head from side to side. "Jes can't tell you right now."

"You mean you won't even trust me enough to tell me what it is I'd be doin' that's so damned dangerous you came out yourself to recruit a maniac like me in the first place?"

"Sumthin' like that," Parker mumbled back. He took a deep swig right out of the bottle, losing all the refinement he had so carefully cultivated over the last decade in his rise to the top. But it tasted good. Tasted better that way. Brought back memories of other days when he had been more savage, not so tamed. And after a few more glasses of the burning liquor, a few more toasts to lost comrades, a few more songs about grunts and whores from downtown Saigon, they forgot about all the problems of the here and now—and lived only in the past, the drunken sweet, twisted past, that had felt so horrible living it, and yet felt so inexplicably wonderful in the recalling.

Chapter Five

"Don't drop the uranium, you asshole," a figure clad in a heavy radiation protection suit from head to toe screamed out from atop a high aluminum ladder that stood in the center of the vast floor of a warehouse. From there he was directing the unpacking of a number of different crates and cannisters—all of them stolen or bought from black-market sources. And contained within these supplies were the ingredients for one atomic bomb—blend carefully, stir slowly, and get the fuck out of there. But if the forklift handler didn't watch his step, they wouldn't even get the thing in the oven. For the heavy-fork-driver had nearly let a large silver cannister, six feet high, slip from the fork's grasp as it hovered a good ten feet above the ground.

"Slowly, slowly, like you're carrying *eggs!*" the man perched up on the ladder yelled down through a battery-powered PA speaker that he held in one hand. Moving at about half the speed he had been going seconds before, the operator eased the load forward so it was set atop one end of a hundred-foot-long, ten-foot-wide steel machine table. Numerous other objects had already been loaded on top of it—a factory's worth of high-tech parts. The man on the ladder checked off a long list on a clipboard and then looked up and down the table again. It was complete. Basically. Oh, there were lots of odds and ends needed, wires, bolts, circuit breakers . . . But the big stuff—the plutonium, the U235, the high explosives for sending the two halves of a steel globe together at super speed, all that was *really* needed—was there.

The man pulled off the hood from his rad suit, exposing his neck and head, and addressed the dozen similarly suited figures who continued arranging all the items by function below.

"A moment, a moment of your time," he said, banging the side of his clipboard against the top of the ladder so it made a sharp gavel-like sound. "Please, it is important that you all stop what you're doing," the white-haired scientist said, his dry lips stroked constantly by his nervous tongue. The workers put down their boxes, stopped their movements, and formed a rough semicircle around the ladder, which stood in the center of a wooden floor a good 40 feet wide and over 200 feet long, lit by dusty skylights from above.

He licked his lips again, a habit he had gotten into to punctuate thoughts when speaking to groups of people—something he had done much in his years, first as one of the junior scientists on the Manhattan Project, which built the first atomic bomb, and later as a professor lecturing Ph.D. students in nuclear physics in his post at MIT. The days before the trouble. Before . . . He pulled his mind away from the less pleasant things and smiled at those who stood below and around him. For better times, greater times were here again.

"We have reached the second stage in our mission," Professor Markus said crisply, enunciating each vowel the way a professor who has said the same words over and over—"atomic fission, nuclei, bombarding protons"—must play with the language or he would surely go mad. Over a lifetime it was only the little games, the manipulations of one's mind, that kept one from going off the deep end. "The first stage—the collection of materials—is complete. We have the prerequisites to make a functioning atomic bomb—minimum size one megaton." He let the words sink in as the dozen or so men and women looked around at each other, filled with a fanatical pride that they had even gotten this far. They weren't playing in the minor leagues any more, that was for damn sure.

And a strange lot they were, even those who made up the revolutionary attack squad had to agree. Revolutionaries, disgruntled Communists, even ex-Fascists—from political terrorism gangs around the world. There were two from the Baader-Meinhof gang of West Germany and three Red Army followers from Japan, all fluent in English—and physics, as they had all been grad students at MIT. Throw in a few Palestinians, two or three Weathermen still kicking around from the sixties—now gray-haired and almost softspoken unlike their more strident youthful counterparts, and two Neo Black Panthers—a splinter group of a splinter group of . . . All that Professor Alex Rawlings Markus cared about was that they all had degrees in some branch of science related to the building of a nuclear device.

"I think we can all feel proud," he went on with a little cough, his face flushing as he let himself feel his own pride for having gotten what was just a mad idea but a few years before. Now, under his guidance, it was actually happening. It was really happening. They would leave a burning wound on capitalism that it would not soon forget. And the other deans and full professors back at the University—oh, wouldn't they be in for a surprise. "Proud that we've been able to bring our project to even this much fruition. As you all know, there are plenty who talk the talk out there but don't walk the walk." The words were his attempt at "communicating" with the younger members of the team, although he knew as well how ridiculous they sounded as they tumbled from his lips.

The members of Revolutionary Cell 12, as it called itself, looked around at one another and reached out and shook hands. They felt, at least for a few moments—before their fanatical minds again felt the deep hatred that drove them all—a kind of mad joy that they had done what all their picketing and screaming, their petitions had not. They had gone out there and taken the bull of bourgeois capitalism by the horns, ready to go at it head to head, atomic-style.

"But this is only the first stage. And we must move on—not tomorrow, but now. Must finish sorting all the materials, placing them in the proper order. Must begin listing the wirings on schematics as I've gone over with you. There is much to do—and little time to do it. You know who the heads of each bomb-team operation are—Chemistry, Explosives, Machine Tooling, and Additional Parts Gathering. We'll work in shifts of twelve hours on, four off from now on. No one will leave the building other than those authorized to gather supplies or food. Is that all completely and clearly understood—so there are no mistakes?"

He looked around. They were a tough bunch. Two had died already, stupidly, unnecessarily. How many more would go before the project was completed? How many might he himself have to kill? For Professor Markus knew, after all the unstable personalities he had worked with in his lifetime of collaboration with other scientists, that there were too many volatile personalities there in one place, too many freewheeling zealots with their own precise idea of revolution burning in their brains for it all not to explode somewhere down the line. But he had his own ideas too. Only thing was—his were going to come out on top. And the silenced 9mm H&K pistol beneath his oversized white lab coat would see to that when and if it came down to it.

"Professor, should we continue to wear the rad suits?" Tina Ferrantz, of the Radical Arm of the Women's Action League and an M.A. in explosive shock wave manipulation—if Professor Markus's memory served him right—spoke up. "I mean while we're working around the table, handling the sup- plies—and the radioactive materials."

"As far as protection goes . . ." The Professor laughed, coming down the ladder and stepping out of his suit completely now that the direct transferring of the materials was complete and nothing was likely to fall over and pop open, spilling its glowing guts all over the place. "That's up to each of you. If you want to keep wearing the suits, that's your decision. But as for me, I feel that those who truly believe in World Revolution, those who are completely, one-hundred-percent will- ing to give their bodies, their lives to the forwarding of the revolution, will not worry about such mundane things. It is not in our hands. We are after all but tools in the hands of an inevitable historical evolution." The others listened half spellbound—all of them either students or ex-students of the professor's, or people he'd contacted through the underground cell network. He seemed to have an almost mesmerizing effect on them, saying the words they wanted to hear. He made them want to do what he asked, to take any risk to contribute.

It hadn't been easy to assemble this crew. They were not only ideologically ready to go the full mile, but among them possessed the skills to build one of the

57

atomic monsters of the twentieth century. What a feat. They might hate him, but Markus knew his name would go down in the physics books forever when all was said and done. Yes, they would curse his name every time they saw it in print—but he was about to be as immortal as the earth spinning around the sun, as the electron around the proton, as the splitting of the atom.

"To work, to work," Professor Markus shouted, waving his hands toward the table. He saw that all but two of them had taken off their rad gear. He noted the two who kept them on—Ayakita from Japan and one of the Black Panthers, Karlson, a chem whiz from Harvard. He would keep a close eye on them. They were thinking more of their own flesh, were still trapped in the illusions of the bourgeois body—that the self was more important than the group, that the flesh was more important than the evolution of man to the next stage in economic and social inevitability. Such men he did not trust.

Chapter Six

Colonel Parker leaned back in the pneumatic leather and nickel reclining chair, seated in front of his black marble desk inlaid with computer and video monitors built along its entire surface, and let out a stream of curses.

"What the hell do you mean Interpol can't promise us access to *all* the European cities we've requested radiation searches in?" Parker exploded out at his right-hand assistant, who stood on the far side of the desk, not looking very happy about being the recipient of his boss's wrath.

"Sir, I'm sure this is the last thing you want to hear— but we've been getting very poor cooperation from a number of countries. Everyone thinks we're trying to sniff out their power plants, their hidden nuke stockpiles, or some damn thing. No way in hell can we make them believe otherwise—or even that there's a real threat to everyone's security. You know how politics is. Some of these bastards would let a rattler bite them in the ass—if it was politically called for. We've got our own Air Force brass allowing us to hook some new infrared radiation-detector equipment to their AWACS flights. But I don't know—it's going to pick up a hell of a lot of bullshit out there—every

59

nuclear reactor, even hospital cancer machines doing radiation therapy. I don't think it's going to give us less than a thousand pins in the European haystack."

"Look," Parker said, punching up the absolute zero data that his summary of intel reports put together by all committees had showed to date. They were getting nowhere fast. "I don't want to hear the words 'not,' or 'can't' anymore around here. We're working with impossibilities. Everything's impossible—until you do it. Let's try it from a whole different angle—our street info sources all over the globe. I want them all used. I want every cop who owes us a favor, every bastard we can bribe or blackmail. I mean this is it, man. Pull out all the stops and go for fucking broke. This is the one. Put out the word—we're looking for stolen stuff that glows. That's hot. Guys wearing weird white suits. You know—anything in that direction. Even sightings of monsters." He chuckled for a moment at the thought of how a few of those rad-suited hijackers would look to some backwoods peasant. They'd be noticed. The bomb-builders weren't going to get away totally undetected no matter how good they were.

"Tell them—big reward money. I mean big—if it's what we want. Say—a hundred thousand dollars— that's American dollars—tax free."

He grinned and Saunders grinned back. The chief was tough—but he was getting to like him more. The stuff they'd taught him back at Harvard Law, and then his Ph.D. in the Destabilization of International Terrorist Cells, hadn't quite prepared him for the real world. The double-dealing backstabbing, no-holds-barred way the "game" was played out here. But he was starting to learn.

"Sir, what about the press? I'm afraid we've got a few reporters nosing around on the plutonium story. The German press is really making a stink about a supposed U.S. Army 'chemical leak' at the restaurant—the whole area, by the way, is sealed off there now. But everyone and his mother knows something is up. Just don't know what the hell it is."

"Fuck the press. I don't give a squirt about them. I'm worrying about an A-bomb blast—I don't care what they write or do. Nothing goes out from here, from this whole damned place. And you can get the word out to everyone in this Buck Rogers cave down here—I find out there's *one* newspaper article that gets out, and the source is us, and that man is through in the Agency. And maybe he's through altogether. I'm not kidding, man. This isn't game time anymore."

Saunders sensed the fierceness, the almost savage intensity of the warrior, the super-fighter that Parker was reputed to have been—saw it suddenly glow in his eyes as if he were back peering through the stinking lilly pads of some godforsaken jungle. And Saunders knew at that moment that Colonel Parker would do anything he had to to carry out his duty. Would even shoot Saunders himself right between the eyes without blinking—if that's what was called for. And suddenly the overeducated intelligence grad took his job very, very seriously, more seriously than he had ever taken anything in his life.

The phone to the right—set into a large panel console which contained ten mini-television screens, all tuned to the main TV news programs around the world with instant English translation by computerized language chips—rang. Cursing again, feeling more pissed off by the minute at every obstacle he was running up against, Parker picked up the phone.

"Yeah, what the hell is it?" he barked into the receiver. "What's that—a guy named Harrison with my private number? Yeah—yeah, patch him through. I'll take it." The colonel motioned with his head for Saunders to get to work on all the possible angles of tracing down a factory for making a bomb. The subordinate saluted in a half-hearted sort of way and turned on his heels. He saw Parker make a little snort at the salute—but Saunders was perceptive enough to see that the man actually enjoyed it. He had never been so alive as during the years he had been out in combat—leading other men, going right into the firestorm and walking out again. The salute meant hierarchy, teamwork, survival. And in a silent way, an acknowledgment of all that Parker had been through out there.

Colonel Parker turned in his chair and regarded the myriad of computers and the men and women tending them around the great War Room—with its immense global maps hanging thirty feet high from floor to ceiling and bursting with blips and dots of lights of red, blue, green. Each color representing the tracking by five different satellites of every ship, every missile, every potentially hostile plane, truck, or submarine on the entire planet containing radiation or radioactive cargo. The number of blips was overwhelming.

"Yeah, pal," Parker said, picking up the magnesium receiver built into his desk when a light blipped on and off letting him know the call had been transferred. He grinned as he heard Harrison's voice again. He couldn't help it—he liked the son of a bitch. "You what?" He laughed, his mouth stretching out into a wider and wider smile, though he knew it was nasty to be so enthused about someone else's misfortune. "Your band broke up because the drummer got popped for coke? The YMCA dropped your course due to lack of funds—and interest? And you're already down to a thousand bucks and that's trying to fly out the window right now?" The CIA chief laughed long and hard until a few tears came to his eyes. He rubbed his thumb and forefinger over his nose trying to relax, and realized he was half cracking with anxiety over this whole damned thing. At least something was going right—for him, if not for Harrison.

"Does the offer still stand?" Parker echoed back. "You bet your right ball it does." Parker banged his fist on the desk and a few pens rattled around like they were thinking of jumping off. "Can we try an introductory offer? No doubt about it, pal." The CIA chief laughed again. It felt good. "How about—we say a four-week training course—then one lousy case just to see how it all works out. Then if you want, you're free to split—only you're thirty grand richer. If you stay—you can go on salary plus all you might earn in your deep penetration role of being a pro wrestler. It's a no-lose proposition. Who knows, if you're any good at it, could be big bucks." Parker could hear the other man coughing, hemming, and hawing as if he was trying to make up his mind. But the CIA chief knew that he wouldn't have called if he wasn't a hundred percent sure. The guy was sometimes slow deciding— Parker had found that out the hard way in Southeast Asia. But when he did, he stuck to his guns with the tenacity of an alligator with its jaws around a squealing pig. That was one of the reasons, aside from Harrison's innate toughness and fighting abilities, that Parker wanted him in on all this. He might just be the only damned one who could actually take on the odds and the kind of ruthless opposition they were up against without losing his nerve. Maybe.

Harrison at last spoke up again, and even through the static of the phone line from New York to the underground info-gathering center in southern Virginia Parker could clearly hear the answer as if he were only inches away.

"Fantastic," the CIA chief said softly, letting himself breathe out just a notch and realizing just how tense he was. "As is oft said—you just made my fucking day, pal. Nothing's been going right the last few days. But that's not your problem—it's mine. Now you get your ass on down here—and fast. We'll get that beer belly in fighting trim before you can scream, 'It hurts.'" He laughed again, remembering the old days, and suddenly realized there were about to be some new "old days"—and no doubt some bad ones.

"I'll give you over to one of my subordinates—she'll tell you what to do, how to get here. And Harrison," Parker said, as he motioned for his Chief of Security Operations, a stunningly good-looking redhead, Lisa Backman, to take the call on the scramble line on the far side of the desk. She stood there with a notebook in her hand waiting to get Parker's attention on a number of security questions.

"Listen, thanks. Thanks a lot," Parker said to Harrison. "It sounds like bullshit sometimes—but your country really does need you, man. I can promise you that much anyway. This is a no-bullshit mission. And that ain't the half of it. When the time comes you'll get every iota of information that we've got on it." And maybe wish you hadn't, Parker didn't add as he clicked off and looked down at the glistening surface of the silver-veined black marble desk with a somber expression. A few yards away Lisa Backman clicked into scramble mode—so if anyone was listening they were going to hear some peculiar and painful sounds—and began talking to Harrison, who was standing in an ice-covered phone booth in Manhattan, with its walls kicked out, the glass on the sidewalk around it like a field of diamonds. Even over the phone line Backman could hear the cold wind whistling across the mouthpiece of his phone. In spite of herself she shivered inside the temperature-controlled underground world of the CIA headquarters as if cold herself. She waited a few seconds for the howls, the choruses of sound created by the wind rushing over his mouthpiece, the hissing static that sounded like nothing less than screams of warning from a choir of lost souls to die out before she continued.

Chapter Seven

Harrison stood frozen like a park statue in the center of the Alexandria, Virginia, bus station searching around for his contact in the milling crowds of travelers, transients, bums, and a few mentally disturbed individuals who ranted and raved at the grease-coated, lime green plastic walls shaking their fists at demons who were hidden inside. He was used to the New York scene being bad, but this seemed just as weirded out—in quality of madness, if not the quantity that the Rotten Apple possessed.

Then he saw her. He knew it was her right away. Not that there was anything CIA about her. If anything she downplayed the whole thing. But there was a presence, a regal bearing that bespoke class, and pounds of it. Of course being a knockout didn't detract attention from her. But there was nothing she could do about that short of getting an "ugly" operation. Long red hair fell down her left shoulder. Slim but toned legs stepped out from an expensive and flattering simple skirt and jacket made of the finest Harris Tweed. As he scanned her he saw a bum make a sudden lunge for the pocketbook that she carried tucked under one arm like a fullback with a football at the one-yard line. Harrison started to move forward to stop the imminent crime when he saw her twist suddenly out of the way so the guy sort of stumbled past her. Then she gave him a quick little push from behind as he lurched forward and sent him flying into a garbage pail filled to overflow with sticky soda cups and newspapers, sending it and himself tumbling over in an avalanche of garbage.

Harrison had to suppress his laughter as people gathered around the struggling would-be felon who was flailing away at the garbage with both arms and legs pumping as if he was swimming in the stuff. At the top of his lungs he shouted utterly foul statements about everyone in the place as if he had just gone completely mad. The woman, meanwhile, didn't even look back, but just walked on with a satisfied smile on her face. Harrison whistled under his breath as he saw her slowly making her way across the room. She was good. If this was representative of the kind of operative Colonel Parker had working under him, maybe this whole damn thing was going to work out after all.

Harrison made his way around a few benches where old women with lines as thick as earthquake crevices on their faces sat waiting endless hours for buses that never came, speaking to their dead loved ones, ghosts, as if they were sitting right next to them.

"Hi, I'm—" Harrison began to say as he approached the woman from the side.

She turned sharply bringing both arms up in a striking motion, and he had to jump back quickly back to avoid a sharp strike to the throat with both hands.

"Hey, easy, lady." Harrison laughed, holding up his arms to show they held a suitcase and duffel bag—all of his worldly possessions. His smile and twinkling eyes showed he didn't have any mischief in mind. Not that kind anyway. "I'm Harrison, Rick Harrison. If I'm not mistaken you're from the Kenningworth Agency." It was the code name they had told him to use.

"Oh—sorry—I—" She suddenly seemed totally flustered, her cheeks growing red with embarrassment. She prided herself on her efficiency. "Have you got the dogs?" she asked, her part of the code.

"The dogs, the dogs," Harrison sputtered for a moment, trying to remember just what they had told him over the phone. "The dogs are coming by train—they'll be here in a week," he suddenly said, smiling at her and liking the way she looked, the curves that just snaked in and out up and down her body like they were in constant motion.

"In three weeks! Three weeks!" she chided him, but her face relaxed a little as she realized it was in fact the right man. "I'm sorry for being so aggressive," she began by way of apology as Harrison walked up alongside her, the baggage dangling at the ends of his muscular arms, hidden beneath an oversized stretched-out black sweatshirt and brown bomber-style leather jacket. "But some moron already tried to do a number on me back there."

"I know, I saw it all," Harrison said coolly. "You handled yourself very well, very well indeed."

"I didn't know I was being so closely observed," she replied with a trace of annoyance, both at being watched without being aware of it and at the fact that it was she, as an operative of the Agency, who should be doing the watching—not the other way around. Her cheeks flushed again, against her will, making her even angrier than she already was. Her nostrils flared as she felt herself growing furious at Harrison for no reason whatsover. What the hell was wrong with her?

"Anyway—I guess we should head on out," he went on, trying to cool her out. He sensed that his words had pissed her off in some incomprehensible female way.

67

"Before someone takes a grab at some of my luggage. Not that they're going to find more than a few dozen pairs of dirty socks and my favorite torn and unwearable T-shirts of the last decade that I can't bear to part with, plus of course my *Playboy* bikini underwear—collector's item." That seemed to make her relax a little and the iron shield came down to reveal a smile, a beautiful one at that, with even rows of pearl teeth, wet with a moisture that made them gleam alluringly.

"Come on, mister," she said putting her hand on his arm for a second to guide him off toward the left side of the terminal, toward the exit where she had her car parked. "Let's get the hell out of here before the zombies start riding down the escalators."

"Hey, I like that." Harrison grinned, something he found very easy to do when looking at her. *"They Came from the Third Floor.* We'll get backing and have a hit movie. You can be executive producer, I'll star—but not as the monster."

"Oh, a live one." She laughed at Harrison's exuberant energy, not to mention his strong six-four body, the sheer power of which she could feel moving like a big cat beside her. He had a different energy than the men she worked around at the Agency. Not that there weren't some hunks there as well, but Harrison— there was something different about him. She couldn't quite put her finger on it. Just something hard, rock solid. Something about not giving, not breaking. The kind of man a woman could wrap herself around like a tree around a mountain. But she had repressed her erotic feelings so long, trying to be professional, cool, cold—the way the others were, the junior personnel at the Agency—that she had almost forgotten how to feel attracted to a man, to allow those feelings. It all made her a little more pissed off in spite of herself, so that by time they reached the car, parked outside in a rectangular dirt-bottomed parking lot, she was in a real funk.

"Hey, the Agency really splurges." Harrison laughed as he threw his bags in the back of the crumbling station wagon, circa early 1970's, with fake wood paneling peeling back and sand all over the floor like Mom and Dad had just taken the kids to the beach.

"We should drive a fleet of Mercedes?" Backman asked with an annoyed little smirk as she sat down in the driver's seat and Harrison got in on the other side. "We really like to keep things low-key. This is the perfect car for getting around in—absolutely bland and nondescript. Won't get a second look in a traffic jam. The money I assure you—as you will soon see—is available for all the necessary things."

"Sure, sure," Harrison said, stretching out his long legs, which didn't fit all that well in the narrowly designed station wagon's front foot space. "Don't get touchy about it. Just making conversation." He shut up, and watched with interest as she started the car up and headed out of the parking lot. He had no idea where the hell they were going. He had never even been in this part of the country—Virginia. In spite of himself, he was actually starting to enjoy the whole thing.

She pulled out onto a four-lane highway and within minutes they were hurtling along in a direction that appeared to be south. Within fifteen minutes it was surprisingly rural, with large stretches of woods and not all that many houses. Once they were firmly set on their route south, she seemed to relax a little and, glancing over at him through the rearview mirror, spoke up, trying to sound friendly again.

"So, you're a wrestler, I hear, Mr. Harrison? Colonel Parker has told me a lot about you. We're all very excited that you're—joining the team."

"Oh, now wait a minute, I'm not a wrestler. I suppose with a few months' training, a hell of a lot of padding strapped all over, I could fake my way through it—but no, I'm not a real wrestler. The kind you see on TV." He laughed as if the whole idea were really quite ridiculous, and again she became tongue-tied. It seemed impossible to get a conversation going with the big slob.

"Surely you have some fighting experience—professional, that is," she said, a little confused. She swore she had heard Parker say that Harrison was a ring vet from way back.

"Well, I have had a few tough-man fights here and there. You know, down in the basement, behind the candy store. Made a few bucks. It's not what you would call a career. Now when I was younger, in high school and college, I was on the wrestling team. In fact I won All Regional two years in a row, and National once in my weight class—before I got called up to the service. That was that as far as being a master of the mat. And that was—oh, crap—at least twelve, thirteen years ago or something."

He could see that she was still having a hard time keeping it going with him, for whatever reason, so he turned and asked her a question.

"And what about you? What's a nice girl like you doing in a business like this?"

"Sorry, Harrison, can't talk about myself at all. Company policy," she replied, fixing the rearview, which had jarred loose on the decrepit old wagon.

"Oh, I see," he said with a snort. "You can ask me any damn thing you want about my life, but I can't know a single thing about yours?"

"Something like that," she replied coolly. "My life's very boring, I assure you. An overeducated brat who

70

got into the business because I couldn't stand going to another society banquet, attending another debutante ball. I'm rich, you see. Or was. My father disinherited me when I joined the Agency—for reasons I won't go into. But I really didn't—and don't—care. When you're wealthy from birth, with servants to literally bring you toast in the morning, it soon loses its luster, becomes as meaningless as the kind of socks you wear. My education in deciphering ancient Sanskrit and Latin inscriptions had led me without knowing it into being a linguistics expert. And when certain people heard of my skills, one thing led to another and I discovered that what I had done in translating what civilizations thousands of years ago were thinking could be applied, via computer—the operational mode in which I work—just as easily to breaking contemporary codes and ciphers.

"So here I am. I also fill in as Assistant Chief of Security Operations. Don't even ask how I fell into that one. But that's how it is. Lisa Backman, Junior Cipher Decoder, and Assistant Internal Security Chief of D2, so pleased to meet you." Talking about herself had again loosened her up a little and she lifted her head and gave Harrison a genuine, unarmored smile for the first time.

They headed steadily into the hinterlands of Virginia and Harrison continued to be surprised at how wild it was getting. Once they were off the main highway, the dirt road they hit after a few miles of two-lane paved was nearly overgrown with vegetation. They headed into the foothills, rising higher, until off in the distance Harrison saw a whole range of mountains rising up into the very clouds above.

"Where the hell are we going?" he asked her, knowing she wouldn't tell him, but having to ask anyway.

71

"Into the Appalachian range. We don't have too much longer to go. Maybe"—she glanced at her watch—"forty-five minutes. Do you have to go?" She asked him mockingly, a smile dancing across her full lips.

"No, as per instructions I went twice on the bus," he replied just as mockingly back to her. She snorted and put her eyes back on the road. They rode on in silence as Harrison tried to figure out just where the hell they were going. Not that he knew the region anyway, but still, a man liked to know what state he was in. He saw a sign pointing to the right: Culpeper. Now, he'd heard of that. Cowboy book title—Culpeper Station. Nah, there had to be another one—that one was in Texas. Wherever the hell they were heading was away from civilization.

The dirt road got more rutted, filled with holes, the brush reaching over from both sides so the twigs scraped along the windshield and sides of the car as if trying to drag them off into the dark woods.

Then they were actually rising up into the mountains, no question about it. Going up, up, winding around curves until he was half afraid to look down, for the down elevator was long and covered with rock-hard jagged outcroppings at every floor. They must have souped up the station wagon's engine, Harrison realized, for there was no way it could climb some of the steep angles they started hitting when the road took off nearly straight up as if only mountain goats need proceed from there on in. The car chugged and shook and made all kinds of noises but somehow it kept going, and they rose higher and higher until it seemed as if they were on a highway into the heavens, the clouds floating around them rather than above them. Harrison stared out fascinated. It was beautiful. He had become used to the hard beauty of New York, had become hardened in an aesthetic way so he didn't think about beauty too much. You couldn't walk in the grimy streets of the city and feel a great love for nature's bounty. But out here, high in the mountains, his brain started to feel like it was unwinding, his eyes taking in the peaks, the valleys, the plentitude of harshness and life that stretched off all around him like some great epic painting. Now he could allow himself to feel a touch of beauty. At least for a moment.

They seemed to reach some sort of summit and then were heading down again. They'd gone hardly five minutes down an inner slope with only inches to spare on one side—and miles to fall—when she turned off onto an equally ramshackle road, with a hand-lettered sign: Culpeper Agricultural Station—though the sign looked faded, many years old—and drove past into what looked like sheer brush. Harrison involuntarily threw his arms over his face as the whole car seemed to be submerged in branches scratching at them wildly at every window. But after about twenty seconds they were through, and emerged at a gate with two men casually sitting in front of it on half-broken armchairs, reading books. The car stopped just in front of them and one of the men—a farmer by the looks of him, wearing long denim coveralls and mud-splattered boots—got up and walked over.

Harrison knew the guy was supposed to look like a farmer—and maybe he even had been one once. But Harrison's quick eye saw the way the big fellow placed his foot flat down as he walked, the mark of a fighter, and the bulge in the side of his oversized denim farm outfit was clearly a pistol. Yeah, these guys were friendly straw-chewing dirt-diggers, until the shit hit the fan—and then the 9-mm's would come out spitting. Probably had a bazooka or two stashed away somewhere in the slopes that rose around them.

"Here with groceries," Laura said with a smile, leaning out the window of her door.

"And what kind of groceries would that be?" the big man asked, leaning over and resting his hands on top of the car as he gave Harrison the once-over.

"Don't worry, there'll be plenty of pie for the kids," she replied, giving the words for the day in a bored litany. The stuff always seemed like bullshit. But the colonel insisted on it at all times. Codes had saved people's lives. His own included.

"Pie for the kids." The farmer laughed, patting his big stomach as he stood up and waved them on. She drove for about another forty seconds until they came to a small ancient barn, a two-story affair, with faded wooden walls and a round silo where grain or tobacco had once been stored. The entire antique structure stood about sixty feet long, maybe twenty wide. It looked deserted as far as Harrison could see—other than a few scrawny dogs running around the dusty yard snapping at flies. He was just starting to wonder how the hell there was this whole big fucking CIA complex out here in the middle of Hell's toenail, when she drove up to the front of the structure. The door opened by itself and the wagon edged inside the dimly lit barn with gardening tools, hoes, and old rakes all over the wooden plank walls. She drove the car over to one side until it fit inside the outline of a square of dark sand, set the car in park, turned off the key—and just sat back and waited.

"Listen I don't mean to be—" Harrison began to say after about ten seconds. Then the whole car seemed to vibrate slightly, and before he could blink his eyes the car and the whole piece of ground on which it stood just sank right into the earth with a deep whir. Harrison's eyes nearly popped from his skull as they moved down, trying to keep up with the sights that were flying past him. For they were in some sort of tremendous manmade cavern carved right into the center of the mountain. And on every level—which he could see through transparent walls—men and women were rushing about tending to banks of monitors, computers, radar screens, all beeping and clicking out a flood of information. Backman watched him out of the corner of her eye to gauge his reaction to it all. He looked like a gawk-eyed tourist in the city gaping up at the skyscrapers. He had never in all his days seen anything quite like it outside of a James Bond movie.

They seemed to go down forever and he turned to ask how many floors there were—but before he could even get the words out, as if reading his mind, she spoke first.

"There are twenty manned floors, and four subbasements for power-support systems, supplies, and a firing range. Takes a minute to get down. We go slower than necessary to let the inner eardrums adjust to the pressure changes. You can bust your whole internal balance chambers by going up and down in these mountains too fast."

"I'll have to remember that." Harrison laughed as he suddenly felt that in his ears were in fact popping—the back of his throat all dry and clogged up. "About going up and down in the mountains, that is." He looked at her in a good-natured lewd way. She sniffed, and moved away from him. The guy was cute, she had to admit. But when it came to refinement, the mailroom boys had him beat by a mile. She hoped Colonel Parker knew what the hell he was doing.

They reached the bottom level and the elevator came to a complete stop, followed after three seconds by a little bong and a green light on the wall next to the dirt platform signaling them to get off.

"Come on, grab your things out of the car," she said.

75

Another plot of dirt with a car on it began rising even as he walked around to the back of the station wagon and took out his bags. She led him forward across a shining marble-textured floor. Harrison couldn't tell if it was stone or some kind of ultra-hard plastic, but the stuff positively gleamed. The whole fucking place did, with satin-smooth black metal and tinted glass everywhere. It looked more like the inner workings of the Starship Enterprise than the inside of a tree-covered Virginia mountain.

Well, they had to spend the money on something, Harrison thought with dark humor as she led him through the streams of Agency operatives who rushed around the floor like ants. The flood of information both in and out of the place was clearly overwhelming, almost out of control. And the shifts of workers had that kind of crazed look of people who were living on the edge, floating in a dazed world of cigarettes, black coffee, and overly sweet doughnuts. People who didn't necessarily plan on making it to the old-age home. Harrison felt at home.

Chapter Eight

Then they were in the colonel's plush private office, and Harrison saluted the man as he always had in the field—even in the mud several times, when given an order that he'd not agreed with but had sarcastically carried out. Parker threw a perfunctory salute back.

"You came," the CIA boss said, shaking his hand hard.

"Yeah, said I would over the phone. You should know me by now—after all this time. Like you—my word is something you can bet the house on."

"Yeah, guess I nearly forgot," Parker said softly. "There's a lot of people these days who don't operate under those rules anymore. A whole lot of people. But let's not get maudlin on your arrival. Come on, let me show you around. I can't take more than a few minutes. But I can show you some of the main features of our little world down here—some of the chief players in this game of backstabbing and assassination."

"You sound bitter, pal," Harrison said as he looked around for somewhere to stash his bags, which he still held in his arms.

"Bring 'em with you," Parker said. "We'll head down to your quarters." Lisa looked sort of pissed off at suddenly being pushed out of the action, and wandered off out to the floor, disappearing in the rush in seconds.

"Yeah, I guess I am a little bitter," Parker said, leading his charge out of the room and off toward a raised platform at one end of the War Room where a smaller version of the main room was in operation. This one with maps of just the United States, focusing only on domestic intelligence-gathering. All news reports, police reports, hospital stays—everything was taken in electronically, grabbed up from interstate computer lines, and intercepted by D2.

"I've seen too much, Harrison." He laughed. "I never really understood that old thing from Adam and Eve. You know, knowledge of the tree of good and evil. Believe me, most people are better off *not* knowing what the hell is going on out there. It's not a pretty picture, what men will do to each other. And I've got to go through it all, look at it all, digest it all, no matter how revolting and distasteful. I think I'm a harder man now than the one who fought alongside you back in the land of black pajamas. But that's it, man—when you bite into the pie, you got to swallow the pits too. Some of them are bitter."

"I spit the bitter ones out." Harrison laughed, hefting the bags a little higher as Parker led him up some magnesium stairs and stepped up to a door which opened automatically, giving them admittance to the Domestic Op room. After that it was a whirl of faces and introductions. "This is Ralph Finkerstein, this is Paul Tolson, this is Cora Rolling, this is . . ." Harrison shook hands with so many people that he felt like a politician. But he also felt good, took some pride in the fact that the boss of the whole damn show was introducing him personally. Showing them that he wanted them to look out for the bastard. Harrison heard phrases like "the first of the deep penetration

78

agents. Will be shown every respect . . ."

The faces became a total blur as Parker took him from room to room, level to level—showing him at least the main attractions of the place. The library with its ten million books and periodicals on microfilm—and access to virtually every library in the world, with instantaneous electronic phone transfer of whole books possible. Parker showed him the training rooms, the judo mats, showed him the firing ranges. Showed him an entire operations department and control center shoved into twenty stories of solid granite.

After noticing that Harrison's eyes were starting to roll back in his head from the endless introductions, Parker took him to a small elevator—one of about ten for internal use—and then to Level 8. They emerged and headed down a gray-carpeted hallway with dozens of identical doors on each side with numbers above them.

"This is one of the living quarters. No one really 'lives' here. But the shifts go weeks, sometimes a month or more."

"You mean all those folks are stuck down here for whole months at a time? Can't even go to the surface?"

"That's right, pal. Like you," he added with a sardonic laugh. "You won't be seeing natural daylight again for at least a month. 'Cause you're about to begin O-fficial Training. You're back in boot camp, boy. CIA style." He laughed heartily. As they came to Room 8007A, Parker took a magnetic card from his pocket and waved it at a light in front of the door. He then pressed Harrison's right index finger and thumb against the other side of the card, then handed it to him.

"This is your pass card. The door will open only to your card—then press your thumb against this panel." He guided the big man's thumb to a glass monitor on the wall. The whole thing lit up and a camera lens came

79

into view behind the glass shooting his thumb. In a second or two the door slid silently open and Harrison walked in, expecting to find a suite or something.

He nearly smashed into the steel bed suspended about chest high just a few feet into the room. For it was hardly a room. More of a cubicle, equipped with all the latest appliances. A high-tech coffin not more than seven feet long, four wide, perhaps seven high at most. It seemed more like a closet than a place where a man could rest his bones and stretch his feet.

"A little on the small side, huh, Parker?" Harrison said, looking around and trying to find a place for his bags, but not seeing any in the midst of all the futuristic dials, screens, and buttons, not to mention the folding bed with gears and pulleys that now lay out in down position with sheets and pillows all ready.

"Bags go up here, I believe," Parker said, pressing one of a row of twenty buttons on the wall. The steel wall above the bed slid open and Parker threw both of Harrison's bags up there, one after another. Then the unit whooshed closed again.

"There—pretty fucking good, don't you think?" He waved his arm around the room, but had to stop so as not to hit Harrison in the face. With two of them both in the room at the same time there was hardly any freedom of movement in either direction.

"See—the TV's up here, stereo system here, tape learning unit there. Over here at this end an entire combo kitchen/bathroom unit: a sink that doubles as a cooking stove, a shower that doubles as a toilet, a . . ." Again Harrison felt his brain start to go numb. "These buttons control the . . ." Parker went on ad infinitum.

Harrison lifted himself up onto the bed and then pulled his legs up, lying all the way back to see if he could even fit in the damn thing. He did, barely, with his booted feet hanging about six inches over the end.

"Not too bad," Harrison grunted, bouncing up and down on the bed a few times.

"See—a regular 'Lifestyles of the Rich and Famous.'" Parker laughed. "Sorry if everything's a little squeezed. We try to maximize efficiency and function down here. We've got a hell of a lot going on, and not all that much space to do it in. But this Survival Room, as we call them, will provide you everything you need for sleeping, grooming, relaxation. It's really quite an amazing little setup. Based on the Japanese Mini-Hotels—only they put their guys into fucking space capsules. This baby would be a mansion over there."

"It'll do. I'm not looking for luxury here," Harrison said, putting his arms back behind his head—or trying to. "Anyway, the bucks I save from not having to pay goddamned rent I can use for myself later. It's a good deal for me, pal. I'm not complaining."

"Good, good," Parker said, seeming to be genuinely pleased. "You always were basically a cooperative bastard. Stubborn—but not moody and neurotic like half the people I've got to work with these days. It's not like it used to be, Harrison. I swear it's not. People just aren't as—tough anymore. I'd take one old-timer any day for a dozen of these 'Intelligence Engineers' as some of them are calling themselves now—though not in my hearing, you can bet your sphincter on that." The CIA chief paused for few moments, wondering just what the hell else to say. "Well, look, gotta get back to my desk. There's a hell of a lot of shit hitting the fan—and I'm the one who gets paid to get sprayed by it."

"Just what the hell *is* going on?" Harrison asked, propping the pillow up behind his head. "What am I being trained for? I've got a dozen questions, man."

"And I still can't answer any of them right now, sorry," Parker said as he reached out and held his hand against a glass screen. The camera scanned him and the door whispered open. "It'll all become clear—that I promise you. By the time you get out there—you'll know every bloody fact that I do. That's *my* promise. And you know what that's worth."

"I do," Harrison said simply. He knew. The promise had been worth enough for the colonel to come back when he had escaped from a prison camp and could have run. Had made him return for Harrison, who was about to meet a most painful fate, and against overwhelming odds save him. Save both of them. That's why Harrison was even here today. Because he trusted the man down to his bones. And though he never would have actually said it, he knew he probably would have followed Parker into hell itself if the son-of-a-bitch asked him to.

"I probably won't see you too much after tonight," Parker said pausing at the door, his hand resting on the clear plasti/aluminum frame which seemed almost translucent with little flecks of color embedded within. "In fact, probably not until you're done with training— four to five weeks. But I'll be keeping an eye on you. And rooting for you."

"Rooting for me?" Harrison asked curiously. "I didn't know I was in a football game."

"We've established a training and testing program for all deep penetration agents—or would-be agents. I'm sure you'll pass. But you'll have to go through it just like any other recruit would. It's tough, very tough. We had to make it that way to weed out all the . . . incompetents. Better they flunk out in here than out there, where a bullet in the head is the most likely reward for a fuck-up." He looked hard at Harrison. "You, you can do it—I've got faith in you. You'll start 'basic training' in the morning."

"Whooppee," Harrison said, waving a finger around in the air in a little circle. "I'm in school again."

"The cafeteria's down the hall. They serve food—not the greatest—but hot and injected with all the vitamins and minerals for strength and sexual virility known to man." Parker grinned, turned, and headed off, moving at quick acceleration to get back to the War Room, to his next crisis, his next flaming car bomb, his next D2 operative gone, swallowed up without a trace in a most muderous world.

Harrison just let himself lie there. He had to admit, as cramped as it was, the Survival Room was cozy in a sick kind of way. As long as you didn't look at the walls. After about twenty minutes he rose and tried to figure out how to use the shower/toilet unit that was at one end of the cubicle. A small digital sign with green characters dancing across its screen pointed that way. He reached the end and waved his hand in front of an electric eye. It beeped softly twice and a wavering mechanical voice spoke up enunciating each word.

"Please place your thumb against the glass to your right. Please place your thumb against the glass to—" He put his hand out with a pained grin. For the life of him he couldn't understand why you would need ID to use a toilet. The camera behind the screen scanned the thumb. The words "Positive ID" flashed across the screen—and instantly the whole back wall opened up and out with a rush of air. Harrison laughed out loud as he saw the "bathroom" that stood within. The whole thing was about the size of a telephone booth. Somehow they had managed to fit a shower, sink, toilet, mirror, electric razor, and numerous other miniaturized items together into one huge interconnected appliance. He took off his clothes, which was itself quite a feat as he bumped into walls and buttons all over the place. He stepped into the shower unit and waited.

Nothing happened. If he had been hoping for some

sort of auto-shower—he was wrong. There were panels and buttons set in along the stainless steel wall, but he could understand the function of none of them since they only had letters on them—H, C, U, D—whatever the hell that all meant. He pressed one. Suddenly water shot out from hidden valves on two of the walls, bathing him in ice-cold liquid. Half screaming from the frigid shower Harrison quickly washed himself and then rinsed off in the icy fingers of water. No matter how he poked at the buttons he couldn't get the hot water working. Maybe it was compact and shining—but damned if there weren't a few bugs in the damn system. He'd have to talk to the colonel about it, when they talked again. Hardship was one thing, no hot water another.

He toweled himself off and headed back down the cubicle, where with some great difficulty he found the buttons to open the drawers set into the lower wall below the bed. A fresh set of loose-fitting camouflage-patterned slacks and a thick sweater lay folded inside, along with socks, fatigue jacket—everything a well-dressed CIA trainee might want. Harrison put the stuff on, and instantly felt a hell of a lot cleaner than he had for days. He put on a pair of low boot/sneaker-type footwear, also apparently unused, which fit perfectly. He combed his hair back in the fluorescent mirror which enlarged every pore of his face, lighting it with a merciless white brilliance that made him look as cratered as the moon, quite horrible. He'd have to talk to Parker about that too.

It must have been dinner time, because even as he held his hand toward the ID monitor and the door slid open, people were already heading en masse toward the dining room. When Harrison reached it after walking with the crowd for several hundred feet, it looked hardly different from a college chow hall, except for the stainless steel, the tinted glass, the chromed edges everywhere. If nothing else, the high-tech seamless joints, the quality of the alloy steel, and the crafts-manship—and money—obviously put into everything made the underground complex look like it would last a thousand years or so. Maybe in the long run, the hundreds of millions that must have been spent down here would actually pay off.

Harrison joined the line that slowly moved past the serving counter that ran down one whole wall, glass shelves behind it filled with a variety of foods, hot and cold. He took some of just about everything. He knew he was being a pig about it. But number one, he hadn't eaten anything more than Reese Peanut Butter Cups for about thirty-six hours. And number two, he didn't give a shit. When it came to food, having to supply a 260-pound frame that cried out like a whole treeful of hungry birds for food, he didn't let anything get in the way of himself and a good, preferably large, meal.

He found an empty table among the rows of tables and began eating gustily, dipping bread into gravy, mashing rice and potatoes together into a little mountain. In general having a good time. He had been at it for about five minutes when he looked up and realized that several of the people eating at the tables around him were looking at him, smirking from the corner of their eyes. As if he were below them, different. And he realized in a flash that of course they would see him as a freak. An unkempt, muscle-bound, non-college grad who wasn't worth their spit—when Harrison knew the opposite was true. Nonetheless, it made him feel suddenly out of place and lonely—an emotion he hadn't felt for a long time.

When the door closed behind him back in his little coffin-like space capsule and he washed and got into bed, he started feeling even weirder. Like he was a kid at camp—and was homesick for Ma and his pals and the dogs. Only, Ma was dead and the dogs too. And his pals, where were they all now? He didn't want to think about it all. He managed to get the TV built in over the bed switched on, and grunted with satisfaction that, along with everything else when it came to the appliances they hadn't been cheap either. It was a huge color twenty-five-inch, crystal-clear resolution and brilliant color.

The only problem, Harrison discovered as he tried to focus in on what appeared to be Tom Selleck dancing with Daisy Duck if his eyes didn't deceive him, was that the unit was so close to him, it was like sitting in the front row of a huge Super Screen movie. The Sony blasted out the image and sound, a weird disco cha-cha into his brain, exploding out from stereo speakers on each side of the bed. Whoever had designed the installation had clearly never actually gotten into the bed with the thing only a foot from his face. It felt like his brain was being microwaved in an oven. He pulled his head back into the pillow as far as it would go, somehow managed to get the sound down to a dull roar, and tried to look up at the picture two feet above his head through half-closed fingers.

It *was* Tom Selleck, he could see clearly now. And he *was* dancing with Daisy Duck. They were dancing, as a flashing neon sign behind them proclaimed blindingly, in *Money for Dying Children*—a worldwide television fundraiser to get money for the dying children around the world. Harrison would contribute to that. Damned sure. He tried to get something else. Anything else. But for some reason the Sony only got static on every other channel. Only the Selleck fundraiser—and a Puerto Rican Baby Racing Show where mothers coaxed their infants down long runways screaming at them in Spanish every crawl of the way.

Harrison didn't know if he was being entertained or not, but he watched them both, alternating back and forth until he thought he would go blind. He fell into a stoned daze with his eyes quivering beneath the luminous rays of the TV, strange moans coming from his snoring mouth. He fell fully asleep only after hours of restless tossing and turning. The images from the TV and from the long day, the faces he had met, the mugger bum from the bus station, the nasty looks in the dining room, the five pounds of food he had just eaten—everything swirled around inside him like a whirlpool churning down in the pit of his stomach. A whirlpool of gas and nightmares and near-religious visions as he squirmed and rolled over and over, like a turning spit roasting a metaphysical chicken over the fires of fear, indigestion, and revealed self-truth.

Chapter Nine

When Harrison awoke he was punching at the air
and kicking up at the gleaming stainless-steel ceiling
only a few feet above his bed. The television was still
on, glaring down at him as if he were in a tanning salon,
only now instead of Daisy Duck, filling the video
monitor was the broad scowling face of an extremely
strange-looking fellow. He had curly black and gray
hair cascading down both sides of his head to his
shoulders and a big fat face with scraggly gray
mustache and small beard coming down from his chin
like Freud's goatee. But even more bizarre, the guy had
rubber bands all over his face—a blue one around the
beard squeezing it tight in the middle, red and purple
ones hanging down from his left ear like rubber
earrings, and a green one on a hook right through the
middle of his left cheek. Harrison blinked several
times, wondering what program this could be—he
could hardly imagine. Morning TV shows usually
didn't have big ugly scowling faces stare at you
intensely and not say a word.

"Rise and shine, asshole," the man suddenly spoke
out in a deep rasping voice that sounded like he was
gargling ball bearings. "Or does Sleeping Beauty want
to get in another hour or two to smooth a few more

wrinkles out on his greasy face? Well, forget it! You look like shit anyway." Harrison could hardly believe his ears. Was this some new early morning programming he knew nothing about? Some new-wave exercise show where they cursed and insulted you into shape?

"That's right, BB Brain, I'm talking to you," the raspy voice said again. "You're Harrison, right? Rick Harrison?"

Harrison's eyes widened in horror. It was a dream, a nightmare. Some byproduct of the terrible damage the electromagnetic programming of the night before had done to his brain. But he answered back cautiously. "Y-yy-eess, I'm Harraldson," he replied sleepily, slurring his own name as he was still not all in this world.

"Harrison? Haraldson? Hinderson? Hinkenstein? Which is it, worm mouth?" The face was scowling even harder now, peering deep into the camera, pressing up against it so the rubber bands were flattened against the camera lens and the scars on the cheek loomed into view. The man looked insanely familiar, though just where he would have seen such a face of aesthetic mismanagement before was beyond him.

"Let's get those decayed and frayed muscles, if any, into gear. Come on, Mr. Harrison." The huge face in the screen less than twenty-four inches above his head said slowly, mockingly, enunciating each syllable clearly. "We've-got-a-few-chores-for-you-to-do-to-day."

"Sure pal, anything," Harrison groaned, trying to find the button that shut off the damned glaring eye in the ceiling above him.

"You've got five minutes, puff-eyes. Then there'll be someone at your door—me. And if you ain't up, I'm going to have kick that lard butt right out into the hall. You don't want to make the Captain angry, do you, Hinkerstein?" Even as Harrison stuttered out "nooo," the screen went dead. Whether Harrison had somehow hit the right button, or the loud-mouthed guy on the screen had terminated it, he didn't know. He rolled over toward the side of the narrow bed—and tumbled off as he suddenly lost his balance. He fell, crashing into the wall a few feet away, and slid down its smooth plasticized surface like an omelette down the side of a teflon-coated frying pan. When he came to a cursing stop he found himself on the floor, his face pressed between the grates of two heating/air-conditioning units set into the floorboard. Thank God it wasn't churning out any heat right now or his nose would have been nicely grilled.

Rising up carefully, he realized he'd better move very, very slowly in this place or he was going to wind up losing a nose or an eye or some damned thing that he'd rather keep. He couldn't help but wonder whether or not this was all some kind of mental torture, testing him—to see his reaction to small places, to stress, to God knows what. But then Harrison, unlike most of the others who had or might come through these training halls, had already been through the real thing.

He headed toward the Buck Rogers crapper in the back, figuring out after nearly two minutes how to fold the shower back so that the toilet slid out, all aluminized with chromium handrests and recessed automatic toilet-paper dispenser which beeped out a single sheet every time one held one's hand up in front of an electric eye. Frankenstein would have felt at home here, Harrison decided as he lowered himself onto the impossibly small seat. He wondered if they were keeping an eye on him through cameras even in here. This was after all the CIA, and they loved to play with surveillance. Well, if they wanted his toilette pictures—they were sure as hell welcome to them. He made a huge mugging face straight ahead at what looked like a camera lens in the wall, though he really had not a clue as to its actual function. Then he settled down on top of the astronaut-sized seat. If they were

90

videoing him they would think he was crazy. If they weren't looking at him he was crazy.

He had hardly finished up in there and gotten his clothes on when the promised knock came, only it was more like a starving gorilla banging, searching for bananas. Harrison opened the door to find the very man himself who minutes before had been assailing him from the miracle of the television screen. The dude was big, wide as a table at the shoulders, with a huge stomach hanging right out of his unbuttoned garish Hawaiian shirt that had to have at least two dozen colors and twenty-three patterns mixed into its blinding surface. Well-worn blue jeans and huge sneakers that looked like they'd been stomped in for the last five years finished the outfit. Not exactly your standard CIA garb. The rubber bands bounced around on the wide face as the man took two steps backward and looked Harrison up and down. He puffed hard on a long cigar he bit between his teeth and let out a cloud of gray smoke right into Harrison's face, setting him to coughing violently. It smelled like something Godzilla might smoke to freshen his breath.

"Well, you look pretty terrible this morning," the man growled out. "But then if you look at *this* face with over seven hundred stitches—from my steel cage matches—you know I wrote the book on ugly. But at least you're a good size—that's a start, I suppose." Suddenly the scowl vanished and a warm smile replaced it as the man held his hand out. "Well, good morning to you anyway, ya potbellied sucker." Somehow Harrison knew that was quite a friendly greeting for the man and held his own hand out. "The name's Captain Lou. Captain Lou Albano."

"Damn!" Harrison grinned hard as he took the hand and shook it. The guy's grip felt like it could crush toasters. "You're Captain Lou!" Harrison echoed dumbly, suddenly comprehending just who he was talking to. Just about the most famous wrestling figure of the 1980's with his jive doubletalk, his crazy race-around-the-ring antics, his managing of numerous champions and tag teams. Harrison wasn't a fanatic about wrestling but he sure as hell had seen his share of matches. It was good stuff.

"The man's got the genius of a moron," Captain Lou growled up at the ceiling, letting his eyes roll. "But I've had worse to work with, though offhand I can't quite remember when."

"I thought you were in wrestling," Harrison said meekly, not wanting to get the guy shouting at him again—Captain Lou spoke every word as if he were yelling to someone from one mountain to another. "On TV, I mean. Why the hell are you down *here?* I mean . . ." Harrison felt more and more like an idiot with every word he spoke. His brain and his tongue just weren't making the right connections this morning.

"My government called me—and I answered," Captain Lou said, turning and starting to walk down the glistening corridor as Harrison followed alongside. He moved slow, and though a big man—he had to be 300-plus—the Captain moved with the centered ease of a bear. Harrison could see that within the slow body was tremendous strength—and speed if needed. "I still manage some wrestlers here and there," the Captain went on. "But in spite of my raw exterior—I'm a patriotic son of a bitch—and I guess a sucker in my own way too. But they needed someone who knew all the ropes, every aspect of wrestling from the weight room to the dirty tricks and everything in between. Well, I wrote the book, made the movie, and got out the bubble gum cards when it comes to wrestling savy, Harrison. You may not know me except in my recent years as a manager—but in the fifties and sixties I was kicking booty from Oshkosh to Kyoto. Me and Tony Altamore were in a tag team called the Sicilians. Made

92

it all the way to the top. And we did anything to get there. Things I guess I'm even a little ashamed of now. But history is pastory, so . . . Now Uncle Sam wants to put some of my wrestling expertise to good use. They tell me the very security of our country is at stake. I can't say no to that."

"So, you're going to show me some moves, I take it?" Harrison asked hesitantly as he walked slightly behind the slow-moving captain.

"Baaaby, I'm going to show you, throw you, flip you, trip you, suplex you and duplex you. But later—I don't believe a man should get his brains pounded into putty until after lunch. And first we got to attend some classes." He said the word "classes" with a snort of derision as he led Harrison to a bank of elevators and held his thumb up to the glass, which scanned it. The door slid open with just the slightest hiss of air. "Required attendance for all new trainees. Teach you to tell your ass from your elbow."

Harrison chuckled as the elevator rose slowly in that patient, mechanized way that everything moved in down here. The elevator stopped at Level 14 and the doors slid open. Captain Lou chewed hard on his cigar, letting out a trail of foul blue smoke that followed them along down the long corridor. The CIA ops who were rushing around were clearly put off by the crazy getup of the captain and his big belly poking out. Somehow Harrison already liked the guy, and felt absurdly proud to be walking alongside him like they were two weirdos in a land of the blond blue-eyed clones. Captain Lou led his charge down the long hall to a doorway with the sign "Main Lecture Hall" over it. Though the place was big—built to hold hundreds if necessary in long rows of seats like a theater in some suburb somewhere—there was no one else that he could see, just a few guys milling about on the stage with a large chalkboard behind them. And a set of books sitting in the front row—

apparently waiting for Harrison, he realized to his displeasure. They looked big and technical. The last things he could remember having read were various issues of *Playboy*.

"Please be seated," a man suddenly said from the stage. Harrison looked up to see a tall, angular-looking fellow in full suit and tie who paced back and forth looking at a vest-pocket watch which he kept winding as if something was wrong with it. Harrison gulped and sat down. The man reminded him of his teachers in school. Dry-lipped, tight-faced, impatient. This one had a tweedy look, an academic paleness about him of someone who had spent decades indoors, without sunlight, in libraries, classrooms, lecture halls like this.

"Good morning, sir," the man on stage said crisply. "I had expected you five minutes earlier." He again looked at his gold antique watch circa 1895, and pushed it back into the side pocket with a final little stab. "But then these days the requirements for entrance to the Agency have obviously become more lax. At any rate," he went on, looking down at Harrison and Captain Lou, who had parked himself a few seats away, slumped far back in the seat like he didn't want to be there anymore than Harrison did, puffing hard on his cigar so a funnel spiraled up to ventilation ducts above and was sucked in. "I will be your 'intelligence tutor' for the next few weeks. I am Dr. Clarence Marshall—Director of Training. We will try to teach you, instill in you some absolute bare-bone basics as to what we're all about. We will try to teach you the background information that is imperative to every Operative of the Agency." Every time Dr. Marshall said the word "Agency," he placed a great emphasis on the A so the word came out sounding like a religious institution, something worthy perhaps of worship. "Usually this takes an absolute minimum of a year—I repeat, one year before any agents are allowed to engage in actual field work. We will be doing it, or attempting to do it"—he clearly smirked—"in one month. So do pay attention—even if it's difficult."

Clearly there were political divisions within the Agency about the wisdom of bringing in outsiders like Harrison to work for them as fully operational field agents rather than just informers or paid "consultants." Colonel Parker had obviously won—for the moment—as was also shown by his hiring of Captain Lou. But there was clearly a lot of opposition and bad feeling toward Harrison's admittance to the hallowed halls. What was he going to do—sell the secrets of their mini-toilets to the Russians? That would go over well over there in Siberia, where their asses would freeze solid to the chromium seats faster than a yuppie can buy a condo.

"Well, I certainly will do my best, sir," Harrison said, leaning back in his front row seat, which was just four yards or so from the raised platform atop which Dr. Marshall was about to launch himself into his audio/visual presentation. And from the moment the guy began, Harrison was lost. He didn't know what the hell the bastard was talking about. It all had to do with "Intelligence Processing," "Hierarchies of Conceptual Foundation," "Concentric Circles of Operational Dynamics." Marshall had slides shown by his assistant, projected onto a pull-down screen—charts, graphs, numbers all over the damned place. Something to do with "Target Population Segments and Counter-Operational Functionalism—the New Mode of Operation." Each of these little segments as far as Harrison could tell had all been term-long classes for the more "normal" agency recruits who had passed through these hallowed high-tech doors.

The deeper they got into it all, over the next hour—then two hours, three—the more Harrison grew lost, until he felt like Alice in Wonderland in a world in which he couldn't understand a single word that was being said. At last, with a trace of pity Dr. Marshall looked down at Harrison, nodded to the assistant to click off the projector, put his pointer down, and asked, "Any questions?"

"No," Harrison replied, stifling a yawn as he pulled himself up in the seat. "No, sir. That—that was excellent. Excellent presentation. I've learned a tremendous amount just this first day," he lied through his teeth. The one ability that Harrison had picked up in his last decade of scrounging around the country with his band, hanging out with people of all classes, races, and fortunes, was the ability to relate to people. He was, in his own slightly uncouth and no-bullshit way, quite charming and even honest. Most of the folks he had met, traveled with, and ate with had liked him. So when Harrison looked up and smiled his most sincere as he lied about the lesson, Dr. Marshall almost believed him, and his own demeanor softened just a trace.

"Now, those books"—he pointed down to the two-foot-high pile of hardcover volumes—"are for your digestion. They must be read in the order they're numbered on the side so as to keep up with each day's lessons. At the end of the month we will have a written and oral test—which I will administer. I do hope you study those books hard, because I have never let a man through those doors who didn't pass. Not once in the twenty years I've been in charge of Training and Evaluation. So, don't think this is all equivalent to some kind of athletic scholarship at some Southern U.—because it isn't." With that he clapped his hands together and headed to the door. "I will see you tomorrow morning. Please be on time, or I'll start the lesson without you." Since there wasn't another person to hear the professor's words—other than Captain Lou, and he appeared to be sound asleep, letting out snorts and snores every once in a while—Harrison couldn't imagine just who the man would be "teaching." He rose up and sort of half saluted the Director, realizing that he shouldn't in mid-motion.

"Ehh—look forward to seeing you, sir," Harrison mumbled after the CIA'er, but the man was already through the side curtains of the stage and heading toward a hidden elevator. He was a busy man and had already "wasted" far too much time on a very poor prospect.

"Wake up, Captain." Harrison grinned, leaning over and tapping one of the broad shoulders. "You can look now." He laughed. "The Creature From the Incomprehensible is gone—until tomorrow."

"Is that tongue-tying professor done with his word stew?" Captain Lou asked, stretching and yawning in his seat as he patted his belly, which hung out of the multicolored Hawaiian shirt like it was sunning itself beneath the overhead lights. "Colonel Parker tried to get you out of it," Captain Lou said, standing up and making his way with some difficulty past the seats, which made all kinds of creaking and grinding sounds like they might just pop free and fall over as he wriggled through them.

"But the powers that be would only go so far," the Captain went on as he reached the aisle. "Colonel Parker's got power here—mucho power—but he's got plenty of dudes like to see his ass nailed to the floor with railroad spikes. And I'm not shittin' you on that. He's a strong man, and men like that make enemies. Do the best you can with this bull. Parker knows it don't mean diddly out there in the jungle. Anyway, once I get you into my training—you'll *wish* you could go to class. But next, at least we'll have a little hands-on education." He led Harrison—who let the books lie where they were stacked, he'd come back for them later—down along the hall to another door, which opened as he held up his hand to the ID Verification.

Inside were numerous shop machines: drill presses, lathes, jigsaws, grinding machines everywhere. An elderly man with whitish stringy hair, wearing a dirty white smock, walked over and greeted Harrison warmly.

"This way—this way," he mumbled half incoherently as, limping slightly on his right foot, he led the two men over to the shop machine he had already set up with dozens of locks held in vises which were attached all over it.

"That's R.T., as he likes to be called," Captain Lou whispered to Harrison as they followed along behind. "He's the lockman—genius when it comes to breaking through any security system." As many words as the professor had had, R.T. was a man of few. He would just grunt, and then show Harrison what he was doing, picking away at the inside of locks, guiding his student's hand when Harrison tried. It didn't take long to see what the guy was getting at. There was a certain circular back and forth motion to lockpicking. It was more the feel than a particular methodology—like making love to a woman. And by the time their hour was over, Harrison was actually picking open at least simple turnkey locks within a few minutes.

"Good," R.T. said as a beeper rang on his wristwatch/phone. "Tomorrow—electric eye and sonic alarms. Simple stuff." He smiled and walked off.

"Come on," Captain Lou said out of the corner of his mouth as he marched ahead puffing hard on the cigar. "Got one more to go before lunch."

"Before lunch? I haven't even had breakfast yet," Harrison protested, feeling his stomach growling like an unfed hound.

"Well, to tell you the truth," Captain Lou said with a nasty little laugh, "I bin told to kick some of that lard off your butt, send the pizza and beer that's taken up residence in your stomach into the land where fat goes when it dies. You'll survive a devildog or two less."

"Now wait a minute," Harrison said, stopping in his tracks. "You mean I can't eat but you can? I see a whole pizza truck inside that eye-damaging shirt that you're wearing."

"Three-eighteen before I shower," Captain Lou said, proudly slapping the roundness with loud resounding smacks. "Only thing is"—he laughed—"I ain't going into the ring with guys that could break a grizzly bear's back with a single snap. But *you* are, BB Brain, aren't you? Didn't they even tell you what you were getting into? A snack now could be a broken head later."

"It could?" Harrison gulped, realizing for the first time that this whole thing, which he had heretofore seen as sort of a big joke that would make him some nice bucks fast, was in fact going to be dangerous. Probably extremely dangerous. Captain Lou led him further down the hallway, which seemed to contain a different sort of expertise behind each door. Even as they approached the last door of the corridor, Harrison could hear the subject matter of that room—firearms. Every kind imaginable, from the sounds. The noise was deafening as they walked inside and saw rows of men firing away down the large open cavern filled with targets from twenty feet off to hundreds of yards back—almost lost in the jagged slopes of the wall of the mountain which had been blasted open with dynamite.

Captain Lou introduced Harrison to his firearms trainer, Bill Sweezy, who handed his student a holster containing a Colt .45 Government Issue. "This has the stopping power of the old Colts—but it's newly retooled, a sleeker, lighter version with all the grizzly dropping force retained. And now you can go to full auto with twenty-, thirty-round clips—even sixty-round bananas for bad days."

"Sounds great," Harrison said, liking the full solid feel of the handgun around his waist. Sweezy looked on, satisfied that his pupil at least knew how to strap the thing on, how to let the handle of the weapon fall to just the right length for quick draw.

"Parker told me that you two had fought in Nam and a few other places together. That you were tough. Do you know weapons, the modern stuff?" the trainer asked as he took out his own similar Colt out of its holster and gripped it up near his right ear, silenced muzzle pointing up at the uneven granite ceiling some fifty feet above.

"Tell you the truth, I haven't really fired a weapon since the late seventies—that was mostly revamped M-16's. We had a few NATO 9mm's that weren't half bad. But no, I haven't been carrying a gun in NYC. I might have used it."

"Well, we'll practice with a variety of firearms, from this light stuff all the way to some missile-launching systems that can take out a jet. You'll have your final say on what you want to pack. Today—we'll start with what I use." He let his hard face relax for a second and turned forward. A target dummy—a large potato sack filled with sand and a smaller one atop for head, with various parts of the anatomy stamped on them in full color—was standing about seventy-five feet away.

"Now the .45 isn't supposed to be accurate beyond forty or fifty feet at most. But that's bull. I say with these new shock-resilient pistol grips and the sleeker design—I can go seventy to a hundred feet—and make a clean hit." He suddenly pulled the trigger six times and Harrison could see each tearing slug rip sections of the sacking apart so that it suddenly exploded out in big gushes of sand. When the smoke cleared there wasn't much left of the thick burlap bags, just a pile of sand on the ground and some ripped material.

"See?" he said turning to Harrison. "It works." Harrison turned toward and sighted up a target. It had been a long time, and he could feel his hand shaking a little to remind him that he was not the most relaxed of fellows. He wondered if they had a jacuzzi here—maybe with a mermaid or two. He pulled the trigger and let his hand go back with the kick. Sweezy was right. With the complete restructuring of torque lines and the thick double-cushion gripping, the damned thing had less of a kick than a .38. He clicked it to full auto to see what that was like, and squeezed softly on the trigger. The whole twelve-shot clip emptied in two seconds into the burlap, sending the sandman and the post behind that held him up disappearing in a storm of sand and splinters. When that smoke cleared there was also nothing.

They trained for an hour and a half with the Colt, silenced and unsilenced, though as Sweezy pointed out, it made sense to use it silenced since the element of surprise was always retained. Then Harrison was shown a few quick handlings of some new super-mini-submachines with even greater stopping power, and the light tripod machine guns up to 50-caliber blunderbusses. Captain Lou, who had been working out with his own Ingram .45 Mini-Sub over at the far end of range, came over and told them time was up.

"I don't know about you, but I'm damned hungry," he said. He caught hold of his charge's arm with a solid grip like he was ready to throw him into the wall and half dragged him out into the hall, then down along the carpeted corridor until they came to a door that read, "Side Exit, Restrooms/Refreshments." In the hall were dozens of coin-operated vending machines, side by side, which dispensed everything from hot coffee to sandwiches, heated-up cans of soup or ravioli, along with the usual candy, cigarettes—and even prophylactics.

"This is lunch?" Harrison asked with disbelief, leaning over and looking at the selections.

"Damned right." Captain Lou chortled. "I told you,

101

it's diet month for the old boy."

"And what's that? What's that box you're taking from behind your back?" Harrison asked, as his nostrils flared from the luscious smells that emerged.

"It's a lunch box from the dining room. They make 'em up. But not for you, Brahma bottom, we gotta get you down at least twenty or thirty pounds—and fast. How much you weigh now?" the Captain asked as he slid down against a wall until he was at the bottom, thick legs extended out on each side of him. He took quick huge bites of stew, or whatever the hell was in there, so that gravy drooled off his face and pieces of meat and potato swirled around in the churning mouth like they were in a washing machine.

"Two-sixty," Harrison answered, his jaw hanging open, his stomach growling like a baby panther.

"Well, when you get to two-forty, then you can have this." Captain Lou held a big forkful of the most delicious scented meat in some kind of wine, and Harrison felt himself start to move forward. But the Captain pulled it back, slammed the meat into his mouth like an anaconda taking down a whole pig, and stared at him through mocking eyes.

"You want a few quick bites—be my guest," Captain Lou said, nodding his head toward the rows of dispensing machines, which motion made more carrots and peas roll from his mouth and down his beard. And even as Harrison's mind said "no," his stomach screamed "yes, yes!" Quickly, before he could stop himself, he flung mountains of quarters into the coin slots of half the vending machines, and then sat down right on the floor of the hall against the cinderblock wall, slurping down minuscule bologna and cheese sandwiches on white bread that looked like they could pass for playing cards, and entire steaming cans of microwaved mini-raviolis floating in blood red sauce.

Chapter Ten

"You mean I have to get into the ring with that son-of-a-bitch?" Harrison asked with very dry lips as he stood next to Captain Lou, both of them about twenty feet away from a large square wrestling ring with ropes and all. It was at one end of an immense gymnasium that took up nearly the entire floor space of one of D2's levels. Here, all the physical training—martial arts, gymnastics, boxing, judo, whatever—was taught. There were weight rooms, saunas, all the latest equipment that could be found in the ritziest of health clubs—and plenty of stuff that couldn't. The entire level, all 20,000-plus square feet of space cordoned off with mobile walls for one activity or another, was filled with the odor of sweat and the grunting and breathing sounds of men and women working out.

"Yeah, him." Captain Lou smirked as he pointed toward the large fellow who was bouncing from rope to rope like a cannonball inside the ring. Large was not the word—the man must have stood six-ten and come in easily at 350, 375. He made the "Fridge" look like a picnic cooler.

"He knows his stuff, Harrison. He's my main man. Was a pro wrestler for about thirty years. Me and him even worked together in the old days. Between the two of us we can show you wrestling from the inside out, from the medulla to the oblongata, from the spinal to the sternum and back again. He's not a bad sort. Of course, he hasn't had anyone to throw around for a while." Captain Lou folded his huge arms and grinned with intense satisfaction as if he was curious as to just how long it would take the Destroyer to squash the "bug" who walked slowly forward with a weird expression on his face.

Harrison had on a wrestling outfit that the Captain had made him put on in the dressing room. As he walked he looked down at his pale legs and his stomach filling out the material like it was going to burst. He had thought himself in pretty good shape. But then most men like to think that—that's why they look in the mirror with the lights out. Harrison tried a limp sort of smile from outside the ropes as he stood there feeling as ridiculous as if he were naked. Then he grabbed hold of a rope, jumped up, and stepped into the ring.

"All right, now walk around, let me see just what the hell we got here, what kind of raw material I'm going to have to kick into shape." Captain Lou could see how nervous Harrison was getting, his face actually growing pale, his knees trembling slightly. The guy was afraid. It was time to bull him.

"Looking good, Harrison, real good. Look at the size of your biceps, your triceps, you got good lotisima dorsia. In fact, walk around the ring." Harrison complied, though he felt about as moronic as a man could feel, especially when two shapely women walked by giggling loudly. "Let me tell you something. I'm Captain Lou Albano, the trainer of champions and well-versed in the field of professional wrestling. I've been in it for thirty-five years, baby—as a wrestler

104

myself, and one of the nastiest there ever was—and as a manager. I've had three Intercontinental Champs and seventeen Tag Team Championships. World Champions all of them. And I wouldn't even mess around with anyone who couldn't hack it. Look at those calves. I haven't seen calves like that since Iron Thighs Johanson. You've got a future, boy. Man, do you have a future."

In spite of himself, Harrison felt pumped up by the words of the Captain, who stood at the edge of the ring pounding his fists against the mat, bellowing out the compliments like a used-car salesman extolling the virtues of the worst car on the lot.

Harrison grabbed hold of the ropes and tested them for bounce. The other man slapped himself hard on his own arms, then his shoulders. Then he smacked his face with hard thwacks, as if trying to get his blood going for the "match."

"Now this here is Rick Harrison," Captain Lou yelled up to the giant, who was flexing his muscles, which were as big as a linebacker's thighs, as he gave Harrison a largely toothless smile. "And Harrison—this is Bad John Grizzly—once one of the hottest pros on the circuit—better known to the masses by the nom de plume of the Destroyer."

"Pleze ta meet ya." The Destroyer smiled, though it came out more like a snarl as he started forward toward Harrison.

"Now show him some moves," the Captain said, leaning forward at the very edge of the ring, his bare chest pressed up against the lower rope. "But don't kill the son-of-a-bitch." He laughed. "Or even seriously maim him. Just jam, not jelly."

"Oh yeah—take easy." The Destroyer laughed as he held out his hand, and Harrison reached out to shake it, trying his biggest smile on the hulking brute just to show that they were really meant to be friends and everything was going to be just—

Before he knew what hit him, Harrison found himself being swung right through the air as the Destroyer grabbed his hand in a wristlock and flipped him over his hip. Harrison landed with a loud thud on the mat of the ring, making the flexible wood foundation beneath give in an inch or so and then spring back.

"That's it, you're doing great," Captain Lou screamed out only inches from his ear so that it felt like a garbage truck was going by. The mat cushioned the fall to some extent—though he could feel the blow slam through his bones. Harrison had taken plenty of falls years before in judo training in the service. But that was years ago. He knew before he had even risen from the first slam that his body was going to feel like shit that night and for many nights to come. And as he reached forward to lock up with the Destroyer, the wrestler moved his own arms forward and spoke up.

"First trick—never trust no one in the ring! When you hold out your hand, when you turn to look at the ref—then your opponent can take the opportunity to smash your face, trip you, even take you out completely with choke hold." The Destroyer lowered his head as he locked arms with Harrison. "On neck see scars," the huge man said as Harrison glanced over the wide shoulders to see the ugly red scar that ran all the way around to the man's back. "Got that from whole table this guy, a Samoan, picks up when he's losing a match. Caught me with it when I was being hassled by the ref—and—voom!"

And again, as the Destroyer had Harrison's attention, he suddenly lowered his head and charged in, striking Harrison's chest with a head smash. Captain Lou for some reason thought this was quite amusing

106

and let out with a gale of laughter. This time, at least, his pupil was slightly faster than on the last attack. Harrison managed to turn his body just enough to the side that he was able to guide the charge past him and the bull of a man went into the ropes about four yards off.

"Good, good," Captain Lou said, banging his fist into the palm of his other broad hand. "See? You're made for the ring, Haraldson—I could see it from the moment I laid eyes on you." The Destroyer laughed as he extricated himself from the ropes, his toothless smile even larger. "You all right—going to have fun today. Lots of fun." He put his hands up so he and Harrison entwined fingers. Then he reached forward and suddenly twisted his right hip under the smaller but more agile man and flipped him again. Try as he might to counter the move, Harrison felt himself once again flying right up into the air and coming down with a loud slam onto the mat.

Over the next two hours, the Destroyer flipped him and tripped him and catapulted him every which way as Captain Lou kept yelling out how good he was doing, how he had never seen a student progress so quickly in all his thirty-five years. Harrison came down on his head, his nose, his back, his shoulders, and his ass. But slowly, like a rock being rounded into place through sheer weathering—and pain—he began tucking the right things in so when he fell he didn't slam on the edges of his body, elbows and shoulders, but spun along like a top, albeit a lopsided one, using his rounded arms to guide him along. He began to hit the mat with the fleshy parts of his thighs and the sides of his upper arms, slapping hard as he took each fall or coming down on his arched back. His whole body would bounce up off the mat like a stone ricocheting off the top of a pond. The pain wasn't too bad—but it

107

sure made a hell of a lot of noise when you fell from seven feet in the air.

The Destroyer showed him suplexes and duplexes, showed him shoulder throws and hip twists, leg sweeps, and drag downs. Showed him head-grabbing and ankle-twisting—all the basic techniques in any self-respecting pro wrestler's repertoire. Other agents working out in the gym gathered to watch the wild match, until after about half an hour a crowd of about twenty had formed. They stretched around the ring and made jokes, yelling out odds to one another over which of the two would win each little bout. Harrison couldn't tell for sure, but he swore he saw Captain Lou taking bets on how many times a man could be thrown in a minute or some damned thing. Harrison didn't see any of them volunteering to climb into the ring and go a few rounds with Goliath.

But once the big guy saw that Harrison was ready to mix it up, and could take it, he seemed to loosen up a little and slowed down, explaining things a little more, showing his pupil just how to set the hip against the other man's hip so it caught the notch of bone—and then turn fast. Showing him how to keep his arm always slightly bent both for strength and falling, since it could better absorb the force of a blow. Showing him various little tips that when put all together meant everything. Then he even let Harrison take a shot at giving him some throws. When Harrison did it right he could feel the gravity-less sensation, the weightless feel of even the huge bulk of the Destroyer as he turned the great mass on the fulcrums—the human levers—of joints, elbows, and wrists.

Suddenly, what Harrison had always seen as just a mass of pretzel, like arms and legs crawling around a ring, he realized was in fact a science—an art—with infinite possibilities, infinite ways to throw a man, and to counter that throw. He found himself, almost against his will, becoming interested in every move, in understanding just what the hell the big guy was doing and how he was doing it. And as Captain Lou saw that he was really getting into it, he began explaining the dynamics of each move as the Destroyer put it on. And after a while it started paying off—as Harrison, following instruction, was able to get in an increasing number of sweeps and shoulder throws on the Destroyer, which both surprised and delighted the big fellow since he had been looking forward to an extremely boring month having to move like he was handling an egg so as not to break its shell. But that was clearly not the case.

Harrison, though not near the top conditioning of a wrestler, and with a gut that could use some liposuction, was tough. In the Destroyer's eyes burned a flame of respect. And in Captain Lou's as well as he saw that the guy had guts for just staying in there, taking a beating. The man might actually have the makings of a fighter if one of his arms didn't get popped right out of its socket like a broken doll's, or his head twisted around with everything inside snapped. Being a wrestler demanded not just incredible physical agility and gymnastic ability—but a strong, tough body. A body with muscles made of case-hardened steel, tendons made of cable. For the human frame was not meant to twist the way it did in wrestling. Was not meant to fall on its neck from eight feet in the air. And if Harrison was going to flunk out, let him do it here, when he might have a chance at walking away, instead of discovering he had a weak vertebra in the ring and being carried out on a stretcher, a quadriplegic with no chance of ever walking again.

But though Harrison took a large number of falls right on his head, neck, and back with great force, nothing seemed to break. He was solid as brick—inside. That hadn't changed. That had always been there. He knew it even if they didn't. The outer edges had frayed a little, the gut had ballooned up, but the inner workings that had taken him through Southeast Asia in one piece were all still functional. And as more and more of it came back to him, how to move just right, how to get out of the way, how to time his body with the other man's in perfect synchronization so he could catch it and fling it in almost any direction he felt—Harrison for the life of him found it all it exciting, even thrilling.

"That's enough," Harrison heard Captain Lou yell out from below after how much time he had no idea. "My turn now. Before he's all tired out."

"What the hell are you talking about, man—your turn?" Harrison asked. "I've been in here for at least two hours." He grunted, breathing hard. The moment he stopped he could feel his heart pounding, his face beet red and pumping out sweat like there was no tomorrow.

"Try three hours, dog breath," Captain Lou said, stripping off his Hawaiian shirt and jumping up into the ring so his belly bounced around. "Let me tell it like it is, Harrison. You're in the Super Concentrated Training Program. Like the man said this morning, we got to try to do with you what we usually spend a year—or more—doing to get fully trained wrestlers. For better or worse—you're in for the Three-Ring-Circus approach."

"Come on," Harrison said, letting his sweating shoulders slump down a little. Things were starting to hurt already. "Have mercy. At least let me have a sandwich, a cookie, a quick nap, a—"

"You're in training, Harrison," Captain Lou bellowed out as he came at him like a charging rhino.

Chapter Eleven

The waves slapped softly against the Marseilles docks, making green-mossed poles rock around like swivel sticks and the half-rotted piers above them, here in the poorest, most rundown section of the French port city, creak and groan with a ghostly sound which echoed down the cobblestone streets. Half-collapsed warehouses which had once housed a thriving, now almost dead shipping industry lined the sides of the streets. Within one of the warehouses, a long and quite wide one, a rat came scampering out through a tiny hole in its base. Other than that not a sliver of light emerged from inside the triple-boarded-up windows. Not a sound could be heard stirring from within.

Those on the inside could dimly hear the occasional horns of the passing boats in the morning fog, the tankers and delapidated tugs carrying their loads of coal and lumber up and down along the coast. But nothing else. For the thirteen people within the warehouse walls were completely sealed in with countless sheets of plywood and insulation over every window and door. There was only one way in—or out. That was through the basement hallway, which exited above ground some thirty yards away in another building so anyone passing by wouldn't see activity of any kind around the warehouse. A lot of time and money had been spent to make the place secure. But then the building of an atomic bomb required privacy, a certain amount of peace and quiet. A strange prerequisite considering how little of those things it gave back to the world.

A large cannister, nearly five feet high and about two feet wide, was being opened, unscrewed by two men wearing thick gloves but no rad suits or other protection. They had all made their decisions concerning their "loyalty" and willingness to "sacrifice" for the revolutionary cause—and they had all discarded the protective equipment. The ghosts of Mao would protect them. And if not—then it was not meant to be. History would use them for its revolutionary purposes and then they would be burned up, martyrs for the workers of the world. One of the men reached in with a long steel gripping device and began maneuvering the much smaller egg-shaped chromium cannister about as large as a football inside the large cannister. Using the block and tackle system they were operating manually—stolen, as was most of the bomb-makers' equipment—they lifted the egg over onto a long steel table that ran down the entire center of the warehouse, a good two hundred feet long. They slowly lowered the load inside a bucket filled with a high-density mixture of sand and lead particles.

"Good, good," a sweat-coated suit-and-tied man screamed down from atop a ten-foot ladder. "Just don't mix up the damned uranium with the plutonium— I told you that yesterday. The first thing is organization—with a capital O. Do you think Lenin survived the prisons, Stalin the Fascist armies, Chairman Mao the enemies of the revolution—without organization?" Professor Markus grew dizzy again, as he often had recently while trying to run the whole damn show of assembling a working nuclear device. He stood up on his high steel ladder like the director of some early Hollywood film, shouting down commands, guiding the whole show from above. He had rigged up a long

112

wooden plank on top of the ladder, and had a whole slew of books spread out before him, their pages open, pads with quickly scribbled notes all over them like the scrawlings of a madman. All the technical information needed to make a bomb.

"Yes, Professor Markus," one of the men—the German, Hauser—shouted up. "We have the uranium marked with a big U on the side in magic marker. And I'll just throw a nice big F on the side of this stuff here," he said as the container holding the softball-sized chunk of plutonium settled into the sand-and-lead mixture. "We're marking everything just like you said. And then adding it to the master chart."

Professor Markus inspected the schematic he had managed to obtain from a high-security-clearance access file that had been stored on microfilm at the University's technical library. The security on the computer system had been laughably easy to overcome. A good hacker with anything bigger than an Atari could have gotten inside. Working with one of his assistants, Ted Thornton, ex-Weatherman and one of the first "followers" of the professor's Mission of Fire—who also happened to be one of the top computer whizzes around—he had logged into the microfiche system via modem. Using Thornton's own deciphering program on an IBM, he had been able to gain access to the charts within twenty minutes. They had fed the digital signals into a FAX machine in the professor's office. And lo and behold, ten minutes later—How to Make Your Own A-Bomb in Ten Easy Lessons. Yield—1 megaton. Which would be plenty. More than enough. Why, the Hiroshima bomb hadn't even been that big.

Professor Markus took a few final anxious looks at his notes, knowing he had to get the damned project started. It had all been a fantasy—until now. An impossible dream. And yet now it was within his grasp. He alone could make it happen. The sudden realization

113

of how much power he held in his hands made him swoon for a few seconds up on the ladder. The search for and grabbing of power—to carry out his utopian visions of a workers' paradise—had always been the quest that carried him forward, that pulled him through his worst times, through his drinking. And now it was all within reach. Power, pure unadulterated white-hot power.

He looked down over the dozen pairs of eyes that were raised up toward him and licked his tongue back and forth, wetting the dry white lips. They were a motley crew. Oriental faces, white, Germanic, a few blacks, the Bulgarians with their wide-open features. Half of them could barely communicate with the other half. But they were committed. And each was an expert in his or her field. Still, he shuddered deep inside, though it was not visible to the others. Though he didn't believe in God, being a devout atheist—a "historical scientist," as he thought of himself—he did believe in a sort of Revolutionary God who doled out justice just as fervently and harshly as any Bearded Fellow in the sky. And he knew that this atheistic god, like the other, had given him this group to work with as his "cross" to bear. It was the overcoming of all the obstacles in his way needed to make it happen that would make it all worthwhile, make his entire life up to this point worthwhile, all that he had done. His physics, his years of fuming at the government, the University—where others were promoted to deanships while he remained always the popular but lowly Professor Markus. "How are you, Professor Markus? Nice day, Professor Markus." Nice fucking day indeed. They would pay. Everyone would pay.

"All right then," he said slowly, flavoring the words since he knew this was an historic moment for all mankind. "Now we begin." Yes, that sounded good for future generations. He stopped to write down the words as the others looked on, getting a little bored as they wanted to get going. The sheer involvement for all of them—scientists covering a half-dozen fields—was in itself a major event in one's "career." How many junior Ph.D.'s or chemists or budding nuclear engineers got to make a fucking nuke?

"All our equipment is before us on the table," Professor Markus said with a dramatic flourish of his hands. "We will begin our countdown as of now. The large calendar you see on the wall shows us the number of days left before we must be finished. *Must be!* For there will be no second chance on this. The timing must be precise. So we work fast—no mistakes—but fast."

"All right," he went on, taking a deep breath, pointing with the long slide rule/calculator/computer that he waved around like some physicist's magic wand. "Bring the main shell over onto the center of the table." Two Japanese wheeled a large shining globe about three feet in diameter. They carried the thing in a motorized pulley, two large canvas straps holding the thing up as they guided it carefully along on high rubber wheels. The globe wasn't that large—but it was heavy, reinforced and shielded on the outside by alternating layers of lead, titanium stripping, and more lead. It was meant to be as detection-proof as possible, and to achieve that goal had to have the weight of nearly 250 pounds added to its 75-pound frame. That plus the additional 100 pounds of bomb that would be built inside of it would push the atomic package over the 400-pound mark, making it bulky. But the professor had no choice. Anything smaller would have been a joke, a mere pop in the dark night. He needed something that would be a spark seen around the world, a fire in the heavens.

"So this is our egg, ladies and gentlemen—all the workings of the bomb must be fit inside this. All your calculations from here on in will use the constants of both the dimensions of this globe and the room needed for each of the concentric stages of the bomb—outer high-explosive charges, inner ring of one-hundred-percent-pure U238 particle jell, and a nucleus of plutonium with its own set of charges inside of it—so that as the outer explosives go off, the inner ones will as well, sending everything flying toward each other and creating a nuclear reaction. It's an extremely complex procedure. Make no mistake about it. All measurements must be within the millimeter range. Anything doesn't fit—perfectly—do it over."

"Professor." One of the dour and stone-faced fair maidens of the late Meinhof gang spoke up, a .45 set inside her belt like a permanent fixture. "How ze hell do ve know dat ze bom vill vork? Perhaps ve built a zekund bom und test it virst?" She had been challenging his decisions from the start. The professor had taken an intense dislike to her rigid Prussian ways, her stiff shoulders, the way she always marched around as if part of some invisible army. He'd have thought she was a Neo-Nazi but for her track record of armored car holdups in the name of the Cause. She had killed three guards all by herself. Made the cover of *Der Spiegel* two times in three years. Of course she had had plastic surgery since then, although it didn't seem to have made her more pleasant-appearing. Nor her dark-mooded twin also from the Meinhof gang, who followed her around like a shadow. The professor himself still didn't trust women in high-tech work—feeling them inferior ultimately in mathematical reasoning and analysis areas in which the male was supreme. But they were what the Revolutionary God had given him, and thus they would be what he used.

"Hey, fraulein, why don't you get a nose job?" one of the black chemists said, chuckling out loud as they all took their places at their work stations side by side along the wide industrial platform.

"Fuck off, blackie," she snarled back, giving him a look that made even the tough Black Liberation Army man, six-foot-plus himself, draw back from her as she walked by. There was something in her eyes, something as cold as a midwinter's night. Colder. His laughter died out on his lips as she took her hand off the butt of her H & K 9mm and walked on to join her twin. Professor Markus looked down, not missing a thing. He had been around students all his life. The Japanese didn't seem to be getting along with the Bulgarians, the German twins couldn't stand the black chemists. There were tensions. And plenty of them. Tensions that could explode as the project went on. For all of them were on lockup duty now—no one except for his two "security" assistants could leave the warehouse—until the bomb was built. The problems among them all would grow, become exacerbated by each passing incident. Like the one that had just occurred. But that could be a plus too, if it could be controlled. They would be competitive with one another, each group trying to get its work done faster than the other. And a man who could control those forces, those explosive energies—like the bomb itself—a man who was a leader, could channel them into miracles.

The Manhattan Project had been like that. Oppenheimer—the man who had put it all together at a base in the desert that grew from 500 to 50,000 people before World War II was over and the two bombs that ushered in a new world were born—had done it. Oppenheimer had known how to use that quality, that tension between his work teams—somewhere between fanatical enthusiasm and nervous breakdown. Markus had been a young physicist then, the peach fuzz not even in full growth on his cheeks. He had seen it. He knew it could be done. He had felt the heat from its spiraling atomic cloud that afternoon in the New Mexico desert.

Chapter Twelve

Harrison's eyes flew open with fear as he saw that he was encased in metal, in a tomb. He gasped hard trying to breathe—and suddenly woke up. He was in the Survival Room—and someone was pounding on the door so that the sharp bangs amplified in the tiny space.

"What, who the hell is—" he sputtered, trying to rise and bumping his head against the television screen, which, thank God, he hadn't had to endure all night this time.

"It's your favorite person, Captain Lou," the raspy voice bellowed from outside. "Time to get rolling. The CIA won't wait. And I won't wait." The fist kept pounding and wouldn't stop.

"All right, all right, I'm coming, damn your eyes," Harrison yelled back feebly as he tried to slowly get out of the metal bed without slamming into the high-tech obstacle course. He was completely unsuccessful in that attempt—cracking his right foot into a radio speaker, his thumb against the instant-coffee dispenser along one wall, and his elbow hard against the laundry chute built into the door by the bathroom. Harrison crawled to the can on all fours for sheer survival and slowly pushed the buttons and levers, trying to recollect just what the hell he had done the day before. Suddenly the shower stall folded back, the sink pushed up, and the toilet slid down and opened outward, filling instantly with a little autosquirt of mentholated, sanitized, degermed water.

All things considered, he came through it all relatively unscathed and emerged from his room six minutes later, almost walking right into Captain Lou's still-pounding fist. He swore the door's case-hardened steel/plastic alloy had been bent in slightly by all the attention.

"You look even worse than yesterday," Captain Lou said, squinting at Harrison and pulling nervously at his beard. Harrison was all puffed up, eyes bloodshot, knees quivering like reeds in a roaring river. He hadn't moved as much in the last ten years as he had yesterday. And now—he had to go out and face another full day. They had not yet begun to fight.

"Got any aspirin, Captain?" Harrison asked as he felt himself already starting to get a headache just standing beneath the hard fluorescent lights.

"Sure, man, always carry a pack with me in this place." The wrestling showman/CIA trainer laughed from between his cigar-clamped teeth. He looked even stranger than yesterday, if that was possible. With brightly colored orange, blue, and gold rubber bands— the giant-sized ones—hanging from ears and cheek, and two of them around his beard squeezing it like it was about to be scythed off and stored for the winter. His half-opened shirt was a camouflage-pattern green-and-gray combat material, only it had been colored in to make it look Hawaiian. Black jeans looked like they were having a little trouble holding it all together at the seams, and his purple sneakers had yellow streaks running along them like bolts. The guy sure as hell wasn't going to be on the cover of *GQ* anytime soon. He took out a little tin of Super Triple Strength Plus Excedrin and handed two to his charge. "Here's some coffee for you to slug it down with," he said brusquely, reaching into a paper bag and pulling out a steaming cup of dark brew.

"Thanks," Harrison said with a smile. He hadn't yet been able to figure out how the InstaCoffee Dispenser in his room worked and he was sure he never would. Maybe the caffeine jolt would get some of his gears going. It seemed to work. Captain Lou led him down the corridor walking slowly—one leg, then the other, like some bear looking for berries—toward his morning classes. Between the aspirin and chugging down the not-half-bad coffee that they brewed in huge vats in the kitchen, Harrison felt his brain if not his flesh start to come to life. Enough so that he actually had a notebook out and pen in hand by the time he reached the auditorium where Director Marshall was just coming in himself from between the back curtains. Captain Lou slid in one of the rows of seats about halfway down, and proceeded to slide back into it like he was preparing himself for a Grade-B movie.

"Ah, I see you're not late today. That thrills my heart no end, I assure you," the Director said as Harrison slid in just a few seats from the aisle and sat down. "At least I can bid you adieu knowing that you've been able to adapt at least slightly to the way things are done here at the *A*gency." He allowed himself a smug little grin as he stepped to his lectern and threw a good half pound of notes down on its wooden top. "Yes, bid you adieu, Harrison—for I've been informed by the powers"—he said the words with distaste—"that you are not going to go through the full training of regular agents, but instead will concentrate on the hands-on training programs that you've begun. So today, I will attempt to

120

squeeze even a little of the very basic concepts of this Agency into you. Please pay attention." With that Dr. Marshall began his dissertation on "The Function of the Intelligence Community as It Interfaces with the Global Political Realities."

Harrison tried, he really did. But his right eyelid began twitching and fluttering down within five minutes after the guy had started. Harrison glanced over and saw that Captain Lou was already deep in dreamland. The bastard had mastered the art of leaning his head on one hand and sort of turning his face slightly to the side and down so it looked like he was awake and in rapt concentration as he listened. Harrison was not nearly so good, and kept finding his head falling all the way over to the side like a junkie on a nod. He would jerk it up straight again, hear a few words about "contextual operational modus operandi," and then would begin the slide back down into Nod.

Not that Dr. Marshall really gave a shit. He had already categorized the man as completely uneducatable. Why try? They wanted a fighting bull, not a trained agent. That was clear. Just look at the disgustingly fat wrestling trainer they had brought in, who was obviously sound asleep. So be it. It wasn't even so much Harrison himself that repulsed the "old man," but what he represented to him. A lowering of standards, an acceptance of "beasts of burden" into the Agency for the first time in its existence. He shuddered to think where it would all end. But he was getting old. It would not be *his* pain to bear. At least there was solace in that. So he went through his lecture hardly even looking up, but going from notes to chalkboard, where he drew in Power Circles and how to infiltrate them, then back to notes again, all as if carrying out some Shakespearean soliloquy addressed not to men,

121

but directly to the uncaring gods themselves.

At last it was over. Marshall coughed loudly and slammed his pointer down on the lectern, so both men suddenly sat up in their seats like they'd been goosed with hot pokers.

"Excellent, excellent," Harrison mumbled. "I really learned a lot of vital information," he said as sincerely as he could, knowing it couldn't hurt to get as many of the bastards on his side as possible. You never knew.

"Yes, I'm sure." Dr. Marshall smirked with ultimate skepticism. "Well, I don't think it really matters how much you've learned," he said with sarcasm, "because undoubtedly you'll be dead before you even get a chance to forget any of it." With that he gathered his things together, said "good-bye" with utmost coldness and civility, and headed back out through the curtains which covered the back of the stage.

"Come on," Captain Lou said, wiping his mouth and scratching his big stomach, which poked out like a whale looking to beach itself. "Let's get us some real education now." Within minutes they were at Harrison's next lesson—Visual and Electronic Espionage.

"This is—I can't tell you his name for security reasons," the Captain said as they came up to a thin, sunglassed man who held out his hand to Harrison. "He's from a company called CCS. They supply all kinds of electronic gizmos to diplomats and corporate types heading overseas. Security stuff, things that go bump and beep in the night. Kind of stuff that would give James Bond wet dreams."

"Glad to meet you, Mr. No Name," Harrison said, taking the man's hand and shaking it firmly.

"You too, Harrison," the CCS rep replied. "Heard a lot about you. You're hot stuff around here. We're going to give you some of our newest items, stuff that's been debugged so you won't have any foul-ups. To say

122

the least, in the business you're in, if something goes wrong—you're history. That's what we want to avoid."

He led them to a table that contained all kinds of gadgets, many of them incomprehensible to Harrison.

No Name pointed out the different gadgets—and their functions, from X-ray attache cases to night-vision goggles. Then he zeroed in on the use of a number of different spy cameras—from big super-computerized jobs to minicams that could fit inside a thimble. He instructed Harrison in the use of a 35-mm camera that was inside a normal-looking watch. The lens was built into the face of the watch, the shutter snapping open when one pushed the hand in on the side. The thing automatically forwarded to the next frame, and when the roll was complete it gave off with a low beep. He showed the Captain and Harrison the clear and vivid photos taken with the watch cameras.

Then it was on to the audio side of the spy game—mini-tape recorders with microphones hidden in tie clips, shoes, or even rings. The things could run silently for up to forty-eight hours recording conversations on a tiny filament reel. Harrison couldn't help but be impressed. And in a way he felt a bit of pride that they had pulled him in on all this.

"Now, this baby took a hell of a lot of miniaturization," No Name said as they reached the middle of the long stainless-steel gridded table. He picked up an unopened pack of cigarettes and held it in his hand as if offering it to Harrison.

"Sorry, don't smoke," the wrestler-in-training replied.

"Me neither," No Name replied with a smirk, his eyes hidden beneath the dark glasses. "But then these aren't for smoking. It's for detecting smoke—or what could become smoke, atomic-style. It's a geiger counter, sophisticated, able to measure down to the milli-rad.

123

Can pick up even low-level radiation sources once you're within ten, maybe fifteen feet." He showed both men how the side of the pack slid back revealing a whole row of inset buttons and readouts. It looked complicated and Harrison groaned inwardly. But after just ten minutes of instruction he was able to make the thing go beep and store the results in a mini-computer built into it.

"Now, you don't want anybody ripping the pack apart," No Name cautioned Harrison. "'Cause not too many packs of Marlboro 100's have diodes and wires inside them. But otherwise—it's indistinguishable from any other pack."

"Son of a bitch," Captain Lou kept muttering through his unlit cigar. He seemed amazed by the miniaturized miracles of modern technology.

The electronic-gizmo operations class went on for about two hours, then lunch again. No Name bid them adieu until the next class. This time Captain Lou took Harrison to the dining area, one of the smaller dining centers on each level. At least it wasn't the vending-machine sandwiches, Harrison thought as he greedily eyed the steaming stainless-steel cannisters filled with chow and started to give his order to the kitchen help behind the counter.

"No no," Captain Lou said, nodding his head sharply so the rubber bands spun around like tassels on a stripper. "I sent in my order yesterday—the 'Special Menu.' You better have it, baby, or else my man here is going to be hungry—and mad! You don't want to get him mad!"

"I'll—I'll check," the young blond man said nervously as he eyed the two huge men, and particularly Captain Lou, with some trepidation.

"What the hell do you mean, the Special Menu?" Harrison asked, feeling the blood surge angrily to his

124

skull, his head starting to throb again—and he'd only been up hours.

"Listen, bison butt, you're on full training now—Captain Lou's Champion-Maker Program. And I've made more champs than any other men in history. You're going on less than twenty grams of carbohydrate a day. No fatty foods or desserts, lots of vegetables, whole grains, juices . . . But you don't have to worry about it, Harrison. The Captain's a gourmet chef from way back. I whipped up my Super Vitamin and Mineral All-Purpose Training Gruel. You're going to love it. Won prizes at several contests." Just where the Captain's super gruel might have won contests was something Harrison didn't even want to think about.

Within a few seconds the kitchen guy came back with a frighteningly small—as far as Harrison was concerned—bowl covered with aluminum foil.

"Here—here it is, sir," the young man attired in white kitchen garb said. "Sorry about the mixup. I'm new here and—"

"Gimmee!" Harrison snapped out as a whole flood of acidic digestive juices cascaded into his empty stomach. He reached out and grabbed the tray, ripping the top off the bowl like a scavenger tearing off the top of a treasure chest. His face dropped like a fallen souffle as he stared inside.

"This is enough for a mouse," Harrison said, his face flushing. "Not a two-hundred-sixty-pound man."

"Eat it and be lucky there's anything. On my Extra-Super, Double-Elongated Training Program, they get *no* gruel, just steamed lettuce and water for a month." He glared at Harrison, who glared back, then slammed a spoon into the stuff, and lifted it to his mouth, dropping it inside like a garbage man throws trash into the mouth of his truck. It tasted horrible. For the sheerest second Harrison felt like spitting it right into

125

the face of the Captain, who chewed away lustily, slamming steam-shovel-sized forkfuls of anything he stabbed on the plate. The man ate like a conveyer belt. But even as the urge came up in him to spit—Harrison's stomach told him to swallow. And in arguments between the stomach and the brain, the stomach always won.

It wasn't that it was that horrible. Harrison had probably eaten worse things. It was that it wasn't really mixed. He could taste the separate products the Captain had put in: ground-up soycake, powdered vitamin pills, various juices—tomato, celery. . . . The texture was the worst. Oliver Twist's famous gruel had nothing on this.

"There gotta be more than this, man," Harrison said with desperation after he had quickly finished off the foul swamp. "I mean, I usually eat this much before I brush my teeth."

"That's it, pal," the Captain said with absolute finality from behind his moving fork. "The colonel's orders. You gotta get to fighting weight. Or my ass is grass. You're in Weight Watchers Anonymous now—whether you want it or not."

Harrison was in a mean mood by the time they reached the wrestling ring. The Destroyer was already waiting up there, jumping up in the air and slamming down hard on the mat. But Captain Lou stopped him as he started to climb in.

"We start conditioning today, Buick butt. Sit-ups, push-ups, chin-ups, all the things that I'm sure you hate. And when you're done with that—we'll put you on the stair machine over there, a treadmill made of stairs. It simulates running up the Empire State Building. You'll hate that even more." And the Captain was right about that. It was hard, sweaty, and grunting work and his muscles felt like they were all going to pop. At last it was time for some ring work, but to his surprise as he climbed up into the ring, Captain Lou came in on the other side, stripped down to cutoff lime green jean shorts, round stomach poking out above them.

"Today, I'm going to try to impart the wisdom of the genius of Captain Lou," he growled, slapping himself on the arms. "We'll work with the ball first." The Destroyer threw a big medicine ball to the Captain, who caught it and instantaneously heaved it across the ring at Harrison. The ball slammed into Harrison's chest driving him straight backward, as he had been unprepared for its sixty-pound weight, thinking it was a beachball. He didn't go down, but flushed as he bounced off the ropes and held the ball at chest level. The two ex-wrestlers stared at him like he was a bug in the jello.

Harrison threw the ball back again. Instantly the Captain flung it straight back like it was made of paper. And Harrison again braced himself, this time at least not stepping backward. But he let out a big grunt of air as the thing hit him in the solar plexus. It hurt, but he didn't show it, stretching a strained smile which both men knew the meaning of across his face.

"We've got to get you strong, Harrison. Really strong to survive in the ring. Otherwise—they'll rip you like you were a rag doll." He made a ripping motion with his hands, grinding them together like he was squeezing a wet towel. Harrison threw the ball back hard. But the Captain didn't even use his arms this time, just sort of jumped forward, slamming his entire stomach into the medicine ball, which sailed backward like it had been kicked by a mule. Harrison braced himself for all he was worth and took it again without going over. But it felt almost like it had cracked a rib or two. Thus it went for an hour, with the pupil taking shots to the chest and stomach and even the face over and over again, until he started feeling like a handful of grain that was being ground down into flour.

At last Captain Lou slammed the ball with his stomach and flipped it sideways so it flew right over the side of the ring. Even the Destroyer, who was standing in the corner of the ring, applauded the move. He knew even more than Harrison the kind of skill and inner musculature it took to do that.

"Today, you poor stinking slob," Captain Lou said, walking up to the sweating Harrison and patting him on the shoulder like a priest would a condemned man, "I'm going to show you some of *my* moves."

They faced off and locked up arms, and Harrison could smell the strong breath of the Captain right in his face. The bastard had eaten half the garlic on the East Coast for lunch. "First thing—wrist locks and holds," the Captain said. "Most opponents will try to grab you with both hands. *Use that to your advantage!*" the Captain bellowed. "You got an ace from the start." To demonstrate he whipped right around behind Harrison, grabbing his right arm in both of his hands, and with a simple twist the trainee felt himself flying right through the air. He came down about eight feet across the mat, where he slammed down hard. His body shuddered from the first shock. It still hurt like a mother from the day before. Every joint, muscle, and other part of him capable of feeling pain was doing its utmost to do so.

"That's a simple wrist flip." Captain Lou smirked. "Now the other wrist." Harrison walked back and stretched out his other hand to grab the Captain's thick wrist. But again he had barely made contact when he was airborne, not fully understanding how he had gotten there. Then it was on to arm locks, neck holds— which could kill if done at full strength. Captain Lou showed him the Double Scissor and the Indian Death Lock to the point that the pupil's eyes were half bulging out. The holds hurt, with a kind of inner bone pain that he had never experienced before. For there was no pain like the twisting of joints. Wise men and warriors had known that since the dawn of time.

After the various locks and holds had been demonstrated two or three times, Captain Lou allowed his pupil to try them on him. It was hard to even budge the wide and low-centered man. He seemed more like a mountain than a human being. Yet by trial and error, doing it over and still over again, he was at last able to bend the Captain's wrist back, get him in a double arm lock, and swing him around so the Captain had to slam down flat on the ground. It suddenly dawned on him that, as tough as he had been—and he had won every bout he had ever had—he could get to be a lot tougher. Be one of the tops. God only knew where it might lead. And deep inside he began feeling as he hurtled around the ring that there was a sense of rightness about it, and his body slowly began to fall into the proper movements.

"All right—now aside from instilling in your cranium a whole menu of wrestling moves—a man has to have two or three that are his ace moves. That he can go to when the shit hits the light bulbs—and come out in one piece. You hear what the Captain is saying?"

"Two or three moves," Harrison echoed back, his eyes staring ahead but hardly seeing as he panted hard like a sled dog.

"So I'll show you mine—and you better know that's a privilege and a responsibility."

"Privilege and responsibility."

"First—the Sleeper." The Captain threw his arms around Harrison's neck so the crook of one arm was pressed right against the side of his neck, and then

129

locked around the second arm. The Captain pulled back hard and Harrison felt himself blacking out as flashing stars filled his eyes. There was a whooshing sound and then the whole world was coming back into the light.

"There, feel it?" the Captain asked as he kept his arm there but loose.

"Uh, uh, uh," Harrison mumbled, his tongue not quite coordinating with his teeth.

"Here, feel it again." Captain Lou tightened and again Harrison felt himself slipping into dreamland. It was scary going out like that. Then again he came to. It felt like he had been out for minutes, but he knew it was only seconds. This time the Captain released him and stepped back.

"The Sleeper has been proven medically to be a devastating hold," Captain Lou said. "It cuts off the blood to the brain—blood from the cerebellum to the medulla back down to the pulmonary arteries going from the left ventricle to the right ventricle—and this can leave a man helpless, cause paralysis or even death."

The Captain let Harrison try it on him and also showed him how to counter it—by turning the chin in toward the pulling arm so it couldn't get the right angle around the throat. Harrison did it without actually applying much pressure dozens of times from each side of the head before the Captain would let him stop.

"Now you'll work on that every class with the Destroyer, who'll be your day-to-day wrestling partner. The Captain, for all his skills, is getting a little too old and fat for the pounding." He patted his belly like a prized possession.

"But I want to show you the other move I've picked out for you. In its own way as devastating, maybe more so, than the Sleeper. It's the Claw, Harrison." The

130

Captain shaped his right hand into a claw and then slammed it into Harrison's stomach. The pupil/victim gagged as his tongue popped out of his mouth and his whole gut felt like it was on fire.

"See? Amazing. Makes the whole body react. If you strike deeper"—he showed again, but only started to poke up under the ribcage—"you can actually seriously hurt your opponent by ripping into organs. And to show you the power of this move—there's this monk Yakamoto or something. The guy can't weigh more than a hundred pounds, his arms are like pinkies, he looks like he's dying. He does this big ceremony in Japan every year where he puts a calf on the platform and—aiieee, aeeiii. Rips the heart right out of the animal and holds it up for all the world to see. If this guy used his claw strike on your head, it would open it up like a coconut."

"I believe you, I believe you," Harrison yelled out each time the Captain poked the claw into some part of his anatomy and squeezed just enough so he could feel it.

"Now the other places to strike with the claw are . . . the neck." He pushed the claw against Harrison's throat, but very carefully. "The face itself." And the meaty fingers clamped over his nose, eyebrows, and upper lip. "Or the top of the head, around both temples." That was the worst one of all as it made his whole skull feel like it was under incredible pressure and his brain might erupt out of his ears, nose, and mouth. But again the Captain was careful. He knew how to gauge his moves down to fractions of an inch. Then he let Harrison try them on him. But as much as the pupil squeezed, even though he thought he was strong, the Captain just stared straight ahead like there were mosquitos buzzing around him.

"Here, take this ball," he said as the Destroyer threw

him one, this only about as big as a baseball, but very hard. "Squeeze that every day whenever you're not doing something else. I put a guy on this regimen once and we built him up to 7.098 pounds of pressure per squre inch. He could take a pair of pliers, hardened steel, put a piece of wood between the ends—and then squeeze so hard the thing would snap right in half. Just imagine what that could do to a man's skull."

"I'm imagining, I'm imagining," Harrison mumbled as he squeezed at the rubber ball and let the blood drain back into the top of his skull, which felt like it had been squeezed into orange juice.

"Now—for some dirty tricks," Captain Lou said. "I don't say you should use them against a man in a fair fight. But if *he* uses 'em first—you gotta know how to fight back." In quick succession he showed Harrison the eye gouge, the ear slap, the knee to the groin, the head butt, the spit in the eye, the sucker punch, the rope scrape, the ring post smash, and an assortment of other moves that they don't teach you at Harvard. Harrison felt like he was a test dummy in one of those car crashes to find out what horrible things can happen to the human body when it gets smacked around and mangled up.

But Captain Lou didn't let up. He knew that his charge had very little time to learn a hell of a lot. An incredible, impossible amount. To make a man a professional-level wrestler—and a good one—in one month or less, was a Herculean effort. He felt a deep responsibility for the man. It was one thing to throw him to the wolves—it was something else to not even give him the slightest of fighting chances. So the Captain pounded the sucker around like he was a basketball on a court. For another two hours he gouged him and tripped him and threw him from one end of the ring to the other—and then back again,

132

bouncing him from the ropes like he was human slingshot ammo. Until Harrison didn't even know what planet he was on.

"Now your turn," Captain Lou said through the spinning fog around Harrison's head. "Try a Fireman's Carry." The pupil was able to get one hand on the Captain's thick arm and then his lower leg. He lifted as he turned, trying to get him up, but had gotten only about halfway there when his knees collapsed out from under him and the whole huge load came crashing down on Harrison as he crumbled to the floor like an accordion folding up on itself.

"All right, that's enough," The Captain said as he rose up from the pancake that was Rick Harrison lying in a state of horrified shock on the mat. "You're all right, Harrison," he said, sounding almost kind for a moment. "All right to fight a tag team of grand-mothers." He bellowed instantly, "Got a long way to go sonny boy. Damned long way to go." Captain Lou lumbered over to the ropes and then stepped out of the ring as the Destroyer helped Harrison to his feet. "Don't know," the Captain mumbled as he left the ring and headed toward the showers. "Don't know, don't know, just don't know."

Chapter Thirteen

Colonel Parker stared at the reports in front of him and then looked around at the three men who sat on the opposite side of the black marble desk.

"It's irrefutable. These prove it," he said angrily, holding up computer printouts. "Missing shipments of irridium, tritium, neptunium. A hijacking of super-conducting coaxial wires. Several missing shipments of super-high-explosive artillery shells—which could easily be modified into shaped charges. These things are the ingredients for only one damn thing—an atomic bomb. It's no hoax. These bastards, whoever the hell they are, are really going to do it."

"*Try* to do it," Miller, one of his European liaisons, said from across the table. "The sheer possession of these materials does show intent—but it doesn't say anything about the ability to use them. Not at all."

"Yes but these attacks—on a train, two trucks, not to mention breaking into a high-security warehouse containing nuclear fusing connections among other things, these events occurring in four different countries—France, Germany, Britain, and Norway—all within the space of the last six weeks, show a highly organized group at work. Our analysis boys, working with a Cray Supercomputer, have been going over information worldwide on the theft of atomic-related materials. Didn't even put it all together the first time around. Can you believe that there's still no international reporting on many of these events? A lot of countries don't want us to know what the hell's going on behind their own fucking borders—and they're our allies."

"Lord protect us from our friends," Hendricks mumbled from across the table as he puffed hard on his Marlboro. He and Parker were just about the only son-of-a-bitches who even smoked around the War Room. The rest, the upcoming yuppies of the Agency, were all so damned health-conscious with their vitamins and bran and jogging and no smoking. Thank God Parker still ran things in this section, Hendricks thought. When he was gone, the last of the hard-drinking, smoking, often carousing men from the old days would be gone. Then they'd ban Hendricks's foul blue smoke, make everyone jog at six A.M., and have Stock and Tupperware parties which would be *de rigueur* for all career-minded agents. Thank God he'd be gone before all that rot, Hendricks fumed, lost in his own momentary anger at the future.

"They're organized enough for me to sit up all night worrying about it," Parker said, looking around at some of his top men. "And sending me back to two packs a day—when I'm supposed to have quit seven days ago." For a moment the faces around the War Table relaxed, and smiles shivered through tense mouths. But within seconds all faces looked quite grim again.

"Sir—" a man interrupted, walking from the Satellite Synch Intercontinental Comm Room with a FAX'd printout in his hand. The hand held out the sheet and Colonel Parker took it with a scowl, not liking to be disturbed in conference unless for the utmost emergency. "Sorry, sir." The man shrugged, a new face that Parker didn't even recognize. "The Shift Chief—Carlson—said you would want it pronto."

The CIA boss looked down, puffing hard on the freshly lit cig in his mouth so that a little chimney of smoke rose above his head, making him look almost as if he was on fire. A few of the men seated across the table exchanged amused glances. Parker's eyes scanned back and forth over the communique, and then his face lit up like he had just been delivered his Christmas presents early.

"Get your parachutes, boys, we're flying to Belgium. And I mean pronto. Just came over on Interpol Scramble Code. That limey bastard, Chief of Interpol Counter Intelligence Eric Stallenworth—he owes me one. They got word that something big—and I mean *big*—is going down at midnight tonight right at the French-Belgian border. Got a whole battalion of Interpol and European Security Forces out to bag 'em. They think it's Baader-Meinhof, and that they've got arms—big ones. And we're invited along for the ride. This could be it. I tell you this could be the break." He was suddenly in a good mood, and stamping out the cigarette before it was half smoked, yelled for his assistant, Saunders, as he began lighting the next one.

"Take over operations, man," he said as he ordered up one of D2's fleet of jets over his phone—this one a de-armed F18, experimental, on "loan" from the Air Force.

"Yes, sir," Saunders said, rushing over from some microfilm files on a wall about twenty feet behind Parker's high-tech buzzing and beeping Central Com desk-table unit.

"And, Saunders," Parker added as he tightened the strap of his hidden shoulder harness and made sure the

136

.44 mag inside was secure enough to cross the world. "Don't burn down the fucking store, okay?"

"No, sir, of course not," the man stuttered back, not quite sure how to respond to such a request. But Parker was already heading off, his eyes glistening, his cheeks flushed with excitement. He was heading out into the combat zone—if only for a few hours. It had been a long time.

Colonel Parker and his three boys picked up some ultra-light bullet-proof chest shirts and then took the elevator up to the top of the mountain. A chopper pad had been built off to one side in what looked like a daisy-filled meadow—but which could accommodate a fleet of choppers if necessary, with hidden landing lights and a flat runway beneath the inch-thick layer of dirt over the area. Their ears all popped as the elevator lurched to a stop, and then they were standing inside the darkened cobwebbed barn. They headed outside, and the chopper was already there, hovering just feet above the ground, sending down an eerie amber light which couldn't be seen for much of a distance. The four leaped aboard the rotating craft, Parker noticing with disgust that two of the men who worked for him could hardly climb aboard. They were soft, a little scared of jumping up. Afraid they might hurt themselves.

Within ten minutes they were boarding the super swept-wing F-18, a mid-sized jet fighter altered for transport. It had the speed of a missile. They were cleared for takeoff and within a minute of boarding, the craft was tearing ass down the runway like a competitor in the high jump in the Olympics. Then it took off and went a hell of a lot higher than any high-jumper would dare dream, shooting up at almost a ninety-degree angle like a rocket heading for the moon. The four men, grimaced as the g's of the acceleration pushed them back hard in their seats, made it hard to

137

even breathe.

Then they were in the clouds, piercing them with the needle nose of the low-slung craft. The F-18 straightened out slowly, and then they were hauling ass so fast it was dizzying. Even from 20,000, then 30,000 feet as the plane rose up, the earth, the towns, then the ocean and tiny boats below moved by with incredible speed. But then, at 2,500 miles an hour, things will blur together a little.

Before they seemed to have even peaked out high above the clouds, so that the earth's very curve could be seen below, the oceans slowly rounding off into mist, they were descending, getting clearance to head into a Belgian Air Force base just thirty miles north of Luxembourg. They shot down out of the sky like a stone. It seemed too fast to the passengers and all of them, even Parker, tensed up as the craft hurtled down. But the pilot threw the brakes on at the last second and the stripped-down jet fighter seemed to suddenly just float above the runway for a few seconds before it touched down smooth as a feather.

They were whisked by a Belgium Security chopper to the site of the "event" that was to take place in exactly one hour, a four-lane highway that ran across the border near Saarbrucken. There was an army of paramilitary agents already hidden behind barricades and low hills on each side of the road. It was going to be a regular old-fashioned ambush.

"What the hell do you got?" Parker barked out as he walked up to a group of three men—the leaders of the entire operation.

"Ah, Colonel Parker," said General LaFitte, head of French Special Forces, whom Parker had met before and found to be a decent and tough hombre. "Let me introduce General Boicrreaux of Belgian Security, and Karl Pauls of German Interpol."

138

"Gentlemen." Parker nodded, quickly shaking hands with each. "So what's the fucking story?" He laughed, reaching for a smoke. "I just traveled further than Columbus did to discover America. I hope it ain't bullshit." Parker knew he pushed his tough-American thing to the hilt sometimes. But he didn't care. That was how he was. A no-bullshit man. If it raised eyebrows—maybe it would also help stop the bullshit from drowning him.

"It's not exactly clear what it is, to be brutally honest," LaFitte said with a cough. "But it's a big operation. That's why we called you in. We captured a German terrorist. We could have him on death-sentence charges. He knew it. So he talked. Spilled his guts, in fact. Probably going to be able to pull in a good dozen or so 'bad mothers' as you Americans like to say. There's a group of some Combined International Struggle Forces as they call themselves—of three different underground groups—and they're moving in force tonight, carrying some kind of cargo. Should be here any"—he looked down at his watch—"minute."

Parker took out the mini-geiger counter he had brought with him and switched it on, aiming it toward the highway. Nothing.

"They're coming, they're coming." He suddenly heard voices hissing all around him in the half darkness as agents from five different countries all cocked their guns, pulled back the safeties on their rifles and shotguns and rapid-fire autos, and held their breaths. A convoy of three cars and a big moving truck in close formation came shooting around the curve at a good seventy miles an hour. Then they saw the border-crossing gate a half mile ahead and began slowing down. They had all the proper identity papers, clearances, etc. They knew there should be no problems. And if there were, the ten men who had commandeered the vehicles had the firepower to blast their way out again. There was no stopping this convoy.

But as they slowed, a rush of cars suddenly tore out from service roads on each side of the highway and cut them off, nearly a dozen vehicles forming a line right across the roadway about a hundred yards ahead of them. The convoy screeched to a halt and began wheeling around, vehicles following one another like four lost little ducks, but more cars shot out behind them from other service roads. They were blocked off at both sides within seconds—and the high slopes of the low hills that ran along each side of the highway made it impossible to drive up them. They all knew, those in the convoy. All knew instantly. And didn't hesitate as they ripped out weapons from within jackets and beneath seats and came out firing.

The firefight was fierce and bloody but the terrorists didn't have a chance. Not with two hundred men opening up on them from every side with an absolute fusillade of slugs, whistling gas cannisters, and whatever the hell else they had been able to drag out. And even with those odds, the terrorists managed to get off a few grenades and set up a 50-caliber and spray the hillside. Before they were terminated loudly and bloodily.

When it was all over, ten terrorists lay riddled with bullets, their fingers still twitching at being pulled out of this life and into the next so suddenly. But they had gotten their licks—five security agents lay dead, up to another eight wounded. It wasn't exactly a bloodless victory. Parker had stayed back as the fighting occurred. He wasn't armed for it—and it wasn't his day to die. He had too much to do. But he moved in as soon as the pops of automatic fire stopped, as soon as the last quivering terrorist finger could no longer pull another round. He came out from around a hillside with the geiger out at chest level in front of him, praying that it would pick something up. He rushed around to the truck where two Belgian Federal Officers were already trying to get through the lock with picks.

"Pardon, pardon," Parker said with a quick smile as he somehow got himself between them and the lock and pushed them back with a little move of his hip. He whipped out his .44 and aimed it at the case-hardened padlock that held the steel door in place. Parker fired as the plainclothes, flak-jacketed officers looked on in amazement. This was not quite how they did things around there. But Parker didn't have time to fart around. Not when nukes were involved. The lock exploded apart and flew off in pieces to the roadway.

"Better get back, boys, could be hot," Parker said to them both, but they apparently didn't understand a hell of a lot of English as they just shrugged and gave each other funny looks. "Warned you." Parker grinned as he pulled the door open about a foot, just enough so he could lean in and hold the rad collector unit into the truck. He looked down at the meter. Nothing. It didn't flicker the width of an eyelash.

"Shit," the CIA boss muttered as he flung the door open wide. There was something inside all right—missiles. Heat-seeking surface-to-air Chinese Silkworm II's if Parker's trained eye wasn't mistaken. A great catch. But not what he wanted. He turned and walked away in disgust, folding the geiger back and putting it in his pocket. He headed toward the three Operations Leaders, who were heading toward the truck from their Operations command post where they had supervised the attack.

Though no one else saw it, Parker's trained combat reflexes, still working though a little rusty, made him jerk his head around as he caught just the glint of something streak across his peripheral vision. The muzzle of a 9mm assault rifle, and the bloody bastard who was holding it wasn't dead. Fucked up, maybe— but he was sighting up the three men and looked long enough for this world to pull the trigger.

As the three Operations Leaders watched in horror, thinking for a moment that Colonel Parker had gone completely bonkers and was about to assassinate them, he ripped out his .44, screamed out "Dive!" and aimed just to the side of them into the gully formed at the edge of the roadway. He fired nonstop, emptying his entire seven shots in under three seconds. A single shot glowed orange in the grayness, firing back. Then there was nothing. As Parker let the pistol hang in his hand and started forward, the others rose from the concrete road where they had flung themselves and wiped the dust off their clothes.

"Sorry about that." Parker smiled as they all reached the area where the assassin had been targeting them. It wasn't a pretty sight. Every one of Parker's huge .44 slugs, dum-dum'd and siliconed, had hit something. They all looked shaken, their faces a little white. Even LaFitte's charming demeanor was gone, his mouth set in a hard expression as he wiped sweat from his brow with a monogrammed handkerchief.

"Thank you," he said in a near whisper to Parker, who was reloading the .44 with an insta-load. Then it was back in his holster within seconds. "Of course you'll be given full credit for being part of this operation. It's an historic capture—a dozen functioning missiles, an entire mobile combat cell of the underground. Medals and promotions"—he grinned— "for everyone involved."

"Thanks—but no thanks," Parker said, as he looked around for his underlings, who seemed to be wandering around in a sort of semi-daze at the actual combat that

142

none of them had ever engaged in before. The smashed-in faces of the dead, the blood pouring from the opened chests and stomachs like fountains bubbling were not exactly like the John Wayne movies. Not by a longshot. Two of them had to walk into the shadows and puke.

"I'm of course overjoyed for all of you. It is a great catch. It's just not what I'm looking for. You boys know what I want. The hot stuff. Anything that glows or has a half-life—let me know about that. I'll be back here in a whore's minute. But as far as mentioning me in reports or the media, please—don't. Forget it. Keep the credit for yourselves. It was *your* operation. I'm not even supposed to be over here. Why, if one of them damn Congressional committees caught me flying some souped-up F-18 halfway around the world—and then back again all in time for dinner—I'd probably lose half my fucking pension."

Chapter Fourteen

Harrison spent the next two weeks in a kind of zombie-like state. He hardly knew where he was half the time—and maybe it was just as well considering the torturous training schedule they were putting him through. Up every morning at six for two hours of physical conditioning with the Destroyer—hundreds of sit-ups and push-ups done in series of fifty each. Rope jumping, then weights. Captain Lou could see that Harrison was basically already strong as a tank. The goal was to sharpen that strength, reinforce it, use the strong hips to be able to uproot opponents, the powerful thick arms to be tightened, stretched, and tightened again under his guidance, until they were like steel cables capable of nearly twice the power he had already. Captain Lou and the Destroyer made their pupil work out to the very limit of his endurance, bench-pressing first 350, then 400, then 450. . . . And when he was almost dead from that, his body sweating up a waterfall, he was put on reps—fifty-pound weights in each hand up, down, and sideways so the muscles in his arms were half popping out of his flesh as they were twisted all over the place.

Then it was morning classes—advanced lockpicking

and security-system neutralizing. Then his camera and surveillance instruction—he had graduated already to doing microfilm slides of schematics—how to hide the film itself inside Band-Aids, the caps of bottles. . . . Next a first-aid/survival class tutored him in self-treatments—combating of poisons, treating gun and knife wounds—should, God help him, he need such aid and none was available. There were also one- and two-day classes in specialized subjects—one of which was radiation-detection equipment and its usage. They seemed to go over that in detail, the use of geiger counters and their various cousins and the interpretation of the data.

Then there was Morse code and other communication/cryptographic techniques, and a smattering of language-comprehension tutors who taught him the roots of a number of languages so that he could recognize certain key words almost anywhere in the world. If he could remember what the hell they were. He had never done all that well in school, though he had to admit he had gotten smarter as he'd gotten older. Still, it was rough going. His brain felt like it was coming out of his ears.

But the wrestling—that was something else. By the end of the first week he felt ready for the morgue. But by the end of the second week, Harrison swore he was getting better at it. The Destroyer systematically showed him new things each day, with Captain Lou pacing around the ring, puffing madly on his omnipresent cigar and shouting out one suggestion or another nonstop. They taught him back-breakers, bear hugs, knee-drives, piledrivers. The leg locks, the scissor holds, the trips. They showed Harrison the infinite ways of throwing, pinning, creating pain in a man with moves whose names boggled the mind: the Double Ouch; Gori's Siamese Twin; Stocks, Sitout, and

Forward Neck Crank; Standing Indian Death Lock. Others were straightforward and self-descriptive: Knee in the Back Hand on Chin Lift, Hair Grab and Rib Crush with Knee, Fall Back Downward Arm Crank with an Inward Wrist Twist, and Leg Over on Your Back. Some had names that were just plain nasty: Hair Grab from Behind, Claw Squeeze around Larynx, and one of Harrison's favorites—after it had been performed on him a dozen times with instant control and command of his body—the Behind Nose Rip and Throat Claw. And the Captain wasn't averse to showing him the extra-nasty stuff either—the throat bite, the eye tear, the ear rip, the balls smash. . . . He'd clearly been quite a son of a bitch in the ring.

The Destroyer and Captain Lou tried to teach not just technique, but the living feel of wrestling—the way it really was. How to move, bounce, always be alert for motion—and trechery. And aside from learning how to take falls, rope work was just about the most important thing. They worked on it endlessly, bouncing back and forth from the ropes like billiard balls, learning how to incorporate the three stiff nylon cables that surrounded the ring so that they became part of one's natural ring environment. Captain Lou and the Destroyer had been through a hell of a lot, had spent over thirty years in the ring, had started in the days when men had fought to the death. Captain Lou's scarred face and body and the Destroyer's smashed nose and cauliflower ears testified to the fact that they were the real thing. And that was why Harrison allowed himself to listen to them him, learn from them. Go through what would have broken most men within days, hours.

And he was slowly picking it up. The Destroyer could see it. The dude was getting him one out of every three times now when they grappled. And as Harrison gained confidence and strength he began trying new

146

things, putting his full power into it. He got good at certain types of moves and concentrated on those a little extra—figuring when the shit hit the fan it would be good to have some aces in the hole, along with the Sleeper and the Claw, that he could move to fast. And one day, to his amazement, as he flipped the Destroyer up onto his shoulder ready to swing him down onto the canvas, Harrison suddenly gripped him in both hands and pushed straight up as if he were pressing weights in the gym. The Destroyer was suddenly overhead looking down with some anxiety in his eyes as he was, with Harrison's arms fully extended, almost nine feet off the mat.

"Fllyyy the friendly skies of . . ." Harrison laughed as he turned one full circle in the center of the ring while the crowd that always gathered when the two worked out stood and watched in amazement. "United!" Harrison finished the tune and flung the man forward with all his might. The Destroyer flew halfway across the ring—and would have sailed right out of it had not his steel hands reached down and grabbed hold of the corner rope at the last second. He swung himself right over the top and came down hard on his booted feet on the apron outside of the ring.

"Damn if you ain't starting to turn into a regular asskicker," Captain Lou said, walking over to the ring and leaning in, puffing up a storm. "You're starting to get some of your own moves going, aren't you? That's good, real good. The sign of a champ. You keep at it, keep finding out what feels good to your body shape and strength—along with what we show you, of course." The Destroyer squeezed back under the bottom rope. And Harrison could see for the first time respect—make that a touch of fear—in the man's eyes. Maybe even in Captain Lou's eyes as well.

Suddenly there was a cough from the far side of the

ring and a short but very wide man was standing there with trunks and a sweatshirt on. He was bald, with wide handlebar mustache and a barrel-sized chest.

"Hey, Bulldog," Captain Lou said with a big smile. "Harrison, I want you to meet Bulldog Williams, ex-boxer, ex-bull-breeder, ex-bear-trapper, ex-just about everything. And now he's ended up like me, giving fighting lessons a thousand feet below the dirt."

"That's right, mister," Bulldog said as he climbed in through the ropes. "And now it's *my* turn. Boxing!"

Whatever machismo Harrison was able to resurrect within himself through his wrestling accomplishments quickly evaporated once he started putting on the gloves, tied on by a trainer at the edge of the ring, a thick-Havana-cigar-smoking old cut man with a poked-in face like a squashed cauliflower, no ears, and a nose that had been broken at least a thousand times. He introduced himself simply as "Cut" and told Harrison to "jab, jab, jab," against the fast-footed Bulldog, who proved surprisingly fast considering his bulk and short thick legs. But though Harrison snapped his left hand again and again, the shorter Bulldog was able to easily deflect his punches with what looked like hardly more than light taps.

And once Bulldog got going, once he started sending in his own combinations of lefts and hooks to the chest and stomach, and then quickly up the body to the head, Harrison saw that he was completely outclassed. The guy was able to get off three, four, five punches to his one. Harrison couldn't even imagine how someone could punch that fast. He thought he had been pretty quick in his back-alley bouts. Bulldog would have kicked ass all over the place. But although he peppered the younger man with blows, Williams didn't throw them too hard. Just hard enough to let him know what he could do if he wanted too.

"All right, chief," Harrison said, half laughing as Bulldog pushed him back against the ropes for the third time, unleashed a volley of blurred punches which just slapped in against his chest, and then danced out again. "So I *can't* get through your defenses, and you *can* get through mine. Show me how to change it, okay? I surrender."

"Just wanted you to feel what a good boxer can do. That's the thing about it, see—you can use jabs, speed, the focus of boxing in life itself. A way of countering everything that comes at you—fast and with minimal energy. Then striking back just as quickly. The Japanese use kendo, stick sword fighting, to harness that explosive momentum, that sudden burst of energy. But for Westerners—guys like me and you—boxing's the thing. When I'm through with you, son, you're going to be able to go out there and into a wrestling, or even a pro boxing, ring and whip booty. 'Cause you got it. Your body, weight, innate strength, and speed. You're strong enough to take on the best. Just need to be hammered into shape—and learn a few nasty tricks.

"Now, the first thing is to get relaxed. Most guys throw a punch—their arm's all tensed up, muscles bulging. That looks good on TV when you got grease on the muscles, but in real life—the street, the ring, whatever—it's much better to be loose. So just try to let your punches float out there. Your hands should feel like rocks tied to the end of ropes. Everything relaxed. See what I mean?" Bulldog had Harrison throw out hundreds of punches as loosely and untensed as possible. It was hard to do it, Harrison discovered, and saw that he had been using far too much muscularity in his fighting and not learning the finesse, the actual abilities of fighting. It had worked so far. But now he was going to be facing guys even tougher than the Destroyer back there, and Harrison knew he was going to need every bit of technique he could get.

"Yeah, like that," Bulldog said, as they began circling each other again. Bulldog threw flurries of punches coming from all over the place, but this time Harrison was able to fend them off more easily. He saw what Bulldog meant. The lighter he moved his arms the faster they went. It made sense. He didn't have to bang the damned punches out like he was using a sledge-hammer, just moving the body and throwing them quick, almost slapping them out, would do fine. And within half an hour he felt a lightness he had never experienced before, as he boxed with less tension in his whole upper body and arms. Once in a while he even got in a few quick jabs at Bulldog, who had to bob and weave and duck fast to avoid his little love taps.

"See, dance, weave, jab, dance in and out, hook, then out, weave, head up and down, everything always moving, never make yourself a target. Never let the other man know where you're about to go next." Bulldog never stopped moving. Every part of him was in full motion.

Suddenly Bulldog really got going, testing Harrison with a volley of punches, this time a little harder. Harrison had to block them or else. But some got through, to the chest and stomach, and they hurt. Bulldog began snorting at the mouth as he came in closer, pounding at Harrison. Then the pupil saw where the teacher had gotten his nickname, for as he closed in he began growling and then barking, making wild dog-like noises as he attacked. Harrison laughed, and suddenly Bulldog was on him in the corner and let loose with what must have been two dozen hooks from each side right up and down Harrison's body. They were only at about half-strength but the recipient felt them and finally collapsed half laughing, half punched out, and totally out of air. Cut rang the bell and the slightly crazed Bulldog, still barking away, headed back toward his corner, where he stood, his eyes blazing with the ring fury of the once-and-still-proud warrior.

"You okay?" Cut asked, concerned as he leaned through the ropes and poked around Harrison's lip and eyes. But he didn't see any blood, other than a trickle from the man's nose.

"Yeah, I'm all right, man," Harrison said spitting into a bucket that Cut held out. "I just didn't know I was going into gladiator training, Roman style." And with Bulldog still barking away and stamping his feet on the ring mat in a boxing frenzy—and the Destroyer standing outside the ring, his immense muscular arms folded across his massive chest, as if he wouldn't mind a little bit more of Harrison himself, and Captain Lou grinning—the subject of all their attentions wondered if he was even going to get through school alive.

Chapter Fifteen

On the Saturday afternoon of Harrison's third week, as he and the Destroyer were just completing a ropes workout, with Captain Lou screaming from the sidelines that he was "moving like a snail on drugs," several of the custodial workers walked over in their white coveralls.

"Ring's down for the night, boys," one of them said with a smile, not saying the words too loud as he was addressing two men who could tear him apart with one finger. "Got to start disassembling it for tonight. Have it together tomorrow—first thing, I promise. Before noon." With that, the custodian directed his assistants to the four sides of the ring, where they began unscrewing the supports.

"What the hell's going on?" Harrison asked Cut, who stood waiting at the outside of the ring to towel him off and check for any cuts or breaks.

"Don't you know?" Cut laughed, as he found a raw spot all along Harrison's right shoulder blade where he had taken a hard fall. It was bruised and purplish already. Cut took out a strong-smelling salve and smeared it onto the man's back. "Every year they have it—at least for the three years I bin working for D2. It's the Annual Terrorists' Ball."

"Who—what?" Harrison growled as he winced in pain from the rough way Cut was putting the ointment on. He could see other custodial people around the large floor taking down the moveable walls so that the entire level could be opened up into a huge loft space. Banners and balloons were already going up along the walls and some sort of platform was being built in the center of the space.

"The Terrorists' Ball," Cut repeated as he finished his repair work and wiped his charge off with a towel, then stood back. "It's this crazy party they have here. Everybody comes in costume. They imitate some famous terrorist or criminal—alive or dead. It's a lot of laughs. Everyone gets drunk, they got prizes for best costume, the worst costume. . . . It's a chance for the whole crew to let off steam. You see what it's like down here. It's a pressure cooker, and not just for you, pal. So Colonel Parker allows 'em to cut loose, go a little crazy for one night."

"So go make yourself a costume," Captain Lou grunted. "You're through for the day here. Got yourself a whole night of R and R. But don't get too drunk, now. You have to be back in the ring first thing tomorrow."

"Yeah, right," Harrison said with a grimace as the salve began really working its way into his skin. Now that he had actually stopped wrestling he couldn't imagine taking another fall. He took a quick shower in the locker-room and changed into the second camouflage jumpsuit that had seemed to magically appear in his auto-open drawer one day. He was too tired to attend the festivities. But just the chance of a little rest sounded wonderful. Harrison headed toward the mess hall and saw that it was almost empty—people were apparently getting their outfits together for the evening. He filled himself with every damn thing he wanted, Captain Lou not being around to keep an eye on his diet. Roast beef, meat loaf, three helpings of homemade mashed potatoes with mushroom gravy, eight biscuits, real butter—none of the laboratory-tasting "low cholesterol margarine" that half the slobs in the place swore by—a malted milk, and two orange juices. By the time he was finished, he was in a state of bliss—just bites from total enlightenment. And he knew he had just gained five pounds in a single sitting.

Burping like a machine gun, Harrison headed back to his little cubicle in the wall and dragged himself up onto the bed. He knew his way around the place enough by now to not keep smashing into everything. Given enough time, it was said, a monkey could write all of Shakespeare. The moment his head touched the pillow he was in dreamland. He slept deeply for about three hours and then woke with a start as he heard something coming from the hall. Singing. In a place like this. But that's what it was. Old rock and roll songs too. Suddenly Harrison felt more at home here than he had anytime since he'd been staying in the overlit cavern of a world.

And oddly, he wasn't tired. He had been doing nothing but training for twenty-one days without stop. He deserved a night out. So what if he didn't get along with most of the bastards here. He could still pour down a few and watch them all make fools of themselves. But, he'd have to wear something. A costume, a costume. This had always been a problem going back to his very first Halloween. What kind of costume to wear or buy that 1) wasn't completely idiotic and stupid so that everyone else laughed, or 2) wasn't exactly what everyone else was wearing. Those were the only rules he knew about. "The sheet," he mumbled to himself, looking down and fingering the

154

synthetic zero-percent-cotton whitish sheet beneath him. No ghosts—that was copping out, chickenshit. Anyway, what famous ghost could he think of? Only Casper, and as much as you stretched it, Casper the Friendly Ghost was no terrorist or murderer. He tore through his mind searching for possibilities.

Suddenly he had it. The movie *The Terminator,* with Arnold Schwarzenegger. The Cyborg assassin who had come back from the future to kill everyone in sight. Harrison's black leather jacket was similar to what the psycho killer had been wearing in the film. Yeah, and his boots too. He just wouldn't wear his shirt, go bare-chested, and put a little oil on. He got out of bed and put the things on, and then some ink from a pen around his face so it looked smeared and dirty. But it was still missing something. When the Terminator had begun to get shot up a little during the course of the movie, its eye had popped out and a red light beneath had been revealed in all its mechanical horror. He went to the far end of the room and managed to pry out one of two small light bulbs that lit up a row of shelves. He took the red bulb and, using scotch tape from a neat row of writing supplies inside the sliding wall desk unit, actually got it taped in place over his right eye. He looked in the mirror. Not bad, not bad at all. Even if it wasn't exactly the Terminator, it sure as hell looked disgusting.

Harrison left his room and headed over to one of the firing ranges, where he convinced one of the instructors to let him borrow a laser sight pistol—a fake, of course; it was for tactical field games where they could all shoot one another and not get hurt. Like the Terminator's gun—this one sent out a red beam of light which formed a dot on the target just before one fired, giving almost perfect accuracy. Harrison took one of the mini-elevators to the Gymnasium level, which had now

155

been completely stripped of all its exercise and training equipment and was festooned like the senior hop.

The joint was sure as hell jumping, people everywhere laughing, with drinks in their hands, or dancing to the music of a slightly ragged band that was manned by CIA operatives. And every person in the place was in costume. There were Arab-headdressed Palestinians with Kalashnikovs, mad-looking black-hatted anarchists with round black bombs with big fuses poking up from them. There were assassins with long range-cardboard rifles. The Rosenbergs, the controversial spy couple, were there, with ropes around their necks. There were pirates and warlords, Al Capones with double-breasted suits and toothpicks in their mouths, Maos with simple gray suits and little red books in their hands. Che Guevara, the symbol of the worldwide revolution, had bandoliers of bullets strung across his chest. Some of the costumes were simple plastic masks brought from novelty stores. The women wore everything from Marie Antoinette gowns—a few of them quite elaborate and stunning, with the women holding fake heads in little baskets at their sides—to the clothing of gun molls of the thirties. There were black pajama'd women, veiled Arab women with fake dynamite inside their loaves of bread, women in Nazi SS gear.

He headed across the floor searching for the booze, and at last saw a table where men in white tuxes were pouring out drinks with wild abandon. As he headed across the floor Harrison playfully aimed his red-dot laser sight at the backs of women's low-cut dresses, or into men's noses. Some of them didn't notice—there was nothing to feel—but a few did and scowled his way as the red light zipped around. He ordered a double scotch and a double brandy, and held one in each hand slugging alternately from them. Now that was what he

156

needed. It tasted wonderful. He hadn't wet his whiskers in nearly a month. And he suddenly realized he hadn't even really noticed it, hadn't had time. Well, maybe it was all to the good. He had been quaffing down a lot of the brew. It was more enjoyable when it was once in a while. And he realized he liked it that way.

"Hey, big butt," a voice shouted in his ear and Harrison knew who it was before he turned. But he wasn't quite prepared for the creature that stood before him. It was Captain Lou in a ridiculous body-length pumpkin costume. He had a huge round orange piece of material that must have been draped over a wire frame as it formed a globular pumpkin shape that curved out all around him. His legs and arms poked out and they too were covered in orange. His head was inserted into a real pumpkin about eighteen inches in diameter so just his nose, eyes, and mouth were visible in the carved-out spaces within it, sort of a vegetable Roman legionnaire's helmet.

"What the hell are you?" Harrison asked, his jaw hanging open.

"The Great Pumpkin," Captain Lou mumbled from within. "My great-great-great-and-a-few-more-greats-grandfather Basquince Albano invented the art of pumpkin cutting many centuries ago. I'm carrying on the family tradition. Looks pretty good, eh?" He did a little pirouette in front of Harrison, who though he might lose his mouthful of liquor, but managed to gulp it burningly down. "The pumpkin is hand-carved, the costume material is unborn virgin wool with laminated nylon stitching, hand-sewn, hand-stitched, hand-made."

"Looks—amazing," Harrison commented. "But this is a Terrorists' Ball. What's so terrible about pump-kins?"

"I think people will feel pretty terrible when they see

157

me," the Captain barked back. He took a slug of beer from a can through the pumpkin mouth and headed back off into the crowd looking for people's senses to assault.

Harrison shook his head back and forth a dozen times. Just when he thought he'd seen everything . . . He drank and watched the CIAers dance and cavort and lose their usual straight-faced, cooled-out demeanors. But the sheer pressure of having to push so much down for the whole year erupted out in shrieks and little screams and lots of boisterous laughter. Harrison could see why Parker let them have their day of madness. There was a hell of a lot of steam to let off. When he'd finished his drinks and was gnawing away on a second set of doubles, he suddenly felt the music of the band start hitting him. It was like he just suddenly wanted to get up and dance. He stood up from the bar seat, holding the two drinks in one hand and the laser red gun in the other, and joined the action as hundreds of people danced and jumped up and down to the song "I'd Like to Meet the Man Who Put the Bomb in Castro's Beard," a raunchy tune against a hot funk bass-beat, all distorted and piped through the level's PA system so it blasted out rocking throbs of noise that made the whole place shake.

Within seconds Harrison had let himself go and was spinning around in the sea of people, laughing loudly. Like a whirling dervish, he just sort of lost himself in the pure sensation of being in the rhythm of the drums, jumping around mindlessly with the others. Suddenly a voice pulled him out of his mystical ecstasies.

"Rudolf the Red-Eyed Reindeer, I see," the voice yelled, and Harrison focused his eye—the good one— the other one taped over with the light bulb poking from it. The stunning woman before him looked like . . . Patty Hearst, that's who it was. With that same

158

little cap and the small submachine gun around her shoulder, and a peacoat like the real Patty had worn. But though the outfit was good, Harrison knew instantly who it was. The face and the figure, the flowing mane of red hair were impossible to disguise.

"Lisa." He grinned in a lecherous dumb way, but not really caring as he held out his hand offering her one of the drinks. To his surprise she took it in a flash and chugged the whole thing down with one big sweep back of her head.

"And you are . . . the Terminator," she said with a flourish, sweeping her hand back so that she threw half the drink he had just given her on the nearby dance crowd. She was already half looped. But then so was he and everyone else in the place, for that matter. They danced together to the hot beat of the music, lost in the sweating crowd. The noise level grew louder and the whole place seemed to shake as more and more people joined the dancing in the middle of the floor. Then suddenly she moved in close against him on one of the slower numbers, and before he knew it his arms were around her and her arms were around his wide and muscled back. Then her lips were nesting in his neck. And before he even really knew what was happening, their lips met and her tongue was wild inside his mouth.

"I want you," she said suddenly, urgently. "Tonight, now. While we're all mad—and can do what we want."

"Sounds good to me." Harrison grinned happily, trying to pull himself a little bit out of the alcohol daze he was swimming around in. "Let's go." He took her hand and headed out through the crowd, making way with his big frame. Then they were moving through the halls, all the lights bright and everything blurring together as they hurried with the frenetic urgency of animal desire toward his room. He slammed his hand against the ID panel and the door whooshed open. He pulled her inside, forgetting for a second how tight it was in the room—her back slammed around and right into the side of the bed.

"Oh, shit, I'm sorry, sorry," Harrison said, his face growing pale, afraid he might have broken some ribs since she had made a loud sound when she hit.

"No, no, s'quite awright." She smiled back. Drunkenness had protected her by making her body so limber and giving it could take a hell of a lot more than when sober. "S'nice place ya got here," she lied. And they both laughed simultaneously. But she didn't care about the furnishings.

"Here, I'll get up first. A girl has to ready herself," she said coyly as she raised herself up onto his disheveled bed, which he suddenly wished he had at least made. He heard rustlings from above and then her Patty Hearst clothes came flying down. He took off his duds as well, standing there stark naked in the near-darkness waiting for her call.

Suddenly she made a raw throaty sound and he leapt up there. A little too hard—for he came down on top of her with a whack and the air pushed out of her hard. He pulled himself up above her, letting her catch her breath, but there was hardly any room at all as his shoulders and head were bumping into the ceiling just two feet above him. Of course, he had to hit the TV switch accidentally, and the whole TV screen lit up just above him, suffusing his whole body and the bed with bright colors which flickered and changed from red to blue to yellow as the scenes on the screen behind them, from a travelogue, unraveled for the late-night viewers.

Suddenly she just sort of rolled him over and straddled on top of him, without any preliminaries. She grabbed hold of his maleness and thrust it into herself beneath him. He let out his own sounds as the sensation of purest ecstasy coursed through his veins.

160

Then he was moving fast with her—and then too fast. For in the throes of their passions, the pair tumbled right out of the narrow bed and down the two-feet-wide space between the aluminum-coated bed and the magna-steel wall. Fortunately for Lisa, Harrison hit the carpeted floor first. With all he had been going through in the ring, it wasn't even noticeable. Then she came down too, still attached to him by the act of love, and slammed down hard on top of him just as she had been in the bed.

She waited there a moment, sort of leaning back and forth, trying to get her bearings. Then she laughed out lustily as she realized the situation they were in.

"I'll try to get up," he croaked up from the floor, where he was just starting to get comfortable. At least the TV wasn't blasting into the back of his skull, though it was still shooting down its bright images from about seven feet above.

"Don't bother, Terminator." She laughed as she began pumping up and down on him, grinding with a fiery madness. "I'll take my licks down here." With that she shut up and began moving fast like she was atop a bucking bronco in a rodeo of the flesh.

Chapter Sixteen

The German woman, Fraulein Hauser, was the first to lose a tooth. And she didn't like it at all.

"What the hell is this?" she asked Professor Markus at their morning self-criticism session in which they "confessed" to any mistakes they had made the day before in work or relations with one another and vowed to work harder for the cause, for the glorious future. She threw the tooth down on the round table where they ate dinner. It was covered with blood, the whole bloody root and stump were still attached like a freshly picked monstrosity from a garden.

"And some of the others are loose," she said, glaring at him.

"I told you from the start there were dangers involved in all this," the professor answered coolly, finishing his toast and taking a sip of orange juice. He had slept a little later than usual on his cot, having stayed up half the night assembling wiring and fuses. There was so much to do.

"Dangers—yeah, but this is too fast. This isn't cancer twenty, thirty years down the road. I'm not ready to go today!"

"Or this," one of the Weathermen said, a pale-faced

youth hardly out of his teens, with thick glasses. He held a clump of hair in his hand. A large clump. "This morning I brushed a few times—and got all this. I didn't brush again." The rest of the crew looked around the table at one another. Some appeared concerned, others didn't seem to care. Being a revolutionary terrorist didn't make you the most health-conscious of people. Still, the professor knew he had to nip this whole thing in the bud.

"I told you, you all had choices in the matter. You may use the radiation-shielding equipment or not, as you desire. It will not affect your standing in this revolutionary cell. We always believe in democratic rule—that is what separates us from the Fascists." Professor Markus would let them believe they were democratic. They thought they were. In fact he had them all in the palm of his hands. It was easy to manipulate the masses. Especially fanatical minds, so young, so impressionable, especially when he offered them the cool rational father figure they had all been seeking so long. For the professor was not just a revolutionary—but a Freudian as well. And it gave him the ability to see far deeper into men's souls than most men are able.

"All the great fighters of the working class, all the great revolutionaries of history were willing to give their all. Their *all!* That means their flesh, their bodies, their very cells consumed in flame, or hung, or electrocuted—or worse. We are just lucky to have the opportunity to join those illustrious ranks. It is an honor to do so. Feel yourselves proud to be part of such a mission—the Mission of Fire. The fire of the workers which will proclaim their power throughout the world. And we shall go up with it. Shall join with the pure and beautiful energies of economics.

"The fire of the workers," he said as he finished his

163

last bite of toast and wiped his mouth with a paper napkin.

"The fire of the working class," most of those seated at the table answered back, their fists raised high. Ah, revolutionary zeal—it was such a simple furnace to tap, the professor thought, amused, praying to his atheistic god again with thanks.

"Now to work. We've done well. Incredibly well," he said, looking at them proudly. "The device is nearly ninety-percent complete. And all tests so far indicate that we're completely on target. Keep it up, all of you." He spoke softly, as he had learned to do in the classroom, making them quiet and lean forward to catch his words. "And if a few swollen bumps appear, or a cold that won't go away—a few hairs on the brush in the morning—these are small enough things to sacrifice for the cause. Trotsky gave his life."

From the other side of the table Professor Markus heard a spitting sound and then a sharp intake of breath.

"Anuther vun of my vucking teeth," the fraulein said with a trickle of blood coming out of her mouth. "You old bastard. You're just suckering us on. We're all dying of radiation poisoning." She looked strained, like she was going to crack. The professor decided to give her some private counseling.

"Come now," he said with a cheerful smile. "Now is hardly the time to falter—when we are so close to success. Just hours away. Now get to work, all of you." He rose and walked around the table patting them on the back, rubbing his hands through their hair. Markus knew the young, the radical, the way lion-tamers know their animals.

"Come with me, fraulein," Markus said, walking toward one of the exit doors. "I have some ointment, some pills that will help that. Your sister too—if she

164

wants some." The other German woman nodded affirmatively. She looked as tense and drawn as her sister. The two had clearly been talking about getting out of the place. The rest of the bomb team dragged themselves tiredly off to the worktable. They were all feeling dragged out these days. Even countless cups of coffee kept flowing from an automatic forty-cup pot didn't seem to help as much as it used to. Nor the sugary pies they had all been eating for the last month.

Professor Markus nodded to the guard on the outside of the door—one of his personal security people who was bound by his oath to protect the professor. He led them down the hall to one of two locked steel doors. Neither of them had ever been in that room before, not even knowing of its existence. They looked at one another nervously but followed the aging man inside. He turned on a single trembling light bulb hanging from a wire in the ceiling and shut the door behind them.

"Yes," he went on, continuing where he had stopped a minute before. "In fact there's been a lot of research done on radiation in the last few years. What all the medical authorities recommend is potassium iodide shots mixed with megadoses of Vitamin B to fight white blood cell loss. Just happen to have that very thing." He smiled at them reassuringly as he went to a locked cabinet and extracted a vial and two hypodermic needles. Just the fact that he was responding to their fears seemed to calm them both down a little. And they let their shoulders relax, their hands draw unconsciously away from the pistols sitting inside their designer jeans.

"Here we go, mein frauleins," the professor said with a smile. He walked back across the floor squirting little streams of the liquid in the hypos into the air. "Now roll up your sleeves—and we'll have you feeling better in no time." They rolled up their black sweatshirts with karate symbols on the front, for both women were tough as nails in Goju Karate and street-fighting. They had been around. The professor leaned forward, slamming both needles into their upper arms simultaneously so they both winced together.

"There, isn't that better already?" Markus smiled as he stood back. "You're going to start feeling dizzy right around now. Because sodium cyanide is amazingly fast-acting, isn't it?" And they saw even as he spoke that the chemical was in fact terribly fast. Already they found their lungs constricting, their hearts feeling as if they were bursting and about to erupt out in blood. "Now, you'll start to gag," the professor said with a little chuckle, as he put the hypos back into the chest and closed it all back up again.

"And now you'll be flopping down onto the floor like suffocating fishes out of water, your faces turning all blue and purple. And just about now—" he paused dramatically as was his classroom style—"you'll be dead. Yes, twelve seconds should be completely . . ." He walked over and looked down. They were dead, all right. The contorted blue-faced corpses looked like something out of the devil's dreams, their tongues black and extended from their mouths like snakes trying to jump out, their eyes bloody sockets out of which the egg-like optical systems had erupted in a spasm of slime.

"You caused trouble," the professor scolded them both, wagging his finger. "I warned you, didn't I? You can't say the professor didn't warn you. But I just couldn't allow the others to get panicked. We're too close. You are but individuals, single separate beings. And individuals must always be sacrificed for the cause of the greater good. History decides all. And now—you are history."

Chapter Seventeen

As Harrison started to spread the ropes of the ring apart and step up in for his daily workout with the Destroyer—he couldn't tell if it was his fiftieth or his thousandth lesson—Colonel Parker suddenly appeared at his side, smoking up a storm so that a trail of grayish blue wafted its way back to the elevator doors about eighty feet behind.

"How's it going, sucker?" Parker asked with a lopsided grin. "Been a month. Can you believe it? A fucking month already?" The CIA chief puffed hard and pulled a few more graying hairs from his already well-plucked scalp as he realized that it had been a month and he wasn't one step closer to the atomic terrorists.

"I can believe it." Harrison laughed as he jumped back down from the apron of the ring. "My body sure believes it. It's these two butt-kicking son-of-a-bitches you hired for my private tutors." The Destroyer laughed, his mouth a frightening black hole though his expression was warm toward his student.

"Don't let him fool you, Parker," Captain Lou said as he walked over to Parker, blowing smoke from his own stinker into the colonel's face. Between them they were putting up a good smokescreen. "This guy is as good as they come. Destroyer's been doing most of the ring workouts with him—and he's been the one running this last week. I swear we've trained our boy here into a regular bodysmasher. Fact that's what we've taken to calling him—Bodysmasher. Smash for short. I tell you, when he opens up, you wouldn't want to be in there with him."

"Well, a punch is worth a thousand words. Let me see what you can do, pardner," Parker shouted up to Harrison, who was inside the ring. "One for the Gipper and all that shit." The CIA chief sat back in a folding seat, cigarette dangling from his lips like a flaming toothpick, and a worried look on his face. A lot could depend on how well Harrison had gotten it all together. How well Captain Lou and the Destroyer had done their work. But the CIA chief knew these two were the best there were in the field. If they hadn't been able to do it—no one could have.

Harrison managed a grim grin. He thought he knew how good he'd become. He'd let it all hang out today, or see if he could.

"Do it, baby, do it to him," Captain Lou screamed as he began pacing the outside of the ring in his usual manic style, banging hard on the apron with the heel of his hand so it sounded like a drum beating over and over. Only Harrison wasn't quite sure who the hell he was rooting for. The two men came to the center of the ring and put their hands pressed out against one another so their fingers laced together. Destroyer tried to use the pure strength of his big hands to force Harrison down. It seemed to work for a few seconds, but then the younger man twisted his fingers forward and got the leverage. His muscles strained like they were going to pop out of his arms—and Parker could see that Harrison had put on a hell of a lot of mass in his upper arms and chest in just four weeks. He'd have to hit the weight room himself if he was going to get results like that. He took a deep drag on the cigarette, feeling oily gray smoke clog his lungs in a most satisfying way.

Suddenly Harrison squeezed hard and put all his weight forward, and the Destroyer—for the first time in his entire wrestling career—was forced down to his knee, from the Closed Full Hand Grip Submission hold. Falling to one knee, the Destroyer mouthed out, "Give! Give!" Harrison let go of the bent-back hands and jumped back slapping his palms together. He was enjoying this already.

"That's my fucking boy," Captain Lou screamed proudly across the ring to Parker. He had a lot on the line too, his whole rep as a trainer and manager. Even he was a little surprised by the intensity which Harrison was putting out.

The Destroyer came lunging at him with a straight arm, but Harrison caught it coming and spun around, swinging the big man right across the ring, where he slammed into the ropes and ricocheted back again like an elephant shot from a cannon. On the way back Harrison gave him a Clothesline—an outstretched arm like a roadblock right in front of him—which slammed into the huge wrestler's upper chest with a resounding boom. The Destroyer went flying backwards as Harrison jumped around the ring, his juices flowing now. He remembered how it had felt. The old days, the wrestling matches he had competed in, with everyone screaming and the girls' eyes wide with fear and desire. The rush of adrenaline felt good, like fine wine surging through his veins.

"You're doing it, baby," Captain Lou screamed out, his face getting red now as he pounded the sides of the ring even harder. "Speed, speed, keep using your speed.

169

That big ugly old son-of-a-bitch could kill King Kong if he could catch him. Don't give him no room, baby, no room."

The Destroyer circled a little more slowly, now trying to find his opening. He had trained his pupil well when it came to trying to find a vulnerable spot. Harrison circled, moved on his toes, keeping the Destroyer just off balance, just out of range. Suddenly the big man made a wild charge forward, feinting to the right and then instantly jumping back to the left. He caught Harrison's right ankle and pulled hard at the same time that he slammed a palm into the younger man's hip. Harrison fell down hard, slamming into the mat with a loud thwack so that the whole ring shook for a second and Parker, eight feet away, eye level with the slamming wrestlers, winced and had to look away for a moment. He took a deep lung-filling drag before he could look back again.

But by the time the CIA boss's eyes focused on the two, Harrison was already free and had taken his ring teacher into a Boston Crab, the Destroyer lying flat on his face and chest while his legs were being pulled up from between Harrison's legs, where he held them in his arms twisting the squirming Destroyer into a backwards V.

"I submit, submit!" Destroyer screamed out, slapping his hand hard against the dirty mat. Harrison released his instructor and danced back to his corner, throwing out quick jabs to the air. The Destroyer rose, and this time he was pissed off. He wanted Harrison to look good for Parker and the Captain but he didn't want to come out of this looking like a complete asshole himself. He rose and slapped both of his hands against his thighs, letting out a little roar. Harrison saw that he had gotten the big dude slightly riled up. The Destroyer suddenly charged in like a maniac on speed

170

and grabbed Harrison right around the chest before he could make a move to escape. The big man linked his hands behind Harrison's back and began squeezing. Bear hug. Harrison could feel his strength draining as his breath was squeezed out. His whole face grew red, but squirm as he might, in the man's steel grip he just couldn't budge.

"Submit! Submit!" The Destroyer demanded, spraying spittle in his face.

"No way," Harrison croaked like an apoplectic frog. "Fuck you, pal." At the word "pal" he let out a spray of spit right into the Destroyer's eyes. It was cheap, it was tacky, it was hardly worthy of Harrison's great talents. It was one of Captain Lou's dirty tricks—but it sure as hell worked. For just an instant the Destroyer was startled and, forgetting what was happening, started to release one arm to wipe his face. The moment Harrison felt the slackening, he slammed an elbow into the wrestler's rib cage, which drove the Destroyer back about five feet. With a snarl he came forward again, and was upon the still slightly groggy Harrison before he could get his act together. The Destroyer swooped down like a big steam shovel and caught Harrison on the inside of his leg, gripping his upper arm with the other hand.

Suddenly Harrison found himself lifted a good eight or nine feet in the air as the Destroyer turned with a happy smile emitting from the half-toothed mouth. Again Parker winced from his seat as the wrestler pulled back and threw with all his strength.

"Don't squash him," Captain Lou screamed out, biting down hard on his cigar so it split in two and the front end of it fell down to the floor. Harrison was suddenly flying about six feet up right over the top of the ropes. But he hadn't been an attentive student of the big man who had just thrown him for nothing. Even as

171

he flew by he grabbed hold of the top rope with one hand. The trajectory swung him over and down, but even as his feet start coming down on the outside, he came on down the bottom rope.

The thick nylon triple wound rope bent down nearly two feet and the whole ring seemed to bend that way an inch or two. Then the rope snapped up again and, like a bow launching a human arrow, Harrison was shot right back in the direction he had just come from. He traveled a good twenty feet through the air as Parker, Captain Lou and the Destroyer looked on in complete amazement. Then, before the Destroyer had a chance to react, Harrison was coming down on his head. He landed hard right on the wrestler's shoulders and slammed both his thighs against the Destroyer's head at the same time.

"This is my Head-Breaker." Harrison laughed, looking down at Parker, who stared up, the cigarette dangling from his lower lip. Harrison slammed his legs again, but not that hard. He knew he could exert ten times as much power if he wanted to. But the Destroyer was a friend. Harrison fell backwards, pulling the Destroyer with him, and then rolled away as the big man fell on his back. The hulking wrestler got up and the two faced each other from opposite sides of the ring, letting little smiles move around their faces. This was it—whoever won this one was the stronger. And that would decide that. They didn't say a word but just charged forward with everything they had. Both Colonel Parker and Captain Lou looked on in tight-lipped concentration.

The two banged hard into each other like sumo wrestlers, and each reached down and grabbed the other man's leg trying to uproot him. They strained and puffed and cursed. Then a shout and sudden burst of energy from Harrison, who was in overdrive, lifted the

Destroyer right off the mat. The moment he felt the feet come free, Harrison continued the upward movement of the wrestler and pressed him right up over his head.

"Been eating your fucking Wheaties," Parker yelled up with a laugh from the seat, which made the cigarette in his mouth send out sparks and ash shooting everywhere.

"Damned right—intravenously," Harrison yelled back. "And this is—my coup de grace." He groaned as he struggled under the weight. "My finito bandito." With that he spat out a stream of curses and threw both of his arms out at the same instant that he pressed up with both legs as if preparing to jump. The combined force of all of his energies focused with all his weight behind it sent the Destroyer into a rising orbit up and over the ring. He flew a good ten feet across the center of the mat—and then right over the ropes. The flight pattern was too high for him to grab hold, and his hand missed. The Destroyer slammed down about ten feet outside the ring onto the wooden floor, which, luckily for him, had exercise mats scattered all over. Still, he let out with a strange sound as he hit the floor and lay there groaning.

"All right, all mother-chucking right," Parker said, rising and clapping his hands together for a good ten seconds. "I'll join your fan club." He laughed as Harrison came to the edge of the ring, grabbed hold of the top rope, and with a single fluid catlike motion jumped right up and over the rope and down onto the floor next to the CIA chief and Captain Lou.

"By the way, Colonel Parker, that was my special Champion Diet, not Wheaties, that gave our boy his power in there. You should really let me take over the whole commissary," Captain Lou said with a wry look in his eyes.

"There are T-shirts in the lobby." Harrison laughed.

"Yeah, I think I've taken pretty good to this wrestling stuff. But then I've had two of the best working with me every inch of the bloody way." He grinned. The Destroyer walked over, a little groggy from the fall.

"Some son-of-a-bitch, heh?" the Destroyer said, not without a little pride as he himself realized for the first time just what kind of fighting machine he had helped to put together. Not that Harrison had it all together. Not by a long shot. There would be guys out there bigger, tougher than even the Destroyer. But he had a fighting chance now. And that was all anyone could hope for. Now it was up to him.

"You taught him well," Parker said. "Very well. There'll be bonuses, big ones—as I promised." The CIAer looked over at Harrison.

"You've gotten through the wrestling part of it, pal," he said, resting his hand on the sweat-coated man's shoulder. "But that's just the start. You've still got to pass the Graduation Exams." Parker seemed a little apologetic." I tried to clear you through on this. But I've got my bosses too." He shrugged, not liking to have to make the admission. "Even with your combat experience—they said everyone takes the same final testing. And I guess maybe they're right. Every D2 Field Operative should have to go through the same thing. There can't be any favorites. Even though I sure as hell know what you're capable of."

"I'm ready," Harrison said, folding his arms across his rising and falling chest. After his bout he was ready for any damned thing.

"Good luck, pal, You'll need it. *Dingh tien,*" he added softly, the secret phrase that the two men had groaned out to one another between the bars of their bamboo cells when they had spent a little vacation with the VC a few years back. The words basically meant, "Hang in there, asshole." And it had meant a lot. Each

174

man knew he would never have gotten through it all without the presence of the other. Without the words, hissed and defiant even when they had been hardly more than red carcasses about ready for the fish of the Mekong River.

"*Dingh tien,*" Harrison replied just as softly, his eyes growing dark for a moment as a universe of pain was recalled in his mind's eye. "*Dingh tien.*"

Parker's beeper was ringing and he was off again in his usual Mad Hatter style, lighting up a cigarette in full flight as Captain Lou trailed after him, the two of them talking a mile a minute about some damn thing or other. Harrison started toward the lockers, a lot of mixed feelings coursing through his veins, when the Destroyer stood in front of him, blocking his path.

"Hey, no hard feelings," Harrison said with a smile, putting his hand out. The Destroyer took it and clasped it firmly in his own.

"You're a good man. Very good. I'm not ashamed to lose to you. I had my day—and now you. . . Who knows, Harrison, maybe someday I read about you in the papers, see you on TV. Just remember an ugly dumb bastard who taught you most of what you know. You could be up there, mister, at the top. I know it. I've seen them come and go."

"Well, I sure appreciate those words." Harrison smiled back, letting his hand rest on the big man's shoulder. The Destroyer hesitated for a moment, seemed to think about something, and then spoke up.

"Dere was once giants who roamed de earth, Harrison. Men whose powers was far beyond what fighters today can do. It was a different time, a different world. Men with the power to do incredible damage— or great good. The Werrieux is what my great-grandfather used to call them. The Bodysmashers. You'll never read about them in books. They're forgotten. People don't believe that stuff no more anyway. Men whose punches could kill, who could take on a dozen men, could do tings men today . . . can't even imagine." He hesitated again, looking up at the rock ceiling as if not sure he should be saying all this, as if he was perhaps revealing too much—and thus was checking to see if any of his distant ancestors were scowling in ghostly clouds. He saw none.

"I think you might be one of those Werrieux. I'm not sure. But—you must be careful. Get strong, very strong. And tough as nails. Dere are others out there and not all of them are . . . good. If they find out about you—they'll comes after you—and try to kill you."

"I hear you," Harrison said, standing next to the Destroyer, who was staring into his eyes from only about a foot away with a burning intensity. "Although I must confess I don't like what I'm hearing." Whatever the man was trying to communicate to his pupil—he sure as hell believed in deeply enough. Harrison could see that. It gave him a strange chill that swept along his spine several times before vanishing into the nether regions of his soul.

"There's—one more thing," The Destroyer said firmly, as if making another decision. "One more technique I must show you. I had decided not to—but now—I see that I must. For you is my equal. If you ever do go up against one of the dark ones—you'll need every fucking ace you can grab hold of." He led Harrison back to the center of the ring, and slowly and carefully demonstrated the secret technique, the technique his father had taught to him that he had shown no other men in his life. And it had to be shown slowly—or the recipient of the technique could easily wind up in a pine box.

Destroyer grabbed Harrison's arms from behind—pulling them both back together. When he had

Harrison in complete control so that the man was up on his toes starting to grimace from the pain, the Destroyer jumped up in the air, slamming both feet deep into the center of Harrison's back. Harrison's face grew white as they fell backwards right out of the air—for he knew he would be a dead man when they hit. But at the last second the Destroyer bent his legs in and to the side so that Harrison slammed onto the man's side as the teacher himself slammed down onto the center of the mat.

"The Double Kick Death Drop," the Destroyer said softly as he rose up to one knee.

"I can see why it's called that," Harrison whispered, rising slowly as he realized how easily the man could have taken him out if he'd just driven his knees into the taut backbone. Sent him up to Pluto and beyond.

"Now you try it," the Destroyer said. The sheer fact that the bastard trusted Harrison enough to let him try the move made the pupil feel unworthy. And not a little scared. It was a weird feeling to realize that with one slight miscalculation you could just snuff someone. He imitated the hold with the arms pulled back far behind the Destroyer's back, then jumped up, ripping up both booted feet into the mid-back of the wrestler. He fell backwards, pulling the man down after him, and could feel as he hit the ground with his back and started to drive his boot up into the spine that he would crack it into pieces—send the damned thing exploding off like ivory shrapnel if he completed the blow.

But Harrison was enough of an athlete to snap his legs straight down, and experienced the pleasure of the huge gorilla falling flat on top of him backwards, knocking the air out of Harrison so that he couldn't breathe for a few seconds.

"Good," his teacher said, rolling off. "Now—you must swear to me never to use this technique unless

177

your very life is in danger. You understand me?" The Destroyer looked suddenly fierce and seemed to grow even taller. "It is the pledge that all in my fighting family had to swear to . . ."

"I swear," Harrison said—feeling a little stupid about saying the words and wanting to hold up his fingers in the Boy Scout salute, but realizing that he'd better not because he didn't think the Destroyer would find it amusing, "not to use the Double Kick Death Drop unless my life is threatened."

"Good, good." The Destroyer grinned. He slapped his pupil hard on the stomach. "Must tighten up even more. Should be able to have me land on your gut and bounce me right off again—with your body. Like Captain Lou. You see his stomach power. You're going to have to be able to do it in the pro ring, you can bet your balls on that. Cause that's what you'll be betting with."

Chapter Eighteen

The "entrance exams" for the Agency were to begin at once. Harrison wasn't even allowed to change from his ring outfit. That was part of the whole game. As in life—things happened just when you *weren't* prepared. He was led sweat-coated and hungry, and feeling mean as shit, by two grim-faced men to the twelfth level—the Testing floor. When the elevator doors opened, Harrison could see no one else on the floor. The two led him down the winding corridor to a room, sat him down in a rickety wooden chair, walked out, and closed the door behind them.

Harrison sat in the creaking chair and looked around him. He was in a room about twenty feet square and the whole place was painted white as the inside of a piece of Wonder Bread. With the bright fluorescent twelve-foot lights that took up half the ceiling it was very bright, almost blinding. He waited for whatever the hell was supposed to happen—but nothing did. And realizing that there were no rules to any of this he got up and began walking around the place. The door they had closed behind him was locked tight. There was another steel door at the far end of the room, no other entrance or exits. So it appeared they wanted him to go

179

on through the next door.

He walked across the room, getting himself on guard for what might lie on the other side. But when he turned the knob, he found the thing was locked as well. Didn't make sense. Why would they just lock him in?

"All right," Harrison mumbled. "there's gotta be some way to get through the door." He walked over to it again and scratched his fingernails along the sides looking for any opening. There—a thin seam. Harrison pried with his index fingernail, pulling back a little square of metal which opened to reveal a numeric keypad such as one might find on a computer, with numbers from 0 to 9 and a plus and minus symbol filling a square of twelve keys.

He began madly banging numbers out on the thing, but though an amber light blinked on and off above it, not a thing happened. There had to be a way to figure all this out. Somehow the information to tap into the pad was in the room. He searched all around the place, along the floor, getting down on his hand and knees and sniffing along the thick plasti-tile floor, white with black and gold flecks. After traveling around the place twice, he found a small, almost invisible piece of plastic tucked into one of the corners. Harrison pulled it out carefully, holding it between two fingernails like tweezers. He held it up to the light above.

The thing definitely had writing on it of some kind, but so damn small there was no way in hell he could read it even if he held it right next to his eyes. "Shit," he spat out. The bastards stymied you at every turn. Still, there was method to their madness. These guys knew just what the hell they were doing. He wondered for the hundredth time since he'd been in the subterranean world if he was on some video monitor somewhere, and was sure that he was. These guys liked to see you squirm, liked to watch you pinned down like a fucking

180

butterfly under a magnifying glass.

Suddenly he remembered his camera and surveillance classes. They had spent a few lessons on the theory and use of lenses, how they worked and all. Harrison glanced up at the curved fluorescent tubes of light that rested above him, long shimmering spears of flickering white. What if he could somehow fashion a lens out of the glass? He felt like an idiot as he jumped up and tried to grab one down from the fixture. But it was difficult, as the cylinder kept just slipping from his fingers. At last he grabbed hold of the long tube and pulled hard. And the thing flew down from the ceiling and right out of his grasp. As it exploded into a thousand shards on the ground, Harrison was just able to turn his head to the side and cover his face and eyes. The shower of glass flew everywhere, and a few little gashes of red appeared on his arms and chest, but none were deep.

He turned around and stuck his tongue out at whatever camera might be following him, then crouched down looking for any likely candidates for a lens. There were enough pieces to choose from as the glass was all over the place. He searched for shapes that were similar to lenses with angles of curvature that he had been shown. The first two he tried just distorted the plastic writing—but the third seemed to be the right idea as it magnified the scrawls in the microfilm a good ten times. Still not enough. It took him nearly ten minutes until he found just the piece that did it. He held the film up to the remaining bulbs above and then looked through the three-inch curved fragment of glass.

There—he could see something now. He had to turn it around a few times to get it all lined up—and then the number was clear. 19888777653. He memorized it. Then ran over to the keypad swearing that he'd forget it in the ten feet that separated them. He slammed his fingers down on the numbers, stood back, and waited. There was a dull whir from the doorframe—and lo and behold, the damn thing slid open silently.

He stepped through, pulling his fist back ready to take out anyone who might be waiting to attack him. He had no idea what to expect. That was also clearly part of the testing procedure. But there were no muggers waiting on the other side, just a dimly lit hallway, only about two feet wide, so he had to turn his broad shoulders sideways as he walked along it. Harrison had gone about thirty feet when he came to a juncture of narrow halls all going off at ninety-degree angles. He made a split-second decision and took the right-hand one. Everything leaned to the right—hadn't he read that somewhere? But again after walking less than thirty steps, there was another turnoff, and then another. It didn't take long to realize that he was in a maze. A fucking human rat in a maze. Only the rats probably would have done better.

Because for the life of him, as much as Harrison tried to figure out where he was going, he just seemed to get more and more hopelessly lost in the innards of the maze. After about half an hour he gave up and slumped down on the ground, pissed off and getting more claustrophobic by the minute. There was one thing he had never been too fond of, and that was tight spaces.

He looked up, noticing for the first time that the walls of the maze didn't extend all the way to the ceiling about twelve feet above. There was a space up there, a good foot or so between the top of the walls and the flat cement ceiling. He might be able to crawl along it. But there was no way he could get up there. Perhaps with a running jump, but he could hardly squeeze through the corridor, let alone run ten yards to get his momentum up. Suddenly he remembered that he still had his thick leather weight-lifting belt on. He had been using it earlier—to protect the muscles of the stomach and groin when pressing large amounts of weights.

He undid the belt and let the buckle fall to his side. The he snapped his arm up sideways and tried to hook the edge of the buckle up over the top. In theory it was a great idea, but the implementation of it was something else. He swung a number of times, but not until the sixteenth try did the edge seem to hook onto something—an errant screw not completely set down. Gripping hard around the belt, Harrison knelt down to the floor, compressing his legs like springs. Letting out an exhale of breath, he propelled himself up from the floor, at the same time pulling hard on the belt.

The whole wall groaned as it moved back and forth an inch or two, unsure whether or not it could hold the kicking weight. Harrison threw his other hand up and over the edge, curling his fingers around the smooth plastic surface. His face contorting with the great effort of pulling his entire body up with just his fingers made him turn red, then almost purple. But somehow he did it—and was suddenly raising his chest, then hips up onto the top of the wall.

Now he could see the whole damn maze—the forest instead of the trees. The wall shook around a little as he edged forward, crawling along the narrow six-inch top like a caterpillar along a garden fence. It was hard going—especially as the top of the wall was pressing right into his gut and groin. He could see that the maze was in fact impassable from below even as he slithered along the top of it. For doors kept changing, walls moving. The pathways were continually altered by computer, no doubt. A man could be lost in there for the rest of his life. So, this was the only way out. Or were there others too? Perhaps, depending on each man's abilities and skills, there were different answers to each part of the test.

After pulling himself along for about five minutes he reached the end of the maze and jumped down. But he had scarcely hit the floor when a hiss hit his ears and a stream of mist began emerging from several grills set around the floor of the white-walled room.

"Son-of-a-bitch," he snarled. Gas. They wouldn't off him—but they *would* knock him out. Still, there had to be a way out. He looked quickly around the room. There was a table off at one end. Some objects on top of it. He ran over even as the thick gray mist began filling up the whole floor of the room, already rising to his knees. On the table he saw some half-empty styrofoam coffee cups with a few dregs still remaining. An ashtray stood at the side. Five cigarettes—Parker's?—half smoked and then stubbed out.

Suddenly a light bulb went off in Harrison's head. And again he didn't know if he was a total idiot—or a brain of the highest order. Charcoal—charcoal filters were used in gas masks. There was charcoal in the charred remains of the cigarettes. And the filters from the long-100's butts had plenty of cotton in them. The gas was rising as he looked down, coming up for him, and he knew when it reached his head he'd be out like a fish hit with a hammer.

Harrison ripped open the butts from their paper containers and spread out the cotton fibers. Then he reached over and took the burnt end of one the butts and rammed it into the cotton, getting the two all mixed together. When the two filters were completely saturated, blackened, inside and out, Harrison lifted them both to his lips, and blew hard—getting at least the outer residue of dust off. Then saying a silent prayer to the gods, he slammed both charred filters up into his nostrils. And almost gagged. It tasted horrible, sending a coating of oily tobacco carbon to the back of his

184

throat, burning his tastebuds with the sour wretching taste. But when he sucked in hard, he got air.

Remembering also that some gases are heavier than air, Harrison pushed the table into the corner and climbed up on top of it, getting his head as high from the rising mists as he could. They came up for him. Within three minutes the stuff floated up over his head and the room was completely filled with it. He sucked slowly through the nose tubes, trying to breathe as slowly and shallowly as possible so he wouldn't take too much of the gas into his lungs. He just stood up there and waited. After perhaps five minutes the mists began dropping, being vacuumed back down into the same grills that had released them.

"Damn," Harrison muttered as he jumped down from the table and sat for a moment leaning back against the wall. He took a deep breath and snorted out hard with all his might. Both plugs of ash-coated cigarette butt came flying out of his nostrils and shot halfway across the room like little projectiles.

A door clicked open at one side and he rose and walked through it. A plastic globe sat atop a thick metal pedestal in the center of a circular room. As Harrison walked closer, he could see within one of the laser target guns. He reached out and touched the globe that surrounded it. The thing was some kind of plexiglass inches thick. Pulling his arm back he slammed forward with the blade of his hand. It bounced off as if he'd hit concrete. He got down on his hands and knees and examined the thing closely. Not a seam or trace of an opening.

Suddenly he let out with a wild Rebel yell and charged at the thing with every bit of power in his muscled legs. When he was about two yards away he suddenly jumped up in the air, slammed out sideways, and delivered a smashing side kick with his right leg.

185

The sheer power of the blow and the momentum of his airborne body slammed into the thing and knocked the globe right off of its pedestal. It flew down to the floor, smashing into pieces like a broken fishbowl, and the laser-sighted "fish" inside rolled out onto the floor.

"All right." Harrison grinned as he rose from the floor and picked up the futuristic pistol. He raised the gun, sighting up along its streamlined muzzle, and began firing in every direction, pulling the trigger so that a red beam of light kept dancing around him on the walls, the ceiling, wherever he sighted.

"Come on, motherfuckers," Harrison yelled out to his unseen audience. "Bring it on! You haven't seen shit yet."

Chapter Nineteen

As if in answer to his curses the entire wall on one side of the room suddenly just seemed to collapse into the floor, and there was a huge open space on the other side. Harrison stared through in amazement. It was an immense labyrinth of multi-levels, platforms, tunnels—like some kind of insane funhouse. He could hear gears turning softly, things whirring around deep in its shadowy innards. With curiosity and paranoia in his gut, for he had absolutely no idea what to expect next, Harrison started slowly forward, the laser target gun held loosely at chest level in his right hand ready to move fast.

He didn't have to wait long. He had gone less than twenty feet when there was a sudden click from what looked like a beat-up two-story shack made of plywood off to the right. Suddenly a figure rushed from the front door with similar laser gun in its hand and fired. Harrison was on the move like a lightning bolt. His combat experience was paying off again. Once you were under "real" fire—you didn't have to be told again for the rest of your life when something clicked, burped, or snapped nearby—you dove to save your fucking ass.

187

A red cylinder of light tunneled through the air right where Harrison had just been standing, but he was already three yards to the right and firing as he rolled over, searching for the target receptors on the man. Even as he tumbled along the floor, Harrison realized that the attacker wasn't a man at all but a mechanical representation, attired in Al-Capone-type duds. Suddenly Harrison's red beam found a small red circle about the size of a quarter on the thing's throat. He stopped rolling and fired twice. The first shot missed, but the second found the target receptor and the figure stopped moving and dropped "dead," both of its arms and its head falling loosely to the side. Then it dropped back down into an opening in the ground and was gone.

"Son-of-a-bitch," Harrison muttered as he moved ahead in a crouch ready to fire at the slightest motion. It was like he was moving through a bizarre assortment of sets from different Grade-B movies—about a hundred feet of Western ghost town, with little ramshackle huts; on the other side of the "street" a row of fake tenement buildings, three-story affairs with sooted brick walls, garbage piled in front of them, steps disappearing into dark, and spiderwebbed basement. It was crazy. He half expected to see Bugsy Malone step out with machine gun blazing from one side of the street and Jesse James with six-gun in hand from the other.

He had scarcely visualized the image when there was another click from one of the tenement windows and a shotgun suddenly appeared, aiming down from between some checkerprint curtains. Harrison fired once, twice, three times into the fluttering curtains as two red beams of light tore down from the sniper. But the human made target acquisition first. There was a sudden clanking sound and the artificial figure, clothed like some twenties hood with a cap and knickers, tumbled forward out the window and down onto the ground. Harrison had to hand it to the CIA bastards—they had a sense of humor. More than he would have given them credit for. Realizing he was not actually going to get hurt, at least in this part of the "exam," Harrison allowed himself to relax and enjoy it a little.

Another figure popped up from a basement and fired. Harrison saw the beam of light sweep across his right leg. Shit! He didn't know if he was supposed to be "dead" now—or if they were just scoring points. But no voice boomed down from any hidden loudspeaker telling him to lie down like a corpse, so he just kept firing back at everything that moved, taking out nearly a dozen of the attackers in about a hundred feet. He knew he was taking a few shots, saw the attackers' red pinpoints of light stab some part of him, felt the heat from one on his back for an instant. But he just kept on. It didn't hurt after all.

Suddenly there was something in front of him, appearing so fast that Harrison didn't even see where it came from. It was strange. Like a man—but not. He could see the shimmering edges of the thing—like a three-dimensional living image. It was a hologram, one that could move around. There must have been a laser projection system set up around the place—able to create this mobile 3D projection of a quite nasty-looking fellow who was raising what looked like a goddamn bazooka. But Harrison had already starting moving even as he took in the thing with wide eyes. He tore to the left, zigzagging fast, and the "man" about thirty feet away turned back and forth holding its holographic mini-missile-launcher.

It fired—and the image seemed to shake as a loud roar filled the air right beside him, but it was just coming from a hidden speaker. A world of make-believe violence that could set a man's heart to skipping a few beats. Harrison stopped in his tracks while the holographic figure tried to find him, and turned the bazooka this way and that. Harrison rushed right at the thing firing up and down, not seeing one particular target. The hologram began swinging its bazooka toward his chest, and as Harrison approached to within ten feet of the ghostly apparition, he knew that if it fired first, however many points he had accumulated would be wiped out. They'd have to scratch you for a bazooka shot to the face.

So he fired into the apparition's face first, getting the creeps as the closer he got the more the thing looked somehow alive, like a being from some other dimension trapped in this one, held in place by the magnetic beams of three lasers. Its skin had a greenish quality to it, its face was twisted, with an almost corpselike appearance. One of Harrison's shots hit paydirt, for as his red beam landed on the thing's right eye, the hologram let out with a piercing scream and then instantly disappeared like a popped bubble.

That seemed to be the last of the "attackers," at least for the moment. The buildings disappeared and the cavern narrowed, until he came to a moat about thirty feet wide, perhaps ten deep. But rather than being filled with water, the damn thing was filled to the brim with sharp stakes that poked straight up. He put one foot out, still wearing the wrestling boots he had had on in the ring, and gingerly tested the tips of the "punji sticks." But he had hardly put more than a few pounds of pressure on them when he felt the needles start going right through the leather.

He pulled his foot back. There had to be other ways. The tests seemed to have multiple solutions. Harrison looked over the moat and toward the far side. It was hard to see, as the lights had been dimmed, but it looked like targets. He got down on his stomach and steadied his laser gun with both hands, lying at a sideways angle to the shadowy targets. It was a long shot—with a beam of light *or* a bullet—but Harrison began firing. The red funnel of ruby light shot out nearly a hundred feet over the spikes and toward one of the light targets set up on small stands. It missed. The next too.

But as Harrison's eyes adjusted a little more to the low light he kept at it. After about a minute he actually hit something. There was a little bong, then the target pulled down into the floor. He started trying to sight the next one, which stood ten feet further back. It took an hour to shoot the bullseyes of all seven targets that had been set up, the last one being back nearly two hundred feet. But when that one was finally hit, there was an instantaneous and most gratifying reward. A bridge of solid steel two inches thick and a yard wide emerged from the floor beneath him and edged its way out over the top of the spikes until it reached the far side.

Testing it to make sure the damn thing was seaworthy, Harrison made a running dash across the span, praying that they weren't playing with him, about to send him flying down onto the cacti of death. But no such double cross was in the works. He reached the far side, and walked along a dusty corridor for about fifty yards, until it opened to a wider space about a hundred by a hundred. Fake boulders were strewn all around, along with fake trees and bushes. Everything was made of plastic. It was weird, like the terrain of a model-train set. Only this was all life-size.

Harrison started forward slowly, and suddenly lifted his laser pistol fast as he saw a figure step from behind some of the "boulders" twenty yards ahead. The man had a gun strapped to his waist, and he was also clearly not human. For he raised his right hand and swept it in front of him in a mechanical motion.

"Hey, you polecat, how about a gunfight?" the robot intoned speaking through mini-speakers in its mouth.

"Sure." Harrison laughed. He had tried these "gunfighters" out at the arcades on Forty-second Street. The gunslinger who takes you on for seventy-five cents, and screams, "You got me, ya blasted varmint," if you hit him. This one was the advanced model. It could walk on its own feet. And as it spoke on, he saw it could sense the environment around it as well.

"Well, how about puttin' that shooter of yours away and we'll draw, pardner. Draw like—real cowboys."

"Sure." Harrison laughed, smiling up at the ceiling and wondering again where the fucking cameras were that were taping him for Allen Funt's "You Are an Asshole" series. Harrison slipped the laser pistol into the waist of his wrestling bottoms and tested the handle a few times to make sure he could pull it out.

"How's your mother?" Harrison smirked as he let his hands drop to his side. He wondered if you could get a robot riled up.

"Fine, thank you—how's yours?" the Old West gunfighter, dressed all in black with a double-holstered pearl-handled six-guns, asked.

Even as Harrison searched his mind for a clever retort to a machine, the thing reached for its pistols. Both hands moved fast, like lighting bolts. Harrison barely had time to get his laser gun pulled free of his pants when the retorts of the cowboy gunner's double firepower erupted in unison. And as Harrison saw the puffs of smoke burp from the shining pistols, and felt the whistling of hot lead steaming past his ears, he knew that this one was not fucking around.

"Oh shit," he spat out as he dove forward and did a triple somersault, taking him all the way to the edge of the cavern and up against a rock wall. He came out of

192

the somersault in a crouch and turned, firing madly back at the robot, which was walking slowly toward him, its mechanized mouth, he swore, twisted into a smile. He knew he had hit the glass target circle in its chest and its neck. There was a little flash of red light which should have signified "hit." But if the robot killer was dead, he didn't seem to know it, but just kept coming forward firing one shot after another from his steaming six-guns, as if he had all the time in the world to take out Rick Harrison.

Harrison tore ass along the wall as slugs tore into the rock just behind him. This was getting serious. A switch had clearly blown somewhere, a computer chip malfunctioned. They'd all be very apologetic later—there would doubtless be an investigation and all that shit. Only Harrison would be dead. He rushed behind a nearby boulder and, catching his breath for just a moment as slugs poured off the other side, hefted the laser pistol in his hand. Well, if the red light didn't do diddly, maybe the thing itself could be used as a weapon. Harrison leaned around and suddenly poked his head out.

"Yooo hoooo, sweetie, over here," he screamed. As bullets tore into the boulder, Harrison dove back toward the opposite side and jumped out into the open. He pulled his right hand back hard like he was throwing a discus and let the Buck Rogers pistol rip. It flew in a spinning arc right toward the gunner, who was only about twelve feet off. The robot tried to duck but its mechanisms were too slow to respond to something so fast. The butt of the pistol slammed into its face, the edge ripping out the orange eye of the robot, continuing on along the nose and cheek as it tore up a few wires. The whole face began to smoke as sparks shot out through the ears and nose.

Still it kept firing, and Harrison jumped the other

way, weaving and ducking like a maniac. But though the gunner fired, it was wild now. Its brain was burning up, melting. Suddenly the figure was jerking wildly around on the floor in a grotesque and horrible death dance.

"Would like to fight, polecat. Fight, like to. Draw your. Like to. Please, pardner." It screamed out from the electronic world, and Harrison swore he heard real pain lost somewhere in the mechanical words. Then the figure burst into a showering funnel of sparks and it toppled over dead, as its fingers and legs smoked and shook violently like a prisoner in the electric chair.

"Man, oh man," was all that Harrison could find to say as he stood above the smoking husk of a thing, looking at its inner wirings and switches, its gears and steel backbone, which were all visible as the plastic-coated flesh burned away above them in a bubbling noxious stew.

A door suddenly opened in one of the walls and Harrison turned, clenching his hands into fists, ready to take the head off whatever it was, blood in his eye.

But it was Colonel Parker, rushing forward with a cigarette glowing red hot as he ran.

"You all right, man? You shot?" He rushed up to Harrison and looked him up and down quickly. There was just a drop of red along Harrison's upper arm, but upon inspection it wasn't even a flesh wound, just a piece of slug that had danced along the epidermis and then ricocheted off again. A Band-Aid would be enough. He had been lucky, damn lucky.

"Something went wrong," Parker said angrily, rubbing his left hand through his silver hair as his right pumped away at the cigarette like a baby on a nipple.

"Oh, really?" Harrison laughed, letting his chest relax for the first time since he had entered the murderous funhouse. "I hadn't noticed."

"No, it's not just a malfuction," Parker said, looking around at the three men who stood looking on behind him. "That thing should never have had real guns or bullets. It was a setup. The laser pistol was replaced with the real thing. Only a human could do that. Only someone in my organization. You were meant to die, Harrison. It's a fucking miracle that you're here."

"So I guess that means I passed?" the candidate asked wearily, just wanting to get back to his sardine can of a room and take a shower and lie down to calm his jangled nerves and his pumping heart. Being shot at like that had brought up a lot of old war memories. Things he'd thought were long buried.

"Yeah," Parker said, suddenly looking down as if he couldn't meet Harrison's eyes after all that he had just been through. "The first half of it anyway," he added with a barely audible mumble.

Chapter Twenty

All of the terrorists had teeth falling out now. And hair too. And bloody gums that oozed with red when they ate or brushed their teeth. They felt strange, all of the bomb makers. Real strange, like they had silly putty in their blood, LSD in their brains. They knew they were dying. But none of them dared say a word. Not after the frauleins were iced. They shut up—and committed themselves even more to the "Project," came more under Professor Markus's spell, just as he had planned. For they couldn't allow themselves to think that they were dying without purpose. No, it all had great revolutionary significance. This Mission of Fire would be the greatest blow struck for the worker since the Paris Communes of the last century. A fiery symbol that all the world would see. So it was right that they all go out in martyrdom. A dozen heroes who would live for eternity in the hearts and minds of the peasants and workers of the world.

But still, they kept the things that fell out of them. Kept them as if someday they might put them back in again. Each of them had their little hidden pile of teeth, of hair, of fingernails. Their minds didn't seem to focus quite as well as they once had. But then it didn't matter any more. The bomb was complete. Now delivery was all that mattered. Delivery to America—to the World Games in Flushing Meadows. Everything was going according to plan. Even the plutonium poisoning of Professor Markus's entire staff.

"Watch it there," Markus croaked in the darkness as they pushed the big trunk containing the nuclear bomb out to the end of the warehouse, and then out through a wooden door on a large cart. There was a private wharf out back as the place had once loaded its cargo right onto ships that docked in Marseilles harbor just beyond. A twelve-foot aluminum dinghy with out-board motor sat bobbing in the water about eight feet below the wooden dock, which seemed to move about beneath their feet as light waves rolled in from the sea.

"Careful now, careful," Professor Markus commanded through the windy and dark night, storm clouds starting to writhe around in the sky. Something was brewing up there. But they had no choice. The freighter was sailing at six A.M. They had to load up now, there would be no second chance. They swung the 500-pound black metal trunk out on a block and tackle attached to its mobile platform, and started slowly cranking it down to the boat below. There two Oriental-looking men clad in thick seamen's sweaters and wool caps waited with upraised arms. The Bulgarians—the other end of the operations team. Without them Markus's plans would have gotten nowhere.

"That damn little boat big enough?" Markus yelled down to the two men as they bounced up and down in the skiff. Already it seemed not all that steady—and it wasn't even loaded.

"Don't vorry," the seaman below shouted back with a wave of his hand. "Ve carry bikker tings before. Now shud up—and lode der boom." Markus prayed to the god of revolution hidden behind the high clouds, and motioned for his men to go ahead and load the atomic egg. He had put a quarter of his life into the conceptualization and implementation of this mission. The bomb was like his child and he felt a deep love for it, could hardly stand to see it depart. He walked to the very edge of the wharf and climbed down the ladder, making sure the lowering trunk didn't bang against the wood bulkheads too hard. Not that the nuke device wasn't cushioned in super-firm three-inch-thick foam, but still . . .

The steel shipping trunk reached the outstretched hands of the two Bulgarians, and they grabbed hold of it at each end as the block and tackle continued cranking down. Suddenly it was down in the boat, dead center. The professor could see the whole craft sink down a foot or two. Oh, please—don't let it sink. The two seamen released the steel cable from the trunk and then untied the rope holding them to the wharf. They started up their small outboard motor, and headed off down the channel and out to the much larger shipping area, where a large cargo freighter stood anchored, smoke rising from its stacks in back. The two seamen cruised over slow as turtles, under Markus's nervous gaze. The boat stood nearly two miles off, already churning up a white foam behind it as it tested its engines for the transatlantic voyage.

The Bulgarians didn't worry about the ship steaming off without them. One of them was the assistant coach of the wrestling team from Bulgaria. The other—the ship's cook. Men will go to sea without their wives, dogs and children. But not without their cooks. And when the big trunk was loaded up through one of the low service doors, just eight feet above the water line, it was hardly considered. "Cookie" often brought on last-minute supplies of perishables, or a sudden windfall of vegetables, even a few crates of good French wine. The steel door frame had a pulley system, and it quickly pulled the trunk into the innards of the ship, to be hidden along with the other equipment of the Bulgarian team heading for the games. It wouldn't be noticed. Not when one of their own was the equipment manager, with everything under his lock and key.

It was an international effort. That's what made Professor Markus feel the proudest as he watched the freighter set sail and head out of Marseilles harbor toward the darkening Atlantic. That when all was said and done—when the atomic ball of fire rose into the sky over the Games, starting a war between the U.S. and the Soviet Union and putting a quick end to the warming relations between the two superpowers—they would all be the reason why.

A war that would purify, and from the ashes of which a workers' paradise would follow. A paradise that those today were sacrificing their teeth, their lips, their bones and blood as though they had been in a barbecue too long. When all was said and done, history would be able to say that this great and beneficent bomb was built on the sweat and blood of men and women from every land. Japanese, Bulgarian, German, American, white, black . . . Revolutionary terrorism wasn't prejudiced. It would kill anyone.

Chapter Twenty-One

"Get ready to jump, pal," the co-pilot of the chopper that had ferried Harrison out to the middle of nowhere said at the very instant that he pulled the blinds off his eyes. They had been placed there so Harrison wouldn't be able to see where they were taking him. The sky was cloud-covered, murky, and it took a few seconds for his eyes to adjust enough to see what the hell what was going on.

"You give a guy a lot of time to get it together." Harrison said, smirking as the man hit him on the shoulder.

"Go, man, go—out the door," the suited CIAer screamed above the din. The chopper was suddenly hovering just yards above the ground, sending out a storm of sand and leaves. Harrison leaned over. At least they weren't a thousand feet up.

"No, supplies, nothing?" he asked, holding his hands up, wishing they'd at least give him a fucking pocket-knife or something.

"Out," the copilot said impatiently. He looked as if he was ready to push him out in a second or two.

"All right, all right, I'm going," Harrison snorted, putting both hands on the side of the chopper and swinging over and down. He hung there for a few seconds, trying to make sure he wasn't going to come down on some boulder in the darkness of the woodlands below. It was lit only by a sliver of moon above trying to slice through the clouded night. But he didn't have the chance to pick his spot—for the chopper suddenly rocked violently back and forth, dislodging him from the side like a dog trying to shake a flea from its hide. And as he fell, Harrison swore he heard the son-of-a-bitch in the open side door of the chopper scream out, "North!" and point with his finger as if that was the way he should head. Harrison tumbled down about six feet and hit the side of a hill, rolling down the slope another eight yards or so before coming to a quick stop right into a tree. He rose, half dazed, and shook his fists up at the helicopter, which was already disappearing over the misty mountain peaks that rose all around him.

"Assholes! I'll remember your faces!" he shouted up. Which was a lie since he hadn't even had time to look at them, being so preoccupied with seeing just what the hell was below him, where they were telling him to jump. He suddenly felt in just about the foulest mood ever. It was dark all around him. He didn't know where the hell he was, except that it was somewhere in the midst of a fucking mountain range because there were towering granite peaks all over the place. And just to add a little icing to the cake of misery, the storm clouds that flew above his head seemed to be dropping ever lower, threatening to burst open with their stored-up dams of moisture at any moment.

Well, he had to start somewhere, so Harrison tried to figure out which way was north. That's all they had said—"north." Great! That was a big help. The first question was how the fuck to figure out which way north was without the aid of a compass. He looked around as his eyes slowly adjusted to the little bit of light from the moon and stars squeezing through

201

spaces in the galloping storm clouds above. He was up on a plateau of one of a group of foothills. And beyond were more mountains, dim shapes disappearing into gray shadows as far as he could see all the way to the horizon. There was not a sign of life, no light burning. Nothing.

He was in the thick of trees, with brown vegetation still clinging to life in a few spots before the worst of the winter storms buried them in sheets of frozen white. He'd had a compass at least in the jungles of Asia. But now . . . What the hell was the saying? Moss grows on the western side of the tree? The eastern? Some side. He got down on his hands and knees on the wet dirt and looked close. There—there was some fucking moss. He decided it must be the west, because the stuff would probably get a bit more sunlight on that side. He prayed it liked sunlight. That meant that north was *that* way. He looked in that direction. It felt like north, had a certain colder, silvery edge to it in the sky. All right then—that was officially designated as north.

He began walking along the plateau. The night was alive with the calls of insects and the rustle of wings, nocturnal birds or perhaps bats feeding in the darkness. Harrison couldn't see clearly, perhaps it was just as well. He had never liked the close-up pictures of bats' faces he had seen in nature magazines. There was something demonic about them. But if they were above him, they didn't seem at all interested in his blood or anything. He saw a branch lying on the ground and picked it up. It was a good three inches thick and nearly as straight as a pole. A little too long perhaps. He bent down and placed one end against a low boulder, then slammed down hard with all his might with his booted foot. The thing snapped, although he felt a jolt of pain arch up his ankle as it bounced back slightly before it gave.

He picked up the stick—perfect—spinning it around

as they had done in his weapons classes. Just having the solid feel of the six-foot-long staff in his hands made Harrison relax just a little. Being out in the wilds, the first time he had really been out there since the war, was bringing up ghosts again. Damned ghosts would always be with him. But that's what being a man was. Having your ghosts follow you—and learning to ignore them.

He headed into the dark woods with rustlings everywhere around him. There sure as hell were a lot of nightime crawlers. It was like New York—St. Mark's Place at three A.M. He grinned to himself, trying to keep his spirits up. The occasional pair of yellow eyes that he could see glowing through the bush did not make Harrison feel particularly settled in his churning stomach. It was hard going through the forests. Dense was not the word. Every branch seemed to have knotted together into a spiderweb of vines and twigs. Maybe he should have gone around the slope. Within another five minutes he was going about a foot a minute, having to slam his way through with the staff, like Dr. Livingston going through the jungle of Victorian Africa. The slower he went, and the more he had to hack his way through the tangle of growth, the more he knew it was a big fucking mistake. But it only somehow made him stubborn. *This* was north. *This* was the way he was going.

It took Harrison three hours to go a quarter mile. And when he emerged into a clearing he was scratched up like a voodoo doll that had been poked with a hundred needles. That was the last time he did anything that dumb, he vowed to himself. There wasn't room to make mistakes out here. His macho plow-ahead style might be suited for the wrestling ring, but not out here. Mother Nature laughed at the toughest that humanity had to offer. He was already tired from his efforts, exhausted. He looked at his watch, which they had allowed him to keep, along with a normal outfit of clothes, sweater, jacket, even his boots. How nice. At least he didn't have to go through the Appalachian Mountains of West Virginia or wherever the hell he was barefoot. It was four A.M. He should sleep, wait until dawn. The sun would awaken him. His brain wanted to go on, but his stumbling muscles and fuzzy brain were somewhere else. Harrison found a nice high boulder about eight feet high that looked flat on top. It would make a good nest for the night. He took a running jump and leaped up with all the strength of his steel legs.

His fingers caught around the edge and scraped hard, the fingernails making a horrible sound as they slid right off coming toward him. Harrison pushed up with his shoulders, kicking against the side, and suddenly was atop the thing, the tips of all his fingers bleeding.

"Great!" he bitched, licking them. He had read that saliva had antibiotic properties. It seemed to help. The fingers stopped throbbing, and within minutes the bleeding ceased and the tips began scabbing over. Harrison scanned the barren rock slope around and above him. Didn't look like much of anything was going to be able to get him up there. And once he'd convinced himself of that fact, saying it over and over in his mind, he actually was able to fall into a very uncomfortable doze for about two hours.

Suddenly he was awake, and could see that it was morning from the dull glow of the rising sun behind the cloud cover. The clouds seemed even lower this morning, more swollen, the air so wet with moisture that he swore he could throw some instant coffee up and catch it as liquid in a cup. If he had any fucking coffee—or a fucking cup. Already he was freezing and pissed off as hell. His body—as he rose it felt like it was set in concrete. Everything ached. Sleeping on the cold rocks had tightened his muscles up like overwound clock springs. Harrison began doing some simple stretching exercises atop the rock—stretched his legs, then his arms, did circles around himself with his whole upper body, and swinging arm circles just to get the blood going. Then he jumped up and down until he could feel his heart speeding up, sweat starting to ooze from his skin.

There, that was better—everything was much more heated up inside. He jumped down, landing on the pebbled slope, and after finding some fresh water in a nearby tree trunk and filling himself with its sweet liquid, he started north again. He made good time. The stretching had helped. At least until he rested again. He'd just have to keep going, not stop, not allow himself to get slowed down. His body would keep putting out heat.

After twenty minutes he reached the top of the mountain he had been climbing and was able to see down over a vista that stretched off as far as the eye could see. It was breathtaking, awesome. Like some pictures from the very dawn of time. Mountains just stretched off, ridge after ridge, like some great scaled beast made of sheerest stone. Mists covered their lower slopes, and the silver sun which beat dimly through the clouds lit it all with an eerie shimmering curtain. He had to get through *that?* Yeah, sucker—you have to get through *that!* he answered his own mental question. Suddenly $30,000 didn't seem like enough. Not nearly.

He started down the far slope, gritting his teeth hard. Mad at the whole world and using that anger to fuel himself forward. Well, they might be assholes—but *he* was the one who was out here, Harrison grumbled. He flew down the slope toward the valley of trees about a half mile long leading to the next slope—and the next— and . . . So *he* was the one who was going to have to watch out for his own damn ass. 'Cause no one else was. And you could bet the house on that one.

He knew it was going to rain—if not instantly, sometime that day. If he allowed himself to get drenched in this cold weather, when night came he'd be a frozen popsicle within hours. As he passed a grove of trees with many of their dark leaves still hanging on he reached around into the thicket. Ripping here and there, he assembled a little stack of branches about three to five feet long, all covered with smaller branches containing thick leathery leaves.

He found some vinelike vegetation which when twisted around formed cord that was strong—he couldn't break it pulling on two ends. Harrison spread the branches out in a circle, and then wove together a crude stitching with the vine cord in between them, kneeling as he made his way around the circle. When it was completed he started another stitch about a foot lower down so that the very center of the branch complex was joined at the top, and then a second anchoring twine several feet down.

When it was all done and the knots tied tight and wound around themselves, Harrison stood back and looked at what he had wrought. It looked like some huge jellyfish made of wood with its tentacled branches spreading out in a circle that was nearly eight feet from one side to another. Harrison got down on his knees and slithered beneath one side of the thing. It felt strange in the half darkness inside, like he was being stroked by hundred of hands as the thick leaves swept against his body. Then he was in the dead center of the thing, and balancing the structure on his head and shoulders, he stood up.

The damn thing seemed to work. He knew he must look like something from a monster picture, *The Tree from the Living Dead*. But not only did the maze of branches that formed an umbrella coming down on every side of him seem as if it would protect him from rain, it was already warming him up, the thick leaves acting as insulation, little heat reflectors. The only problem was—he couldn't see through the branches.

He had forgotten to put in a visor. He reached up, not wanting to take the whole thing off again, and broke off twigs and leaves here and there right in front of his eyes, so that after a minute or two he could see, as if looking out the slit of a pillbox.

"All right," Harrison congratulated himself as he started walking forward. The bottom of the branch umbrella came to just about the midway point of his boots, and with the whole thing sort of draping outwards as it swung around him, it wasn't all that difficult to maneuver. Still it did weigh a good hundred pounds, so he had to remember to compensate when he jumped across small holes or over rotting logs.

And his fashion creation hadn't been completed a minute too soon. For as he reached the valley between the two mountain slopes, the storm hit fast, and fierce, like an attack, a violent barrage against the world below. The clouds hurtled down until the peaks around Harrison suddenly disappeared into the swirling blackness.

Then the deluge came. Sheets of water, streams, rivers, waterfalls dropped down from the erupting skies. Harrison could feel the winds, the sheets of water fly into the leaf umbrella, nearly toppling him over. The wind whistled through the cracks creating eerie sounds like a hundred flutes all playing against one another. But though he could feel the liquid wetting him here and there, the invention did its job. It kept him basically dry and warm, safe from the ravages outside. He walked on, carefully now, having to contend with the wind as well, although the way the "umbrella" fell evenly all around him, it almost seemed to *add* to his balance, the weight pulling down from every side. Thus attired, he headed up and down the foothills and mountains toward the north, not stopping as the rains came ceaselessly down.

Chapter Twenty-Two

After hours of trudging along feeling this surely was how the cavemen must have traveled, Harrison could feel the rain start turning to sleet, and then hailstones, and finally snow, a transformation that occurred over about four hours as a cold front swept in from the north—the direction he was heading, as if into the very jaws of the reaper. But the umbrella continued to keep him about eighty-percent dry, and a hell of a lot warmer than he would have been unprotected. He wondered if he could patent the damn thing when he got back to "civilization." Maybe market it. "Your Original Vegetable Body Armor Umbrella." Then he could just retire like all the other fat cats, down to Miami or the Riviera with a bevy of beauties on each arm. Harrison could get used to the idea.

Being able to get his water supply by just opening his mouth and tilting the mobile treehouse back a little, he could drink all he needed. He had enough surplus in his gut to go a couple of days without chow, though his stomach sure as hell was protesting, making all kinds of angry growling noises. It had basically been getting all that it wanted for years now. A few days' abstinence might teach it some fucking humility and patience.

He kept on, up one slope and down the next, as the snow turned the world around him nothing but white— white sky, white ground, white as if he were buried inside a piece of chalk. It was impossible to see a thing, but he knew that the hills ahead of him were all basically stretched out in an east-west orientation. Thus, as long as he kept going up and down, he should be in the right direction. And even in the middle of a blizzard you can still feel gravity, the angle of a slope.

He entered a sort of dream world where he wasn't even sure anymore what was real and what was not. It was hard to keep his eyes focused on the gray whiteness as they kept going out of focus like a camera lens that can't get a fix on anything. The storm just seemed to grow more blinding, more fierce, as if the skies were after Harrison himself. Somebody up there sure as hell didn't like him. For he had just reached the bottom of a long snow-covered slope and was crossing a valley floor several hundred yards wide when he heard a cracking sound beneath him.

He was on ice—it was beneath the snow that he was walking on. Harrison carefully started walking backwards, when there was a loud snapping sound all around him and he was going down. It was a strange sensation, to have the ground, or what you thought was the ground, suddenly disintegrate beneath your feet. But when the ice water hit him he knew it was no dream. The umbrella which had been protecting him these last hours was suddenly about to become his death suit. For the leaves became almost instantly saturated with water—and heavier. They swelled up all around him, and seemed to reach out and press at him even as Harrison kicked furiously in the water to stay afloat. But he could feel that the waterlogged leaf umbrella was winning. It grew heavier by the second.

Harrison realized that there was no way he was going

209

up—at least not here through the maze of twigs and branches around him and above him blocking a way out of the hole he had created in the ice. He took a deep breath and pulled down into the freezing water slipping out from beneath the umbrella. He swam into the mind-boggling cold water about eight feet down, and then ten feet or so to the side before starting up again. The cold was squeezing at his lungs, forcing them to open. And he knew that when he did—when he breathed in and took in that ice water—it would be his last breath on this earth.

Harrison reached the surface of the ice about twenty feet from where he had gone down. He slammed at the ice, which gave off a dim light filtering down from above. It was as hard as . . . ice. He couldn't make a crack in it. His eyes grew wide in fear as he knew he had only seconds left. He swam like a manic porpoise just beneath the surface of the ice slamming up at it every few inches, knowing he was about to be on sale in the frozen fish department of your favorite neighborhood supermarket.

At the last possible second, when his lungs were screaming with fire and his face was blue with freezing madness, Harrison slammed with his fist—and it cracked through. Twice more he threw out punches that would have cracked a cinderblock, and then slammed his head straight up. The top of his skull emerged from the ice sheet like some Arctic seal looking for a place to land. He took in deep gasping gulps of air. For even as he sucked in the freezing air, the water on his face, eyes, and lips all began freezing into solid layers of ice, like a sheet of the stuff was hardening on his exposed skin. He could feel the rest of his body, the muscles in his arms and legs tightening up like rigid steel that wasn't going to keep bending a hell of a lot longer.

Harrison reached up with his hands, trying for a hold on the surface as the snow cascaded down from above in vast blankets of great crystal flakes. He caught both elbows up on each side of him as he kicked up with his feet, trying to force himself up. But the ice broke even as he lifted himself. He kept pushing in that direction, but the damn stuff kept cracking right beneath him, not allowing him to get up. This little game went on for about twenty feet, until at last Harrison won and the ice grew thick enough to support him. With a heave he came lumbering up onto the snow covered stuff like some great fish that can't quite get along on terra firma. For now that he was out, all that Harrison had done was throw himself from the refrigerator into the deep freeze. His waterlogged clothes, hair, and skin were all freezing up as hard as a corpse in the city morgue.

He made himself keep crawling along toward what he prayed was north—out on the flat surface of the ice it was hard to tell what was what. But he headed in the direction the storm was coming from. He prayed it hadn't changed direction. At last he felt what was clearly more solid ground. There were small roots and bushes beneath the snow. He somehow rose up to his knees and then stood up, feeling no sensation in his legs. It was as if he was standing on pieces of dead meat and when he looked down he saw them shaking and wobbling around like rubber bands about to give way.

Harrison forced himself on toward the shadows ahead. Once inside the thick overlapping branches he found it was suddenly snow free, almost windless. The branches above were catching most of the snow and wind. He collapsed, as his sensationless feet wouldn't hold him up anymore. It was better there. At least he didn't have the intense driving wet snow and the wind. But it was still cold. He'd freeze. After resting just a minute and catching his labored breath, Harrison looked around. It was very dark, but he could see piles of leaves around the base of the nearby trees, leftovers from the fall. It took about five minutes of slow, aching movements with his arms, but at last Harrison had a whole pile of the stuff pulled up over him. He ducked down inside, pulled a last handful around his head, and tried to warm up. He couldn't tell if it was helping or not. But after a few minutes everything began hurting more. That seemed like a good sign. For Harrison knew it was when you *didn't* feel a damn thing that the tissue destruction of frostbite had begun. And once it set in, toes, feet, fingers, ears were quick to go. But it just kept hurting, every part of him, like razors were racing up and down his flesh.

He lay there unable to sleep, shivering like a freezing fetus as the sun slowly came up and the sky began brightening. And if Harrison needed a miracle, he suddenly got one. For as the sun came up, the storm clouds suddenly seemed to expend themselves. What had been raging black mountains were suddenly mere wisps of moisture, and within minutes were gone. The snow stopped falling, and even as the golden sun began rising to the east, Harrison rose to catch its life-giving rays.

Like a lizard in the sun after spending a frigid night beneath some cold desert rock, Harrison stood there at the edge of a meadow and received the warming beams of sun. By eight A.M. he could move his fingers and elbows. By ten he was stretching out and his clothes were half dry. He gave it another half hour or so, turning around like a chicken on a spit just to get every part of him feeling vaguely human again. Then, to celebrate the sheer fact that he was still alive when he shouldn't have been, he began running. Slowly at first, just so he could feel the sensation of hot blood coursing through his veins after being so close to not having any.

212

The sky was clear now that bright ball of the sun had begun dissolving the freshly fallen snow, sending sheets of water down the slopes.

He ran nearly twenty miles, exulting in the sheer power of his own body as he didn't seem to tire, was able to keep going at a steady clip. Suddenly he knew he was getting close. He didn't know how he knew—he just knew. There was a feeling of human presence ahead, though he wasn't sure how far. But the sudden awareness that his "test" was almost over suddenly made Harrison slow down as he realized that once he left this wilderness he was heading into even more danger. He might not come out of it at all. And suddenly, far from feeling threatened by the wild environment around him, he felt as if he were in a paradise—and he ran slower and slower as the human presence ahead grew stronger.

Perhaps it was because he was enjoying the view *too* much that he didn't watch his step quite enough. For another denizen of the mountains was engaged in licking honey from a fallen bee's nest and didn't see him either. And when Harrison came running right into the 320-pound black bear and sent it flying, and himself as well, it was hard to say who was the more frightened, him or the bear, as they scrambled around in the dirt.

But when Harrison got a look at that huge black face and the open jaws which looked as if they could swallow him whole, it was definitely the human who was the more frightened. For the bear stood up on its hind legs and came foward one dramatic step at a time, swinging its great claws in the air, as if it wanted to scare the shit out of him before they even fought. Which Harrison had to admit it was doing. He backed off slowly, mumbling "fuck, fuck, fuck," to himself over and over under his breath, like some sort of insane mantra to the bear spirits.

He had read that you weren't supposed to run from a bear. Which was probably true and all that, but a little hard to put into practice when the hairy dude was coming straight at you swinging those big mitts like he was ready to swipe Harrison's head into the next state. The bear came walking in on those two huge pillars of legs, standing a good six feet at the shoulder. Harrison leaped to the side as if he were shooting right over the ring ropes. And not a second too soon. The right claw of the beast ripped in like a guillotine right where his head had been. He had pissed this bear off, and it wasn't about to stop now.

Harrison began running, but within seconds he could see that the animal was going to catch him. Bears were faster than the fastest man—another fact he suddenly, unfortunately, remembered. He looked around for trees to climb, but there was nothing for a hundred yards taller than something the bear could knock over with a single stiff push. Even as he tore ass with everything his driving legs could muster, he sensed the big shape right behind him. And before he even had a chance to turn around, the beast landed right on his back and slammed Harrison forward into the dirt. He landed hard on his chest. Only the training he had just completed made him instinctively throw his arms out in front of his face or it would have been creamed. He bounced back up, using the force of the ground to spring him up again in the "Throw Off" move that wrestlers use to dislodge a man who's holding them down. It seemed to work just as well with a medium-sized black bear, sending the creature over onto its side with an angry roar which echoed through the hills.

But that was just one fucking move, and the bear didn't seem particularly hurt by it, just angrier. It rose up and came forward again on all fours, its foaming mouth snapped and snarling like it hated Harrison more than anything on this earth. As the bear came in, Harrison knew he didn't have any more time to flee. So he pulled back his arm as far as it would go and let out with just about the most wicked punch he had ever thrown, right into the snout of the beast that was coming in fast. Bears are walking armored vehicles. Their thick fur and hides are impervious to any but the most powerful weapons. Only the bear's snout is open, defenseless to the world. It has to be, for it's the animal's link to the universe. A bear lives through his nose. All other senses are secondary.

Thus, when the blinding pain of Harrison's blow came in like a missile and smashed the big black bulb for a second, making a squishy sound, the animal went bananas. It reared up on its two back legs and let out an elephant-like sound. Then it came down and ran around in wild circles, snorting and howling up a storm. Whether it couldn't even see him anymore in its blind terror or had had enough, Harrison didn't know, but the animal tore ass down the hill they were on and into the woods as if in search of an emergency room to fix its pained nose.

Harrison felt a sharp stinging sensation in his right shoulder, and looked around to see that the son-of-a-bitch had gotten him on the first flying attack. Its five claws had dug a good half inch into his upper back, sweeping down five inches or so. Thin trails of blood dripped down from the gashes. He had been that close to death. If the animal had gotten those dagger claws in another few inches, it would have ripped his whole back and lungs out, sent his heart sliding around like a bloody bowling ball.

"Harrison, Harrison," he suddenly heard voices yelling from the other side of the hill. He had done it, he was there. There was no more. And if that maniac Parker had any more CIA tests he could shove them up

215

his . . . Harrison stumbled up the side of the slope, the adrenaline from his encounter with the bear flowing through his veins, making him feel like he was about to pop. He reached the top and waved down at three men—one of them he coud see was Captain Lou by the big belly hanging out of his customary open Hawaiian shirt.

The three men stood about a hundred feet down, stamping around in the cold with hunting jackets on in front of an old beat-up station wagon, apparently D2's favorite mode of transportation.

"How'd it go, mister!" Captain Lou yelled up with a laugh as he clapped his hands together in mock applause.

"Oh, no big deal," Harrison yelled back. "Just your usual sub-freezing-blizzard, fall-in-the-ice, freeze-to-death, bear-attack mountain hike. Everyone should go on one. Really, I hope you all try it some time."

Chapter Twenty-Three

The same storm that had rocked Harrison to the roots of his existence continued eastward at a record speed, and straight off the East Coast across the Atlantic. The big freighter, the *Svetlanya,* carrying the Bulgarian team's supplies, was hit by the brunt of it. The ship was tossed and turned like a cork in a baby's bath, and even hardened seamen were sick to their gills, leaning over buckets down below deck as the ship lurched from side to side, rose and slammed down again with tremendous roars that reverberated through the steel halls as if the entire hull might rip apart at any moment.

And while they were puking their living guts out—and the Romanian captain was popping valiums up in the bridge as he stared out the curved tinted-glass window watching the boiling ocean all around him and unable to do a thing about it—a terrified man sweating out sheets of garlic-scented moisture, which covered his face and neck with a sheen even in the coldness of the storm-racked Atlantic night, was far down in the sub-bulkheads of the *Svetlanya,* with his left hand resting on a crate and a bottle of vodka in his right hand. Every time the freighter lurched up in the air and slammed down again, making the crate and its contents shake, shimmy, and roll like they were about to burst out of their contents, the man rolled his eyes and took a deep slug of the burning liquid.

He had a Mongolian-looking face, all rounded and savage-looking, with almond slits for eyes and a hard-set mouth that looked like it had seen a hard life. The man could have been one of the descendants of the great barbarian hordes which had swept down from northern Asia numerous times during Europe's long and bloody history. With his stubbly face and glowing Oriental eyes, he could have been one of Ghenghis Khan's forward infantry. But that was over a thousand years ago. And the crate that the teary-eyed man rested his arm on could have taken out all the great Khan's armies in one blow as if they were so many burning leaves in the wind.

"I don't want to die," he croaked in the dialect of Northern Bulgaria, the Dobruja region. He was drunk, drunk as hell. He had come down when the storm began and had sat next to the crate, thinking in the peasant wisdom that he still carried in him from his small town of Novi Pazar that by talking to the beast, reasoning with it, could assuage it, calm it, control it.

"Don't explode, bomb. Please, I beg of you." The freighter lifted up and came down as if the bow had crashed a good fifty feet down into the ocean. The box actually lifted up into the air, and came down with a loud smash on the steel floor of the bulkhead. Samokov took another deep drink from the bottle, shielding his eyes with his palm as if he feared the atomic fire that was about to follow. But still it didn't come.

"Don't explode! In the name of the Burning Angel, I beg you," he pleaded drunkenly with the thing, slapping it on the wooden back, cajoling it with his drunken tears. "I want to see my Mingya again, my little Tuskevh and Magvar. You are a good bomb, I know it. A fair bomb. You will not go off until you have reached New York. Please, oh, great bomb, please." He stroked it like an old dog, and even poured a little of his vodka atop the wood, thinking somehow that the exhibition of such generosity would impress the bomb.

"There, now that's better, isn't it, bomb?" he slurred as he patted the crate on the side. "We're both a little nervous. A storm at sea is never fun. Not for you, not for me. Ah, but we've plenty of vodka, haven't we!" the Bulgarian said enthusiastically, taking out a second bottle from inside his thick pea coat. "And we've got all night to tell stories, to tell of our families and children, the lives of our grandparents." He took another huge gulp, finishing the bottle off, and threw it over his shoulder into the corner, where it shattered. But the sound couldn't be heard over the thunderous roars of the ocean crashing into the metal skin of the ship just yards away from him.

"Well—let *me* begin," Samokov said, opening the second bottle and sniffing it to see if it was as fiery as the first. He tasted it. "Ah—the perfect elixir for an evening of conversation. Yes, I am the oldest of three boys," he began, "born in the village of Novi Pozar in the year 1947. The story of my village is a long one, beginning with the takeover of our region by Tsar Alexander IV in . . ."

Thus, the Bulgarian drunkenly lectured the atomic bomb through the long stormy night, as the freighter edged its way forward, one crashing watery step at a time, through the towering seas. Fifty- and sixty-foot waves battered at the vessel like black spears set on ripping it asunder—like the tridents of Neptune, god of the sea.

Chapter Twenty-Three

"I'm embarrassed, Harrison," Colonel Parker said as he paced around his private office off to the side of the War Room, turning now and then to face the inductee who sat on a black leather couch looking up with bemusement. "Embarrassed for the Agency, but mostly embarrassed for myself. I brought you in on all this. It's hard enough without having to worry about watching your back. That's something you and I never had to worry about when we were out in the hinterlands, you can bet your balls on that."

"Amen, pardner." Harrison grinned wearily from the couch, holding up his right hand with the thumbs-up sign. He was still just a mass of aches, pains, and bruises. The bear-claw wound didn't help matters any although the med people had treated it with a shot or two, and bandaged the whole thing up. Considering all that he had been through in the last month, it was amazing to Harrison that he was alive at all.

"Damned embarassed," Parker went on. "Clearly someone has infiltrated D2. I don't know who the hel¦ it is. Tell you the truth I find it hard to believe. I'm the bastard who put this whole damned unit together from egg to chicken. I mean, part of the reason the boys upstairs gave me a free hand was because I was so critical of other branches of the Agency, which I believe are riddled with foreign agents or incompetents—or both. The presence of a single provocateur in D2 means my security is flawed as well. Somehow—some way. Damn!" He spat out the curse and pounded his fist into his palm with such force that he actually hurt himself, although he didn't acknowledge it, just let the hand fall dangling to his side. He had never showed pain in front of Harrison. Not even when he was undergoing the living tortures of hell back in the jungles of God's little burning acre.

"Hey, don't sweat it," Harrison said, waving his hand with a look of disgust. "Look at it this way. I'm alive, and you flushed out your rat. He failed at his mission, but he's out of the closet. He'll be running scared. He'll slip up. You know how it is, Parker, it's all the same with gorillas, rats, coons, or men. Just set the trap—they'll come to it."

"Son-of-a-bitch." The CIA chief laughed, walking over and giving Harrison a mock punch on top of the skull. "I'm the one who's supposed to give the advice."

"If it's good, take it. Advice is the same, no matter who gives it." Harrison had quoted the phrase that the Colonel had always used on him in the old days. But the CIA chief was already turned away and pacing the well-worn Dhuri rug.

"Yeah, we've flushed him out. But now we need a trap." Suddenly he caught himself as he realized he shouldn't be talking about this in front of Harrison. "Oh, forget it, that's my problem." He laughed, throwing himself down in the plush red leather armchair that sat about five feet in front of the couch Harrison was slumped back on, sipping some brandy in celebration of his successful completion of the training. "*Your* problem is that you're through here

221

and ready to head out, pal. It's combat time."

"Already?" Harrison sighed. "I was just getting used to my pad. You know, found a way to roll over in bed. Met a few girls. My shoulder still hurts, it's . . ." Harrison reached up with his hand and rubbed around his shoulder.

"Forget it, pal. Talked to the doctors already. They said as long as you keep the wound clean, it should start healing up within days. They threw some new glue-type stuff in there too so it's setting, and according to specs you'll be as good as new within days. Good try." Parker laughed as he extracted a butt from his jacket pocket and lit it with a big metal table lighter in the shape of an eagle—pressing the wings so that flames shot out of the opened beak. He got the cigarette smoking like a blast furnace, took a few good puffs and went on.

"You may have been wondering just what the hell you've been training for," Parker said, putting one leg up over the other as he leaned back trying to relax himself, though not being nearly as successful at it as Harrison was.

"Yes, it has crossed my mind," Harrison answered, throwing back another quick slug of the burning liquor. He'd always had a soft spot for fine brandy.

"Well, I didn't want to tell you at first—because you had enough burdens on you what with all the damned training, and then the final 'exam.' But now you'll be one of only five men in America who know the truth. Some sort of atomic device is being brought into the United States, to the International Games, the wrestling and weightlifting competition that's about to be held in New York—or so we've come to believe."

"Yeah, I remember reading about it before I came down here. Was thinking of going and watching a few matches."

222

"Well, now you're going to be in those matches, pal. It's all amateur wrestling, you know, with gold medals and everything. There'll be competing teams from around the world—nearly eighty countries are involved. You're with the American team—it's all arranged. There's a cot waiting for you in the Games Village and your very own entry number. You're set, pal. You're going to be in the All-World Games."

"Damn," Harrison groaned, throwing his head back and putting his palm over his eyes. This was getting crazier by the minute. "And just what is it that I'm looking for?" he asked after a few seconds, spreading his fingers apart and peeking through as if he were a kid looking at a monster picture.

"I don't know," Parker said dryly, finishing his own brandy and pouring another. The golden liquor sparkling like ephemeral liquid fire beneath the subdued lighting which suffused the private suite. "I don't know what the hell these bastards have planned, what their motives are, where the bomb is—nada, zip, zero, nothing. We know that the materials to make such a device were in fact stolen over the last few months in various European countries. After that, almost nothing. Just traces, tantalizing clues that go nowhere—a pair of hot gloves in Belgium, a dead cat with a stomach as radioactive as Hiroshima the day after, found floating in the English Channel. Who the hell knows. I don't . . ."

"So I'm supposed to go to these Games, compete with half-ton peasants from the Ukraine, search for infiltrators of unknown nationality or description, and find an atomic bomb which could be hidden anywhere within a hundred-acre village with more levels and tunnels than a fucking anthill?"

"Yeah—something like that," Parker snorted back. "If you want to be so blunt about it."

223

"I like being blunt when it concerns my life or death. I'm weird that way." He poured himself another as well, drank it down fast, then looked across at Parker with a lopsided grin. "Well, when do I begin?"

"Tomorrow, pal," Parker said with a sheepish grin, knowing he had given Harrison less than thirty-six hours of R and R from his survival exam before the main battle began. "Sorry about that. You know how it is. Things always fall a little behind. I had wanted to give you a week before jumping into the fray. But that's the bad news. The good news is that Captain Lou will be going along to keep an eye on you, be your contact man back to us with any information you dig up, and to give you—God help you, pal—some advice when you actually get in there with those wrestlers. He'll be going incognito. He's too well known to the masses. He'd attract too much attention to you. You're just supposed to be a country hick coming in for his shot at the big time. But he'll be around, as will other of our agents, also undercover. Here's his beeper number. You can contact him twenty-four hours a day. And something else—from our CCS pals." He took a ring out of a small plastic box and handed it to Harrison. "Try it on."

"I'm not really into rings," Harrison said skeptically as he slipped the medium-sized garnet-topped ring over his middle finger. It fit perfectly.

"It's a tracker. This will transmit your location to the Captain twenty-four hours a day on a pick-up device he's got. It's just a little extra insurance. Don't take it off, okay? Even when you're taking a shower—or getting laid—or whatever."

"Well, that's something," Harrison said, admiring the ring from different angles, taking a final sip from the glass. "How will I know Captain Lou if he's all disguised up?"

224

"Oh, I'm sure you'll pick him out." Parker grinned. Then his face grew somber again, and he started wrenching at his hair again. "Listen, pal, I—"

"Don't worry about it," Harrison said. "So when do I get the thirty thou?" he asked, letting the top of the glass rest against his chin.

"How about this?" Parker said, leaning even further back in the $2,000 chair. "I'll give you twenty thou now—ten when you complete the assignment. Put it in your account, whatever you want. And if you're crazy enough to want to continue after this mission, then you go to full salary, like we said. Plus full medical, dental, wraparound, brain-transplant coverage—you name it, it's yours."

"I better have full wraparound." Harrison grinned back, reaching for yet another glass. He was getting a little looped. There was no doubt about it. And he didn't give a shit. For all he knew this might be the last time he ever would. "Cause I have a feeling I'm gonna need it."

Chapter Twenty-Five

To say they had fallen a little behind schedule was the understatement of the year, Harrison discovered after he was flown to New York. He carried his bags of gear for the Games along with a few hidden items such as a geiger counter built into a wrestling belt buckle and various spy gimmicks hidden within a shaving cream can and a transistor radio. By the time he took the cab from LaGuardia to the Games grounds, the place was packed with people and cars. The immense domed stadium that had just been completed months before— the Apple Dome, the biggest in the country—now stood rising like Mt. Vesuvius from the middle of an immense complex of buildings and athletes' living quarters that stretched off in every direction. Dozens of acres of running tracks stood to one side with viewing stands alongside them.

The cab drove further, up to barricades and heavily armed guards. Harrison had to show his pass—a plastic ID card with photo and name, prints, blood type, and other vital information for the security and medical bureaucracy of the Games. The cabbie had to go slow, for there were raised bumps every twenty yards or so to slow cars down—which was a good idea, as there were countless people rushing all over the place. It was like a madhouse, filled with powerful-looking men and women, wrestlers and weightlifters from around the planet. Perhaps the best of their breed on the entire earth. All here to see who was the best, the very best. The first such Games in the world, with eighty nations participating and as much media coverage as the Olympics themselves.

Another set of guards, with submachine guns hanging from their necks and one hand on the weapons at all times, checked his ID again. "Got your bags in there?" one of them asked. A dour no-bullshit face looked in through the window.

"Yeah," Harrison answered apologetically. "I'm just getting here—you know—bad plane connections—"

"The others have been here a week already, most of them. There always gotta be a character, right?" He smirked. "Well, I'll have to check your bags, if you don't mind," the man said, standing a few feet away as Harrison opened the door of the cab, took out the bags, and paid the cabby. The cabby took one look at the weapons and got out of there fast, wheels squealing. He had been held up twice in the last year, at gunpoint, and just the sight of a weapon seemed to set off a wild fear in the man.

The guard led Harrison a few yards to a small building about fifty by ten, made of still-shining corrugated steel. He pointed to a conveyor belt, and Harrison put both bags up on top and watched as the belt carried them along. Scanners, radar units, devices that measured for explosive and gases—whole arrays of measuring equipment were trained on the bags. As the baggage moved, the guard walked along on the other side of the measuring screens, checking out their readings. At the other end he said, "All right, you're cleared," and handed Harrison a small bright red medallion.

"This is your I.D. pin. You don't want to lose this

'cause it's your internal ID. You need it to get everywhere, to food or the Games. Now come with me. We'll find out where your group is. He went to a small computer at the end of the single-story structure and punched in all of Harrison's information.

"Let's see, you're with the American team, weight class five—that's Barracks Z-171. You can take one of these buses we have that runs through the complex." The guard pointed out the window and Harrison saw a cross between a mini-van and a golf cart pull up to a small bus stop with a blue sign with the picture of a wheel in it. Only international symbols were used here, pictographs that could be understood by an Eskimo as easily as a Watusi.

Harrison ran, his bags slowing him a little as they were filled with almost 150 pounds of junk. But the driver of the twenty-passenger open-air bus waited until he was aboard and had slammed himself down into one of the uncomfortable plastic bucket seats that ran down both sides of the vehicle. A quick glance around the bus showed two monstrous Russians or Eastern Europeans—to judge by their talk—sitting just ahead of him. There was also a group of female weight-lifters who looked Eastern European and were giggling like schoolgirls as they eyed the hunks of muscle walking by everywhere. Never before in history had so many awesome physiques, male and female, been assembled in one place. That in itself was making the Games an event, a must-see-or-die happening, for which people were flying in from all over the U.S. and overseas. Helicopters buzzed constantly overhead as reporters tried to find interesting footage for the Six O'Clock News.

Harrison couldn't help eyeing his opposite numbers. There were gorgeous women parading all over the place like they were falling from the honey trees of heaven. They were in the absolute peak of condition, their bodies toned to a perfect cutting edge. He lost his heart at least a dozen times in the next three stops. The Games Village was arranged by blocks in alphabetical order, so Z-Block was nearly at the end of the line, about a five-minute ride. There were two-story barracks along each side of the street, extending back into more rows than he could see. The place was like a mini-city. It was absolutely amazing.

Finally they reached Z Block, and Harrison exited the bus and asked a few people directions. The huge stadium dome loomed behind him, reaching up into the sky like some mountain just plopped down in the flatlands of Queens, New York. Even as he walked forward he heard tremendously loud noises blare out from the top of the dome, sounding like the dead rising. It was in fact the PA system being tested for the next day's opening events. He came to a corrugated building, Barracks Z-171, and walked through the steel door that pushed in on springs. Although the place held forty beds, twenty on each side, running down the walls, only two men were inside. They were on bunks, getting out of sweat-soaked clothes they had just been working out in. They were big fellows, one of them, a black man, bigger than Harrison himself.

"Help you out, fellow?" the black man asked, as he slipped off his sneakers and pulled on a pair of fresh thick cotton socks. He had muscles that looked like they were out of a Sylvester Stallone nightmare.

"Yeah, I think I'm supposed to bunk here," Harrison answered, letting his bags drop to the floor with loud thuds. "Name's Harrison, Rick Harrison. I know I'm late but—"

"Late ain't the word." The other man, a blond, blue-eyed, all-American-looking guy with barrel-sized biceps laughed. "The whole fucking shebang starts tomorrow at ten A.M. sharp. You ain't even practiced for the parade or nothing?" They both looked at

Harrison with pitiful expressions, shaking their heads from side to side.

"Gimme a break, okay, fellas?" he pleaded, not in the mood. "Where's the empty bunk? I need to rest my ass for a few minutes."

"Let's see—I guess you could have that one over there," the black man said, pointing to a corner of the barracks. "That one by the window in the corner. There's no one there. Of course, Connors, the guy next to you, snores like a moose in heat, but—" he shrugged his shoulders—"guess that's one of the consequences of being the last one. The early bird catches the—"

"Look, pal," Harrison said as he walked over to the bed and threw his bags down onto the plywood-sheet floor that had been only nailed down days before. As tired as he was, he just wasn't in the mood for bullshit. "I've just been through a hell of a lot the last few weeks. I didn't even know I was going to be here until twenty-four hours ago . . ." Suddenly he realized he was saying more than he should, was blowing his cover—the first thing they taught him not to do at the Agency. Shit, he'd have to be more careful from now on.

"The guy who was supposed to come from my college got sick," "so I'm just a sub. That's why I'm late," he added brusquely, throwing himself back onto the bed. At least the mattress was soft, though the springs of the steel-framed cot gave out squeals and his back seemed to sink down about six inches.

"Where you from, sub?" the blond asked as he threw on a clean Game Sweatshirt and matching exercise pants. All the athletes wore the same official uniform, purple stripes running down the arms and legs of jet black material.

"From Michigan," Harrison answered, telling the truth. The Agency had said he could basically tell the truth about everything. It was easier not to create an entire cover—too many lies to remember, too many

230

possibilities of a slipup. Especially for a relatively untrained agent like Harrison. He had already made one slip. He'd have to watch his tongue as if he were holding a guillotine over it. "Marquette College up on Lake Superior. Cold as a witch's clit up there, man, I'll tell you." They looked at him a little suspiciously for a moment—he looked a little old to still be going to college. On the other hand there were loads of guys competing in their twenties, early thirties. It was basically a non-professional tournament. That is, you had to be an amateur to compete—either a college wrestler or a club wrestler who hadn't turned pro. The Russians had "college students" in their forties, big beefy guys weighing 400 pounds who looked like they had been eating steroids for twenty years.

The black guy grinned and walked over, holding out a hand. "Name's Carter, Lenny Carter," the black Samson said, reaching down and gripping Harrison's. "Don't mind us." He laughed. "We're known as the ballbusters of the barracks by all the guys."

"I'm Samuels, Peter Samuels, from Southern Cal. Glad to meet you," the blond guy said as he finished putting on his sneakers and stood up straight, stretching his arms overhead to get a crink out of the rows of bulging muscles. "Like he said"—pointing his foot, which he held straight out in front of him toward Carter—"we're just a bunch of hot air. Glad to have you aboard. We need every sucker we can get—the Eastern Bloc nations look awesome this year. You look pretty tough, dude. Wrestling, weights?"

"Rasslin'," Harrison said, lying back, feeling his whole body sink deeper and deeper into the mattress. "Though how tough I am remains to be seen."

"Well, if you want any food you'd better come now. That's where we're heading," Carter said, putting his leg up on a window ledge about four feet above the floor and stretching it out, leaning his body almost all the way forward with great dexterity.

"Shit, I was just getting comfortable," Harrison groaned, making his eyes open and his body slowly rise up like a corpse from a coffin. He had to eat. He hadn't had more than dogs and fries in the last twenty-four hours with his plane transfer getting all screwed up and whatnot.

"Yeah, I'm coming," he said, spinning around and putting his booted feet wearily down on the plywood floor. "Tell me where can I get one of those nifty outfits both you guys are wearing." he asked as the three of them headed out the door.

"It's on the way," Carter answered walking alongside Harrison, the blond weightlifter falling in behind them. "Should have a few left—there were truckloads of them last week."

"You been here a whole week?" Harrison asked as he looked at the amazon-sized women who were stalking around. They looked hungry too. Like a lot of hot action was going on in the trampolines at night.

"Yeah, I was one of the first," Carter replied. "I'm also working with the Games Committee as an Assistant Coordinator of Wrestling Supplies. Some title, heh?" He laughed. Harrison liked the guy. He seemed like a no-bullshit type. "I've been through this before. The first one—four years ago. Though it wasn't nearly as big as this one's turning out to be." As if to accentuate his words, flashbulbs went off to their right where four spandex-attired lovelies from the Scandinavian lands posed with their chests pushed out hard against skin-tight tops, the immense stadium forming a backdrop.

"You never turned pro either?" Harrison asked, knowing by the guy's bruises and scars that he had to be a wrestler.

"No," the black man answered, turning to the right to a building marked Equipment and Supply. "Have a family—a good job—with my own garage, maybe two soon. Just like to compete, I guess. Won the bronze last time, but I was just getting in shape then. *Now* I've trained my ass off for four years," he said, flexing a muscle. "I'm going for the gold."

"Ain't got no argument from me." Harrison laughed, seeing the huge bicep in front of his eyes as big as the trunk of a fucking tree. He didn't think he could remember seeing an arm quite so strong before. He wondered if the guy used steroids, which were completely illegal at the Games and grounds for instant elimination, but didn't ask. What a man did with his life and body was his own business as far as Harrison was concerned. That's what America was all about. The freedom to make your own choices—even if they killed you.

They walked up to a corner where a bored-looking elderly woman sat reading a romance novel with rapt attention.

"Come on Clara, honey," Carter yelled out, banging his fist down on the wooden counter. She stopped reading and looked up annoyed. "Harrison here needs a set of duds."

"Oh, you," she scolded him. "I was just getting to the good part where he—he—" She blushed and put the book down.

"Let's see. I'd say you need an XX Large," the matron said, walking a few feet and getting a uniform from a bin. Clara waddled back with a set of the purple-striped black all-purpose jumpsuits. Harrison took it, went into the dressing room, and put it on. When he walked out and looked into the mirror, Clara whistled as she climbed back up on her seat, her overly made-up face glowing even a deeper red.

"Hey, this guy's got some body." She whistled, making Harrison blush.

"She's right." Carter laughed. "Didn't realize you

233

were that well defined. You're more compact than me—but I swear you sure as hell look like you got it all packed in there."

"This thing's too damned tight," Harrison said, growing more self-conscious by the second. It fit him well, but everything sort of clung to him. He was used to baggier clothes, things sort of hanging off him.

"Well, man, you can look at it two ways," the black wrestler said. "One, you get the baggy kind and drift into the background. Two, you get the ones you're wearing, the tight ones, like every other narcissistic son-of-a-bitch in this village. Because then you get noticed, and interviewed, and photographed. Then you get in the newspaper and on magazine covers. And suddenly skin-bracer manufacturers, tire companies, sneaker conglomerates all want you to endorse their products. And suddenly you have your second home, your wife's clothing allowance for a year. I mean you're set, pal. The front of the Cheerios box or bust. That's my motto."

Harrison laughed at the guy's frantic rap. "I'll take the tight one," he said, looking down at the uniform, trying to get used to the tighter, enclosing feel.

"Where are the photographers?" he asked mockingly as Carter led him back out to the main thoroughfare, which was crawling with people. If Harrison had ever felt like he was part of an ant colony, this was it. And even as he spoke, bulbs were going off on a grassy knoll a hundred feet to the left, where a dozen athletes had formed a gymnastic pyramid, four layers of muscle men rising up thirty feet in the air. They had just gotten it completed, although the whole thing was trembling violently—and a few bulbs had snapped—when the entire stack of strong boys came tumbling down. They flew all over the place—fortunately for them, landing in thick grassed lots that had been left to add a little greenery in between all the steel and concrete.

234

"Here we go, Harrison," Carter announced, marching sharply to the left into an immense building that had lines of athletes going in and out. Once inside, Harrison let out a whistle. The place was huge, stretching as far as the eye could see, a twenty-foot-high, single-story affair that was a good football field long. There were counters of serve-yourself foods on every side of the room, and as they headed in deeper, Harrison heard conversations in every language under the sun— Russian, German, French, Spanish, Arabic. It was the Tower of Babel.

"There's too many fucking people here," Harrison shouted above the din to Carter, who was leading him down the main aisle past table after table of diners chewing lustily at piles of food. Everyone in the place was a horse. It was like being in a land of giants. Harrison had always felt big around people. Had always stood out in a crowd. And now many of them were nearly as big—and some bigger. And suddenly, for the first time in his life, he felt small.

"There's more damn races here than you could count on both of our fingers and toes put together," the black man said, laughing. "There's the Norwegian table, look at 'em all so blond and blue-eyed, like a remake of *Heidi* right here in our dining room. And there, that's the African contingent from Zimbabwe—brought their own medicine man." Carter laughed. "And what's more, I used him—and he works. Guy's Harvard-educated—uses a mix of Western medicine, African tribal herbs, voodoo dancing, and shiatsu that's out of this world. Over here," he went on as they neared the end of the aisle, "is the Chinese contingent. As you can see, most of the competitors tend to sit with their own, although there is more mingling at social gatherings— of which, as I'm sure you'll find out, there are plenty."

"I must be going crazy," Harrison said as they stopped at the end of the aisle and faced the long curved

235

counter which ran along the whole length of the wall. The other side of it held pot after steaming pot of food, and lines of people were going past taking huge helpings. "But I swear every table we passed was eating a different kind of food."

"You saw right, mister," Carter said as he waved to a redheaded woman who gave him a deep look as she passed by. "People gotta keep eating their own chow— otherwise they get sick, can't compete. So all these steaming vats of food there"—he pointed around the immense dining room, which fed only a quarter of the village, the rest having similar feeding stations in their own quadrants—"are the foods of a number of nationalities. It's great. You can eat Chinese one night, Upper Volta the next. Why, in this one week I've been here I'd say I've sampled at least a dozen different cuisines. It's one of the perks that makes all the hassle worth it. Anyway," he said, rubbing his big stomach, "what's it going to be?"

"I'll tell you, I feel like plain ol' American chow tonight," Harrison replied, looking at the line with anticipation.

"Glad you said that—me too." He led them to the right and walked another hundred feet, then slipped onto the end of one of the moving lines. They both filled their trays with "American" food—four cheeseburgers each, a whole bowl of fries, two malteds, two cups of coffee—and headed off to find a table. They had gone back into the table section, down one of the side aisles twenty yards or so, when Harrison noticed an attractive woman sitting at one of the tables. He didn't know why, but for a moment he was mesmerized by her—the way she looked, the way her hair fell. It was a perfect moment of beauty. Like a dream. And as time almost seemed to slow down, like in a Grade-B movie, he saw her eyes look up at him and fix on his face. Her mouth moved into a smile and there was a sudden glow of tenderness toward him that he could feel fly through the air. There was a palpable feeling of something primal between them. Something Harrison had felt only once before with such intensity.

Suddenly there was a loud bang and his attention was torn to the other side of the wooden table, where an absolutely immense man was rising and staring at Harrison, swallowing something which was disappearing, strands and all, down the great greasy wound of a mouth. The man was ugly and weighed 450, perhaps 500 pounds. He stood a good seven feet one, but Harrison wasn't counting.

"What you luk at, asshule?" the great bald muscle man screamed in broken English.

"Ignore that son-of-a-bitch," Carter said at Harrison's right. "He's Boris Bukowski, the Bull, the captain of the Bulgarian team. Nasty as a hyena in heat, and tough as they come. Always picking fights with Americans—and winning them. That's his girl you were making cutesy at. That's a no-no, Harrison."

"Sorry," the offending American said, totally embarrassed now as the entire table of gigantic Bulgarian wrestlers and weightlifters were all looking at him with forks and knives in their hands. They had expressions that said they wished they were carving him up instead of the thick sausage on their plates. "I thought I—I—recognized her," he said to them as he walked off. "Thought I knew her," he stuttered, walking quickly on as Carter motioned for him to just get the hell out of there. The Bull stared after the two Americans, who disappeared in the crowd. He looked hard as if sending out some magic spell of evil toward them. Then he flexed the muscles along each arm twice, as if to show the gods that the bastards would be squashed flat as moths against a windshield if they messed with him.

237

Chapter Twenty-Six

The *Svetlanya* docked in Brooklyn about midnight that night. The freighter had pushed nonstop through the storm, carrying a combined load of Bulgarian, Romanian, Polish, and East German equipment that had been forgotten on the first ship that had sailed weeks before due to bureaucratic bungling. As soon as it tied up, Eastern Bloc Games officials were at the dock to supervise the unloading of the equipment onto the dock and into the waiting trucks, which would rush it to the stadium in time for the following day's opening ceremonies and competitions. The nick of time was hardly the word for it.

American officials checked out the crates as they were lowered down in large nets lifted up from the cargo holds. Portable X-ray devices and geiger counters were run over everything by nearly a dozen Federal Immigration officials. Dogs were used as well, four of them sniffing madly at everything that went by. Nothing was found. Though one trunk was opened when a dog began barking and scratching at it. Sausages—a whole trunk full that one enterprising Polish fellow had planned to sell in New York. He knew handsome gourmet sausages could bring in tens of thousands of dollars. But the officials had to put his sausages in quarantine for six weeks as required by law. The sausage smuggler was led off crying.

Back in the ship, in the lowest and most forward section of the freighter, crouched the Bulgarian Samokov, clutching his 9-mm Turgenev Soviet Army Issue. He hid behind the wooden crate containing the trunk with the atomic device as tears rolled down his cheek.

"Oh, pleeze, no one come down here. I don't want to kill no one," he mumbled wildly to himself in Bulgarian, punctuated with various curses. Why had he ever become a terrorist? He was too cheerful a fellow to be a murderer. But he *had* joined the terrorist cell—to fight the rapprochement between the East and West which would allow bourgeois America to control the East—with its omnipresent fast-food joints, polyester clothing, brainwashing TV shows that destroyed the brain tissue of its own children. He had joined because his half-brother Pretyor had been killed by Israeli counterespionage agents in Madrid. Taken out like a dog in a doorway by the forces of Fascist Israel—no doubt with American help.

Samokov kept thinking of his dear wife, how she would cry if he was dead—or being in an American prison for the next forty years. How he missed her already. And again the thought sent a torrent of moisture cascading out of his eyes. He looked at the pistol and cocked it. He would—would *have* to kill if anyone came looking for him, for the bomb. He had sworn an oath of loyalty to the cell. To go against it was worse than death. They would track him down and torture him. He knew they would, and they were capable of it. There was no place on this earth that he would be able to hide if they wanted him.

Yes, he would—he would shoot. He had a silencer

on the pistol. If anyone—God help him—came down, he would kill them. There was no way out. He hefted the bottle he had taken from the kitchen. Cooking wine, but it would do. He ripped the cork out with his teeth and took a deep swig. Ah, it was good. Thank God for wine, for alcohol, man's best friend—even more than the dog. It made the madness, the pain of all this, a little easier to bear. Would make killing a little easier as well.

Outside and about twenty feet above where Samokov sat with his back against the crate, the last of the supplies were unloaded and placed aboard three huge transport trucks with Game insignias on their sides. The Federal inspectors milled around the dock until nearly three in the morning, bullshitting, swapping gossip about their colleagues as the last of the big trucks was loaded and driven out toward the Flushing Meadows Sports Complex, diesel stacks spewing black soot into the air. Then the inspectors loaded into three cars and headed off to Donovan's, a local gin mill that stayed open all night. Not a man had checked the ship. There was no reason to. Everything was off it.

Chapter Twenty-Seven

The sky over New York the morning of the Opening Day Ceremonies was the tawny pinkish color of a beautiful woman's breasts. The sun soared into the sharp skyscraper horizon like a glowing meteor as if it wanted to bring the day on fast, get things going. All around the immense stadium, groups of athletes, performers, even animals, were already gathering into their proper groups, into the formations they would enter the stadium in in several hours. Last-minute repairs were made as costumes ripped, banners snapped free of high poles, horses shed shoes as they kicked around, frisky in the brisk morning.

Already the crowds were starting to come into the parking lots, with a steady stream of cars. Subways were dropping off load after load—the Transit Authority had put on double the usual amount of trains for the duration of the event. The souvenir sellers were already out hawking their wares—everything from caps to complete jogging outfits, all with the Official Games emblem on them. The early bird catches the worm—and there were a hell of a lot of worms turning out on this fine morning.

But Harrison was not among the happy risers. He

was pulled from a deep relaxing sleep—the first he had had in over a month—by the sound of someone screaming in his ear, and was torn at the speed of light from a quite interesting embrace with a gorgeous young thing into a world where he was lying shivering in the middle of his bunk, the blankets on the floor and a huge black face about two inches from his nose, its teeth moving and its mouth saying nasty things that hurt his ears.

"Get up, asshole! What the hell's wrong with you? You got five minutes—five minutes, man—to get with your contingent. The Ceremonies are about to begin." It was Carter, the guy who had shown him to the dining hall the night before.

"What—what's going on?" Harrison stuttered sleepily, rubbing his puffy eyes as he sat up on the cot and reached for his sweatshirt at the foot of the bed. It was damn cold.

"Damn it, man, you come in here a week after everyone else. You almost get in a fight with the Bull the first hour you arrive, and now you want to know what the hell's going on?" The black wrestler shook his head from side to side. "Didn't they give you any briefing before you came to the barracks here? Nothing about your place in the parade—all that stuff?"

"No one said a thing."

"Well, you *gotta* be in it, pal. They left a space for one man in the ranks. Heaven knows what it'll look like." He shook his head again and then laughed once before returning his face to its previous scowling expression. "But we'll find out soon enough, won't we?"

Harrison dressed quickly, shaving the stubble off his face with an electric razor the Agency had given him—which had a few other features as well. He used a small cracked mirror that someone had placed along one windowsill, and had most of the whiskers off within about forty seconds. He looked down at his outfit and then over at Carter's. The other man's uniform looked a hell of a lot cleaner. Harrison must have spilled some damn food on his or something.

"Oh, come on," the immense black man said, slapping his hand over his head as he saw Harrison looking down forlornly at his soiled get-up. "No one will be able to see you from hundreds of yards away. Man, there's going to be a hundred thousand people out there today, all screaming and burping up their hot dogs. You really think they give a shit about whether or not you got doo-doo on your sweatshirt? Now come on!" Carter headed out the door, letting it slam back on its overtightened springs with a loud bang. Harrison threw down the razor—didn't even take another look in the mirror, for he knew he'd chicken out—his hair was all a mess too. He'd been meaning to get it trimmed. But now it all cascaded sloppily down around the nape of his neck. Some representative for the CIA. But then he wasn't here recruiting.

He ran and caught up with Carter about two hundred feet away. Even then he had to move his legs as fast as pistons to keep up with the man. Carter had a positively wild look in his eyes like they were on fire. But then this was the day he had been waiting years for, training his heart out for. The day he had kept in his mind like some sort of carrot to lure him on when he swore he couldn't move another muscle. Today—it was all coming to fruition.

Even as they approached the immense flat field that surrounded the massive stadium rising like Everest from the sea of people and cars all around it, they could hear the one hundred buglers who were announcing the official opening blow their long antique horns. The sound was incredible even from nearly a thousand feet

243

away. Masses of athletes were lined up everywhere in their own formations filling a square ten-acre field. Bands rushed around with instruments and batons, their sequined and fringed outfits sparkling and glittering. Harrison didn't know what the hell was going on, and the fact that everyone else did was starting to depress him a little.

"You're with my contingent," Carter said as the two men walked side by side through the crowds, Harrison sticking close by the black man's side. He knew that if he got lost he wouldn't even be able to figure out how to get into the stadium. He had never seen anything with so many levels and stairs and platforms all over the goddamn place. They reached the American wrestling contingent, about 160 men in two rows of 80 each. As Carter walked toward his spot in the middle of the line, Harrison saw the empty space that had been reserved for him on the very end of the left line. He walked quickly to the back and stepped into place, giving a friendly smile to a guy right across from him since he was going to need the bastard's help to get through all this.

The thick-browed face that returned the look, unsmiling, did not exactly look like the best prospect for friendship and aid. The guy looked like something left over from World War II with his face all mashed in and then sewn together again. Something horrible had definitely happened to him and Harrison didn't even want to know what the hell it was.

All around them, the long lines of participants were chafing at the bit to get going. The bugles blew again, followed by a roll of drums, and inside the stadium an incredible roar went up as over 100,000 people all screamed at once. Suddenly from above the opened sliding dome top, what looked like about a million balloons emerged in a flood that shot straight up.

Balloons of every color, representing all the races in the Games, poured out of the top as if the Apple Dome was a giant popcorn machine shooting out its product. As soon as the balloons hit the upper air above the stadium they shot off wildly in every direction, whipping around and bobbing up and down like corks in rapids. Within seconds the whole sky was filled as the balloons headed off in a general westerly direc27on, speading out as they flew.

The horns blew again and a line of horses about a hundred feet to the left of Harrison's crew began moving in through a large open gate in the side of the stadium. There were a good two hundred riders, two abreast atop big beautiful steeds, attired in cowboy glitter costumes to rival anything Liberace had ever dared put on. Harrison could see the horses file in as a roar went up from the crowd within that felt as if it were shaking the very walls of the Apple Dome.

"Uh, buddy," Harrison said, leaning over to the ugly-faced fellow. "Could you even give me a hint of what we're supposed to be doing when we go in there?"

"It be okay." The man smiled a toothy grin that just made him look even uglier. "We practice all week. *Me* know good," the guy said with pride, slapping himself on his barrel chest.

"Well, that's great." Harrison grinned back as he saw that he was going to have to get directions from someone whose brain power was a few rungs higher than an amoeba's.

"You watch me," the man said, as he pretended to march in place, swinging his arms back and forth in an exaggerated fashion like the guards at Buckingham Palace. "Show all the tricks." The fellow looked quite pleased that someone actually needed advice from him. It didn't happen too often.

"Yeah, I'll keep an eye on you," Harrison replied,

swinging his arms with hardly any motion at his sides. Somehow he didn't feel too optimistic about how this was all going to turn out. Soon it would be their turn. The last of the cowboy riders rode in with huge smiles plastered across their faces, lariats spinning in their hands. Next came the majorettes with skin-tight white satin outfits cut low, throwing their batons high in the air as they headed through the wide tunnel that led into the stadium. Then it was just one group of weight lifters, about a hundred of them—and then the American team's turn.

The line moved forward, and Harrison could see that they were in fact all marching with just as exaggerated an arm motion and high leg swing as his brain-damaged companion. Harrison tried to get into the rhythm but kept getting thrown off slightly. They headed into the tunnel and toward the stadium. The tunnel was two hundred feet long, but as they got to the halfway point the roar of the crowd inside began echoing along the concrete walls like they were all going to be blown away.

As Harrison emerged into the blinding brightness of the stadium, the sound was almost terrifying. He had never heard anything quite like it. All one hundred thousand people, just specks of color, were on their feet shouting and whistling and waving pennants, as flashbulbs flashed from countless locations like an invasion of fireflies in the cool morning. He tried to keep pace with the rest, and was just getting into the march motion when he heard a whistle blow from the team leader of the wrestlers. Suddenly they made a sharp turn to the left following some prearranged course. Harrison completely missed the turn, and just barely missed slamming into his ugly-faced pal, who was smiling happily, really into the whole thing. Harrison pretended, as his face turned red, to make a second turn, as if, *being* the end man, he was *supposed* to do something fancy. And then, double-timing it for four steps, he was able to catch up to the back end of the contingent.

He felt like an asshole, but he knew it was true what Carter had said—no one gave a shit about him, to say the least. For as the competitors marched in and birds and balloons flew above in the sky, the immense floor of the stadium, which could hold four football fields, began filling up with the army of humanity. It was impossible to see much of anything. It was more like watching some immense forest fire and just seeing the wall of flame, the instantaneous change of color and motion.

The whistle blew again and Harrison tensed himself, waiting to see which way they would go. They turned right on a sudden ninety-degree angle. Harrison almost made this one, just going a half step off, and he made up for that within two more steps. There—he was getting the hang of it. But he had just started feeling the slightest bit of confidence in his parade abilities when there was another sharp whistle up ahead and the entire contingent did a 180-degree turn on a dime. And started heading back in the opposite direction.

Harrison didn't have a chance. He slammed right into the guy in front of him who was now coming back toward him—a huge fat fellow with a big beard. Ordinarily Harrison would have been able to take even this big boy's advance, but he was off balance, his own feet sort of tangled up as he had been preparing to go either to the left or the right. The wrestler bowled him over, not even looking at him as if there were no one there. Harrison flew backwards, landing on his back. But he did do a rather nice back roll, coming up into a standing position so he was again alongside the end of the group, which was just walking by. Not a face looked at him, though he was sure in his embarrassment he heard some extra loud laughs and squeals coming from his side of the stadium.

But before he could even try to squeeze in somewhere, the whistle sounded again and they reversed direction once more. Harrison stood with his feet going as if he were part of it all, hands swinging out high in front of him until the procession had once again just gone past, and then he swung back onto the line, rejoining his ugly-faced compatriot, who smiled and moved ahead like he was heading for the promised land. The American contingent marched once more all the way across the wide field, and then came to a stop alongside the baton twirlers, who had formed a square about a hundred feet on a side and were twirling flaming batons high in the air, two at a time. It looked as if a fire shower was going on. To Harrison's relief they continued to march in place—but there were no more turns.

He let his guts relax just a little as he looked out over the spectacle that was unfolding on the floor of the Apple Dome. A goodly portion of the assembled participants were out on the field now, parading all over the place. They marched in circles and squares, moving in complex patterns, all intersecting with each other in a mobile spider web of flesh. It reminded Harrison of some of the Busby Berkeley dance routines he had seen on late-night TV in which masses of dancers turned into pure geometric designs.

The Eastern Bloc countries came in after the Americans had paraded through the gate. Russians, Poles, Romanians, Bulgarians . . . They marched all the way around the stadium once, their heads turned toward the crowd. Harrison got a good look at them as they passed by in front of his contingent. They were big. Huge might be more the word. They looked like they were sprinkling something more than yogurt on their bran fiber. They weren't taller than the Americans—but their muscles and flesh were so puffed out it looked as if they'd been pumped up with air. They all seemed as strong as Hercules. Harrison felt his stomach tighten as he realized that *those* were some of the friendly fellows he was going to be wrestling.

It took nearly half an hour for the last of the athletes to march in—a group of Japanese sumo wrestlers, all still non-professional, and thus eligible for the Games. It was unusual for wrestlers to compete under international rules. But these guys had worked out something. They were big, wearing traditional sumo gowns, beautiful flowing robes of silk with dragons and birds embroidered all over them. There were but ten of them, here to make a name for themselves and then go back to Japan to enter the competitive sumo world with a high profile. Everyone was here for the same thing—the prestige, the chance to leave the Apple Dome with accomplishments that could set one up for life. The whole world was a hustle now, Harrison thought a little cynically as he saw them stroll by like hippos just looking for trouble, sneering at the Americans. There were no more innocents. Well, he wasn't any different. He wouldn't be here at all but for the bucks.

When the entire stadium was filled to capacity and he swore they couldn't cram another body inside, the procession at last ceased and they all stood marching side by side. From out of the main gate came a runner, torch held high in his hand. The man had run from California to New York—and the loudspeaker began narrating the history of the games and how this man represented the link with the past, going back to the Greeks. The man ran to the center of the stadium and up to a large round swimming-pool-like structure in the center of the Apple Dome. He waited at its edge for a few seconds in what seemed like meditation, and then heaved the flaming torch right over the side and stood quickly back. The round structure about eight feet high and thirty in diameter suddenly erupted into flame. A cylinder of orange and yellow climbed up a good hundred feet into the air like the beginnings of a volcanic eruption. As the cheers of the crowd built, a great cloud of red, white, and blue smoke followed right behind the wall of fire. For a few seconds the cloud seemed to almost blot out the sky above as it rose into the air.

Suddenly, to everyone's astonishment, doves—thousands of them—flew out of the rainbow smoke and shot off like they were heading for all parts of the globe, countless wings flapping wildly. As the doves reached the top of the stadium and started over, lasers snapped on from the walls and created holographic images which swept back and forth above the field. Images of the flags of all the nations were represented. They appeared to be three-dimensional, somehow, and seemed to flap in the air, first one, then another. Then all eighty flags were blowing around, brightly colored holograms snapping in an illusory wind.

The stadium erupted as if it were going to shatter. And even Harrison was caught up in the emotion of the event, feeling tears edge into the corners of his eyes from the sheer primal power of the event. One thing he had to say for Americans. They sure knew how to throw a fucking party.

Chapter Twenty-Eight

The festivities went on for nearly an hour, with light shows and numerous speeches about the history of wrestling and weightlifting and how they represented the virility and power of a nation. The mayor of New York spoke about the fact that the only thing he ever wrestled with were "oversized bagels covered with lox and cream cheese." Then a slew of other officials went on about this and that. Harrison could barely hear over the PA, which was so loud that any kind of monotone or whining quality—which most of the politicans had—made their words get muddied imcomprehensibly when they emerged from the immense twenty-foot-high speakers that lined the entire stadium below the retractable dome cover.

At last more drums rolled, bugles sounded, and the gathered athletes began marching out again through different exit gates. It looked to the crowd above almost as if they were just sort of flowing away. Harrison's group was told to stay on the side once they got inside the exit tunnel—for the first wrestling matches were to be held almost immediately. The bullshit was over. The bloodshed was about to begin.

Harrison and his team came forward and waited just

inside the tunnel at the very edge of the competition field as entire wrestling rings were hauled in on wheels by small tractor like vehicles with tremendous motors that looked as if they could pull a building. Everything at the Games was mobile, automated, streamlined for quick change. There were so many kinds of events going on, changing numerous times over the course of a single day, that not a single thing could be a permanent or even semi-permanent fixture on the stadium floor. Thus everything was wheeled in and out on wide steel dollies pulled by tractors with huge deep-treaded tires that loomed high over the men who drove them.

Four rings were set up along the center of the stadium floor. There were too many contestants there —and too many spectators spread out over nearly a mile of surface area around the stand—to have only one match at a time. This was going to be a four-ring circus with different weight classes wrestling continuously all along the stadium floor in their respective wrestling rings. The massed crowds had paid their hard-earned dollars to get inside, for tickets were exorbitantly priced, the cheapest seats in the house starting at fifty dollars, and they damn well were going to get their money's worth. Within ten minutes after the last parader had left the field, the amazingly efficient grounds crew had set up one of the large rings right in the middle of the field. Harrison and his teammates were gathered around looking tense, talking nervously to one another. They would wrestle both foreign competitors and each other. The wrestling games were broken down by weight class, regardless of place of origin or any other criteria. Match-ups within the weight classes were random. That way there would be less possibility of favoritism, with a tremendous mix of judges and competitors. It was all in all a fairly

complicated process of elimination—tallied and pro-
cessed by computers. Otherwise it would have been
nearly impossible to keep track of it all. After all, over a
thousand wrestlers were competing, from every wrestling club in the world. It was the fairest way they had
figured out to make the Games really open-ended and
give sheer talent a chance to climb to the top regardless of political considerations.

The ring in the field in front of Harrison had been
completed within minutes, the built-in wheels beneath
it swinging up as large rubber pads descended like
landing pads from the bottom of a flying saucer. There
were two angled support beams at each corner that
slowly raised up on pneumatic tubing until they had the
ring at exactly the right height from the ground, and
then locked automatically in place. The driver of the
tractor vehicle walked around the ring testing the
ropes, kicking at the strut supports. Then he got up into
it and jumped up and down, and the crowd went
momentarily wild thinking the first match about to
begin. But once he saw that everything was holding up
fine he jumped down again. The floors were designed
with rows of springs underneath to be able to take a
sudden pressure of up to ten tons. That was something
on the order of an elephant jumping from forty feet up.

Harrison had scarcely settled himself into a vaguely
comfortable position, leaning against a steel fence that
separated several of the staging areas, when he swore
he heard his name being called. He rubbed his face and
wished desperately that he had some coffee, about a
gallon of it, when he heard it again blasting over the
huge PA.

"Rick Harrison of the U.S. Team will now enter
Ring Four at the south end of the stadium. The first
matches of the day, ladies and gentlemen, are about to
officially begin." The announcer read off the names of

the other competitors who were to report to their respective rings. Harrison walked slowly forward into the light streaming down from the 200-yard wide opening in the Apple Dome's ceiling, as the entire U.S. Super Heavyweight team followed him with their eyes.

"Oh, shit," one voice spat out. "It's the dude who fell right on his ass during the parade." The others laughed and sneered.

"He's going to represent us first? I can't fucking believe it," another said, slapping himself right in the jaw.

"Thanks guys, thanks a lot," Harrison replied, mock-saluting them, turning from side to side as he walked through the rest waiting for their turn. "It's really nice to get encouragement from your own team."

"Ah, leave him alone," Carter shouted just as Harrison walked off. "He's ready to get his head busted out there in front of two billion people watching this thing, just like the rest of us." The others quieted down and looked on, their hearts beating as anticipation of their own matches grew. Harrison paled as he reached the ring. The crowd cheered wildly, jumping to their feet as the first wrestlers walked out from their various spots up and down the long field and entered the four rings. "Two billion people," Harrison thought, growing anxious all of a sudden in spite of himself. Was it possible? Probably. An event like this with entrants from around the planet would attract an immense crowd. And what with satellite hook-ups and TV sets even in the most primitive villages, there might well be something in the neighborhood of four billion pairs of eyes watching his every move.

Suddenly he felt a kind of stage fright, a paranoia sweep over him. It was so *much* attention—the masses of humanity all screaming like banshees, the choppers and blimps overhead all crowding for camera room, and the TV cameras around the field on their own mobile tractors zooming around trying to get every angle. There was motion and sound everywhere. He felt dizzy. They hadn't prepared him for any of this back in the basement spy school. He tried to relax himself as he climbed up into the ring. He put his hand on the top rope and jumped right up over it, landing inside the ring. The crowd nearest him gave out with a roar of approval, which made Harrison relax just a little. At least *some* of them were on his side.

But the instant that he laid eyes on the overgrown, steroided super cruiserweight who climbed up at the other end—a good 325 plus, with arms the size of small tree trunks, and a face that said, "Run, sucker"—Harrison again wondered if $30,000 was going to be enough, even for a retainer. But Harrison couldn't back out now—he was in it for the duration. The man climbed into the far corner of the ring and looked at Harrison with a sneer. He spat, and a gob of stuff flew out of his mouth and down into the center of the mat. So it was going to be one of those matches, Harrison realized as he limbered up by jumping up and down in place. The blue cotton/spandex bodysuits they wore covered everything well enough, but it was cool out and he could feel goosebumps along his legs and arms. Well, he'd be warm soon enough. That was for damn sure.

"Ladies and gentlemen," a referee said, coming to the center of the ring and speaking into a wireless microphone that was attached around his neck. "It is my honor to present the first of the Super Heavyweight bouts. In the right corner, Rick Harrison of the U.S. team. Heavyweight U.S. western division holder . . ." Yeah, right, Harrison thought, groaning inwardly. Only it was about twelve years ago. Oh, well, what the hell did he care. What were they going to do—lock him up for lying on his resumé? Anyway, the CIA had supplied all relevant information to the Games committee. They could sue them. "And in the left hand side of the ring is Alfonso Nastrioni of Italy." A cheer went up a few hundred yards off from the Italian section. All along the stadium, cheers were erupting as different competitors were introduced in their respective rings.

"Now, you know the rules," the ref said. He was a ruddy-faced Irishman with white, close-cropped hair that stood up only about a half inch or so as if it had been sheered off by a table saw. "Clean breaks when I say so. Take down is worth two points, shoulder pins three. Foul takes away a point. The best two out of three bouts—maximum duration of each bout is five minutes. Any lack of immediate response to my commands will result in disqualification from the bout. Got all that?" Both men nodded yes. The ref stepped back, swung his hand down as a whistle sounded, and the first match of the cruiserweight-plus class was on. The Games were under amateur rules, which were different from the pros. No eye-gouging, testicle-kneeing . . . The rules were a mix of Graeco-Roman and Freestyle, the two main international wrestling styles. The International Style—basically all types of throws using hips, shoulders, and wrists were allowed. As well as using legs and the lower part of the body for trips, power takedowns, whatever. It allowed the wrestlers a wide latitude of moves and counter-moves. And since many of them had trained in the particular styles popular in their own countries, it promised to be an interesting week as the contestants battled it out.

Harrison walked forward and locked arms with Nastrioni. The man looked right into his eyes with a laugh and said something nasty in Italian, which Harrison didn't understand but knew somehow had to do with his lineage. Then the ref was standing right in front of them, and he pulled his hand down hard as an electronic gong sounded off next to the ring.

In a flash Nastrioni charged forward trying to just overpower Harrison. He outweighed him by a good sixty pounds and was lower to the ground. And it seemed to work for a few seconds as the American was pushed straight backward across the ring a good seven feet. But just before the Italian could squash Harrison against the ropes, his victim somehow stepped to the side, and using Nastrioni's own momentum, flung him hard into the corner. The huge Sicilian hit the ropes at thirty miles an hour and pushed them out a foot or so. All the air went out of his stomach, which was pushed in by the ropes. Then he came flying backwards as if shot out of a slingshot, and flew a good eight feet before he fell right down on his ass. The ref pointed his finger at the scorekeeper on the side of the ring, who pushed a button. A small beeping was emitted, signaling that Harrison had just received two points for the take-down—making the opponent fall to the mat.

Harrison was on Nastrioni in a flash, grabbing him from behind. He ripped Nastrioni's left arm up behind the man's back. The instant Harrison felt the arm lock up in place he reached around and got the other. The double arm lock from behind was an almost unbreak-able hold. But as he pulled back on the right arm Harrison found out it wasn't going to be that easy. For displaying incredible strength, Nastrioni suddenly leaned forward and dropped down on one knee, so that he swung Harrison right up and over him. The American had to let go of the double lock as he flew into the air. He shifted his weight and tucked his hips fast, not wanting to slam down on the mat and give two points to the Italian. And somehow, like a cat spinning in midair, he was able to land on his feet. The crowd let out with a roar off to the side. Already they were

257

starting to get their money's worth—and it hadn't even been one minute yet.

The two men faced off again, and then charged forward going for the grapple. But as Nastrioni reached out to grab his opponent's arms, Harrison slid down beneath him and threw one arm around one of the massive thighs. He reached around and grabbed one of the descending hands trying to strangle him, and suddenly stood up into a Fireman's Carry. The man felt like a baby elephant on Harrison's shoulders, but Harrison was able to rise to his full height and then turn around three times in a spin. With a great grunt he threw Nastrioni straight forward, still holding onto the arm and leg. When the big Italian hit the mat Harrison was able to pull the arm and leg toward each other so that the man was on his side locked in place like a roped steer. The ref raised his hand signaling a full pin, the bell rang, and the American crowd behind Harrison went wild. Thousands upon thousands of spectators rose and waved little American flags. Down the field someone else had apparently won—this one from the Eastern Bloc, for the Polish contingent started cheering up a storm.

The ref sent the two men back to the center of the ring. That was only the first bout. The best two out of three would determine the winner. They locked arms again, and this time Harrison could see that the Italian was on the defense, moving much lower to the mat so it would be harder to lift him. His eyes looked like they wanted nothing more in this life than to pound Harrison's face into red relish. The electronic gong sounded and the two went at it. Harrison went for a hip throw trying to turn his body to the side to get the leverage. But he had turned only halfway when Nastrioni dropped to the mat like a rock and grabbed hold of Harrison's right calf. He stepped back, suddenly pulling it up and toward him so that Harrison was instantly hopping on one leg and hobbling wildly. The Italian laughed as he stepped backwards and walked around in a wide circle dragging his victim, as if exhibiting him to the crowd. The Italian section cheered lustily. But the Americans booed back just as loud.

Nastrioni's very showmanship was his big mistake. For it allowed Harrison to regain his balance for a second on his other leg, and, letting it relax for an instant, he dropped down about a foot. Suddenly he sprang up, letting the leg uncoil like a steel spring, and shot right up into the air, kicking out with the leg the Italian wasn't holding. Nastrioni saw the foot coming right in toward his face but he couldn't do a thing about it—except let out a little gasping sound. Then Harrison's wrestling boot slammed into the brow of the 325-pounder and sent him flying backwards. As he released the leg he had been holding Harrison was able to snap it up in the air, joining the one he had just kicked with. He swung his hips in and tried to relax just as he had done so many times in the Agency gym with the Destroyer. The flip took him over, but not onto his feet. Harrison landed halfway down on his back and left shoulder. He was lucky the mat was padded and cushioned as thickly as it was for he slammed into it hard, with a thwack that even the crowds could hear, and a murmur went up.

He let out his breath as he hit to absorb the impact, and then rolled right over, not stopping for an instant so they couldn't call it a takedown—or so he hoped. But when he came to a standing position and spun around like a top, his hands extended to take on the charging rhino of a man, there was no one there, no one standing anyway. The kick had sent the Italian backwards until he had crashed into the corner post.

259

Somehow as he had fallen down, knocked out cold, he had managed to entangle his arms and legs in the various ropes so he looked like a sort of human pretzel, his head hanging to one side, his tongue draping out of his mouth as if looking for an insect to snap up. The ref and a doctor who had been seated at a long table on one side of the ring had already jumped up and were trying to pull the man free.

And as Harrison saw the Italian's eyes open groggily, he breathed a sigh of relief. He didn't want to seriously hurt anyone at the games. Suddenly there was a cheer that rocked the stadium. And the pounding feet of fifty thousand as the results of Harrison's bout were announced. And then bulbs were going off everywhere, and fingers pointing at him and up at the air, and people screaming, "Number one, number one!" And for a moment in the midst of all the excitement Harrison felt confused and looked around to see who they were pointing at. And then he realized it was *him*. And that he had won. The first U.S. winner in the whole damn Games. And they were cheering him. Rick Harrison. And in a way, winning that first match was just about the proudest moment Harrison had ever known. And knowing that the TV cameras were undoubtedly trained on him from fifty directions, he looked up toward one, raised his fist into the air, and silently mouthed the words with his lips.

"Thanks, Destroyer, thanks, Captain Lou." Four hundred miles away in the underground world of D2, an aging wrestler's eyes filled with tears for the first time in many, many years.

Chapter Twenty-Nine

Harrison exited the ring, jumping out right over the top rope and then down to the stadium floor in one fluid motion. The crowd roared. Maybe Colonel Parker had been right. Maybe he would get a kick out of all this. As he walked back along the firm astroturf to the American team, which waited on the sidelines, he could see that their faces were different now. They slapped him on the back, smiling. "Way to go, man." "All right, motherfucker, all right." "Where you bin hiding?" And assorted other comments that brought a big grin to Harrison's face. He had gotten them all pumped up. Not just because he had won. But because it set a precedent for the rest. It was a good omen in a sport that had plenty of omens.

Harrison stood back and watched as the next American walked up to the ring and faced his opponent, a tall and muscular Albanian. They linked arms and the contest started. They seemed to be fairly equally matched, and began dragging each other all over the ring trying to gain the leverage, the advantage. Harrison cheered his man on, along with the rest of the Super Heavyweight team, their faces red with excitement.

And so it went throughout the afternoon. Twenty matches were held and the Americans won thirteen of them, the highest percentage of the afternoon for any team. The American crowds were ecstatic, positively beside themselves with joy. For sports brings out the collective unconsciousness of a people, makes them feel a deep pride in the physical abilities of their nation, their people. Makes them walk a little taller.

After a late lunch of way too many hot dogs à la Creole, Harrison returned to the stadium and saw that the rings were already gone for the day and in their place were ground mats and weightlifting equipment. Different weight classes of lifting were being announced as he came out of the athletes' tunnel. His special pass enabled him to walk along the side of the stadium field and see the various displays of strength, the immense lifters with their great bulks and fire hydrant arms that made even many of the wrestlers look like ninety-eight pound weaklings. Some of the weight guys looked like they could just wrap their arms around a tree and rip it right out of the ground, roots and all. Harrison was thankful he wasn't going to have to face any of these elephantine fellows.

Or was he? He stopped as he recognized the baldheaded Bulgarian who had given him the evil eye the day before in the dining room. Harrison watched as the loudspeaker announced the man, Boris Bukowski, the Bull, all 485 pounds of him, and ninety-nine percent looked like muscle. The bastard dwarfed even the giants he had seen down the way. It wasn't just that the Bull was big—which he was, nearly as wide as a table with shoulders that could have rented out as condo studios—but he looked absolutely invulnerable, his neck nonexistent, just the huge head sinking down into the top of the massive chest. Even the man's eyes were sort of pulled back into his face, hiding beneath multiple folds of flesh. He was without question the strongest man that Harrison had ever seen.

He watched as the Bulgarian walked over to the thick platform on which sets of weights were resting and gripped his hands on the bar holding huge metal plates at each end. As the crowd watched breathlessly he squatted down, seemed to focus on another dimension, his eyes staring straight ahead, his lips pulling back to reveal brown half-rotted stumps of teeth. Then he pulled up hard, and as he rose into a standing position, swung the bar around and up so it rested against his chest gripped in both hands. Setting his feet just right, he half screamed as he suddenly swung the weight up, stepping beneath it at the same instant. The poundage flew up over his head—and held. His arms were stretched up and Harrison could see the tremendous muscularity. Bukowski held the weights without making his legs tremble, an indication that the lifter wasn't being tested to his limits.

A gong sounded, indicating he had held it the legal time, and Bukowski sneered and held it another three seconds—just to show he could. Then he threw it down from the air as if just discarding the thing in disgust. He turned and walked away from it before it had even dropped down onto the mat with a great slam. The crowd ate it up and went completely bananas. The man had an aura, a persona that was electrifying. Gulping hard, Harrison stepped back out into the track and headed on.

As he hit midfield, he saw that the women's weight-lifting was going on ahead. Powerfully muscular women stood on rubber mats dusting their hands with powder as they prepared to make their lifts. Again Harrison was goo-goo-eyed, but out of lust, not paranoia. For they were gorgeous. As curvaceous a lot of females as one was likely to see. Like the men, some

had overdone it, with great bulging arms and thighs—
unquestionably from steroid use, which gave the body
a ballooned look, like bread shot full of air. But others
were just plain beautiful.

And strong as well. For as he watched a few of them,
he saw them already hitting weights in the hundreds of
pounds in the overhead press. He was sure records were
going to be set during the course of these Games. And
at that instant he realized that he actually *did* represent
his country. And that what he did mattered. And
suddenly the whole thing seemed a thousand times
more serious and important and he felt his whole
stomach tighten up into a knot. And wished that it was
still a joke to him. It had been easier to deal with it that
way. But it wasn't. And wouldn't be again.

Harrison walked down the sidelines trying to get a
feel for where everything was. One of the first rules of
the CIA training had been to familiarize yourself with
the terrain of operation. Which made sense to
Harrison. Besides, he got to look at all the girls. He had
nearly reached the far end of the field, marveling at its
size, its high-tech features everywhere—built-in lights,
specially designed tilt seats that filled the stands,
underground sprinklers, lasers, even hidden astroturf-
covered platforms that rose up out of the ground. The
place was a miracle of modern engineering.

Suddenly, as he scanned the place, he saw her. The
woman who had so hypnotized him the night before.
She was a lifter too, and was just leaning down over a
bar with two gargantuan weights at each end. It looked
impossible for her to make the lift. Even from the fifty
yards or so that separated them Harrison could see her
face, the look of absolute determination on it. How
alive she looked as she squinted up her eyes, gritted her
teeth, and focused everything inside her. Suddenly
she snapped the bar up, and then without hesitation

brought it up over her head. It looked like the weights were bigger than she was as she held them straight overhead, her legs shaking from side to side beneath the great pressure. And just as she completely set, her eyes caught Harrison's through the crowd, for the contests were on raised platforms that rose up out of the grounds, hers set at about six feet so the audience could see. And their eyes locked for just a moment—which again felt like a thousand years. It's strange what happens to time when your heart is beating double time.

Then the time gong beeped electronically and she let the weight drop down, stepping back from it with a proud smile on her face as she paraded around the mat, her hands held high in victory over her head. She wasn't that big, didn't even seem to have a hell of a lot of muscles, as far as Harrison could see. Just a body that was in incredible shape, and a strength that came from within, hidden, almost mysterious. And Harrison felt the stirrings of something in his chest, his guts, the back of his skull, that he hadn't felt for long time. Then the crowd erupted in a thunder of applause and he joined in, wondering if he was heading for another fall. A full nelson of the heart.

Chapter Thirty

If the daytime scene at the Games had been wild, the nighttime had a Mardi Gras aspect to it, with the entire stadium floor, which had been completely cleared of equipment, filled with athletes for the Official Wrestlers' and Weightlifters Get-Acquainted Party. A chance for the competitors to meet and get to know one another a little, see that they were the same—inside. Part of the Games' intent and meaning was to promote world peace and understanding. A few drinks, some rock bands playing around the stadium floor, a tidal wave of men and women looking for some fun—and you damn well would have some understanding going on.

Peace—that was another matter. For fights seemed to erupt throughout the place. A huge Samoan here accusing some Armenian there of winking at his girl; a Czech weightlifter grabbing the nose of an Australian wrestler for spilling his beer. But for the most part it was fairly good-natured roughhousing, with just a few perfunctory slaps or holds exchanged before the combatants became old drinking buddies, arms around each other's shoulders singing Beatles songs and getting drunker by the minute. Harrison made his way through the crowd holding a big stein of draught beer—pretty good stuff at that—in his hand. It was good to see people having a good time. There wasn't a hell of a lot of that commodity around these days.

Some pneumatic platforms had been raised up out of the astroturf for liquor bars to be set up, and every hundred yards or so along the vast stadium floor rock bands cranked out loud music in four different languages. Harrison felt himself getting in the mood of it all, and he began rocking back and forth as he headed through the crowds winking at pretty girls here and there, who all winked back. He walked past the French band—okay, but he liked the harder stuff. Then there was a band all decked out in glitter costumes singing out tunes that must have been in Norwegian or something because of the large number of model-quality blondes who stood around conversing in an incomprehensible language.

At the far end of the stadium he began hearing more like what sounded like *his* music—hard-driving rock with some maniac on stage screaming out lyrics that went something like:

He's a rocker he's a roller, see him bounce from
    rope to rope-a,
He's a wrestler, out of his waaaay!
Well he goes so fast that you just can't catch him,
He's a wrestler, out of his waaaay!
How many men will he pin todaaaaay?
Wrestling U.S.A, Wrestling U.S.A!

They were really cranking it out with a full band of drums, bass, two synthesizers, and two guitars. The lead guitarist was a weightlifter whose hair was shaved mohawk style. He wore spiked jewelry around his wrists, ankles, shoulders, and neck. Harrison got into

267

the mood as the band took off into the stratosphere, their notes all screaming and blending together as the super-reverbed drums slammed through his very bones. He started jumping with the other dancers around the field, like kangaroos with a little too much liquor all bouncing around.

He looked up at the band while the speaker throbbed in his ear about twenty feet away as if he were listening to a jet plane take off from inside the engine. Suddenly he did a double take—the guitarist was a guy he had played with in his last band before it had fizzled. He raised his arm and caught Calhoun's eye just as the tune ended. The guy whispered a few words in the lead singer's ear, and the punked-out guy nodded, then spoke into the microphone in front of him.

"Ladies and gentlemen, we're lucky tonight to have with us the winner of the first bout for the U.S. this afternoon—Rick Harrison. wrestler extraordinaire. And we're told he's a rock and roll singer himself and would like to come up and play a couple of numbers right now. Come on now, give him a big hand," the spiked-haired guy said, clapping his hand together. Shit, Harrison thought as the dancing crowds all around the field, literally thousands of them, all yelled and roared for him to go on. Harrison walked up the collapsible stairs on the side of the raised platform and took a guitar from a stand, walking to the center mike.

"Do you know 'Don't Fear the Reaper'?" Harrison asked the band members. Enough heads nodded yes for him to know they could fake it. He started playing hard as he looked out over the crowd. As the music began building he could see them start to rock all around him.

"This song's dedicated to former President Jimmy Carter, who was attacked one day while out canoeing in the rivers of Georgia, by a wild rabid rabbit which came right at the President's boat with murder in his eyes—and had to be dispatched by Secret Service agents. 'Don't Fear the Rabbit.'"

> Oh, they say this life is crazy and it's ready to explode.
> I've got to stop that rabbit before he gets into my boat,
> His flashing teeth, his glowing eyes, they burn into my heart.
> I've got to kill that rabbit before he tears this world apart.
> Oh, oh I want to know why they sayyyyy
> There is no way to kill the rabbit.
> Ohh, kill the rabbit.
> Don't fear the rabbit . . .

By the time the band ended, the whole place was going crazy singing along with Harrison, "Don't fear the rabbit, kill the rabbit." Some of them who had had a few too many began hopping around like rabbits snarling and mock-biting at each other. Harrison slammed a quick power chord to end it and dropped to one knee, throwing his arm up and his head down in a dramatic pose. The dancers roared with approval and shouted for more. But one song was plenty. He jumped back down right off the stage, dropping down about seven feet to the ground, where hands slapped him on the back as he walked through the crowd. Well, Parker had said he wanted Harrison to be "high-profile." That was the whole idea of deep penetration. To become well known, blend in through fame rather than anonymity. It looked like he was quickly achieving things in that direction.

He had walked about twenty yards looking for a refill at one of the long bars filled with just about every beverage known to man when a hand caught him at the shoulder and a voice said in what sounded like a bad German accent, "Looking for zumzing, zailor?" Harrison turned fast. It was *her*. The woman he had seen twice now, who had already begun slicing little cuts into his heart.

"I—I—" he stuttered, not sure how to answer the question.

"The cat has svallowed your tongue?" she asked, winking heavily. Her manner was so strange that Harrison was somewhat taken aback. She seemed to be trying to talk like Marlene Dietrich as a Berlin whore in some thirties movie.

"I thought you were Bulgarian," Harrison blurted out, staring right into her crystal blue eyes as the crowds surged all around them, forming chains now as they linked up arms with one another into a long line that began snaking its way around the center of the stadium.

"Oh, zo you know who I yam?" She laughed. "The Americans have been zpying on ze Bulgarians again. Well, do you know my name az vell?" She didn't wait for an answer. "I yam Natasha Stanislau, Champion of Bulgarian Women Weightlifters." She tossed her long black hair disdainfully over her shoulder. She was proud, very proud. Like a wild mare.

"Yes, I must confess," Harrison said with a shy grin, "I *have* been spying on you. But why—do you speak with a German accent—and not a very good one at that?"

"I learned English vatching old American zirtiez filmz. My father iz a commissar in Bulgaria—ve had a VCR. But only old moviez vere ever available—from the zirtiez—lotz of Marlene Dietrich and Mae Wezt. Ztuff like zat." She laughed, and Harrison liked how it looked.

"Well, I was just heading over to refresh myself, Ms. Natasha Dietrich," Harrison said with a little sway to his body. He had already had three drinks on his way up the field.

"Vell, don't mind if I tramp along for ze ride," Natasha answered, swaying her hips at him. With her tight-fitting skirt and navy blue sweater filled exceedingly well she looked like a vision from heaven. She took his arm and they walked to the drinking station, where he got her a Thirsty Savage, a drink of his own concoction which he directed one of the bartenders to make. Bourbon, apricot brandy, cherry coke, and vodka—mix well in shaker, drink. "To your health," he said as he handed her one and took his own. They clinked glasses. "May all your weights feel like feathers."

"And may all your opponentz haf only vun leg." Natasha grinned back. They threw back their glasses, and she nearly gagged but took the whole damn thing down as he did—in fact finishing first.

"Zat's it?" she said, wiping her perfect lips that kept looking more and more inviting. "My village—zat ztuff iz fed to the infantz az baby formula." She laughed, hitting herself on the chest. "Ve carry two-hundred-proof vodka at all timez out in the znow. Need something to varm the zoul." She laughed again, her cheeks flushing slightly, and Harrison swore his heart was dropping into his toes. He felt feverish in her presence, her eyes seemed so magnetic, like he was just losing himself in their seductive depths. Suddenly she reached forward and threw her arms around him. Her lips pressed hard against his and for a few seconds they were locked in a tight embrace. Then she pushed him away and stood back, wiping her mouth with the sleeve of her sweater.

"Zer, big boy. Vat do you zink of zat?"

271

"I think I want more," Harrison said, his eyes a little crazy with lust. Suddenly he sensed movement behind him and turned to see Bukowski, the Bull, charging like one. Luckily for Harrison the man was intoxicated and came in with his head down, face red, ready to slam right into Harrison's chest and rip through it. The American planted his foot as the Bulgarian giant built up to a terrific speed, bowling people in the crowd out of the way. At the last possible second, Harrison turned aside, and helped Bukowski on his way by pushing him hard on the back as he shot past. The big man didn't have a chance to stop himself, and flew right up onto the bar, sliding into and sending flying countless bottles, which spun off in every direction like tenpins as he glided about twenty feet and then down at the other end of the bar onto the astroturf.

Harrison turned to see Natasha laughing at the sight. "Come on, ve'd better get out of here," she said, still laughing to Harrison. "He'll be mad az a hatter ven he getz up." They rushed giggling like children through the crowd all the way to the far side of the field. Within seconds they were far away from the drunken Bukowski.

"I thought you were hooked up with him," Harrison said at last when they slowed to a walk after about a hundred yards.

"Ah, zo you haf been zpying on me," she said, scolding him again.

"Why not? You seem to know a lot about me." Harrison replied a little defensively, if only because he *was* in fact a spy. Though as far as he knew he wasn't after her—at least for security reasons.

"Vell, in fact, your intelligence information iz vrong," she said still in her German accent. Harrison realized it was the way she really spoke English. "I'm not vid zat big ugly mule. He'z been hafter me ze whole trip here—ve are all on the plane, everyvere togezzer. Ze other men on ze Bulgarian team are zcared to effen talk vit me, becauze of dat mskynvka! But you—you're not afraid," she said, looking at him with undisguised admiration.

"Whoa there, sugar-babe-ski," Harrison said as they zigged and zagged through the dancing crowds. "I wouldn't say I'm not afraid of the Bull. Any man who said that would be a liar. Let's just say I'm willing to take the risks."

"Ze riskz for vat?" she asked coyly, taking his arm again as they reached the end of the stadium field.

"You," he answered looking her squarely in the eye. Every time he looked at her Harrison swore she looked more beautiful. There was something sixteenth century about her, almost an innocence, a red-cheeked lustiness that most woman today didn't have.

"Come on," she said softly. Harrison didn't ask where they were going. He didn't care, if it was with her. She led him out of the stadium grounds, and down through a long tunnel that led out to a section of the living quarters. She seemed to know her way well around the place, going through this tunnel, that overpass. It took about ten minutes for them to reach the training building where she and her teammates held their workouts. There wasn't a soul present as they came in through the back door, slowly, checking for security. But it was lax tonight—for better or worse.

"Where are we—" Harrison began to say, but she put her finger to his lips and just led him on. They passed through a large matted gymnastics room, and then on into some smaller rooms in the back, each with its own mattress. She took him into one and slammed the door behind her. She turned the key in the lock and then turned to look at Harrison.

"Ve won't be bozzered." Her eyes were like twin fires

now, her cheeks all flushed and excited. And Harrison was too. She was bold, extremely so. She pulled him quickly over to the small metal-framed cot on the floor that was used for massages, and down onto the mattress, grabbing hold around him, groaning with passion even as he reached to hold her. The bed creaked beneath them, not used to the weight or the energetic gropings that were occurring on it. She was like a wildcat. Ripping at him, pulling him hard against her. And she was strong too. He still couldn't comprehend how such a package of beauty and softness could possess the power that she did.

"How'd you get so strong?" he asked with a laugh, pulling away from her for a moment since he felt like he was in a bear hug. He unclasped one of her hands from its hold around his back so as to relieve the pressure on his larynx.

"Vork, all ze time on family'z farm ven I vaz growing up," she answered, lying beneath him, her hair all spread out, her eyes radiant as she looked up at him with burning pupils. "Lifted tree ztumpz, carried balez of hay, carried calvez and goatz who vere zick. Ate lotz of meat, barley, und beer. It zust zort ov happened." She laughed and pulled him down. "Who carez." She laughed wildly. Suddenly she was ripping at his clothes, and he at hers. And they were naked, pressing against one another with all the mad desire of soon-to-be lovers. The way she felt in his hands, tasted on his lips was driving Harrison to the point of sheer madness. He had always enjoyed a fling here and there, and had never had trouble getting a woman. But this one—there was something special about her. They kissed passionately as she squirmed beneath him like a snake all around his arms and legs, stroking his chest as she made little mewing noises interspersed with loud raw throaty growls like some animal in heat. Then he

274

began to go into her, but she stopped him and said a little nervously and drunkenly, "zafe zex, dahling." She reached around her with one hand into her skirt pocket and pulled out a foil package. Harrison hadn't seen one of them for a while and he looked at it, not really liking the things. But he knew she was right. There was too much weird junk flying around these days not to be careful. Anyway, it was her body, she had a right to protect it. She was just sharing it with him for a night. He took the rubber guardian and put it on his arching manhood. Then she took the stiffness in her hands like a precious wand—and guided him home. The cause of international friendship was advanced mightily that night.

Chapter Thirty-One

By three in the morning there was not a soul stirring around the freighter *Svetlanya,* other than the single night guard who walked along the deck. He checked his watch, and when he saw that it was exactly three, walked over to the port side and signaled with a small penlight down to the dock. A speck of light answered him and the seaman breathed a sigh of relief. He turned quickly and motioned for a second man hidden in the shadows to operate the net that raised and lowered the ship's cargo. It cranked and hummed as the net in the cargo hold below was raised slowly up, and then turned around and set gently down onto a concrete wharf some forty feet below it. Four figures in the darkness undid the net and signaled for the operator above to lift it out of the way. The gears scraped for a second, and then the net shot back up into the air and disappeared over the freighter's side.

"Come on," one of the men on the dock said. They wore ski masks over their heads, with slits cut out for the eyes. They couldn't afford to be seen right now. Not when they were so close to the completion of their mission.

Professor Markus turned to the table-shouldered

Bulgarian who stood beside him. "Let's move it, Bukowski. We haven't got a second to spare. The guards should be making their rounds within—"

"Hold it right there," a voice suddenly yelled out from the shadows. "What the hell is going on here?" As the masked figures turned, two guards, wearing gray uniforms and holding .45's in their hands, marched forward from out of the darkness.

"Well, what have we got here?" one of the guards, a black man in his forties, asked, with a big smile spreading across his face. "Wool masks, a crate snuck over the side from our Commie boat here. Why, I think I'm about to get a promotion. Both of us, Willie," the guard said, looking over toward his partner, who stood nervously fingering the pistol, not quite as sanguine about the prospects as his partner.

As the guard turned his head for just that instant to talk, Bukowski moved forward like a striking snake. He whipped the side of his fist around in an arc that slammed into the man's head, cracking the whole side of his skull to the brain as pink tissue began oozing out. He froze in mid-sentence and slid down to the wharf as though his legs had turned to useless pieces of dead meat—which they had. The other guard tried to get a bead on someone—but the four figures instantly spread out in the shadows and he didn't even know which way to turn.

He didn't have to worry about it for long. Suddenly the huge man who had just taken out his partner was on him from the side. The Bulgarian threw both hands around the guard's skull and pulled hard, twisting it around. The entire head seemed to revolve almost 180 degrees so that its bulging purple eyes were looking straight backwards. There were all kinds of snaps and cracks, and then blood exploded out of the dead mouth, eyes, and nose. Bukowski let the guard drop to the dock, where the corpse shook violently like a fish out of water, flopping around the dock in violent spasms, his head still turned around at a horrible angle.

"Move it, man, move it," Professor Markus hissed in the darkness as the men pushed the crate forward on a dolly. They got it onto a metal platform at the back of the truck they had parked a hundred feet off. A lever was thrown, the lift rose up to the level of the truck floor, and the crate was wheeled inside. The steel door quickly closed down behind it. The Professor quickly penned a note and tore a page from his small omnipresent spiral notebook. He pushed it into the hands of one of the dead guards. Then he jumped into the truck, onto the seat beside the driver, and motioned him forward.

"Get the hell out of here!" They both ripped off their ski masks as the truck moved forward. The driver was a little fast and the wheels skidded making squeals.

"Slow, slow, don't attract attention," the Professor barked. "We're just another dirty truck carrying pickups for the Salvation Army," Markus said, referring to the words painted on the outside of the truck. "*They'd* have no reason to go fast." He coughed into a handkerchief that he lifted suddenly to his mouth. And the driver, Karlson, the black chemist, could see the blood come out. The man was getting sicker. They all were. The Japanese had been left behind in Marseilles. One of the Palestinians was dead, had been weighted down and dropped into the ocean. And the rest of them—though none of them dared talk about it with each other after the "disappearance" of the frauleins—knew they were dying. The world would soon see their devotion, their willingness to go to the grave.

"Good God, Professor Markus," Karlson suddenly said, his eyes bulging in horror as he drove down a

278

darkened street heading toward the expressway. "You're—you're glowing." He pointed one hand toward the Professor's right hand, which was holding the handkerchief. The whole hand from the base of the palm to the end of the fingers was glowing an iridescent bluish green. It reminded Karlson of when he had squashed fireflies on his hands when he was a child at camp. Only these weren't fireflies. The Professor pulled the hand away, slamming it into his jacket pocket.

"Mind your own damn business, why don't you!" Markus said, snapping at the black man. "Keep your eye on the road! If you veer, or crash—you'll ruin the entire operation after all this work and effort."

"Sorry," Karlson said, snapping his head forward. He didn't want to incur the man's wrath. One never knew just how much it might take for him to decide that Karlson was more valuable to the cause dead than alive. Karlson suddenly wondered if *he* glowed. He had been spitting up more blood every day. Three of his teeth had fallen out in the last twenty-four hours. He felt drugged, as if everything was running in slow motion. And though his body had ached terribly for weeks, now it seemed to have cooled out and he hardly felt anything. He didn't know if that was good or bad.

Still, he didn't want to glow. There was something about the idea that sent shivers up his spine. He visualized his rotting corpse in the grave, glowing like a torch in the dirt. Attracting worms and beetles that would eat off the poisoned flesh and crawl off, themselves glowing like little beacons of poison, lighting up the underground passageways like neon signs advertising the madness of mankind.

Chapter Thirty-Two

Natasha awoke Harrison at about five in the morning. She didn't want any of the security people to find them. Besides, she had to compete later that day—thank God not until the afternoon. She kissed him hard, pulling him back a few times, before she was really willing to part with the man who had given her such pleasure the night before. Harrison walked, his clothes half hanging off him, and somehow stumbled back to the American barracks. He had just fallen into bed, gotten perhaps an hour's sleep at most, when there was a great commotion and all forty of the guys in the quarters were up and running all over the place screaming and making a great to-do.

"Come on, pardner," Harrison heard a voice berating him as he tried to pull his head further under the pillow. "Time to rassle, man." Harrison peeked one eye out from beneath his pillow. It was Carter. The black man's eyes were already wide awake and his bulging muscles looked ready to tear down mountains. All Harrison's muscles could think of was sleep.

"Oh, hell," he said, raising himself up so that he sat dizzily on the end of the bed. Everything was spinning in an alcoholic fog that made him think he just might upchuck some of yesterday's dogs.

"Hell ain't going to help you now," Carter said good-naturedly, slapping Harrison on the shoulder so that his brain reverberated inside his skull like one of the bells of Notre Dame. Suddenly the black wrestler leaned over and grabbed hold of Harrison around the chest. He pulled him up, dragging the half-awake man to his feet, and then started hoisting him in the air.

"Just relax now, man," Carter said with a grunt, "going to give you a spine straightening." He lifted Harrison right off the ground and pulled back, his arms wrapped around the man in something approximating a bear hug. Then he proceeded to spin Harrison all over the place, from side to side, around, up and down. Suddenly Carter pulled hard and Harrison swore he heard half his spinal cord crack and fall into place. The black wrestler dropped him back down to his feet and let go with a great exhale of air.

"Heavy sucker, ain't you?" He laughed. "Well, that should do it. Works, don't it? It's the Instant Wake-Up method that my grandfather always used to pull on us when we was just lying around in bed all lazy as shit."

"Well," Harrison said as he pulled his head to a non-vibrating position. "It sure as hell works. If it don't make you puke out last Thanksgiving's turkey in the process." He felt awake, that was for damn sure. Suddenly spotting the ugly-faced wrestler he had seen the day before, who was getting dressed at the far side of the long barracks, Harrison turned to Carter.

"What's the story with him?" he asked as he pulled on his competition getup.

"He's a farm boy from Iowa," the black wrestler said, glancing down at his watch. "Slipped into a machine that grinds up corn husks for cow feed. They got him quick enough, but not before the blades of the thing had chewed up his whole face—and some of his brain too. Half his skull is fake, made of super-tough plastic. But basically, as far as I can see, he's actually a pretty

281

nice guy. Fellows around here have been nice to him. Most of them anyway. I saw him yesterday—son-of-a-bitch can rassle." Carter started toward the door. Most of the team members had already departed. "If you want to get in any chow before the matches begin, better get a move on, man."

Harrison got his ass in gear, though it felt like half the sprockets were rusted, and jogged after the black muscle mountain who strode ahead of him. He filled up on bacon and eggs and a double order of fries—and prayed he didn't have a match immediately. He headed back to the stadium just in time to see the first match begin. It was Ugly Face, and Harrison could hear the crowd gasp as the deformed man paraded around the ring holding his hands high. But the crazy smile on the man's horrid features and the sheer fact that he had the balls to go out and compete quickly won the masses over to him, and within seconds gasps turned to cheers and loud applause. Then his opponent climbed in, an immense Brazilian with a bad attitude who snarled at his smaller American adversary. The ref got the match going, and Harrison winced as the South American leaped right on top of Ugly Face, surely squashing him to a pulp. But even as they both fell to the mat, Harrison saw, with amazement, the American somehow wiggle free so that only the Brazilian hit the mat. Before he could move an inch, Ugly was on his back and had him in a crossbody scissors and arm lock. The Brazilian was clearly astonished as he crashed and struggled wildly on the floor. But he couldn't break free. The ref got down on his hands and knees, slapped the mat three times, and blew his whistle. And just like that Ugly Face had won himself a match against a much bigger man. He laughed like a child as the gong rang, and jumped up onto ropes waving his hands with abandon at the crowd. They loved him. Everyone loves an innocent—even a hideously ugly one.

The American team slapped him high and low fives all over the place, and the man clearly reveled in it. But the next man from the U.S. contingent ran into big, big trouble. The Bull, Bukowski, also a wrestler as well as a weightlifter. The huge 480-pounder stamped around the ring as he waited for his opponent to climb in. The American climbed through the ropes—Jenkins, a 320-pounder from Georgia, a country boy with biceps the size of Roman columns. He looked tough. But he sure as hell wasn't tough enough.

The instant the beeper sounded both men charged toward the center of the ring. But as Jenkins reached for the grapple, the Bull just reached down and lifted him up. In a fluid motion he grabbed the man, one hand around his throat, the other around his leg, and raised him high in the air. Then he dropped down to one knee, bringing the American down on his side right into the immense rock-hard knee that must have been a foot wide high. Jenkins let out a scream as the whole side of his rib cage smashed in. Then, mercifully for him, he passed out cold from the sheer shock to his nervous system. The Bull walked around the shaking man, his arms raised high and a contemptuous smile on his face. The Eastern Bloc audience cheered wildly for their man. He was already legendary in Bulgaria. Now the West, the capitalist world, would see his power as well.

Bukowski exited the ring and a stretcher was brought in for the American to be taken off to the hospital. He would have to undergo five hours of intensive reconstructive surgery on his rib cage.

Then it was Harrison's turn. He felt as awake as he ever would. And though he was a little hungover, the wonderful memories of the night before made him unconcerned about what was going to happen. Which was the way to go as far as he was concerned, loose and easy all the way. Until he saw his opponent climb into

283

the ring.

The man was like a small hippo—a sumo wrestler from Japan. The Games allowed just about any legitimate contender to compete. Thus there were alligator wrestlers from Florida, Eskimo walrus grapplers, and sumos like the one Harrison was staring right into the beady-eyed face of. The man looked like nothing but fat—and tons of it. He stamped around in one corner of the ring, praying to his ancestors and throwing rice all over the place. In general he managed to scare the shit out of Harrison, who leaned back against the ropes and burped out a taste of western omelette.

The ref set them together in the center of the ring, and the Japanese stared into Harrison's face and smiled, revealing a completely toothless mouth, just pink gums that seemed to undulate like worms at the top and bottom of the smile. Harrison groaned under his breath. This wasn't looking too good. The gong rang and Harrison had his hands full—and fast. The sumo style was to drop low fast and try to uproot the opponent. Which this toothless specimen attempted to do with a vengeance, dropping down impossibly low in a flash until he was over at a sharp angle just a few feet above the ground. Harrison too dropped down to meet his drop, realizing what the man was trying to do.

Then they both slammed into each other. And the sumo won. For Harrison found himself being pushed straight backwards as the fat thing wriggled and jumped and pushed forward set over at almost a forty-five-degree angle. The Japanese rammed ahead, driving him back across the entire ring. Harrison felt himself slam into the ropes, and the sumo's head drove right into his stomach. All the air whooshed out of him like he'd been hit with a cannonball, and he sucked in hard, gasping for more. The Japanese rose his head up like a whale surfacing above the water for a second to see how his victim was doing. Seeing Harrison's pained bluish face he laughed, and the gums wiggled around some more.

Then the Japanese grabbed hold of Harrison's right leg and suddenly whipped him up into a single shoulder carry. Harrison knew it was too late to counter, but as he felt the man start to flip him up and over in a shoulder throw, he grabbed hold of the man's long hanging ponytail of black hair. As he fell, Harrison curved his arm so that he hit the mat in a roll—but he pulled the sumo along with him, something the man wasn't expecting at all. The Japanese's head was pulled straight forward and down, driving it into the mat with the full weight of Harrison's falling body and the sumo's own large mass. The entire ring moved around like elephants were breakdancing in its midst, and Harrison came out of his roll and jumped up, turning around on a dime, his arms extended to see what was next.

The sumo was up too. He was too tough to be taken out even by a blow like that—but he had clearly felt it. He had a look of surprise on his face, a look of newly found respect for the American. The Japanese bowed slightly and Harrison returned the gesture. The two men circled each other trying to gauge a weakness, searching for any opening. Then the sumo came charging forward again, very low to the ground. Harrison waited, and then met the charge like a bullfighter—suddenly stepping to the side and guiding the sumo right past. And as he did so he simultaneously tripped the man with his leg—and slammed hard from behind with both palms—so the sumo flew forward completely off balance and shot into the ropes. He slammed in so hard the ropes bent in a few feet, and then came flying out backwards, soaring a good two yards before he crashed down onto the mat.

Harrison was on him in a flash, throwing a left leg

285

wrap around the neck, with a right-arm arm lock from behind. As he pulled up hard on the straightened arm of the Japanese he squeezed hard, wrapping his leg around the fat neck like a python trying to wring the breath out of his prey. The sumo gasped for air as he grabbed at the leg, his face turning a bright red within seconds. Suddenly he somehow turned his head and bit hard at the calf, forgetting he had no teeth, that he had taken his dentures out in the locker room. The gummy feeling was not particularly a pleasant one but it didn't make Harrison release his hold. He forced the man over onto his side, trying to pin the wide shoulders. But it was like trying to pin a blob of jello. For the sumo just shifted his weight this way and that and somehow managed to keep avoiding the pin.

Suddenly the sumo bridged up fast, bending his back and chest like he was a McDonald's arch, and Harrison's hold was cleanly broken as he flew a few yards through the air and came down on his back. The Japanese was on him like a shark on a stunned fish. His immense body came crashing down from what seemed like a thousand miles up, and Harrison slammed into blackness for a few seconds, all the air in his lungs forced out of him in a single burst. When he emerged from the fog the sumo was getting him all locked up with some weird pretzel leg lock plus the sheer immense weight of his obesity, which draped over Harrison like some kind of fleshy avalanche. He tried to move, and discovered to his horror that he couldn't, that the ref was running over from the side of the ring ready to start the count. Damn, he was going to be out of the running before he'd even had a chance to get going.

Suddenly Harrison heard what sounded like someone screaming out his name, and he twisted his head around even as the ref threw himself down on the mat checking to see if Harrison's shoulders were pinned flat.

"Harrison, Harrison, you fleabrain, listen to me,

man." Harrison could hardly believe his eyes. A bizarre-looking fat man was just yards from the side of the ring and he was screaming his lungs out. He had a long black beard like he was some Russian prince from the eighteenth century—perhaps Rasputin, thick sunglasses, and a wide tan trenchcoat that could hardly fit across his broad shoulders. But even in his daze Harrison could see the fat belly poking out, the edge of a Hawaiian shirt underneath the trench. Incognito, right! The Captain stuck out like a neon light in a sewer. He was raising both hands and forming them into claws and then digging them into the air in front of it like he was ripping at it, trying to slash the oxygen molecules.

"The claw, Harrison, use the claw on his fat gut. Use your medulla—the claw, the fucking claw." He clawed back and forth like a tiger at an elephant as security guards came rushing over and started hustling him off. But it was enough to have gotten through to Harrison's addled brain.

"One," the ref screamed as he slammed his hand down on the ring mat and made a thunderous sound right next to Harrison's ear. Harrison formed both hands into the claw and slammed up into the huge gut. He couldn't get much leverage with his arms as they were both virtually pinned down. But he was able to turn his wrists up and drive the claw fingers into the flesh. Then he squeezed hard around whatever he had grabbed. And ten thousand or more squeezings of Captain Lou's Claw Ball paid off. For the fingers gripped the flesh, sinking deep inside like some immense snapping turtle grabbing around the leg of a deer that strayed too deep into the swamp. The sumo let out a scream that could be heard clear around the stadium and involuntarily pulled back.

"Two," the ref yelled and then stopped, holding his hand in midair as he saw that the match wasn't over yet.

Harrison breathed out hard, found strength somewhere inside his half-crushed body, and arched up from the mat, jumping to his feet in a single motion without using his arms. The crowd let out a roar of approval at Harrison's guts. And he felt their energy and tried to charge himself up on it. The sumo was still hollering and jumping around, grabbing at his big belly, which had purple marks where Harrison's fingers had inflicted their damage. Harrison didn't give the Asian hippo a second chance, but dove straight across the ring, slamming into the sucker like a nose tackle into a quarterback. The sumo went stumbling backwards completely off balance and crashed down onto his back, and the whole ring went up and down like it was doing jumping jacks.

Harrison threw his arms around the huge throat from behind, locking one arm over another as the Captain and the Destroyer had shown him so many times while working on the Sleeper. He tightened the grip around the man's throat, pulling even harder so the face went from red to purple. That seemed to take a little bit of the energy out of the Japanese. And suddenly, as he flipped all the way over on his side, Harrison was able to make the pin. He pushed down with his leg as he pulled up hard with his arm, holding the man's arm in a bar lock at the elbow. The sumo struggled furiously—but Harrison's leverage was too good.

"One, two, three," the ref counted. And that was that. The electronic gong sounded. And Harrison had won his second match. He stood up to the wild cheers of the crowd and stared down hard at the side of the ring where Captain Lou had done his gesticulating. But Rasputin was nowhere to be seen. He sure as hell had kept his promise. Even looking like an extra in a *Spy from Istanbul* movie circa 1958, he had been true to his word. He had been there when Harrison needed him.

Chapter Thirty-Three

As Harrison left the ring to the acclaim of the American supporters and his own teammates, he suddenly felt someone rush into him. It was Natasha and she looked terrified. But she didn't even stop to speak, just slammed a note into his hand which Harrison took, his mouth hanging open. Before he could say a word she was already gone—into the crowd. He waited until the rest of the group—Carter, Ugly Face, and the others—had stopped congratulating him, and then headed over to a long bench that members of the American team sat on while waiting for their turn. He found a spot where no one could read over his shoulder and, cupping the note which had been scrawled in erratic English on a piece of toilet paper, read it.

"I hear the Bull talking to man I never see before outside training building. I don't know what I hear, Harrison—but something bad is happen. They have something in Room B234-O, one of basements for equipment storage in training building. They talk about *all* of us dying. Don't know why I tell you—but can't trust own security people. You tell FBI, you are American. Find someone. With love and body still tingling.

"Natasha."

This was the break he had been waiting for. A link to the terrorists. So the Bull was involved in the atomic nightmare. It didn't surprise Harrison. The man had a killer instinct about him. He had seen it in the ring, the way the bastard absolutely annihilated his opponent, not just taking him out—but trying to ruin him for life. Harrison wished—and then didn't—that *he* got to meet the son-of-a-bitch in the ring. But if Natasha's information was true, the Bulgarian would be behind bars long before that occurred. Harrison looked up and around the bench quickly, but saw no one keeping an eye on him, though he knew that someone could easily be watching him from across the stands. The surveillance training he had been through had showed him the power of some of today's binocs and sighting systems. It was a simple enough matter to read a note at two hundred yards.

He decided to move fast—on the chance that the whole thing could blow at any minute. He'd notify Parker later. First he had to see just what the hell was going on. Deep penetration. Well, he was in deep enough. Now for the penetration. He wondered whether to get the pistol hidden in his suitcase, a mini-nine-shot-9mm, but decided no. He still didn't feel comfortable with the damned thing. Besides, he still had no proof. He could start an international incident if he started firing away at Bulgarian athletes. God help him if he actually hit one. He trusted his hands, his legs, his fighting abilities. He'd been doing pretty good so far.

Harrison headed out of the stadium, walking slowly as if he were in no great hurry. He headed about ten blocks to the Bulgarian Training building. Once inside, he took the fire stairs down to the basement, then the sub-basement. The place had been built to accommodate all sorts of electrical wiring and water piping, and the corridors and rooms had been built extra large to allow easy access and the possibility for expansion in the future should they run out of space above. Thus there were miles of these tunnels and basically unused levels below ground, half of them not even lit.

He moved cautiously when he hit B Level, and pushed open a creaking steel door half off its hinges. It was like a set from a Dracula movie inside. Darkness, shadows, punctuated only by an occasional glaring light bulb, hanging by a dangling cord. Spider webs ran along the walls, big ones filled with centipedes and roaches, many of them still wriggling and trying to get free of the unfreeable. He walked in on tiptoe, ready to move in any direction like a cat. In spite of himself he could feel his heart speed up, his face grow cold and clammy. Not even so much from fear of a human attacker—but of a monster, coming out of the misty shadows of the rooms and tunnels. He berated himself for being such a child, and searched around, squinting in the little light that was bouncing around to read the signs at every corner.

There—B Corridor. And there were numbers on the doors. It wasn't that bad. He had the situation under control, Harrison kept saying to himself. But when a huge rat suddenly scampered right in his path, and then stopped and stared up at him, scornfully getting up on its hind legs and giving him the once-over, he started feeling his ticker jump around a little. He reached over for a broom handle he saw leaning against one wall and waved it at the rat, then banged it on the concrete floor. The rodent didn't seem all that scared, but after glaring at him a little more, at last sat down on all fours again and tore across the corridor, into a hole on the far side. Oh, yeah, this was a great place to hold a party. Or to store an atom bomb.

He headed on, growing more tense with every step. He suddenly remembered the geiger counter in the fake cigs stuck in his pants pocket, and took out the pack, clicked the appropriate dial on the side, and held the mini-geiger up in the dim light. Harrison turned the would-be pack of Marlboros around, facing it in all different directions. Not a thing. If there was a bomb down here it was damn well hidden. He walked on, squinting up through the darkness at the numbered doors, at last finding the room Natasha had mentioned in the note. He held the geiger up to the door—and it showed a minute amount of radiation. Not a hell of a lot, but the digital readout was definitely picking something up.

Harrison unscrewed the light bulb in the hall right behind him so he wouldn't make a good silhouette in case someone was waiting inside with a gun. He tested the steel door—it was unlocked. Kicking the door hard with his foot, Harrison came into the dark room in a lineman's rush and hit the floor in a roll. His eyes adjusted to the gray light that filtered down from the fluorescent tube flicking on and off. He came to his feet just behind a wooden box and quickly scanned around. Nothing, not a soul in the place, just crates, some opened, some not, extending as far as the eye could see.

As Harrison walked around he saw that he could have started a flea market down there. There was every damned thing lying around. Construction materials from the building of the immense underground chambers—piles of sheet rock, plywood, metal frames. There were shelves and boxes of nails, screws, power tools, electrical cords. . . . Further on, crates, some of them hastily unpacked, with splintered wood lying around the floor—supplies. It was endless. How the hell did they expect him to find a needle in this dank haystack?

He tried the geiger again—and this time hit paydirt. The thing was sending out red warnings. He was heading into a danger zone of radiation. Without suit or proper protection exposure should be limited to less than five minutes. No contact with radioactive substance should be made. And various other warnings all scrolled out in small digital letters across the side of the cigarette pack.

"Thanks," Harrison said, addressing the Marlboros. Maybe all this high-tech bull that the CIA had wanted him to use worked. He walked over toward a trunk sitting by itself half-hidden behind two large wooden crates. That was strange. It was the only metal trunk he had seen down here, a little out of place. He walked toward it holding out the cig pack. This time it went completely bananas, setting off a beeper.

"EXPOSURE LIMITED TO 30 SECONDS. DO NOT MAKE PHYSICAL CONTACT WITH RADIATION SOURCE. EXPOSURE LIMITED TO 30 SECONDS . . ." The green letters danced across the pack warning him. The thing wouldn't stop beeping, so Harrison had to push a tiny "off" button, which cooled the thing out. He walked around the trunk, and then put his booted foot out and pushed at it slowly. It was heavy, hundreds of pounds easily. Harrison reached out down to the lock but it was padlocked, a big thick case-hardened number. He walked back about fifty feet to some tools he had seen half spilling out of a broken crate.

There—some crowbars—just the thing. He grabbed the biggest one he could find and headed back to the steel trunk. He wedged the end into the lock and stepped back, pulling with all his might. The lock was tough—but not tough enough. It exploded suddenly, the steel ring that ran through the latch of the box shattering into several pieces that flew off and clanked lightly along the concrete floor.

Harrison walked up to the trunk and started to reach down—then decided to be at least slightly cowardly about all this. He stepped back a yard or two and reached out with the crowbar, flipping over the top. It swung back with a loud thwack and he looked down at one of the strangest devices he had ever seen. It was like something out of *War of the Worlds*—a high-tech globe of steel about a yard in diameter, with lights and antennae and digital screens reading out numbers and symbols all over the fucking thing. If he had ever seen something that looked like a super bomb, this was damn well it. So he had found it. He congratulated himself, wondering if this meant he'd get a bonus, a medal, and a kiss on the cheek from the Director of the CIA. He'd take the first two.

Harrison walked around the steel glove, switching back to rad meter, which immediately started making all kinds of clamor about getting the hell out of there.

"All right, all right," he mumbled, snapping it off again. Well, he sure as hell wasn't going to mess with the bomb. He didn't even begin to know how to break into the solid globe of chromium metal. For all he knew it was booby-trapped. They had shown him some simple bomb-dismantling techniques, but those had been for land mines and pipe bombs, not fucking nukes. He aimed his camera watch down and pushed in on the hour dial on the side. It made an almost inaudible clicking sound, and then a GO sign appeared on the face, the only indication that the shot had been successful. They had said that the camera would focus itself and that it could take pictures of radioactive substances, shielded somehow from the X-rays by a special chemical process over the film. He walked around the bomb taking pictures of it from about ten

294

different angles.

That was enough. He didn't want to get himself suntanned into the grave. Harrison clicked back to watch mode, and then walked around to the front of the shining steel egg and kicked the top back over the trunk. It shut with a loud slam that made him freeze, realizing that maybe it wasn't such a good idea to kick the hoods of nuclear weapons. He closed the latch by hand and then picked up part of the broken padlock. By resting a piece of it on the latch Harrison was able to make it look, at least from a few yards away, as if the lock was still on. If anyone touched it, of course, they'd know. But he'd be out of here, on the phone to D2. The game was over.

He walked back out of the storage chamber, vowing to keep this place in mind when he needed construction supplies. Half this stuff was going to rust anyway. He knew how these fucking bureaucracies worked. Anyway, he worked for the CIA now—he was allowed to take a hammer, an electric drill or two. If there were any problems, the authorities could just talk to the President. He'd be 007, with a license to filch appliances. Harrison was starting to feel pretty smug about the whole situation, and wondering why this intelligence stuff was cut out to be such a tough business, when he suddenly heard a sound in the darkened door frame to the right. As he turned around, raising his arms to defend himself, something hard slammed into the back of his head. And as mean little stars danced all around in front of his eyes taunting him not to fall down, another waterfall of pain slammed into his skull, and then another. Then he was sliding down a pit into darkness as black as the heart of midnight.

Chapter Thirty-Four

"Love this watch," a voice was saying as Harrison's brain came from out of an ocean of black into a swamp of gray. Shadowy figures marched around in front of him. For a few moments he didn't know who, let alone where, he was.

"Look at this, Bukowski," the slightly nasal high-pitched voice went on. "This gadget here has at least ten different functions that I've been able to find, and I've only been fiddling with it for a minute." The man he was talking to merely grunted, not particularly interested apparently in such wonders. Harrison's eyes twitched like mating butterflies as he struggled to open them. Finally they seemed to open about a half inch. He could see.

And instantly wished he couldn't. For the four men who stood around in front of him looked like pals of Frankenstein or maybe the Incredible Melting Man. Bukowski was the closest, he already knew and loved the fellow. But standing around him were men whose faces seemed to be melting. They wore sunglasses and scarves—but it couldn't hide the bubbled-up skin, the streams of pinkish blood oozing from their noses and ears. Teeth wobbled loosely inside their mouths as they talked. And yet—they all acted as if nothing weird was going on. Just a typical day rotting at the office.

"Ah, our guest is awakening," a tall thin white-haired man said, walking over until he loomed right over Harrison, who looked up at him with a throbbing skull. "Allow me to introduce myself—I'm Professor Markus, Professor Anthony Markus. You already know Mr. Bukowski, I'm sure, having seen him in the ring. These are my associates, Dr. Rennings and Dr. Ayakita." Both men nodded toward him, their faces hidden, their mouths twisted in obvious pain, though they made no sounds to indicate it.

"Now that we are all introduced, I must ask you—with the creator's narcissism, I confess—how did you like our little bomb?" He put his hands together and smiled down benignly at Harrison with the look that Norman Bates gave Janet Leigh just before he turned into *Psycho*.

"Uh, great. It was really a fine-looking bomb," Harrison muttered, his mouth tasting like cotton dipped in mud. He was, all things considered, not in the best of situations.

"Good, good. I think considering what we had to work with, the constant pursuit by the authorities—all the constraints which are none of your concern—we did quite well. Quite well." His smile suddenly turned to a cough and he pulled out a handkerchief, which had clearly been put to a lot of use lately, and spat into it. A red stain spread across several inches. Harrison suddenly wished he was back in East Harlem basements taking on 400-pound Puerto Rican supers. This was starting to get a little on the depressing side. Which feeling was squared when he tried to move and discovered that he was lashed down with 1/4-inch steel cable hand and foot to a long wooden table of some kind. He struggled hard, suddenly losing control and

297

wanting like a trapped animal to escape. But the steel binds were strong enough to lift a ton. He wasn't about to snap them.

"Of course it is totally useless to struggle." Markus smiled when he had finished his little blood coughs. "We have you so secured not even Houdini would get out, though you're welcome to try. Now, all I want to know is: How much were you able to tell your CIA pals before tonight? How much do they know, Harrison? I'll be blunt with you. You're going to die anyway. You know that, I know that. But there's a hell of a lot of pain between here and dying that I can make you go through if I want to. And I must tell you that both I and my associates here are experts in our own methods of inflicting pain. We have had occasion to use it in the past."

"Who the hell *are* you bastards?" Harrison asked angrily, still struggling with every part of his body, testing the steel cords and seeing just how secure they were. Very.

"We are concerned individuals." Professor Markus snickered. "Representatives of the Third World dedicated to showing the filthily rich bourgeois world that we will not allow the Workers' Revolution to be derailed by capitalistic tricks."

"Could you translate?" Harrison asked, looking around the rest of the room to see what the setup was.

"Of course," Markus said, folding his hands together. "It means we are going to strike a blow for all the oppressed peoples of the world. And a death blow against the rapprochement between the Soviet Union and the United States—the greatest betrayal of the revolutionary cause since Stalin had Trotsky shot. While the peasants and workers of Asia and Africa and Latin America grow hungrier and weaker by the day, the USSR and U.S. decide to get together to divide up the pie a little more. These so-called "Games" being played here are little more than propaganda tools to unite your two decadent cultures. Why, soon, there'll be a McDonald's in Red Square."

"Already is," Bukowski snarled, pounding his fist into his other hand as he stood off to one side glaring down at Harrison with a look of sheer violent madness on his twisted face. Harrison had hoped they'd get a chance to go at it—he just didn't know he was going to be tied up.

"We are going to make a statement, Mr. Harrison. A revolutionary statement. That we are willing to die for. All of us. A symbol to the underclasses of the world— that someone is fighting for them. Perhaps our 'message' will even cause them to unite and overthrow the imperialistic capitalistic ruling governments of the earth. We shall never know that—but at least we will have done our part." This whole crew was crazy as bedbugs, Harrison realized with growing horror.

"And just what is *your* part?" he asked, not wanting to and already knowing the answer.

"Oh, to set off that little globe of hellfire you saw, Mr. Harrison. But of course you knew that. To take out all those so-called 'athletes'—nothing more than pawns of the Czars of Entertainment to keep the masses enslaved. To paraphrase Marx, sports is the opium of the modern masses, Mr. Harrison. And we shall strike a blow against that enslaving drug."

"Let me get this straight," Harrison said, ceasing his struggles at least momentarily, just lying there wrapped up like a caterpillar inside a cocoon about to turn into a very bloody butterfly. "You're going to kill all of the athletes at the Games—and most of New York—so that the peasants of the world will get angry, kick in their TV sets, stop playing sports, and go out and start a revolution or two?"

"Well, I wouldn't put it in those terms, but yes, that would be in any case the results." The professor chuckled, pushing his bifocals, which had begun slipping down his hawk nose, back up onto the ledge of his ears.

"But you'll all die," Harrison exclaimed, looking around the room at the mad crew. "Don't you care?"

"We serve a higher purpose than selfish needs of the flesh," the professor snapped at him, growing a little angry. "The purposes of history, of the inevitability of . . ." He stopped himself in mid-sentence. "Ah, but I bore you. You don't really give a shit about the Hegelian world transference from master-slave to dictatorship of the proletariat. You just don't want the torture to begin." He looked at Harrison's watch, which he had strapped onto his own wrist. "No, we're already running late. You'll really have to start telling us what we want to know or . . ." He nodded to Bukowski, who got a happy look on his wide basketball of a face. He walked right up to the right side of the board Harrison was tied down to and reached beneath it turning some bolts. Suddenly the board turned upright, Harrison strapped to the thing in a standing position, his feet tied down as well, so that he was spread-eagled, completely vulnerable.

"Now, please tell me. How much did you tell them? Who's your contact at the CIA or the FBI or whoever the hell you work for? Who told you there was a bomb in the basement?"

"Hey, whoa, fellow." Harrison laughed as Bukowski stood just inches away from him, making a fist and holding it up in the air as if inspecting it while he turned the immense paw around like a diamond for Harrison to get a good picture of. Harrison did. And wished he was standing and holding a 12-gauge shotgun with seven shells. Because it looked like, even untied, he'd need it against the monstrous Bulgarian. "I don't work for the CIA—and if I did I didn't have time to tell anything to anyone. I'm doing some articles for a wrestling magazine about the Games. I was just snooping around trying to do a story on the equipment used in them," Harrison lied, telling the story that Parker had concocted for him. Which hadn't sounded too bad at the time, but which didn't sound too good while tied to a board in front of radiation-poisoned terrorists who didn't believe a single word.

"Very well," Markus said, pursing his narrow lips together. "You bring it upon yourself. But don't say I didn't warn you." He stood back and motioned for Bukowski to have his fun. The immense wrestler stepped forward and looked down at Harrison.

"So glad to meet you face to face." Harrison smirked, looking straight into the face of the seven-foot, 485-pound piece of oversized lard. "I've seen you in the ring and I just want to say you're the nastiest bastard I've ever witnessed."

"Thank you," the Bull sneered, not quite sure what "nastiest" meant but getting the drift. Suddenly his fist was coming down toward Harrison's nose like an asteroid bent on annihilation. The calloused fist slammed right into the center of his face, and everything inside Harrison's brain disappeared for a few seconds like a light bulb going out. When he came to a second or two later he was in a world of jello, everything just sort of dripping around him. Then the fist hit again, and again.

Bukowski was an expert in the use of hands-on pain. He had killed many men, hurt many more. He knew just how far to take someone without completely destroying them. Thus he toyed with Harrison, slamming him all over his body with vicious blows that were designed more for pain than for termination.

Kidney shots with the elbow, slams with the heel of the hand right into the stomach, followed by a knee for good measure. Blow after blow from fist and foot rained into the American like he was running through a gauntlet of a thousand attackers.

He didn't know how long it went on. Somehow, after he went out a few times near the start, his mind grew weirdly clear in a dull-witted sort of way. And then he couldn't go out. No matter how hard the Bull slammed into him. Oh, he felt the pain, all right. Felt the crunching of ribs, the loosening of teeth in the inside of his jaw, his brain slamming around inside his skull like a potato in a blender after Bukowski delivered a dozen hooks, one after another, to each side of his head. God knew what was keeping him alive. He became just a piece of mental sludge, blood coming out of his mouth as his head snapped from side to side. After a while he couldn't even tell one blow from another or when they began and stopped. Streaks of color that filled his senses were his only indication that the barrage was continuing.

Finally it stopped. He knew it stopped because there was cold water thrown over his face, once, twice, whole buckets of it. He sputtered back to consciousness, his brain and body feeling like they'd just been put through several meat-grinders at once. His eyes rolled back and forth in his skull as he tried to focus on Bukowski, standing a few feet away with a look of supreme satisfaction on his ugly mug, rubbing his red-knuckled hands in one another and covering them with some sort of salve. He had broken a few knuckles in working Harrison over.

"Now, wasn't that just a barrel of monkeys?" Professor Markus asked as he came into dim view at the other side of the upright wooden frame to which Harrison was strapped.

"Yeah, monkeys." Harrison made his lips twitch into something approximating a sneer, though he wasn't at all sure what it actually looked like since his mouth was just a big burning stream of red. His reply sounded like a clever retort. But he wasn't sure about that. Wasn't sure about anything except that he felt like he had just been inside an A-bomb blast at ground level.

"Well, now, I'm sure you're ready to tell me what I want to know," Professor Markus said with a kindly, totally insincere smile on his red-blistered face.

"Professor—if I could tell you—I swear—swear I would," Harrison said. "Not—with the—CIA. Just dumb asshole looking for story."

"Ah, Mr. Harrison." The Professor sighed, looking upward at the ceiling of cement about ten feet above his head along which conduit piping of every size ran off in all directions. "You leave me no alternatives. But let me warn you that the going-over that Mr. Bukowski just gave you was but an appetizer to what I'm about to inflict. Do you understand what I'm saying?"

"Un'erstan'." Harrison smiled dumbly through blood-dripping lips. "Bring on main course. Red wine if got any. Or does white wine go with torture?"

"How clever, how very clever," the Professor replied. "Well, we shall see how clever you'll feel in a few moments." He motioned for one of his melting associates to push a cart forward. It had a strange-looking electronic device and all kinds of wires with little needles on them coming out of it. Harrison didn't like the looks of it at all.

"Put them in," Markus directed one of his underlings, who lifted one of the long syringe-like needles with wires attached to it and held it up so that Harrison could see it. The American didn't even like looking into the swollen red eyes of the mottled face. The man was obviously near death. It couldn't be more than weeks, even days off. His eyes looked like they were in another dimension, like he was completely mad, not even really on this planet anymore. He smiled with a twisted expression and came forward with the needle, digging it right into the side of Harrison's neck. The victim winced as the point sank in. He had never liked needles—especially in his neck.

"Now, what we're doing here is quite interesting," Professor Markus said in a lecturing tone as if he were in the front of a class teaching a lesson. "You've doubtless heard of the pressure points of the body—acupuncture and all that kind of stuff. Well, it's all true. It really does work. There are deep, hidden, nerve systems in the body that carry energy, and they can be tapped and used for incredible strength and health. But they can also be used to create terrible pain. For the same spots into which my assistant is now putting the needles—" As he spoke the lackey was jabbing needles into Harrison's elbows and wrists, his knees, the soles of his feet, until within a minute or two he was completely covered with the things, a human pincushion. "Into the meridian points, the junctures and highways of the body's energy flow. But enough words. Let me demonstrate."

He walked over to the cart and turned on a machine to which all the wires that were coming out of the needles were attached. "It's very simple really. We're feeding electricity into those needles, into your pressure points. Only, instead of using the low-level amount that acupuncturists do, we discovered that if you use, say, a hundred times as much—the results are quite profound." He turned the dial in front of him hard to the right.

Harrison was suddenly thrust into a world of pain he hadn't known existed. Not in his entire life. Not when the Bull had just been using him as a punching bag. Not

304

even when he had been tortured years ago—and he had always thought that *that* had been the worst that a man could endure. Yet this was worse. In a way far worse. For not only was the pain more intense, digging deeper into his nervous system, but it was occurring in every place there was a needle jammed right into his flesh—over three dozen of them. He felt his body jerking and jumping all over the place like some kind of wild animal with rabies. But strapped to the board all he could do was flail against the wood and the steel bonds, his wrists and ankles cutting into the cables as he slammed out of control. He didn't know how long it lasted as he had no longer had a mind beyond the perception of pain, pure and unadulterated.

Then suddenly his body went limp, and he was just hanging there on the board like some kind of dead thing ready for exhibit in the hall of some dusty museum.

"There, wasn't that interesting?" Professor Markus commented as he looked fondly over the top of the control panel beneath him. He waited until Harrison's eyes slowly opened, until the head raised up a little. Until Harrison actually found the balls deep inside to mutter, "My toaster's done worse."

"Oh, has it? Has it fucking now?" the Professor screamed, apparently not able to take a joke when it came to inflicting torture. He turned the dial straight up on the counter beneath him. And again Harrison's body immediately began jerking around wildly like there were a thousand little aliens inside of him all trying to eat their way out at once. His back arched up and his mouth opened wide. And he couldn't even tell for sure if he was screaming or not, but he figured he was. Then he was transported into a world of pain few men know. And like enlightenment, those that do usually can't talk about it afterwards.

Chapter Thirty-Five

The grizzled old guard sitting at a desk in the lobby of the New York City Morgue looked up from his horror novel as he saw two men open the front door. They walked down the long tile floor, their heels reverberating in sharp little echoes up and down the corridor. The guard put the book down as the two approached.

"Yeah?" he said in that brusque New York way that endears out-of-towners to the species.

"Parker," the man said, opening his trenchcoat and holding out some super-official-looking ID that made even the jaded guard take a second look.

"CIA, huh?" He looked both of them over as if gauging them against his own ideas of what a CIA agent should look like. Then he snorted as if to indicate that they didn't quite fill the bill.

"Gotta come at three-thirty in the morning, huh?" he asked.

"What, are we going to wake the dead or something?" Parker snarled at the guy, almost enjoyed his New York nastiness after the endless, smiling, lying faces of D.C.

"Yeah, funny, funny," the guard said, shaking his head. "I've heard the line a thousand times, and it wasn't funny the first time. Anyway, go on in. Just follow the yellow signs that say Storage. There's someone on duty down there." He turned back to his book without another word and put his feet back up on his desk. Parker glanced at the cover of the book the man was reading. *Night of the Living Yuppie*. He'd have to get a copy.

Parker and his assistant walked, heels clicking, down halls, then stairs, and then more halls again. The place was huge. And it smelled of death. Formaldehyde, the after-shave of corpses. *Stank* of death was more like it after a hundred thousand bodies had passed through it. All victims of violent crimes or their own murderous hand. Brought to the city coroner's office for autopsy, legal determinations. You couldn't wash the stench clean, nor the sense that the dead themselves were thick in the air. Their lost dreams, their tearful memories, their final screams, seemed almost to echo with a searing silence through the cracked marble walls of the immense bureaucratic building.

After taking two or three wrong turns, they at last came to Storage, a glass door behind which Parker could see the walls of stainless-steel corpse containers. They walked in without knocking, and several men who were standing around two long sliding trays which had been pulled open looked up. The CIA man walked across the room glancing around at the bodies that lay in their frozen death poses in various large metal trays atop moveable carts. Some of the corpses were cut open, their guts strewn out around the trays like someone was looking for a lost olive inside a triple-decker sandwich. Hearts, livers, brains—all were lined up as if they might be put back in again later and the patient returned to normal. But no one in there returned to normal.

"Oh, Parker," one of the men said, an FBI badge pinned to his collar. "Didn't expect to see you here

personally. Thought you'd send one of your lackeys."
He arched a thick reddish eyebrow at the CIA chief.
The two men had never actually hit it off. But they
cooperated when they had to.

"Hagstrom," Harrison said, nodding his head
slightly as he walked over. "I thought I'd check it out
for myself. Sounded intriguing. What do ya got?" He
walked around until he was alongside the shorter FBI
bureau chief and looked down at the two corpses
spread out naked in the long stainless storage trays. He
found it hard, even as battle-hardened as he was, to
look at the head of one of them. It was twisted all the
way around so it was facing down into the tray, while
all the rest of it was facing up.

"How the hell—"

"Don't know," the FBI man replied. "There are
fingerprints smeared all over the place on the neck. So
obviously a *person* did it. Someone of incredible
strength. To do something like that . . . I mean . . ."
They all looked at one another, not even wanting to
think about the madman who could exert such power.
It wasn't the kind of guy you'd like to meet in a dark
alley—or even a bright alley, for that matter.

"But this is why we sent a telex to your people," the
FBI man went on, walking a few feet to where the
corpse's clothing, no longer needed by its deceased
owner, lay in a neat bundle in a plastic container. Atop
the clothes, encased in thick plastic, was a piece of
paper with writing on it. "This note—well, read it—
you'll see what I mean."

Parker took up the scrawled letter, holding it
carefully at the edges of the encasing plastic, and read
the contents.

To the Pigs,
    You will never catch us because we're already
way ahead of you. These corpses are just a taste of

308

what's to come. Prepare for the light of revolution to burn bright over New York City. You know what we have—try to find us.

The Committee of Revolutionary Martyrs

"Martyr—I hate that word," Parker said as he held the letter up to the fluorescent light that flickered overhead. "It means someone who's willing to die for whatever crazy bullshit they believe in. And when a man doesn't fear death, you can't even reason with him anymore. He's on a different wavelength than the rest of us."

"And there's more to it than that," the FBI man went on, taking the letter and walking to the wall, where he turned off the overhead so that their portion of the room was cast into relative darkness. The thing was glowing like a Christmas tree. Especially the fingerprints that were all over it as if dipped in dayglow paint—which meant that the man who had written it was as high-rad as you could get.

"We already had one of the morgue doctors here. He's doing his thesis on radiation, as a matter of chance. He calculated the level of contamination of the person who gave off this much radiation on a piece of paper. That's why it's encased in this lead-threaded fiberglass. And the doctor's conclusion was . . . he shouldn't be alive. The guy's a walking time bomb himself. A bomb of radiation. You don't even want to stand next to the sucker for more than a few seconds. I mean it's like he's a monster or something. Guy must have plutonium dust embedded in his fingers, his skin, everywhere."

"Plutonium—then there is a damned bomb. And it's here in New York, I'm sure of it," Parker said, slamming his fist down on a body tray so that its inhabitant wriggled around a little as if turning in his long sleep. "Listen, Hagstrom, I don't know how to tell

309

you this, but these two bodies here are just tadpoles in the pond compared to how many there could be within the next few days. We believe that there's a one-megaton bomb—give or take a few thousand kilotons—here in New York. A homemade one, believe it or not. But it may well work. If this guy's is as high-rad as this letter indicates, then even if it didn't go into critical mass, it could still release enough radiation to kill thousands, poison large parts of the metropolitan area. Plutonium is the most poisonous substance known to man. A microscopic speck of it can cause lung damage, liver failure, cancers years later."

"You don't have to tell me about radiation," the FBI man said, his face growing as white as those of the corpses around him. "I was in Hiroshima with the first airborne troops to hit—just weeks afterwards. It was hell. Hell on earth. I was one of the staff photographers. I still dream of what I saw, what I photographed, to this day."

"Then you know what we're up against. Why we'll need absolute cooperation—and silence on all this." Parker looked at the FBI man's subordinate, but Hagstrom nodded.

"No, he's okay. Won't blab, I swear. I agree with you, we have to keep a complete news blackout on this. The city would go into an absolute panic. Eight million people trying to flee—why you'd lose fifty thousand from accidents, crashes, fires. Wouldn't even need a bomb."

"Get your men out there," Parker said, staring at the green fingerprints that glowed so brightly you could almost read by them in the semi-darkness. "Give them geiger counters and just send them the hell out there around the city, the docks, the Games, everywhere. Because we've got to find these madmen before they recreate the very pillars of fire of the Bible. The fires 'that cleanseth all.'"

310

Chapter Thirty-Six

"Wake up, dog, it's time for more," a voice was screaming in his ear. Then Harrison felt a whole bucketful of freezing water slam into his bloody face and chest. And in spite of himself, he was pulled from a dark place where at least he felt nothing to a bright, very painful one. He opened his swollen eyes to see Bukowski standing in front of him. And this time there were brass knuckles on each hand. The big bull-like face snorted contemptuously at him. Perhaps Harrison wouldn't have such smart-ass things to say after the next session. Perhaps he'd have nothing to say.

"Do what you want with him," said Professor Markus, standing off to the side. Harrison couldn't see the bastard, his neck was too swollen to move, but he knew the voice. He'd never forget it. Not that "never" was going to be very long. "He's clearly not going to tell us anything. Kill him—and dump him in the river." Then there were footsteps and the sounds of several men walking off. Harrison heard the peal of a foghorn from a boat nearby, and then the slapping of waves against a pier.

"You and me, we have some fun," the Bulgarian said, stepping forward. The hand with the brass knucks came down and slammed into Harrison's jaw. And though he would have sworn he couldn't even feel any more pain, he discovered to his displeasure that he could. A lot more. For as the knuckles slammed into his ribs, his stomach, his sides—he could feel bones fracturing, blood dripping from myriad gashes in the flesh. The guy was going to pound him into hamburger —economy pack. Just add "Shake N' Bake," cook— feeds a family of ten for a year.

Harrison tried to hang on, even accepting the pain, as he didn't want to slide into the blackness that he kept dangling on the edge of. He was afraid he wouldn't come out of it. But when Bukowski worked his way up his body with the knucks, found his head and began banging it back and forth between his fists like a boxer working on a speed bag, he couldn't hang on. Harrison felt a tearing pain in each side of his skull. And then he was back in the blackness, grinding and terrible.

When he next came to, he was amazed that he was still alive. His body didn't feel like it existed, just a throbbing piece of bloody gristle that was ready for the worms and crows. But somewhere, something in his brain was still taking in information from the outside world. He could hear water slapping nearby, the grunts of a man.

"Kill him," the professor had said. So Bukowski was taking him out in the river now—and that would be that. He tried to feel down to his feet with his mind to see if they were weighted down—but he couldn't even tell. It was hard enough to even keep his mind from going like a candle blown out in a dark wind. He could hear the Bulgarian mumbling and cursing to himself in his native tongue as he worked the small engine on the back of the ten-foot skiff. It had just sputtered to a stop.

"Ah, by the turds of Stalin," the huge wrestler

exclaimed, bending over the small ten-horsepower outboard to see what the hell was wrong. Harrison opened his eyes as wide as the edge of a razor blade. He could feel they were sticky. Blood was coating the outer lids, almost gluing them closed. Somehow he had the feeling he was similarly decorated in red all over his body. He could feel the boat bouncing up and down on low waves, and could see a shore not too far off, perhaps a hundred yards, with cars moving along it and big square warehouses crowding the shoreline for miles. Now—now was the time to make his move. Harrison suddenly felt the thought rush through him as his mind seemed to focus for an instant and he saw the night in a kind of crystal clearness—and knew he had only seconds to live.

He gathered whatever remaining strength he had left inside and pushed up with his arms. They seemed like they were made of rubber, hardly moving at his command. But he kept pushing, kept ordering them and his legs and every other damned muscle to move. And like a slug with terminal polio he somehow dragged himself the foot or two over to the side, and then up and onto the low edge of the small dinghy.

"What the hell—" he heard a voice scream out behind him. But Harrison didn't wait around to find out just what the guy wanted to talk to him about. He shifted his weight and pushed himself over the side. He slammed into the river like a dead weight, sinking down a good six feet or so. The shock of hitting the river woke Harrison up slightly, and he realized that he was in imminent danger of drowning. He just seemed to drop deeper into the impenetrable blackness of the river. He tried to move his feet, thinking perhaps the Bulgarian had already tied a weight around his ankles. But they moved, although slow as worms in mud. It was his clothes, his pants and shirt and exercise jacket—they had become saturated and were taking him down like anchors. And worse—the deeper currents were pulling him along sideways at a fast speed so that he began spinning around as he moved through the foul brown liquid.

Somehow Harrison kicked and paddled upward—and luckily he was caught by another current that was heading up. His head broke surface and he gasped hard for oxygen, the taste of the cool night air just about the most wonderful thing he'd ever tasted. Suddenly a shot rang out, and he turned his head to the right to see Bukowski about sixty yards away firing a pistol and cursing like a Times Square whore. A small flicker of a smile crossed Harrison's face even as he floundered around, shots zipping into the murky waters all around him. It was hard to fuck up disposing of a "dead man," but the Bull had done just that.

Though that situation might not last for long. Harrison quickly found himself being sucked back down by his soaking clothes. He barely managed to keep his head above the water as he was suddenly pulled sharply down the middle of the river. He pulled desperately at the jacket, trying to get it off, but it was hard going. His arms felt like they each had about a thousand pounds of lead weights sewn inside them. He pulled and ripped at the jacket as he was spun around like a top moving along at a good ten miles an hour. He could see both shores now as he turned. He was in the East River heading down along the Brooklyn shoreline. He knew the area well enough. He had gone out with an artist who lived among the converted loft buildings along the river. The city skyline glittered all around him like a billion jewels on fire in the velvet night.

Then just as he started going under again, Harrison was able to tear free of the jacket, and it sank down several yards in a flash. Getting rid of it released a good fifty pounds of weight and he was able to kick his bloodied battered legs, which only worked on alternate commands as if his whole nervous system was short-circuiting. As he spun around he could see Bukowski now over two hundred yards away and fading fast. Without the motor working the bastard had no way of catching up, and was too far out of pistol range. Harrison's sheer desire to get back at the torturers, to wreak revenge for the pummeling and pain they had put him through, gave a little extra spurt of fuel to his endeavors. He kicked and squirmed and groaned his way through the slapping foul waters. It seemed like he was hardly moving at first, every inch forward being negated by a pulse of water which pushed him back, currents gripping his body and constantly changing his direction. But somehow, going under half the time, taking huge mouthfuls of East River water, he slowly began heading toward Brooklyn.

At times his body didn't want to work. He felt electric pain ripping up and down his nervous system like rats through a kitchen piping. His head wasn't all there either, as it kept threatening to topple off into blissful nothingness. Which Harrison knew, even in his semi-stupor would be *eternal* blissful nothingness. And as fucked up as this ol' earth was, he wasn't in the mood to cut his stay here short.

It seemed like he had paddled, floated, gone under for hours and hardly made any headway. An occasional tug moved by several hundred yards away, heading up or down the river, pushing oil and coal barges filled to capacity. But they didn't see him and his screams were hardly more than hoarse whispers, inaudible more than a yard or two away. He was in this on his own. Still, it drove him half mad to know that there were millions of people asleep, behind the steel and stone

315

mountains that surrounded him, and yet he was out here as if he were a trillion miles away, beyond the frigid reaches of Pluto.

It was starting to feel as cold as the ninth planet too. Aside from the shooting pain, which was about the only thing even keeping him awake, Harrison began feeling everything tightening up from the effects of the frigid waters. His muscles he could deal with. It was fine with him to lose sensation in those pain-wracked appendages—it was his lungs tightening that scared him. For as the cold really began setting in, he could feel the lungs contract more and more like a balloon shrinking, and he took in less and less oxygen. Soon he was gasping for air, his face turning blue as he continued to roll like a bottle, tossing this way and that, heading perhaps for far ports in Africa, Asia. Although somehow Harrison didn't think he'd be alive at the other end to enjoy the vacation.

But the fickle currents of the river suddenly whipped him around quite quickly toward Brooklyn, and within minutes he was within forty feet of the high cracked concrete sea wall that ran along the shore line, below the empty factory buildings and warehouses. As he got closer, even through his mental fog, Harrison's nose was suddenly opened wide. It stank. It was as if he was in the midst of a sewer, a bug being flushed through a toilet line. And as he tried to focus his burning eyes, he saw that he was in fact floating in a large flow of garbage and raw sewage. It was a strip about fifty feet wide that was moving right along the sea wall, extending far upriver.

The stuff was bad, Harrison saw with disgust. Feces, used prophylactics, all kinds of rotting and river-swollen half-eaten food, myriad bobbing brown and gray shapes all floating around him like a tsunami of human debris. Even in his state of near-mental collapse

316

Harrison was disgusted by the flowing tide of garbage. He tried to paddle through the foul muck, but it was like trying to get through quicksand—almost impossible.

And suddenly, as if amazed that there was anything else that could happen that could make him feel even worse than he already did, Harrison saw a shape in front of him, and a narrow snake-like head suddenly whipped up right out of a pile of orange peels and cigarette butts and looked him straight in the eye.

"Oh, *no*," Harrison groaned as the demonic, fanged, yellow-eyed aquatic creature stared at him, about six inches of its thick black body undulating around just above the foul surface of the river as its tail wriggled wildly below to keep it upright. For a moment his dazed mind irrationally thought that it was some kind of sea monster. But in seconds he realized what it was—an eel. A big black overtoothed eel. He had never thought highly of the creatures, and had thought they were pretty much gone, that everything living was gone from the Hudson and East Rivers, which ran down each side of Manhattan. And yet clearly they weren't.

"Easy, boy," Harrison hissed as he paddled slowly backwards, suddenly alert in spite of his concussions and wounds. He just didn't feel like getting jawed by the ugly thing only yards away from him. But even as he kept a sharp eye on the baseball-bat-thick river-dweller, another head appeared, and then another, all popping up in various places around the garbage. They were splashing around, ripping up pieces of whatever they found most delectable that floated by. They seemed very aggressive, sinking their teeth around pieces of McDonald's burgers, doughnuts swollen up from the water like cotton candy, ripping them around in the river like sharks slamming down a death blow on a fish—or a man. Some of them fought each other over particularly choice morsels. Bubbles and thrashing filled the strip of garbage all around him, and Harrison felt his heart start doing backflips. And suddenly $30,000—or even $3,000,000, for that matter —seemed far too small an amount to be doing all this for.

Suddenly the eel that had been eyeing him decided to come in for a closer look and wriggled forward, moving fast as it raced across the foul surface of the slowly moving river-garbage tide toward him. Harrison's eyes bulged with horror as the mouth opened and the thing came right at his face. If they all attacked him, he could see the headlines in the *Daily News*. *Man Eaten by River Snakes*.

He reached forward, grabbing a broken bottle that was bobbing by, and, getting a hold with one hand, he hefted the thing up and sliced out at the head of the eel, just as it was speeding up for the final strike. The thing hissed and tried to turn its head as it sensed the weapon. But it was too late—and the sharp ridges of glass caught the eel just below its head. It slammed back down into the water right in front of him, thrashing violently, and Harrison stabbed at it again and again out of sheer terrorized madness. It jerked all around, and he could see that it was long—a good five feet or more. Blood filled the water, and after the eighth or tenth strike—he lost count—it was still. The eel began floating sideways toward its compatriots, who, not being particularly friendly critters even to one another, and definitely not fussy eaters, sank their fangs into their dead brother's flesh. Anything that didn't fight back was fair game for this crew.

As dozens of the eels closed in from around the garbage slick and began fighting viciously over the fresh meat, Harrison plowed foward right through the garbage, seeing his chance. Once the eels tired of their

318

meal, who knew what the hell they would do next. So he gave it his all, knowing there wouldn't be another chance. This was his last burst. After that, it was in God's hands. It was extremely tough working his way through the slick of waste which extended down a good foot or so into the river. On every paddle his hands and feet made contact with sludge or slime of some foul kind. But then somehow—he was through it. And the lights of the fire exits on the huge square warehouses that dotted the shoreline, rising out of the early morning mists like some sort of mythical pyramids, drew closer, until they were just above him.

He bumped into the sea wall with a gasp of joy. He could hardly believe that he had made it, and looked back out for a moment to see the wide dark river behind him and Manhattan like another world far off on the other side. But when he turned back to the cracked concrete wall that rose a good fifteen feet above him, Harrison realized he wasn't out of it yet—not by a long shot. For his strength was expended. If there were stairs, maybe he could crawl up them. But this was a solid wall of cement. There were cracks here and there, but nothing to write home about. He hung on to the side of the wall, digging his fingers into the thickest crack he could find.

After he had rested for a minute he tried to pull himself up the side. But it was a joke. Harrison could hardly get himself more than a few inches up before he fell back into the water. He tried to do it four times. And four times he got nowhere. On the last attempt, he nearly lost his grip on the wall. The current was getting stronger as the tide changed, and he pressed close to the cement wall, hugging it like a barnacle. But now that he wasn't moving, the cold began setting in for real on his muscles and flesh. Within minutes Harrison could feel his legs stop kicking, turn to leaden poles. Then his fingers began stiffening as well, slipping from their niches in the wall.

Suddenly he felt his eyes sort of just roll up in his head, as his battered body told him that it had had enough of all this. His fingers completely straightened out, like a corpse setting into rigor mortis, and he slid down the concrete wall into the dark river. As the shock of his head going under hit him with a final mini-jolt of adrenaline, Harrison tried to move, or at least send the command from his fogged brain to move. But the appendages were having none of that. Nothing would work for him anymore. And so he slipped beneath the water, wishing with what he knew would be his last thought on this earth that he was in bed with Natasha instead of dying out here in this infinitely foul and filthy place.

Chapter Thirty-Seven

Even as he felt himself being swallowed up by the frigid liquid Harrison felt something grabbing at him. A hand gripped around his collar and pulled hard. And suddenly, not knowing what the hell was going on—except that he could breathe again—Harrison broke the surface and was floundering around in a foam of death struggle. The hand kept pulling, and Harrison forced open one water-logged eye and looked up. A man was above him and when Harrison saw him—even in Harrison's near-terminal state—his eye opened a slit further.

For the man was completely tattooed—at least what Harrison could see of him—his arms, neck, everything but his face. And from the way the tattoos extended in under the black silk Chinese-style vest and pants that he wore, Harrison knew his entire body must be covered with them. There were beautiful, brightly colored drawings of snakes and dragons, with archaic symbols inked on between them like terrains around which the tattoo creatures ran and moved. Two immense green dragons curved around each of the man's arms, their heads seeming to bite into each of his shoulders, huge scaly jaws opened wide with red

321

tongues extending out and disappearing around the back of his neck. He was white-haired, with a long silverish beard that came to a point about a foot below his chin. And his eyes were fixed on Harrison with complete focus and lack of fear or panic.

"Relax," the voice said, though Harrison didn't even see the man's lips move. "Don't fight me. Here to help."

"Sure, sure," Harrison spluttered through river-filled lips. He tried to cool out. Not that he had to try too hard. And the tattooed man dragged him up out of the river so they were both sort of hanging on the side of the concrete wall. Harrison didn't quite see what the hell was going on, his eyes not working that well. But it looked like the tattooed guy had tied a rope up top and then come right down the side. Harrison knew he couldn't climb the damn thing. But the stranger didn't ask him to try. He felt the smaller man load him onto his shoulders, in a sort of Fireman's Carry, then tie him on with a long leather thong. Once he was secured, the man began climbing hand over hand right up the side of the wall, pulling up not just himself but all 240 pounds of Harrison.

Even in his near-coma Harrison knew that shouldn't be possible. But it was happening. For even as he coughed up a few mouthfuls of dark water, Harrison saw the wall going slowly by them. It took nearly three minutes—but at last the twenty-foot wall was ascended, and Harrison felt the man pull them up over the side. Then, without setting him down, the tattooed stranger started walking along the cracked streets by the river's edge. Harrison felt pain from the jogging motion as he was draped over the man's shoulder, the motion pressing against his numerous broken bones there, making various wounds bleed again. But he wasn't complaining—not after what he had just been through. After all, he shouldn't even be around anymore. I feel

322

pain, therefore I exist.

Then he was like a bouncing carcass draped over a hunter's shoulder. The man picked up speed even with his great load and they moved along through back streets that Harrison had never seen or heard of, cobblestone alleys filled with mist, along docks, through backyards, down narrow alleyways hardly wide enough to squeeze through. Wherever they were heading, it wasn't getting more civilized, for Harrison didn't see a soul. It seemed to grow ever foggier, the mist rising up to near chest level, as the air grew damp and thick with a strange chemical smell. Then they were at the base of a bridge which towered overhead. He could hear the cars occasionally zipping by, hundreds of feet above them. The man carried him to one of the great stone bases of the bridge—and fiddled with a huge combination lock on a steel door. After a few clicks the lock and then the door opened, and Harrison was carried right inside into one of the immense concrete supports that anchored the bridge to the Brooklyn shore.

He forced his twitching eyelids to open again as he smelled the dampness in his nostrils. The stranger was carrying him down a long corridor made up of huge stones piled one atop another. It was how the insides of the pyramid must have looked. The ceiling was high above, arched with all kinds of metal scaffoldings. Along the corridor, an occasional oil lamp burned smokily up on a wall, creating the only light within the shadowy rock halls. It seemed like they moved along for nearly five minutes before the stranger opened another door.

They were in an immense cavern of some kind. Harrison couldn't even see the far walls. The place was sparsely furnished, to say the least—just a broken-down chair here, a missing-legged sofa there. There were dummies hanging from the walls, mats, targets, all kinds of gear for combat and martial-arts training. But even as the tattooed man carried him to a large mattress in the middle of the great room, Harrison's eyes went on strike. And the last thing he saw as he slipped into darkness for the third time in the last twelve hours was the deep vacuum eyes of the man staring down at him as if from a thousand miles up.

Chapter Thirty-Eight

After that Harrison wasn't sure if he was dead or alive or dreaming or what the hell was going on. He just knew that he was hurt, bad. Everything hurt inside him now that he wasn't trying not to drown. His whole nervous system felt like it was on fire. He knew he was in bad shape, near death. That his system had been so abused, his nerves so overloaded, that his very being was near dissolution. Not that he was thinking it all out very clearly. But he knew.

Then he sank into deep and bizarre dreams. He was floating, floating like a balloon all around the room, above his body, and he could see the immense cavern that the stranger lived in. The man was lighting candles and sticks of incense all around the bed that Harrison's body lay on. And Harrison knew that it was a little weird that he should be able to look down and see himself. And he looked pretty pathetic, he had to say, battered to a pulp with every part of his body bruised and dark purple, blood coating his entire face. But before he could wonder about it all too much, he felt himself shooting up right through the ceiling of the place and into the dark night. It was as if he was in a time warp, being beamed down from the Starship

Enterprise or something. And then suddenly it was as if he couldn't stay aloft, as if his engine gave out, and before he knew it he was falling, falling into a jagged chasm of shadows and screams.

He was in a jungle. It was—it was North Vietnam. He was back again. How was it possible? Hadn't the war been over for—? But he could see the jungle all around him, hear the cries of the birds and frogs in the thick unbreathable dankness. He tried to walk, but found his feet stuck as if in quicksand. And he looked down to see that he was in fact standing in quicksand up to the knees and couldn't move an inch. Only the quicksand wasn't sand—it was blood, human blood. And as he looked down a hand came up out of the blood mud and grabbed hold of his leg, trying to pull him down into the dark liquid which bubbled up from below. Even as Harrison's mouth opened to scream and found that it couldn't, he saw them coming from the jungles all around him—the ghosts, the living corpses of the dead.

There were Vietnamese and Viet Cong, women and children—all dead from horrible wounds and burns, all dripping ghostly blood as they walked, their arms outstretched, terrible moans coming from their black holes of mouths. And even as they poured out, he saw that it wasn't just Asians—but Americans too. The souls of the dead men he had served with. There was Berger and Pauson, both with huge gaping holes in their chests and horrid ghoulish smiles on their faces. There was Hernandez—Harrison had sworn that the man had gotten his head blown off. But as the figure drew closer, he could indeed see that the corpse ghost was carrying its head in front of it at chest level with both hands. It laughed a noiseless sound as it walked, blood spurting out of its opened neck wound like a geyser and flowing down all around it.

326

Somehow Harrison knew instinctively that when and if they touched him—he was dead. That they wanted him. He tried to move his feet from the blood pond, but he was stuck like a fly in glue as the hand still pulled wildly at him from below, grabbing his leg with its clawed red fingernails. And as the lurching corpse army drew closer, he could hear them calling to him.

"Harrison, Harrison, come with us. Join us. It is beautiful here. There is no pain. Is no pain. Just eternal meditation. It is beautiful." They all seemed to talk at once like a Greek chorus. None screamed or yelled or raised their voice. But like talking dolls extolling annihilation, they pleaded with him to come—be one of them. Which idea, as head-banged as Harrison was, was not to his liking. He struggled harder, ripping his feet up, trying to fly up again the way he had a minute before. And with a supreme effort of will, he somehow managed to rip his feet free and rise up above their grasp just as the blood-coated hands reached in to grab him.

Then it was as if his body was just sucked through some sort of pneumatic tube. For suddenly he was back in the great stone chamber beneath the bridge. And he was lying face down on the mattress—with the tattooed guy smearing some sort of green paste all over his body. His naked body, he realized as he felt the chill from the air hit the thick goo. He tried to move, but couldn't budge even a little finger. Harrison prayed that the bastard wasn't some kind of sick pervert. Though just what kind of pervert would want to cover someone with green slime was beyond his feeble ability to comprehend. Once the foul-smelling green stuff was applied so that it covered every square inch of him, the guy stepped on top of Harrison, wearing some kind of weird-textured boots—and began walking back and forth on him like he was trying out a pair of sneakers.

Harrison could feel, even within the pain, bones snapping and popping all over the place. He groaned audibly as he felt his very soul wracked with unbearable pain.

"Ah, good, you feel the pain," the tattooed man said as he continue to walk up and down on Harrison's back, legs, arms. "You are very badly hurt," the man went on. "Perhaps I can help you—perhaps not. But you must fight. Do you understand? You'll black out again soon. Whatever I do in the next hours and days— is to help you. I promise you that. Marshal your strength, half-dead man. For if you've ever wanted to live, *now* is the time to make it known." With that the man began jumping up and down on one of Harrison's legs. He had known it was broken back in the river, as the pain had been absolutely searing every time he kicked with it. The pain now pushed him back over the edge into the gray eternal fog, where the living and the dead meet and battle out the war of survival.

He was on the battlefield again. There were shells landing everywhere, machine-gun bullets spraying by like little lead-nosed sparrows looking for human worms. Right beside him a man, Doral, a card-playing buddy, went flying into the air in a blast of orange and red flame. When he came down he was just an armless, legless piece of red dripping meat with nothing more to say. Harrison flew through the jungle paddy. But the bombs poured down—and he realized with horror that it was his *own* men, U.S. attack choppers, that were sending down this hailstorm. Ahead of him the VC who had been hiding in ditches came pouring out and fled toward the nearby jungle. But the U.S. firepower was just too withering.

All around him VC and Americans were being sprayed down, shredded into Sloppy Joes. He was slipping now as he ran, sliding in pools of blood, stumbling through obstacle courses of pieces of bodies. But he ran. "You must fight to live. Fight to live." The words rang through his head like some sort of sacred mantra and he surged ahead ducking and dodging the bombs that flew everywhere. Suddenly a single whistling shell seemed to have his name written all over it. It tore down out of the dark sky and came down right on his head. Harrison felt himself explode into a thousand pieces, felt his mind, and heart, and all his memories just spray out in every direction as if dynamite had gone off inside his chest and brain.

Then he was back in the bridge cavern. He was still covered with the thick green paste, which seemed to soothe and sink ever deeper into his skin. And he was on his back looking up at the great vaulted ceiling that rose like the ceiling of St. Patrick's as high as he could see, until the stone roof vanished in the dark linear shadows high above.

"Ah, he awakens for the second time," the tattooed man said, looking down at Harrison, as he pushed some kind of dolly on which the immobile Harrison was lying. "You have been out for ten hours. You may actually live. I'm still not sure."

"You must—must warn authorities," Harrison managed to somehow mutter through his swollen lips as he raised himself a few inches. "There is a bomb, atomic bomb—in B basement of Games Village. Bulgarian training building. Do—do—you underst . . ." His voice broke off as he collapsed back down flat onto his face.

"I will warn them," the man said, not breaking stride or questioning such a wild statement. Apparently the fellow had his own way of judging things. Suddenly Harrison felt himself being pushed off the side of the dolly and into something wet. For a moment he panicked and began trying to splash around, though he

hardly got more than a shudder or two from one leg
and a hand twitched slightly before collapsing again.
He quickly realized that it wasn't the river that he was
being dumped back into, but some kind of tank. The
water felt warm instead of the frigid death chills of the
East River. As he settled into it Harrison saw out of the
corner of his eye that he was in a flotation tank, like the
kind those seeking deep states of meditation went into.
Apparently it had other uses besides just calming the
mind.

"You will sleep some more. And heal," the tattooed
man said. And for a moment Harrison could see in the
flickering of an oil lamp on a table alongside them that
the man was dressed in opened black silk vest and
cutoff silk black pants at the knee, with kung fu shoes.
He was tattooed over every part of his body on all the
exposed flesh of the arms, lower legs, and chest. And
Harrison saw that the pictures, which had looked
separated and alone earlier, were actually part of a vast
mosaic of color and ink sliced into human flesh. An
epic scene of Celtic warriors coming at a Roman
phalanx as they rode, themselves tattooed, on horse-
back swinging immense swords and standing upright.
And on each flank of the man were dragons and lions
coming out and eating the warriors. It was a wild
picture—something worthy of the greatest of painters.
A thousand questions rose up in Harrison's mind like a
swarm of wasps, but it all just made him feel tired,
terribly tired. And even as he rested down in the tank,
letting his eyes slip closed again, he heard the man
pouring some sort of powder into the water and it
seemed to foam and bubble against his skin. Then the
top was being closed, so that he was covered all the way
up to his neck. Only his head, supported by a small
floating headrest, was above the water line.

Harrison had to admit it felt good. He was a fetus in

the womb again floating in the hot mineralized water—
in a chemical/mineral bath simulating all the essential
elements of the human body, transferring them into the
heat-soaked, pore-opened flesh.

Then he was with the ghosts again. Only now he was
not even in an earthly terrain, but in some dark
claustrophobic place far beneath the earth. There the
dead squirmed sideways like snakes through the soil
and they were everywhere around him. And they
sighted him, their radar senses alerting them to the
presence of a new soul. They came toward him with
their ethereal dripping jaws opened wide, their skeletal
clawed hands digging through the dirt, digging wildly,
like beasts, trying to do anything to reach him.

Chapter Thirty-Nine

Colonel Parker jumped from the beat-up Valiant that the plainclothes boys had driven him across Queens in. The anonymous tip that there was a bomb in the Games Village, which the FBI boys had received and called him in on, had proved to be false—or at any rate they were all too late. There were traces of radiation in the subbasement—lots of it—but no bomb. No Harrison either. But just as they finished searching the entire basement, a call had come over police radio band that a terrorist situation involving radiation was occurring on Corona Boulevard, about two miles from the stadium. Parker prayed this was it. For the Games only had two more days till the award ceremony, and then they'd be over. If the bastards were going to strike, they were running out of time. And so was he.

"Machine gun," a cop yelled as Parker exited the unmarked car, pointing up toward a five-story tenement building across the street. "He's got a fucking machine gun." There was a sudden burst of fire from an upper window, and slugs crisscrossed the asphalt, bursting car lights, ripping into the pavement. At least two cops took hits and let out sharp screams.

"Dive," Parker screamed out to FBI Bureau Chief

Hagstrom, who was getting out of one of the back doors of the Valiant. The CIA man dove to the ground, grabbing the FBIer by the arm and dragging him halfway under the unmarked car. The windows of the vehicle above them exploded out like a bomb had just gone off inside, covering both men's heads with little snowflakes of glass. Then the bullets moved off again, down the wide street filled with cops and squad cars, their lights flashing wildly in the midnight darkness.

After about twenty seconds the sound of the machine gun stopped, and fifty blue hats slowly rose up over the hoods of their cars to see what the hell was going on. Then fifty pistols and rifles appeared and began firing back up. Parker saw a big red-nosed cop with official-looking medallions all over his jacket and cap and he headed over to him, crouching low. The FBI man followed close behind. Parker headed straight up to the big cop, interrupting the orders he was bellowing out to five of his white-faced subordinates.

"What the hell is going on here?" the CIA chief asked, his face getting as red as the cop's. The Chief of Queens Detectives, Captain Beldings, moved toward Parker as if about to punch him. Suddenly he recognized the FBI man by his side. The Chief of Detectives had had a number of cordial, if not particularly friendly, interactions with him in the past.

"Who the hell is your friend here?" Beldings asked, standing up to show the officer how tall he was. Parker didn't look all that impressed.

"He's Colonel Parker, CIA," the FBI man said. "We heard the call over the police radio, that there's radiation involved. That's why we're here. We can't tell you exactly what our interest is, but I guarantee you it's el primo."

"Yeah, primo, everyone's primo," the cop said with disgust. "There's radiation, all right," Beldings snarled, glaring at Parker for a few more seconds just to let the guy know he wasn't scared of him. "We had a bomb call. Bomb squad boys were called in and picked up some readings on their meters. Why the hell do you think we got so much equipment all over the place?" He pointed around at the big bomb and emergency service trucks that filled one whole side of the street just out of range of the sniper's line of fire.

"Tell me," Parker said, slamming a butt into his mouth as he kept one eye on the window, ready to dive if the machine-gun muzzle poked out again. "What the hell's going on? Exactly what happened? Don't mean to be so rude. But what we're after is of life-and-death importance to every man, woman, and child in this city?"

"*Everyone's* in a damn hurry," the captain said with a snort, his beefy red nose looking like it might just fall off the ruddy face from its own weight. "Well, we got a call from the landlady of the building where our machine-gun-firing crazy is holed up. A Mrs. Rodriguez," the Chief of Detectives went on in a sarcastic kind of drawl, obviously not all that pleased about having to deliver a report to the smooth, expensively attired Parker. "She called in a report that this guy she had rented a room to had some guns and stuff. So we send a couple of guys over—they knock—and boom! He tries to blow them away with some heavy firepower. Both in the hospital, one critical. Everybody in the building empties out. So we get the SWAT team in, plus a tactical unit and the bomb boys. They get the rad readings. They say they're not dangerous to nearby human health, so we're not evacuating the neighborhood—at least not right now. Looks like we're going to have to ice the bastard to get him out. We've been firing for fifteen minutes. The son of a bitch got two more of my guys."

"Did anyone try to talk to this creep?" Parker asked

334

as another burst of firing from the upper window filled the street. Since they were standing behind a large bomb truck they didn't duck.

"Listen, Parker," the cop said, his face starting to glow even redder. "We pull up and this bastard starts shooting. What the hell do you want me to do? Kiss his ass?"

"No, I want all your men to stop firing. Just stop—period! I've got to talk to this guy. He's not a psycho. Not a normal one anyway," Parker said with tremendous authority and command, which made even the cop who had stood up to police commissioners blanch a little.

"Not a normal psycho, jeesh," the cop snorted to himself. He looked over at the FBI bureau head, who just raised his eyebrows like it might be a good idea. And suddenly it dawned on the cop that maybe it really *was* important. These two guys wouldn't be here for Mickey Mouse shit. "All right, all right," he said somewhat reluctantly. He pulled out a bullhorn from behind the truck's door and walked around with it to the street.

"Stop firing! Stop firing!" the Chief said, bellowing like a bull. "A Mr. Parker is stepping out into the street to talk with our pal up there. I repeat, stop firing until further command." The shooting slowly died down until just a few shots were heard. "I said stop!" Beldings screamed so the words came out distorted through the amplifying power of the handheld PA. Suddenly it was eerily silent. Smoke filled the street like a fog. Parker grabbed the horn impatiently out of Beldings's hands and walked slowly out into the center of Corona Boulevard, keeping a wary eye on the gunman's window.

For the first time, as he walked forward, Parker could see how much damage had already been done. The entire street was a wreck. Every window was blown

335

out, most of the cars parked along the sides—and the cop cars as well—had bullet holes like pock marks covering their steel bodies. Even bits of the street and sidewalk had been blown out, making little cement craters the size of ping-pong balls. Parker tilted the horn up toward the window.

"We won't hurt you—if you surrender. We are not your enemy." He waited a few seconds. Nothing. At least the bastard wasn't firing.

"What do you want? Do you speak English?" He waited again. Silence. A stay cat took advantage of the momentary lull in the battle to jump out of a garbage can and run across the street. The can tipped over and crashed onto the sidewalk. Cops everywhere jumped like they'd been goosed—but somehow all held their fire. Parker's heart skipped five beats. He looked around for a good spot to leap to if . . .

"Are you all right?" he went on, speaking in calm modulated tones. He had taken training in hostage and terrorist situations, and if he could just calm things down a little, maybe they would get this guy alive. Parker was itching to get into the room.

Suddenly the man's face appeared at the window, and Parker winced as he thought the guy was about to fire. But he screamed down wild rantings in some foreign language that Parker knew was Arabic after he had heard a few seconds of it. He could see even from his vantage point that the guy was hurt. Hurt and worse. His face was bandaged, but even through the coverings the CIA man could see patches of red everywhere. His hair was almost gone, with big bald patches as if the man had been half scalped by Indians. And Parker could see as well that the man was shaking, jerking around like a puppet on a madman's strings. He couldn't be too long for this world.

"Hey, does anyone here speak even a little Arabic?" Parker asked through the bullhorn, addressing the

336

multitude of heavily armed cops. No one seemed to respond, but after about five seconds, a thin cop with wiry black hair yelled out, "I do!" Parker waved him forward, and the SWAT man let his assault rifle rest in his right arm while he walked slowly forward from behind a nearly destroyed station wagon.

"You speak the stuff?" Parker asked as the man walked up to him with a twisted expression on his face, realizing he was right out there in the middle of the firefield.

"I'm a Jew, you know," the young cop said. "Lived over in Israel for a few years. Yeah, I speak some of that A-rab lingo."

"Ask him what he wants. Who he is. Say anything, just get him talking. And—what's your name?"

"Myron, sir," the cop said, "Myron Barstein."

"Myron—act friendly, okay? However you feel about the bastards is your thing—but this guy's on the edge, to say the least. Act concerned, don't say anything threatening. You understand?"

"Yes," the CO replied, sensing the authority of Parker, the energy that had always made him motivate, lead men. "I'll do my best." He took the bullhorn that Parker held out and raised it to his lips, looking up at the window where the bandaged face of the terrorist was peeking out from between shredded curtains. The cop yelled up a whole stream of words that all sounded like high-pitched gibberish to Parker. The man yelled down, answering for about ten seconds. The cop looked at the CIA man.

"He says we should all go to hell."

"Ask him what it is he wants," Parker said.

The cop yelled up again and the man screamed back in a clearly hysterical voice. "He says he wants to die— but first he wants to kill as many police as he can."

"That's what he said?" Parker said. "Shit. Ask him why. Why does he want to die?"

The cop yelled up again. The gunman screamed down for about twenty seconds, his voice rising to a wild crescendo. The cop turned to Parker, his eyes wide in incredulity. "Well, I don't know if you're going to believe this—and maybe my Arabic is worse than I thought—but he says some crazy stuff about how he wants to die because then he'll be in Paradise tonight. And the more cops he kills now, the more maidens will wait on him and serve him golden fruits, their dark eyes shining like pools in the desert—or something like that. And then he added—you're all going to die anyway. All. That was what he was screaming at the end there. All! All! All! I'm sure that's what he said."

"I believe you, kid," Parker said, patting the young cop on the shoulder. He could see that the cop was getting a little unnerved by the whole translator role. But suddenly the conversation was abruptly over as the gunman opened up again. Parker pushed the cop sideways and down behind a tire-punctured patrol car in the middle of the street just as bullets ripped the air like lead raindrops falling from the very skies. As the scissors of slugs ripped down toward the other side of the street, Parker dashed back behind the bomb truck and up to Chief Beldings, who looked at him with a big smirk on his wide face.

"I told you, didn't I? This guy wants to be shot, needs to be shot—so let's shoot him."

"All right—go for it," Parker said. "But listen—your men have got to be extremely careful. There could—could be a bomb inside. Something fairly large. It might not look like a bomb, might just be in a big box or something. You hear me? I'm talking big bomb here, pal. Real big."

The Chief got the message. Suddenly he realized what this was all about and his face went from red to chalk white in the space of about a second. "We'll try tear gas first," he said, suddenly sounding a lot less

338

aggressive. "We'll try to get him alive." He walked quickly away to his communications unit and gave out orders to the various leaders of the special services squads spread out over a three-block radius. After about five minutes as the cops moved into their various spots near the building, two cops on the opposite roof fired in cannister after cannister of tear gas through all the windows on the fifth floor. Their aim was good, and within seconds thick acrid white smoke began billowing out of every window.

"Rush him. Rush him now," Beldings screamed out, urging the forces on. Ten cops armed to the teeth ran across the street and plowed through the narrow doorway of the gunman's building. They ran up the stairs two at a time, blood in their eyes, their pump shotguns and 9-mm assault auto-rifles ready to blow anyone away. Parker started across the street after them, but Beldings grabbed him by the jacket sleeve and wouldn't let him move.

"No way, Mr. CIA," the cop said. "I'm in charge of the field operations here. You get bumped off, big Washington fellows like yourself, I'm back popping whores on the Bowery. You wait until they've got the place secure." Parker fumed, but put his .357 back into its shoulder holster. The cop was in charge of the situation. Parker could respect that.

The cops ran up the first flight and heard coughing somewhere above them. A white cloud of tear gas was working its way down the rickety wooden stairs, which creaked as if they ached beneath the cops' feet. The gunman had been forced out of his room.

"I think we got him cornered, men," the SWAT sergeant in charge of the assault team said. They slowed down as they rounded the second-floor landing. "Quiet, quiet," the stocky sergeant hissed in the smoke, a dim twenty-five-watt bulb barely illuminating the smoky hallway. They edged tightly along the wall, all pressing against the peeling green paint. The sergeant peered around the bottom of the stairs leading up to the third floor. He couldn't see anything clearly in the cloud of smoke above.

"Masks," he whispered. The cops all pulled their tear gas masks from inside their flak jackets and strapped them on.

"Okay—let's move—but slow." His voice was muffled and far away within the thick rubber mask. They moved inch by inch up the squeaking staircase unable to hear a thing from above. Maybe the terrorist had fallen unconscious from the gas. They were halfway up the flight of stairs when the Arab appeared suddenly like some ghostly apparition from out of the smoke. He looked down on them with scorn filling his black eyes. He had no gun, but balanced a long shining tube on his right shoulder. He was holding it and aiming with both hands.

If the sergeant had been trained in armaments identification he would have recognized the Stinger II hand-held missile-launcher and its deadly red-tipped torpedo-like shell peering out from the end ready to launch itself. Had he known, the sergeant might have turned and jumped to the landing below—or he might have fired instantly. In either case he and his men might have lived. But he waited a half second too long.

What the fuck is that? he wondered as he raised his shotgun up in a quick arc. It was the last thing he ever wondered. A blue-white flame shot out of the back of the tube with a deafening roar, melting the plaster on the wall behind it with a temperature of 2500 degrees. A missile, four feet long, ten inches wide, shot out of the front. As it left the tube, two small fins popped out of each side for stabilization. Within one fiftieth of a second, the projectile was moving at a speed of 360 miles an hour.

In a twenty-fifth of a second the missile slammed

right into—and through—the chest of the sergeant like he was made of butter, ripping right through his ribs, sending his lungs and heart exploding out through his back in a thick soupy spray toward the men behind him.

By one tenth of a second the missile had ripped through two more cops, slicing their heads cleanly from their bodies, splashing their brains into the dark tear-gassed air. By the time it hit the wall at the bottom of the stairs—the first target with enough solidity to make it detonate—the missile was traveling at a speed of 500 miles an hour. The Stinger II was a surface-fired missile intended to take out tanks or jets. The wall was like tissue paper to it, and the Stinger traveled halfway through the crumbling plaster and inner lathing of the decrepit old rooming-house wall before it exploded.

In the small space of the rooming-house hallways, the stairs, doors, walls, and ceiling were instantly pulverized into fragments and dust. A fireball surged across the second and third floor, mushrooming up and blowing the top of the roof right up into the air. A shock wave flew just ahead of the sound blast, rushing down the stairs and knocking the ground floor completely off its supports and down into the basement, where hundreds of deafened bleeding rats ran around squealing loudly.

The remaining cops on the second floor landing were incinerated in the swirling firestorm that descended over them. They didn't have time to scream as their lungs were burnt to the crispy texture of fried duck skin in Chinatown. Their flesh turned black within seconds and dripped like hot tar onto the splintered and flaming floorboards. The Arab, on his trip to Paradise, left his body in a most disorderly way, splattered into the surrounding woodwork as the explosive force from fifteen feet below ricocheted back and melted the flesh right from his chest and face. He didn't have time to scream. None of them did.

At one and a half seconds, the brick facade of the front of the rooming house erupted out into the street, pelting the blue-helmeted cops below with thousands of bricks and twisted bits of glass and steel from the window frames. Pieces of porcelain toilets, tubs, and sinks rained down in huge chunks like hailstones.

At three seconds the release force of the forty pounds of high explosive sent a shock wave out through the windows and walls and onto the street. The cops standing all around were knocked to the ground like tenpins, their flak jackets ripped open by the concussion, a few toupees flying into the air. Smoke poured out of every opening in the barely standing building, black like smoke from an oil fire.

Then it was over. The explosion anyway. Parker slowly lifted his head. He was lying in a pile of rubble covered with dust and bits of broken brick. Another man was sprawled just inches from his face—Beldings. It took him a few seconds to clear the cobwebs from his mind. He stood up, barely able to hold his own weight on trembling legs, though he couldn't really see that he had been hurt. Just sheer shock from the blast. His ears were ringing like a thousand fire alarms going off at once.

The dense smoke slowly cleared around him and joined together, forming an almost mushroom-shaped cloud that extended up a two hundred feet. Bodies of barely moving cops were strewn all around the street like discarded mannequins. Parker could hear moans and cries of pain coming from every direction. As the smoke cleared further he could see the building. Jesus, there was hardly anything left. It looked as if the whole top of the place had been ripped away by a giant claw that had left but a few twisted wooden support beams poking skyward. Flames licked along the edges of the few remaining walls, and he could see beds and chairs

342

smoldering through the swirling dust. Most of the building's outer walls had burst free of the structure, so it was like looking at a dollhouse—you could see each apartment exposed, the contents within—beds, chairs —lying on their sides. Parker headed into the building, moving carefully up the half-collapsed staircase. He knew he was crazy to even be walking around the damn thing. It looked as if it could go down at any moment. But he had to know if the bomb was there. He made it up by grabbing onto things and pulling himself up by hand. But after about five minutes he reached what had been the third-floor landing. The cops were splattered all over the place like they had just been through a butchering factory. Parker had seen a lot of death in his time. But this was something else. Perhaps because of the way they had all been confined to one area, their bodies had been ripped apart like they were in the blast of a jet engine.

Then at the top of the next flight of stairs, where some of the wall had somehow stayed up, Parker saw something that made his skin crawl, his flesh turn cold. Particles. Glowing in the gray air as they swirled around like bugs in the dust funnels. Pieces of the dead terrorist were all over the top of the stairs—and they glowed too. Severed hands, his head, an organ or two—all were shining with a green luminescence through the smoke. The man was as radioactive as a Hiroshima cockroach. Parker picked up a gas mask he saw at the foot of the stairs and pulled it over his head. He didn't want to breathe in the glowing high-rad particles of a dead man. He took out his mini-geiger and checked around the fourth floor, walking carefully, creaking up a storm. But though he found lots of residual readings, there was nothing that could have been the A-bomb. But he knew one thing beyond question now. It existed. And these bastards were crazy enough to use it.

Chapter Forty

Harrison seemed to float back and forth between the world of the dead and the world of the living, like a balloon caught in opposite wind currents that doesn't know which way to go. His body was wracked with injuries. Most men would have died from the sheer trauma of the beating and the exposure to the water and cold he had endured. But Harrison was not most men. His will was stronger, his desire to survive, to live on whatever the pain, was too strong for the grabbing hands of the dead to overcome. Gathering all his strength, Harrison shot up through the ethereal black soil—a million clawed hands reaching for him, a million black eyes sparkling like death stars all around him.

When he opened his eyes and felt the pain ripping through his flesh, he knew he was back among the living—at least for the moment. He was still floating in the pool of warm water. It felt good. Compared to splashing around in garbage with eels biting at his face, this was like paradise.

"Good, you're awake," a voice said, startling Harrison from his dreamlike state. The moment the voice made him open his eyes it all started up again, like fire along every vein. "You must wake up fully now," a fuzzy face was saying. As Harrison's eyes adjusted slowly to the dim oil-flamed darkness of the chamber, he saw the white-bearded face, the tattoos. It all came back to him in a flash—where he was, the rescue. . . .

"Who—who are you?" Harrison asked through slow-moving lips. He felt like he was yelling, but he could hardly hear his own words. "Why are you helping me?"

"Call me . . . Tattoo," the man said, looking down at Harrison with an expression that was neither smile nor scowl, neither friendly nor cold, but more like the absolute neutrality of a mirror reflecting back what it saw. "I helped you because you needed help."

"But where am I? What's going on? Did you notify—" He began yelling in his feverish mental state and writhing around within the flotation tank. It splashed up over the sides and out onto the tatami mat that surrounded it.

"Relax, relax, Mr. Harrison," the tattooed man said, folding his arms in front of him so Harrison could see the snakes intertwining with one another. Every time the man moved he set some of his tattoos in motion. It looked like his very flesh was alive with creatures crawling all over him. "Relaxation is the key to all things—war and peace. Yes—I did notify the authorities of what you told me. Now relax. Breathe out. Breathe out deeply, Mr. Harrison—for you still have a terrible battle ahead of you." Harrison listened, realizing he was starting to lose it. He took three deep breaths, pushing out as far as his tortured lungs would permit, and then lay still in the tank, his head free of the closed metal cover.

"Listen to me carefully," Tattoo went on as he walked around the tank and began undoing clasps on its sides. "What I'm about to say to you will be the most

345

important words you will ever hear. Do you understand?"

"Yes," Harrison muttered weakly, trying to maintain his breathing and not panic.

"You have been near death for two and a half days. You still are very close to the darkness. If you fall completely within its grasp—there is nothing I can do. Now—I have healed the outside of your flesh. Already the skin is closing, the bone fractures are beginning to knit together. But you are hurt at a deeper level. When whoever tortured you gave you electric shock at your pressure points, they reversed your Chi flow. That means the motor that runs your body actually believes that you are dying and is already sending its Chi, the life flow, into the negative direction—or the death flow. You are alive, your flesh is healing, but the innermost energy systems of your being don't even know it. It is a strange situation," Tattoo went on, undoing the last of the cover's clasps and throwing the steel cover back. He helped the dripping, still-green-coated Harrison step out, handing him a thick robe and warm slippers, which seemed to insulate him almost immediately from the cold, and led him a few feet away to a mat about ten feet in diameter.

It was rough going for Harrison, even moving a few yards. His legs were like burning pokers, his feet felt like they had razors embedded in the soles. Every fucking part of him begged for mercy, but he just walked slowly ahead, gritting his teeth and making not a sound. It took nearly thirty seconds for him to walk ten feet, and then he stopped and stood beside the tattooed man.

"Now—there is only one way we can reverse the Chi direction again—to a live flow—and we must hurry, begin immediately. Already it may be too far gone in the direction of cessation."

"I don't know what the hell you're talking about," Harrison whispered through puffed-up lips, "but I'm ready to try. You've already helped me greatly. I guess—I trust you."

"Take this position," Tattoo said, suddenly spreading his feet about shoulder distance apart and holding his arms straight out in front of him at chest level so the palms were facing back toward him, fingers just touching. His hands were curved as if cupping a ball. "There, see the curve of my fingers, hands, arms—and whole body? Curves within curves." As Harrison tried to sink into the posture Tattoo was showing him, he felt everything creak a little in his body, pangs of pain shoot through him like he was being jolted with an electric cattle prod.

Tattoo rose and walked around him, helping him get it all in exactly the right angle. "This is the Standing Posture, the Chi Concentrator. It is said by legend to make the limbs as supple as a baby's—and the bones as hard as steel. When done for extended periods of time, it can create tremendous flows of Chi through the body, almost overwhelming amounts of pure life force. This is what we must do with you." He ran his index fingers along the insides of Harrison's palms, showing him the circular relationships of the hands, arms, shoulders. Circles within circles, the secrets, the building blocks of the universe—and of men.

"Now you must feel the energy flowing between all these points. Between your hands, between hands and chest. Like an electric current, an invisible wave that can amost burn with its heat." Again he aligned Harrison just right so all the angles that the Chi Concentrator Standing Posture called for were correct. Harrison couldn't be a millimeter off in the angle of joint to joint—or the energy reversal might not occur. Tattoo knew how difficult their task was. But he didn't share the odds with the half-dead man standing next to him.

"Now you must stand like this for twelve hours without cease. Without moving, without taking a shit or a piss, without eating—without anything. Do you hear me, Harrison? Do you understand what I'm telling you?" Tattoo kept talking as if he were speaking to a moron, which Harrison didn't appreciate. But he understood that the man was trying to make him take the words very, very seriously. He'd try, though he sure as hell wasn't guaranteeing any results. The idea that he could stand for twelve minutes, let alone twelve hours, seemed a little absurd at that moment, seeing as how his legs were vibrating beneath him like toothpicks trying to hold up a hippo.

He let himself sink completely into the posture as Tattoo did the same about a yard to the right of him. They both stared straight ahead at an immense Tankha—a Tibetan painting—that was mounted on the wall about thirty feet away. It showed a ten-foot tall demon with horns and fangs, holding a circular depiction of all of man's godhead and demonic selves— from total good to utter evil. Each segment was demarcated by a different scene of man's conflict with himself, with good and evil. It was striking.

"Now we will stand together. I have joined you so you will not have to endure the pain, the loneliness of the task alone. You must feel that you are sinking, sinking always further down. As if you were rooted into the earth like a tree, and your legs, your feet are roots digging down into the soil. Your spine and head are the trunk rising up, your arms the branches. *All* is rooted, all sinks into the earth." He let that sink in a little as he settled deeper into his own posture.

"First you will feel just pain. Then a shaking, and a heat in your legs, which will begin to vibrate as if they

348

are out of control. You must keep standing. No matter what happens—stay in posture. Breathe deep. Fear nothing. Nothing." With that the man stopped talking. As if on cue a great gong sounded somewhere in the cavern, sending an icy chord through Harrison's spine and cranium.

He rested into the position, growing more awake by the second from the pain of standing up, of feeling all his fractured bones pushing down against one another. But the pain could be good too. Yes, it was good—would keep him going through the hours. He had to trust Tattoo, though he knew nothing about the man, who the hell he worked for, or even what race he was. He seemed somehow an amalgamation of all races, with a dash of the Orient thrown in with the long pointed beard and silver hair now untied from its long tail and spread out dramatically, flowing down and around his shoulders.

It didn't take Harrison long to begin feeling some of the effects of the Standing Posture that Tattoo had warned him about. The pain lasted just about half an hour, intense wracking pain that made tears come to his eyes as the bones seemed to settle further into place and nerves began feeling again—exquisitely unpleasant sensations. Then suddenly it all seemed to just vanish. And his whole body from the ankles up felt hot, like it was on fire. He welcomed the warmth as his flesh was feeling cold with the green goo still coating it, even within the goose-down full-length robe that Tattoo had draped over him.

Then the shaking began. Harrison could hardly believe it when the first shudders hit him. It was as if his legs weren't his own, like they were made of rubber and were jumping all over the place with minds of their own. He thought perhaps he would fall right down on the cold stone floor. But though the shaking actually

349

began making him pogo-stick up and down so that he felt himself lifting an inch or two off the floor and coming down again, he didn't fall down. It was as if all his body weight were dropping, sinking ever lower and lower into the earth, just as Tattoo had said.

Then the pain began anew. And this time it was in earnest. It was as if wires had been slid through his skin and into the end of every nerve cell in his body. And all connected to a 20,000-volt generator—then lit up at once. Everything was exploding inside, and all that Harrison wanted to do was scream—but he found his mouth frozen in place by the sheer numbing pain that made the jaws lock like a bear-trap. He shook even harder, moving up and down on his legs like he was on springs, so that he began jumping around facing in different directions.

Tattoo, who was also bouncing in place, his posture absolutely perfect, began chanting, a deep guttural sound similar to what Harrison had heard monks chant in Asian temples. It was a soothing sound, contrasting markedly with the jolts of pain coursing through him, taking him to the very limits of his abilities to endure. The deep chanting sounds grew louder, faster—strange indecipherable sounds, like a lost language, a song from the dawn of time itself, with animal sounds mixed in, barking calls and long ghostlike howls. He had never heard anything like it. In a way, the sheer bizarreness of the sounds took his mind off the pain—for a minute.

But when it hit again—it was worse. Harrison swore it was all over. It wasn't just pain—but a terrible crushing sensation coming down on every part of him. He knew in an instant that it was death itself coming to claim him. Making a final attempt to grab him in a choke hold—and not let go. And by the way that Harrison's chest was tightening up as it had in the river—it looked like death was winning. It was as if he was a child again filled with a pure, nameless terror. The terror of the blackness that waits just the other side of life. The darkness beyond the door. The darkness that reached for him now from out of the very depths of time, from out of the demonic face of the rainbow Tankha that stood on the wall thirty feet ahead.

And suddenly Harrison could feel death's hands closing around his throat. They were cold hands, starkly cold in contrast to the great amount of heat being generated by his body from the Chi Posture. The skeletal fingers squeezed his throat, ever tightening so he couldn't breathe. Harrison could feel them—all ten fingers. Death had ten fingers too. At least he knew that before dying. He weakened, on the edge of falling apart as he felt himself start to go over. It was Humpty-Dumpty time, and all the king's horses weren't going to be able to put him together again.

Suddenly, like a bolt of lightning from out of the burning clouds of his flesh, came a sudden feeling of release, of moving from the darkness to the light. And Harrison knew without knowing the words for it that his negative Chi flow had reversed. That his soul, his deepest generating force, the sheer magnetism of the universe itself that ran through the veins of all animate things, had been polarized back to the flow pattern of the living. And even as he felt a surge of almost loving warmth like a mother's hot milk flow through his every cell, Harrison felt the skeletal grip relax on his throat, the shadowy fingers hesitate as if frustrated that they had been so close. And then, as the Positive Chi flow began hitting cruising speed inside him and a deep pinkish color returned to his cells, the hands of darkness vanished suddenly to seek out other souls who would be easier game than this stubborn son-of-a-bitch.

351

Chapter Forty-One

The deep ringing tones of the gong again swept through the great bridge cavern, nearly bringing tears to Harrison's eyes. It was the sheer power of the sound, like an unstoppable waterfall of life. Then Tattoo was in front of him, both of his hands on Harrison's shoulders.

"You can stop now, it's over. You're alive—and will stay that way until the next time. Come over here, lie down on the tatami mat, let your body rest." Harrison followed the Tattoo's directions and lay down flat on his back. Shit, he hurt. As if nails were being pounded into every part of him. After about ten minutes Tattoo motioned for Harrison to sit up.

"Drink this. Zhnaktha herbs. It doesn't taste the greatest—but it will give you energy for the next few hours. Used by the Sherpas for their climbs up Everest, and by monks when they cross the great Himalayan passages.

"After that you will collapse—and sleep for about a week. You've been through too much to keep going for long. But this will get you through one more day." He handed Harrison a cup filled with a reddish liquid. The odor of the stuff wasn't bad, but the taste, as Tattoo had mentioned, was terrible.

"Don't spit it out," Tattoo said firmly. "Drink it down. Drink every drop. It is the only way to get through what you must face today." Harrison made himself quaff the stuff down though he wasn't quite sure it was all going to stay down. He handed the cup back empty.

"Good." Tattoo said. "Good, you've done very well."

"Listen," Harrison said suddenly, as he felt an infusion of energy instantly rush through his bloodstream, making his eyes pop open wider. Even his senses seemed more alert. "I'm sure as hell grateful for all that you've done for me—though to tell you the truth, I'm not sure what the hell it was. But, man, what's going on here? Who are you? What's your trip?"

Tattoo smiled for the first time in their short acquaintance. "You are an inquisitive fellow, aren't you? But then you would have to be. It's one of the top survival traits—curiosity. As to who I am—it doesn't matter and would be too complicated to explain. As to where we are—that I'm afraid I can't reveal. It will be better for you not to know. There are those out there who would do anything to know the location of . . . this place. Suffice it to say that you have your battles to fight—and I have mine. We fight on the same side. Of that I can assure you. But you know that. You can tell what kind of man I am."

"Great, you won't tell me a damn thing, and every time you say a word you just add more confusion to the whole mess." Harrison reached for a glass of water he saw alongside the mat to wash down the wretched-tasting Zhnaktha herbs. He put the glass down and stood up. He was amazed. He could walk. Could move his arms. Everything actually worked. He knew he was still hurt all over, could see the bruised flesh, feel his puffed-up eyes, his split lip. Still, compared to how he had felt yesterday, it was truly a miracle.

"Come," Tattoo said suddenly. "We must go!" He barely gave Harrison time to get dressed in his clothes, which had been cleaned and dried out. Then Tattoo was off and running, leading Harrison on a wild course through basement mazes beneath the highways and bridges of the shoreline. He lost track of where they were as they moved and twisted every which way. Harrison knew that Tattoo was deliberately confusing him. And he made no real effort to memorize the location, not that he could have if he had tried, after the twentieth turn. At last Tattoo slowed down and led him up a ladder. He pushed up on a manhole cover at the top and looked around like a submarine turning its periscope.

"Go, go now. There's no one around." He pulled to the side to let Harrison pass him on the steel-runged ladder, and the wrestler pushed the cover aside and pulled himself up, still awed at how well his hands and arms and everything else seemed to work. Almost as if he hadn't just been through the tortures of the early Christians. Harrison sat up on the sidewalk, wincing from the bright daylight of the noonday sun. He was right on a street corner. A car stood waiting at a light about twenty yards off. Just as he fully pulled himself from the hole, he saw a pedestrian turn the corner and catch sight of him, beaten-up and disheveled, with traces of green goo all over him. The man turned and walked quickly off in the other direction, vowing never to walk down that same street again.

Harrison turned to look back down the manhole— but Tattoo was already gone. Just empty darkness below. With a twisted grin, he pushed the manhole cover back over the opening and headed down the street toward the wider boulevard beyond. He had been gone for three days now. That meant it was Friday, the last day of the Games. He had to get to the Apple Dome and fast. But he didn't even know where the hell he was. Across the street he saw a phone booth and ran over to it, ripping the receiver from the hook. What the hell was the Captain's beeper number that Parker had given him before he left? He had memorized the thing using the special memory procedures of the CIA. But what the hell was it?

He reached in his pockets for money and realized with horror that he didn't have a penny. He had been stripped clean of everything when the Professor had kidnapped him. An elderly man with an umbrella was walking by in a stiff posture and Harrison stuck his head out of the booth and put out a pleading hand.

"Sir, I'm terribly sorry to have to ask but I need a quarter for a phone call that could affect the lives of tens of thousands of New Yorkers. Our nation's very security." He stood there with a pleading look like a Calcutta orphan. The man coughed a few times, looked at the battered flesh and oozing blood in a few spots, and shuddered, thanking the Good Lord that it wasn't him.

"Well, I'll give one quarter as long as it's going to be used for a phone call—to a hospital, I would imagine—and not on wine or crack."

"No, I promise," Harrison said with a puffed-lip smile. "I'll put it in right before your eyes." The man pulled out a quarter from his pocket, looked at it like it was a family heirloom from the eighteenth century, and then handed it grudgingly over to Harrison, harrumphing a few times as he did so.

"And do get a job," he said, turning abruptly and walking off.

"Oh, absolutely," Harrison said with a crazed tone in

355

his voice. "Absolutely. I'm calling the job agency right now in fact to see if anyone needs a human punching bag." He frantically dialed the number and prayed it was the right one. It rang six, then seven times, and Harrison began cursing hard under his breath. "Damn, fucking son-of-a-bitch, lousy—" A couple walking along made a wide berth as they passed him, wondering if they'd bought the wrong condo on the wrong street.

At last a voice came on on the other end.

"This is Captain Lou, baby. I can't be reached— leave a number and I'll get back to you as soon as— beeep."

"This is Harrison, you ugly fat son-of-a-bitch, where the hell—"

"Whoa, slow down, baby, what the hell happened to you?" a voice suddenly said. "We heard some bad news on the grapevine—and I mean bad. My tracker wasn't picking you up at all. Where the hell were you?"

"I can't go into it all now, Captain. Listen—there's trouble, huge immense, mucho trouble at the Games. I don't know where the hell I am—"

"Hang on, Smasher, the Captain's on his way. Don't move an inch. I'll be there before you can say 'kick ass' a hundred times. I'm getting a reading now on my locating device."

The phone clicked off and Harrison stood there, taking a deep breath as he looked around him. He must have looked pretty wired. Everyone who passed made wide circles around the booth like it was a sinkhole in the earth. Harrison suddenly felt absolutely starving as he sniffed a strong meaty scent in the air. He saw a hot dog stand about ten feet away. The Captain would have bucks. His stomach was going to need more than Tibetan healing herbs to get through even a few more hours. He ordered three dogs with everything. And even as he ripped into one with greedy bites and the

356

vendor held his hand out for money, a souped-up van came careening down the street and screeched to a halt with such violent force that its tires squealed like a whole barnload of stuck pigs, sliding sideways a good twenty feet, coming to a stop just a yard or so from the side of the vendor's cart.

"Get in, Harrison—let's move," Captain Lou bellowed out from inside, this time minus the long black Rasputin beard—but with a good set of rubber-bands covering his face.

"Money—I gotta pay this guy for the dogs," Harrison exclaimed, slobbering another of the wieners down.

"Ain't got none, baby," Captain Lou shouted impatiently. "Couldn't get to the bank machine. Tell him to send a bill to the President. Now, let's go, asshole, the whole city could blow."

"Sorry," Harrison said with a sheepish look as he suddenly ran with the last frank, dripping mustard and onions, to the far side of the monster wheeled van. He ripped the door open, feeling a little bad about not paying. "These dogs are helping your country," he blurted out inanely, and jumped in as the van started forward, wheels screeching before Harrison even had a chance to shut the door, which bounced off a car parked a few yards ahead and slammed closed by itself.

The hot dog vendor didn't take a single step after the accelerating monster van. He just stared at it as if in a trance.

Chapter Forty-Two

Captain Lou floored the van across town, flicking the dials on the radio for news of the Games. There—he found it suddenly. The announcer was going wild.

"Here, in the last match of the last contest for the gold medal in the Heavyweight-Plus Super Division, Gregor the "Bull" Bukowski of Bulgaria is absolutely taking Len Carter of Idaho City apart. And I mean apart, ladies and gentlemen. This is almost too terrible to watch. As those of you who have been following the wrestling portion of the World Games know, Bukowski has crushed every opponent he has faced over the last five days. And I mean crushed. Out of ten, eight are in the hospital, and two could use it, but refused to go. Now Len Carter, the last man separating Bukowski from the gold medal—who appeared in the first few minutes of the match to be doing well—has faltered and given the momentum to the Bull. Now Bukowski is delivering a knee to his stomach. Carter is down. The Bull is leaping in the air and coming down with an elbow right on the back of the American's head. Oh, this is terrible, this is just too—"

"There's no time, Captain. No fucking time left for us, we've run out," Harrison said despairingly as the last of the dogs disappeared into his churning gullet.

"Keep your blood pressure down, Mr. Wrestling Man, I'll get you there. Just hang on. The Captain knows some shortcuts." He suddenly wheeled the van up the wrong way on an exit ramp, skidded across a service road, and then got on a four-lane highway, coming into the traffic like a kid in a bumper car.

"You sure you know how to drive this fucking thing?" Harrison screamed out as the motor of the van roared away. "Where the hell did you get this souped-up monster anyway?"

"It's a CIA model, with all kinds of built-in high-tech stuff from our CCS pals," Captain Lou replied with a mad twinkle in his eyes. "Just hold on to your balls and anything else you don't want to lose." He gripped both hands on the wheel like he was at the Indianapolis 500 as he turned wildly back and forth weaving through the traffic. Within minutes, Harrison didn't know how, the Captain had maneuvered the van through three superhighways, across five service roads, around a parking lot, and the wrong way down a city street for eight blocks as cars reeled wildly in every direction. But suddenly they were approaching the huge stadium.

"There's no time to mess around," Harrison shouted as the roar of the van engine grew louder by the second. "We can't go in the regular way—through the guards and all—it would take an hour to explain."

"Don't worry about it. You look like shit, by the way. Don't look in the mirror," Captain Lou grunted as he rested his left arm on the opened window and leaned back in his seat. He was barely able to fit into it as his stomach pressed up hard against the wheel. "We're going in the Captain's way—special delivery. This sucker's got super-reinforced bumpers front and rear—can go through concrete walls." He drove up to the back security gate that ringed the stadium as an outer perimeter of defense, topped with barbed wire and video cameras.

He accelerated the van right toward the thick mesh fence, the weakest point of entry in the place as a single guard lolled around in a chair reading the *Post,* checking his stocks for the hundredth time that hour. He had only a thousand dollars invested, but it gave him great pleasure to follow it as faithfully as any Wall Street tycoon. Suddenly he heard a motor being revved, and looked up with horror to see the monster van with racing stripes painted down each side come bearing down on the gate.

The guard reached for his pistol, but by the time he got it out of the holster the van had slammed right through the gate, sending a whole twenty-foot section flying off as it careened forward down a dirt road that led straight to the stadium. He fired two shots after it, knowing he couldn't hit shit. The vehicle was moving a good fifty miles an hour, and was quickly over a small rise in the road and heading straight toward the back of the towering Apple Dome.

"This is Station 18," the guard screamed into his walkie-talkie, ripping the antenna up on the thing. "This is Station 18. White van has just crashed through my entrance, speeding toward Stadium Entrance A24. Dangerous, priority alert."

Captain Lou floored the van across the wide parking field filled with cars behind the stadium. At the entrance to the stadium itself Harrison saw three guards lining up right in front of the tunnel that led beneath the stands and into the field of competition.

"If they think I'm stopping to pick up fares, they're crazy," Captain Lou said merrily to Harrison. "Oh, by the way—better duck—and hold your nose." He slid down, his big stomach moving under the wheel as his back and head got below the dashboard level. Harrison threw himself down as well as slugs poured into the front of the van. Captain Lou steered, just peeking up over the panel, and flicked a dial on the panel in front.

A spray of grayish-looking mist shot out from hidden panels underneath each headlight and at the guards ahead. The front windows of the van shattered into fragments showering over both of them. But the three guards suddenly stopped firing as the gas enveloped them. They crumpled to the ground as the van shot past them and up into the dark tunnel.

"Gas—won't hurt them, more than a bad headache," Captain Lou said, sitting up fast, and threw the headlights on, honking the horn like a maniac to make sure everyone got out of the way. Then they could see the light at the far end and hear the crowds roaring as the blood match was being played out before their wild eyes.

The van tore out of the tunnel and onto the stadium floor. There in the dead center of the huge astroturf field Harrison could see a single ring and two men going at it tooth and nail. It was the final and most dramatic match, and the attention of the entire world was focused on it—the picture being sent live via satellite hook-up to every corner of the globe. There was intense interest—and betting—on whether or not there was a man alive who could take out the Goliath, the Bull, the monstrous Bukowski.

Captain Lou weaved his way through more security guards who came flying out from every direction like defensive tackles. Which was a little insane considering he had an elephant-sized vehicle and all they had were guns. There were pings here and there, and another piece of glass shattered over their heads. The Captain gave a few more pushes on the dashboard dial and more squirts of the knockout mist issued forth, taking down another half dozen of the stadium security forces.

The CCS-equipped van made it to the side of the ring, where Captain Lou threw it into park. He was out the door before it had even fully stopped, spinning around with a squeal of brakes and tires. Harrison exited on the other side, coming out on the run.

Two security men who were guarding the ring had already seen the commotion and had their own revolvers drawn. But as Parker had always said when they were in the jungles, "If you draw a gun use it fast—otherwise don't draw it." Advice these two should have followed, for Harrison was upon one and had his wrist twisted back before he could even think about firing. While Captain Lou came up behind the second and slammed into him with his huge shoulder, sending the dude flying into some chairs like he was a bowling ball trying to knock them down. Harrison twisted the gun free from the guard's hand, then threw him spinning through the air, flying a good eight feet before crashing to the artificial turf.

As Harrison looked up into the ring, he saw that Bukowski had the black wrestler up in the air by the edge of the ring and was about to bring the center of his back down onto the steel ring post. Carter could easily be a cripple for life—or dead.

Harrison knew this was no time to be subtle. He ran forward and dove, as if he were sliding into home plate, right into the ring. He slid about a yard, as Bukowski turned, lofting his soon-to-be-"destroyed" opponent as many in the crowd cheered lustily. Harrison grabbed the Bulgarian around the ankle and followed the old adage about "when in the jungle do as the animals do." He sank his teeth right into the huge wrestler's right calf. The man let out a piercing scream and staggered backward, losing his balance and letting Carter fall from his grasp—but toward the center of the ring, not the metal post. He slammed into the insulated mat and lay there unconscious from the beating he had been taking from the Bull.

Bukowski hopped around on one foot for about five seconds. Then the pain cleared from his eyes and he looked around like some sort of wild beast.

"You," he gasped when he saw Harrison standing there staring at him with pure hatred in his face.

"Yeah, me, asshole," Harrison replied with a smirk on his busted mouth.

"You're dead—saw you go down in river," the Bulgarian whispered with real fear showing in his face. The TV cameras were riveted on the wild scene that was unfolding. The world was witness to this showdown.

"Not dead enough," Harrison said as he started toward the big bastard with rage in his eyes. He didn't care how big the sucker was—he had hurt too many people. Harrison was mad now. Real mad. He hadn't ever felt like this in a fight before. Like he wanted to take out the other guy, tear him limb from limb.

Bull pulled back to the far side of the ring and bumped into the ropes. Suddenly his whole demeanor seemed to change as he saw that Harrison was all beat up, bruised, with purple splotches everywhere. He wasn't a ghost, he was human—and fucked up. Somehow he hadn't drowned—but Bull would finish that task quick enough. The Bulgarian laughed out loud, and then pounded himself on the chest hard, like a Slavic Tarzan.

"You want fight Bull? All right, my stupid friend. You fight him. Come, come." He waved his hand forward as he spat into his cupped palms and rubbed the hands together in anticipation of eating Harrison alive. A security guard jumped up on the ring apron to climb in and try to get Harrison. But the Bulgarian just batted the man down like he was a fly. The guard went flying, knocking down three more of his own. Not another man tried to enter the ring with the two maddened giants heading toward each other. They weren't fools. Captain Lou kept circling the ring, staying away from them as he kept his eyes glued on the ring.

The two wrestlers charged toward the center of the ring like two trains coming down the same track. Their bodies slammed into each other at a good thirty miles an hour with a resounding thwack like two mountain rams cracking horns. Bukowski was huge, but Harrison had the mad energy of the totally enraged, ready to do whatever it took to bring the bastard down. Thus, it was the American, coming in at a low angle so he could push upwards, who actually pushed the much larger man back a few yards, much to the Bulgarian's surprise.

"You moth," Bukowski snarled, pulling back out of the outstretched arms and raising himself up high, like the bear had done just before it had attacked on Harrison's survival mission. That seemed like another lifetime to him now. "I will crush you with my fist." With that he flew into Harrison with a flurry of blows, each fist as big as a ham hock. Harrison ducked and bobbed and weaved and slid his feet all over the damn place. And suddenly all those exhausting lessons with Bulldog, the boxing coach, back at the D2 gymnasium seemed worthwhile. For he was able to dance around the King-Kong-sized hands, which came in seeking to pulverize his brain. And Harrison had no doubt that they could do it—if they made contact. If was the operative word. For Harrison just kept dancing out of the huge dude's way as he snapped out his own left jabs and hooks to the grizzly-sized rib cage.

He knew it didn't really hurt the big man, not more than a horsefly biting a horse. But still it gave him a satisfying feeling when the Bulgarian grunted or spat out after a blow and grew even redder in the face. He'd let the guy get really mad—make a blunder—then he'd strike hard, real hard. As Harrison reached the ring post and realized he was about to be cut off, he just ducked down low and ran fast right beneath the giant's outstretched arms. The Bulgarian howled in rage as the smaller man escaped his imminent grasp. And he howled even louder as Harrison released six quick pumping punches right into his kidneys as he swung around behind the man.

"You got him on the run, baby, keep up the attack!" Captain Lou screamed out as he flipped two guards who had gotten their mitts on him.

"Come on, you Pillsbury dough boy, you slab of flab, come on," Harrison screamed at the Bulgarian, taunting him to come forward, to lose whatever cool remained.

"Sure I come to you, flea, I come," the Bulgarian screamed, and launched himself right from the corner of the ring toward Harrison like some kind of mutant NASA probe. Harrison was amazed at the speed with which the huge man could move and the velocity with which he took off. But he was faster. He rushed toward the hurtling Bulgarian, and then made a forty-five-degree-angle turn to the right side, kicking out with his foot right into the rib cage of the hurtling murderer. The man's ribs were huge, thick as table legs, but when his great mass met the smashing outstretched foot of Harrison, with Harrison's other foot planted on the mat like a tree, rooted as Tattoo had shown him, the ribs cracked with an audible sound, two, maybe three of them snapping in as the wrestler flew by. For good measure Harrison drove his elbow right down into the man's neck as he hurtled past, slamming it just below the base of the skull.

Bukowski kept going right past his would-be victim and slammed down into the mat face first about ten feet ahead. He hit hard, almost knocked out for a moment by the elbow strike. His nose was a bloody mess as he slowly rose up getting his bearings. Red streamed down the whole front of his body. But then, as Harrison's wounds from the brass knucks the other day were also opening up here and there, they both had plenty of color to lend each other.

"Now, you die," the Bulgarian whispered as he rose and came forward. This time he moved slowly, finally catching on that his rage was allowing the smaller American to take advantage of his speed. This time there would be no mistakes. He moved in a slow careful circle around Harrison, who realized that the guy was getting the right idea. That was bad for him. He didn't want to get grabbed by the sucker. But even as he thought it, Bukowski threw an arm out toward Harrison's shoulder, and even as the American tried to pull the shoulder away, he saw that it was just a feint. The Bull reversed himself instantly and reached out for the right shoulder. He caught it, and closed his hands around it like a starfish around an oyster. And his face lit up like a child's for he knew that now that he had Harrison—it was all over.

The American tried to swing around and put a counter-move on the grab, but the Bull was too fast. In an instant he dropped to his knees and swung his shoulders around. Harrison was flung right over the man's back judo-style and slammed into the mat hard on his shoulder. He tried to roll free but felt that huge hand still hanging on, in fact pulling him back along the surface of the mat like a fish being reeled in over the foaming white crests of the sea.

"Come here, little worm. I want to show you a little trick." He yanked hard on Harrison's arm, and suddenly the American was right beneath the huge chest, the arms grappling with him, getting him in a half nelson and wrist lock. The Bulgarian rose up and stood to his full height, and before Harrison could react he whipped him up and around so that Harrison was staring right down at the ground and the man was holding his legs up in the air wrapped tightly within his arms. He knew what was coming next.

"Bye-bye," the Bulgarian whispered, for the Pile

Driver had sent numerous men to the critical ward. And on this one he was going to add a little extra. A lot extra. Gripping Harrison hard as he held the American upside down, he jumped straight up in the air a good yard off the mat. The crowd gasped as they saw what was occurring. The TV cameras were in tight focus to see the blood, the end in full living color. As Harrison felt himself descending he somehow threw out both hands so they were just beneath his skull and bent his elbows slightly to take the blow. Then he slammed into the mat like a safe thrown from the twentieth floor of a building. He was out cold for a fraction of a second, and then found himself toppling end over end. But his hands and arms had taken enough of the blow not to send him into never-never land. Still, his neck felt like it was just this side of broken, and his whole head sort of tilted sideways like a toy doll kicked once too hard into the closet. He had no illusions. In any kind of drawn-out affair the Bull would grind him down to mincemeat. Harrison had to move fast. Had to move now.

"Still alive?" The Bulgarian laughed as he stood up, one hand on his hips, the other scratching his immense basketball of a head, the toothless mouth moving this way and that as he spoke. "You be fun for Bull," the wrestler said, pounding himself again on the double-barreled chest. "Me be sad you die now." He came forward again, slowly at first, but then throwing caution to the winds, wanting to end the match in dramatic style, he charged ahead in the bull-like fashion that had given him his name—being able to crush men's chests, and kill them, with his head smash. That was how he had worked his way up in the back-country wrestling matches of eastern Bulgaria. That was how he would win the world's gold medal, its highest championship.

Harrison pretended to stand rubber-legged as he waited for the head to make contact, as if he were out on his feet. But he was waiting. Waiting until the last instant. As the head flew toward him like a ramming log on the front of a galleon, Harrison suddenly jumped to the side. As the huge mountain of a man drove past, snorting and stomping up a storm, not even aware that his victim had gotten out of the way, Harrison ripped his elbow around with everything he had right into the dead center of the man's skull. It was like an immovable object meeting an unstoppable force. Harrison let out a little bark of pain as his elbow felt like it was shattered into a dozen pieces. But the long crack that appeared across the entire top of the Bulgarian's skull, he was sure, hurt a lot worse.

The man didn't make a sound, not a loud one anyway. His charge took him right into the ropes, where he bounced off and looked around in a confused kind of way as he turned a few circles along the ropes. The crowd gasped and some women cried out as they saw the large red fissure spreading across the upper surface of the Bulgarian's skull. It was like an egg that had been cracked and was leaking—blood. But the Bull still had plenty of fight in him yet. He shook his head a few times, which sent sprays of red and pink all over his shoulders and chest and down onto the white-surfaced mat.

"Crack his coconut," Captain Lou screamed out. "You're almost there, Harrison—don't fail me now, baby."

"You hurt me, scum," the Bull howled at his opponent. "Now I hurt you—bad." He came forward with murderous intensity in his eyes. But Harrison had other ideas. He lured the Bulgarian forward, taking one careful step at a time, pulling him on.

"Come on, fat boy, come on, almost there." At the last possible second, as the Bull saw that he had the American trapped against the ropes and charged, Harrison jumped up and backwards as if off a diving board. It was the move he had worked on over and over —the one the Destroyer and Captain Lou had chided him for as being too showy. But the move worked. Harrison's feet slammed into the middle rope, and it pulled down a foot like the string of a bow. When it sprang up, it launched him straight up back in the direction he had just come. By throwing his own leg and hip motion into the trajectory, Harrison was able to fly up a good eight feet, soaring over the lunging Bulgarian's head as he grabbed at the air with a mystified expression on his blood-soaked face.

But Harrison wasn't about to give him a second chance. He came down on his feet and spun around and, grabbing both of Bukowski's arms from behind, pulled them suddenly straight back with all his strength. He knew he had only seconds before the Bulgarian used his massive power to pull them back again. But a second was all he needed. With the arms taut and pulled back so tightly they were almost meeting each other, Harrison leaped up into the air and kicked his feet out against the center of the man's spine. As he fell he pulled on the arms and forced Bukowski to fall backward, and they both descended as one great interlocked unit of battling flesh. As Harrison hit the mat on his back he drove his feet out and straight up as hard as he could, his legs extended like pistons. At the same instant he pulled back with everything he had on both huge-muscled arms. The Double Kick Back Breaker—the death blow that Destroyer had shown Harrison as his parting gift to him.

There was a terrible cracking sound, as the great body bounced down onto the booted feet, then another as it bounced a few inches and came down a second time. Harrison kicked up, letting go of the arms, and the body flew up away from him, slamming down onto the mat, dead as stone before it even reached the blood-splattered plastic material.

Chapter Forty-Three

But if Harrison thought it was all over—it was just beginning. For even as he rose to one knee, catching his breath from the fierce fight, he heard a loud whirring sound, and as he raised his head, saw a pneumatic platform, one of dozens of them hidden beneath the artificial turf throughout the stadium floor, start to rise. The turf slid apart, and a large square steel platform came right up out of the ground like a new mountain was being formed from out of the ocean. And atop the thirty-by-thirty platform—three men stood armed to the teeth. But it was the object in their midst that caught Harrison's attention—a bomb. A gleaming globe of chromium steel with lights blinking, digital readouts reading, and antennae poking from the damn thing like it was some sort of alien steel insect.

As the steel platform rose up above the green astroturf the three opened fire, and Harrison flung himself flat on the wrestling mat as the slugs dug in all around him. The guards who had been standing around the ring with their pistols drawn, not sure what the hell was going on, now turned their attention to the firing men. But that was a mistake. For their pistols were no match for the Uzis and Colt assault rifles. The guards' firing only brought attention to themselves, and the three madmen atop the platform answered back, cutting a dozen of them to ribbons. Then they turned their bloody attentions to the crowds on each side of the stadium and began firing madly, indiscriminately into them.

Harrison edged forward on the mat as he saw that they weren't looking his way for a moment. They were about a hundred feet away and not that easy to see as the smoke of their weapons began filling the air around them. But what he could see was horrible. For the men were melting, their skin a mass of bubbles, their mouths bleeding gashes without teeth, their hair all gone so all three were bald as eggs. These were—to put it mildly—men who had nothing to lose. They had already lost it.

He could hear one of them, the tallest one, skinny as a rail and holding a big assault rifle with both hands, screaming up at the TV cameras which were all around him, screaming and waving his fists, as the bravest of the cameramen continued to work, sending the whole scene out to the world, which watched it all mesmerized.

"Peasants, workers of the world—this is all for you. We give our lives as we take the lives of the bourgeois spectators—all for you!" Suddenly the man's picture was being flashed up on the huge screen at the far end of the stadium used for close-ups of the competitors—and now filled with the hideous melting flesh. Harrison knew it was Professor Markus, he could tell by the voice. Though the face wouldn't have given him much of a clue. For just in the three days since he had been tortured by the man the professor had deteriorated drastically. It was worse than horrible—it was a nightmare. The man no longer had a human face. The camera caught the other two for a moment as they sent their firepower across opposite sides of the field with a look of demonic concentration on their red-eyed faces. They didn't look any better.

"For you," the professor screamed, and Harrison could see it all in living color on the huge screen. "We carry out this act of supreme martyrdom so that the ruling classes of the world will feel the wrath of the oppressed. And we strike here—because sports is the opium of the people. It enslaves the minds of the worker. Arise, throw off your chains, ye prisoners of starvation. Behold the power of the worker." He turned and pointed dramatically at the bomb, and a dozen cameras focused in on it. The man turned to look up at the great screen and saw that his words, the image of the bomb, were in fact all being transmitted. His fanatical ravings were going out to the whole world. His entire mission had been carried out successfully. He could die a happy man. It had all worked far beyond his greatest expectations. He swung the huge rifle that he could hardly carry around and began firing again. They would take out as many of the bourgeois swine in the audience as they could—it made for good TV, and the professor was nothing if not image-conscious and aware of the power of the media. That was what this had all been about.

Then the bomb would go off. Oh, the video cameras would catch that nicely, wouldn't they? Before they melted. But the worldwide audience would doubtless get the message. What the working class could do when it set its mind to it. Only six minutes. Six minutes to Revolutionary Heaven, where Marx and Trotsky, he knew, were waiting for him with open arms. They would spend the rest of eternity arguing and discussing the finer points of Engels and Hegel. Professor Markus looked forward to it as he had to nothing in this life. He smiled, though no one who was looking at the hideous bloody face on the screen would have known it.

The crowd was going mad, screaming and running off in every direction. Harrison could see that hundreds had been hurt already. People were falling from upper tiers, crashing down to the seats below. It was a massacre—even without the bomb. Harrison knew he had to move—and move fast. He rolled over and over across the mat as a scythe of slugs ripped into the canvas shredding it as cleanly as a tailor cuts his suits. Harrison rolled right off the side and down six feet to the astroturf below. He was clear for the moment. He looked around and saw Captain Lou, who was helping Carter to his feet. Carter was apparently none the worse for wear, though bloodied here and there, but then who wasn't.

Carter choked out above the roar of the gunfire, "What the hell is going on?"

"Too long a story to go into now," Harrison shouted back. "But we've gotta stop them—it doesn't look like anyone else is about to do the job." Some of the security guards around the stadium had started firing back, until their superiors saw the bomb and screamed out orders not to shoot. They had to sneak up to get a clear shot, and as they tried, they were picked off by the incredible firepower of the three terrorists. They must have had a stockpile from an army truck with crates of ammo around their feet, even grenades. Yet the guards had to try. And after the first minute of the bloody attack twenty of their number lay silent or groaning on the plastic astroturf, some within yards of the pneumatic platform.

"We gotta get those sons-of-bitches," Captain Lou yelled, looking intensely at the two wrestlers. "You with me?" Nobody else was making it across the field of fire. It looked like sure suicide. But they would all be dead anyway, within minutes at most, if something wasn't done. Both men gulped and nodded yes. The three put their fists out for a second and touched flesh. If they had to go out—they'd go as brothers, brothers of the fighting spirit, brothers of the light against the darkness.

"Let's kick ass!" Captain Lou bellowed out, and all three men took off like wide receivers. Harrison sprinted out from behind the wrestling ring he had just hastened the demise of Bukowski in, and shot forward. He had hardly taken three steps on the 150-foot dash toward the steel platform, when he heard whirring sounds all around him. Suddenly he felt the very earth beneath his feet shift and move, and had to jump to the side as another pneumatic platform rose up. They were rising up everywhere now, all sizes, some empty, others filled with sprinklers, tarps, amplifiers for rock bands, myriad kinds of equipment. Dozens of them came right up out of the ground, rising quickly to different heights, ten, twenty feet above the ground, and then sinking back down again just as fast. It was crazy, for within seconds there were dozens of them just zooming up and down, making it seem like the very earth had gone mad, that confusion reigned.

But Harrison saw that this was his break. He sprinted straight ahead now, not having to dive for protection as there were three of the rising and falling platforms between him and the three men's line of fire. One of the terrorist slugs must have hit some electrical equipment—short-circuited something. He glanced around and saw that Carter and Captain Lou were also using the pneumatic platforms to shield their movement as they zigzagged from one to another toward the three terrorists whose own platform was the only stationary one.

Harrison came around the last protective platform, which disappeared back into the astroturf just as he reached it, exposing him suddenly. Professor Markus saw the bruised and bloodied wrestler come out of nowhere and ripped the assault rifle around, digging trails of melted plastic into the astroturf as the slugs reached for the American wrestler's flesh. But Harrison was a little faster than a seventy-six-year-old, radiation-decaying professor, and he dove straight forward, landing just beneath the platform. The square opening below it led back down to the lower regions, and he almost fell in, catching himself with his hands against round steel tubes that held the platform up at the last second.

The professor fired straight down but couldn't get the angle on the man beneath him. The slugs just melted a straight gash into the field material only inches from Harrison's foot. Suddenly the firepower shifted again as the professor caught sight of Captain Lou coming around from the left side like a rhino in full charge. The instant Harrison saw the wall of bullets move away from him he jumped out from beneath the platform, which was a good ten feet above the ground. Out of the corner of his eye he saw Captain Lou take a slug in the side of his arm and fall to the ground, rolling under a tarp for cover.

Letting out a quick breath of air, Harrison leaped up suddenly with everything he had, and his fingertips just caught hold of the metal edge of the inch-thick steel sheet. Without hesitation he pulled himself up, his powerful arms bulging. His fingers felt like they were about to slip, but then his elbows were up and he threw them forward, catching himself on the side of the platform.

The moment he was halfway up he saw one of the terrorists, who was firing with one hand toward approaching security guards, kick down at Harrison trying to dislodge him from the side. The foot came right toward his head, but Harrison was able to catch the ankle in his right hand as he shifted up to bring himself a little higher on the edge of the platform. He felt slightly nauseous as his fingers sank into the man's ankle flesh. The man screamed and tried to lower the pistol, firing wildly as it arced down. But Harrison wasn't about to give him a chance to make target acquisition. He pulled with all his might toward the edge of the platform and the terrorist went flying right over the edge. He hit the astroturf like an overripe peach.

Harrison lifted himself the rest of the way up onto the metal plate and rolled forward as the professor's auto-rifle tried to sight him up, the row of slugs pinging off the metal just behind him. He slammed into the professor's legs and sent him flying down onto the steel floor. The professor, as rotting as he was, still seemed to have the staying power of a true madman. He rose up into a sitting position, firing the rifle with one arm. One of the slugs ripped into Harrison's shoulder, and he grunted but rushed on, diving from about five feet away.

He came down right on top of the bloody husk of the man, amazed that the thing could even still move, let alone see, talk, or pull a trigger. But if Harrison thought if was a match takedown—he was wrong. With the strength of the damned of hell, the professor reached up with his right hand and clamped it hard around Harrison's throat. It was like the hand of death. Harrison could feel it instantly lock around the windpipe, cutting off his air. The man was possessed of uncanny strength. The hand felt like the unbreakable grip of a steel robot.

"Die, pig, die," Markus ranted into Harrison's face, sending a spray of red over it.

"Not yet, you crazy bastard. You die!" Harrison screamed back. He punched with all his might right into the son-of-a-bitch's chest. The punch slammed right through the weakened bones of the rib cage and into the lungs. Somehow the professor's other hand still tried to get a bead on him with the rifle, but Harrison slammed it away with his free fist.

Rising to a standing position, he pulled the professor up, stepped to the side of the platform, and with a great heave threw the man over the side. Markus sailed free of the platform and crashed into the astroturf below. It wasn't something you wanted to take snapshots of to send home to Mom and Dad.

And still the professor screamed out, "Die, bourgeois slime, die," as he rolled forward across the turf. The wild flailing motion of his arms and legs, which still kicked in rage, kept him moving toward the nearest platform, which had just reached its height of fifteen feet and was now coming down like an express freight elevator headed for the basement. The professor came to a stop at the edge of the dark opening, his legs hanging over the side. The bloody head turned and saw the descending platform coming down like a guillotine. It slammed into him, and the meager melting bones were nothing against the pull of the pneumatic pillars capable of carrying twenty tons. The platform sliced through Professor Markus at midsection, taking his legs down into the darkness. The legless trunk, still rolled around, the arms punching at the air, the mouth screaming. For a second or two anyway. Then the madman's violent motions suddenly stopped and he lay there like a sunken ship in the sea of his own blood.

Harrison whipped around and focused his blood-splattered eyes on the bomb, sitting there calm as anything while the world erupted in bedlam all around it. But then it could afford to be calm—it knew that within seconds it would be taking everybody out. He had scarcely gone a foot when he heard a scream and looked up. The third terrorist was about to take Harrison out with a NATO Assault 9mm. Captain Lou, who had issued the warning, suddenly let loose with a rubber band he fired from his thumb. It sailed nearly fifteen feet and sliced deep into the terrorist's melting eye. Captain Lou dove into the bastard, throwing his arm around the head and pulling sharply to the side in a neck-breaking move. But because of his great anger and strength combined—and because the flesh of the terrorist had been so weakened by the radioactive acids—the whole head tore free of the body. As the headless corpse sank to the mat, Captain Lou looked in horror at the thing he held cradled in his arms.

"Oh, shit," he muttered in total repulsion, throwing his arms out so the head dropped to the floor of the steel platform and rolled around as if looking for its better half. But Harrison didn't have time to say thanks. As he continued walking toward the great chromium egg he saw the timer moving silently down on a small panel on the side of the thing.

".15, .14, .13 . . ." Even as he looked, the numbers were dropping down to .00—and you didn't have to be Plato to know what that meant. He dropped to his knees, completely oblivious to the screams everywhere in the stadium, the gunshots that still went off from guards here and there who didn't even realize that the human battle was over. The atomic one was about to begin. Harrison looked over the bomb frantically, his eyes moving around like fruits in a slot-machine window.

He ran his hands quickly over the thing, looking for any dials, switches—anything. But beyond two antennae poking up on the top and meters giving readouts that were all now flashing red with warning signs, the thing was virtually smooth.

".10, .09, .08 . . ." Well, there was, as they said, no time like the present, he suddenly decided. He gritted his teeth, squatted down, and put his arms around the shining nuclear device. Then he lifted. It was heavy, incredibly heavy, heavier than anything he had ever tried to raise before. He could feel every vein in his body pulsing out, every sinew vibrating like the high string on a violin. But there was no turning back. He screamed as he raised the thing to his chest and then pressed it up straight overhead. Then running a few steps to gain momentum, he let out a great roar and threw all his strength into this one final heave. The bomb flew out of his hands and out about eight feet, soaring toward the hard plastic turf. It made a little humming sound as every light suddenly stopped blinking.

".03, .02 . . ." The bomb crashed into the astroturf and made a ripping metallic sound like a huge steel egg cracking. A seam opened all along one side, and there was a violent crackling of wires inside as sparks shot out the opening. Harrison involuntarily flinched and put his arms up over his head as he looked at the thing through squinting eyes. It seemed to roll around like a jumping bean trying to take off. There was a great sputtering inside, and then blue smoke exiting out of the crack like the final exhale of a dying smoker. Then it shuddered once and was still, its digital readout stopped forever halfway between .001 and .00.

Chapter Forty-Four

Harrison stood on the highest of the three round pneumatic platforms that were raised up about three feet apart from one another, his platform being ten feet above the astroturf. He stood on the six-foot-wide disc of chrome with his head slightly bowed. Television cameras zoomed in on the battered face, the purple bruises beneath each eye—but also the proud, unyielding jaw and the hint of a smile. A hand, the hand of the Games Commissioner, who was himself raised up on another round platform right in front of Harrison, reached out and carefully placed a ribbon around his neck. And on the end of the blue ribbon—a gold medal. For winning the highest world title that the sport of amateur wrestling could bestow.

Bukowski would have won the gold, had in a sense unofficially won it when he threw Carter down in the ring. On the other hand Harrison hadn't had his chance to compete—and it was Bukowski himself who had tried to kill him. Most importantly, the Bulgarian was dead. It wouldn't look too photogenic on all the magazine covers to put the medal around a corpse's throat. So without much ado, and as soon as the stadium was cleaned up of the dead and the bomb hauled off by bomb experts to a waiting lead truck, the ceremonies continued. The spirit of man, the best of that spirit lived on. And those receiving the awards were living proof of that.

And the world was riveted. For the story of the day had spread around the planet like wildfire. The Games Commissioner lowered himself with a small lever on the side of his pneumatic platform and placed the silver medal on the next man down—Len Carter. The black wrestler had defeated all until Bukowski. He accepted it with pride, his head bowed. Then the bronze—this to a Russian heavyweight, Minkorv, a tough but fair fighter. The commissioner let the TV people get their money's worth as the crowds went bananas and the entire stadium felt like it might shatter from the sheer volume of the screams and stomping feet. Then they descended. The platforms with the three medal winners came down as the next three winners in a lower weight class were announced.

The three men stood face to face and all simultaneously, as if it had been prearranged—which it wasn't—put their hands together and gripped them firmly for a few seconds. Again the cameras whirred. Great visuals. Colonel Parker, with Captain Lou walking at his side, appeared from the waves of officials surrounding the awards platforms. Harrison grinned as he saw them. The flesh wound in Captain Lou's arm had a bandage around it, but he looked none the worse for wear.

"Maybe it was all worth it in some weird way," Harrison said as Parker walked up to him and put his arm around the wrestler's shoulder. "Though those bastards tried to drive us all apart, they drove us together. A black man, a white man, a Russian. We can get along, can't we, Parker? It doesn't always have to be the way the professor wanted it, does it?"

"I once thought it did," Parker said softly, his smile

turning to a more serious, thoughtful expression. "But as I grow older, I see that we've got to exist together—there's no room for even one war on this planet. Maybe you're right. The whole world is watching. Maybe in some way this all helped. We'll see what happens. But don't get any ideas that it's over. It's not, Harrison, not by a long shot. There are Professor Markuses all over the world. Worse than him. This was just one shot fired across the bow. You two men did a magnificent job," he said. There was genuine gratitude and affection in those usually cold, sentimentless orbs. "I'm more proud of both of you right now than I think I've ever felt in my life. We could see it all on TV, the kind of firepower you guys were up against. It was impossible."

"Don't say that word around me," Captain Lou said. "The whole training program that our Bodysmasher here went through was to never say die. 'Cause once you say it—you're dead." Parker laughed, and Harrison too, at the Captain's way with words. Then the CIA chief's face grew serious again, and Harrison could see how the guy was aging by the day. There was even more gray than the last time he'd seen him, whole clumps of hair looked missing. The poor bastard. Harrison wouldn't trade places with him—for anything.

"There'll be more battles," Parker said. "More madmen trying to take us all down with them. At our best—maybe we can stop them from doing too much damage. I need you guys. Need both of you," he said, turning back and forth to the two men as he gripped their shoulders firmly. "The whole damn country does. By the way, Mr. Harrison . . ." The CIA chief chuckled as he saw a car being driven slowly up past the officials. "There's a bonus for all your busted ribs and black eyes." He tilted his head to the side as the 1988 Mercedes came to a stop. It was silver and sleek as a

382

landbound rocket. Harrison whistled as the driver stepped out, walked around the glistening vehicle, and dropped the keys in Harrison's hands.

"Aside from all the usual luxury features and modified engine that can hit one hundred eighty," Parker said, "it's got CCS offensive and defensive built-ins that will make the hairs on your nose sizzle. But all in good time, my friend. It's both a gift—and a hope that we can work together on future—"

"Not now," Harrison said, cutting his boss off in mid-sentence, waving his hand in front of his face. The last thing in the world he wanted to talk about right now was continuing in this business. Not after what he had just been through. Maybe next week, next month he'd talk about it. Maybe. But not now.

Suddenly a face appeared in the crowd, and Harrison felt a surge of warmth flow right up from his heart. Natasha. She was alive. Somehow he thought the bastards had gotten to her. Though he hadn't had too much time to think clearly about it all.

"You're all right," she said, rushing up to him and into his arms, which closed around her. It felt good to hold her woman's body so softly after being slammed around by the male of the species so much over the last week. She reached up and kissed him hard on the lips, her green eyes flashing like twin emeralds of passion.

"Whoa, I see you've made some friends," Parker said, laughing as she pulled away from Harrison with a loud smack.

"Yeah, a best friend," Harrison replied, feeling the warmth of her flanks as he stroked her lower back with both hands for a second. Suddenly he felt all the energy just sort of slipping out of him like air from a balloon. The effects of the Zhnaktha. Tattoo had said it would wear off after a few hours. Well, it sure as hell was wearing off. Before he knew it his knees were buckling

383

and Natasha had to catch hold of him, draping his arm around her shoulder.

"Hey, you need a rest, Smash," Captain Lou said, slapping him on the back of the head. "You've been through hell in the last few days. You look like shit, you know."

"Here, you two kids," Parker said, suddenly feeling extraordinarily generous. "Take this credit card—it's a company card—go crazy. Take the Mercedes, drive to the Plaza—we have a permanent room on reservation. Whatever you want—it's yours. I'll tell my people to keep the *Do Not Disturb* sign up for the next two weeks.

"How's that sound, Harrison?" the CIA man asked, looking over at the wrestler, who was already half slumped at Natasha's side. Only her great strength even enabled her to hold him up, one of his arms around her shoulders while she held him around his waist.

"Soun' great," Harrison barely managed to mumble. He wasn't just counting sheep. They were jumping all over his brain, pulling him down into deep, deep sleep whether he was ready or not.

"Now you take care of my boy," Captain Lou said gruffly to the beautiful Bulgarian bodybuilder, pulling his shoulders up and scowling hard to show he meant business. "I'll hold you personally responsible for his well-being." She grinned back as she took the Mercedes's keys from Harrison's limp fingers.

"Oh, I'll take care of him," Natasha said as she took the offered credit card and slipped it into the small zippered pocket of her athletic pants. "I'll take very, very good care of him."